# The Fan-Shaped Destiny of William Seabrook

# The Fan-Shaped Destiny of William Seabrook

*A Romance of Many Worlds*

PAUL PIPKIN

All quotations from published books, magazines, and newspapers are genuine. Likewise, the contents of the annotations are factual. This includes data bearing on the "literary anomaly" and discrepancies in the historical record. Otherwise: This is a novel and a work of fiction. The characters and events portrayed in the body of the text either are products of the author's imagination or are used fictitiously.



For information address iPublish.com, 135 West 50th Street, New York, NY 10020.

An AOL Time Warner Company

ISBN 0-7595-5039-5

First edition: November 2001

Visit our website at www.ipublish.com

For Linda, to meet again

# Contents

# Author's Note

At the end of the day, the narrative which follows is a love story; a highly erotic one, at that. Still, a number of idiosyncrasies may prompt some readers to echo the wonderment of Madeleine Leiris (in her *Testament* included in the sixth chapter) and ask, *"Could such things be?"* To those determined to strike out on such a path of higher improbability, I offer such explanation as I can.

William Seabrook and the people around him were actual historical personages. As with the chronicle of the scientific workers and the authors alluded to, I have endeavored to be as faithful to their lives and work as the narrative and its affiliated research could approach.

Seabrook documented the existence of his unpublished materials in 1942. If those notes are still extant, only they can confirm whether they support the narrative thread of *The Fan-Shaped Destiny* fragments purportedly represented in the later chapters.

What of the apparently composite figure that

Seabrook and Ward Greene called Justine? The artist Man Ray wrote fondly of Willie Seabrook: *"It is rare to read facts that sound like fiction—most writers strive for the reverse effect."*[1]

1. Man Ray, *Self Portrait*, NY: Little, Brown, 1963, 1988, p. 154.

*At times I almost dream I too have spent a life*
*the sages' way,*
*And tread once more familiar paths. Perchance*
*I perished in an arrogant self-reliance*
*Ages ago; and in that act, a prayer*
*For one more chance went up so earnest, so*
*Instinct with better light let in by death,*
*That life was blotted out—not so completely*
*But scattered wrecks enough of it remain,*
*Dim memories, as now, when once more seems*
*The goal in sight again.*

—from *Paracelsus*, Robert Browning, 1835

# I
# Happenstance

IN THE AUTUMN OF MY LIFE AND AT THE END OF A dark and bloody century, I had undertaken to make a final accounting of the strange odyssey of William Seabrook, a forgotten literary figure of the Lost Generation. The twists and turns of events that followed from this eccentric project, infused as it was with the dark energy of my personal sorrows, would come to beg expansion. *The beginning?* Such a discrete moment shifts within my grasp. It mocks me still.

For some years, I'd been working in the southern part of Texas as a union business agent, a vocation that had killed better men than me. I was burning out under the pressures of the work and grief over my wife's recent death, a result of chronic alcoholism. I had paid for the ticket with my tears and taken that ride to the bitter end; and it had been so very bitter. I'm not good at "moving on," you see. Venture forth and my steps would only turn again, back toward

Willie's *ever-receding far-away*. When in Laredo, I would sit alone nights on the patio of a bar just beside the International Bridge, reviewing the contradictions of my life. So much of it had been lived up and down the Interstate 35 artery, throbbing with the commercial invasion of the South, that it would often appear in my dreams.

As I stared across the river into the vast mystery of Mexico, I-35 would become that dream highway. Along its dark axis, one just might drive off some night into other times, other worlds. One ramp, four hundred miles and thirty-five years behind me, would exit upon my adolescence and late-summer nights spent reading the pulp science fiction from decades more remote still. Some of those old books and magazines had transfixed me with strange stories, which had worked to reinforce a childhood fantasy. That the past might be only another room, a room which we have exited but whose door may have remained just a little bit ajar.

Some of those boyhood nights had hosted inexplicable dreams, intense enough to linger as dim memories, for years and even decades. One by one and without any other forewarning, they had come true. Such phenomena are not nearly so remarkable as they may seem to those with no experience of them. But, by the time I had reached the far point of my life in that Laredan bar, the last of my prescient dreams had been exhausted. Did that mean there was nothing left ahead? Was the future as dark a void as the highway beyond my headlamps? Such thoughts would suggest that the miles home to San Antonio would also be measured in milligrams, at least five milligrams, of Valium. Then occurred the first event that would shatter the conventional assumptions on which I operated from day to day.

Many threads comprise a life. Worry one from its accustomed position and even the most elaborate tapestry may begin to unravel. I was used to being in the news, from time to time, regarding various political and social issues. One morning I had been quoted in some front-page coverage of a labor conflict. Such publicity always elicited phone calls, so I stayed in the office to receive them. There was only one that mattered.

---

"DO YOU REMEMBER ME?"

My boss stopped by as I was trying to manage the coffeepot with shaking hands and volunteered that I looked like I'd seen a ghost. My laughter on the edge of hysteria, I retreated behind my office door where I could break down and cry.

Did I remember her? Did I remember that first meeting, at a teen dance in the shelter house of a North Texas lake? What we were both wearing, where we were standing, the lights of the power plant across the lake, sounds of the ducks and wavelets against the pier where we held each other amidst the smells of vanilla perfume and chewing gum?

Did I then recall the scented summer evenings that followed, or the blaze of her red hair in the amber glow of fall afternoons, or loving her in the autumn leaves? Later, after she had gone to join the constellations in the night skies of my dreams, she became the template against which all future involvements were to be measured. *Do I remember you?* Oh, maybe just to the extent of all the joys and hurts of my life exploding in me at once!

When I met her for lunch and she raised her lips to mine without reservation, I was lost. You've heard of old girlfriends coming back? Well, get behind this one: Try your first, not seen or heard of in over thirty years. She'd been living on the north side of San Antonio for twenty, and later I would learn of so many probable near misses that I would rage against fate.

Time had not been especially gentle with JJ. I would hold the dear countenance between my hands and hate what years and battery had done. She could never be other than beautiful to me, and I swear that I took no satisfaction. Whatever rejection I may have suffered, I had truly wanted to believe that she was having a wonderful life somewhere.

Yet, when we would make love, before my eyes occurred a phenomenon of which I'd read in romantic literature, never believing it to exist as an actual, literal experience. I sought after rational explanation, blood suffusing the capillaries or whatever, to no avail. The fact remained that, in those intimate hours, I seemed physically to hold in my arms the same young girl I'd known over thirty years before.

During the months of the late-life affair that followed, I allowed myself to believe that some deity, for reasons known only to itself, had taken pity. It's very hard to lose someone twice, to take that second hurt that revives the first—and all the hurts and rejections that have been hung on it in the meantime, like evil ornaments on a malignant Christmas tree.

---

IN FACT, IT STILL HURT LIKE BLOODY HELL, even months later when my good friend Joe, being tolerantly familiar with my obsessions, had persuaded me to attend the upcoming Fifty-fifth World Convention of Science Fiction. It was being held in San Antonio over the Labor Day weekend. For all my early reading in the genre, I'd never been attracted to formal "fandom," or thought of attending such events. This being the convocation that names the recipients of the Hugo Awards, there might be authors present whose brains I could pick.

While Seabrook had never written in the genre himself, I was by then obsessively focused on him as the unacknowledged source of an inexplicably ignored anomaly in the evolution of a particular theme. At the WorldCon, I might hope to pick up unexpected details of the past or current usage of that alternate-realities theme, which had become pervasive in film as well as literature. Internet postings and other queries had been turning up zip, so no avenue had preferred probability over any other. Short of serious literary and historical research that I was without the opportunity or resources to pursue, I'd reached an impasse.

Certainly the proposed diversion of the WorldCon portended an ideal setting for mad speculation. The event was held at the convention center named for Henry B. Gonzalez, the last of the real Democrats, and two Marriott hotels on the adjacent Riverwalk. I was consoled that I could spend hours prowling the booksellers who, among the hawkers and hucksters, jammed the exhibit hall. I attended the panel discussions and presentations at whim, with no particular order or system.

I'd hoped that the venerable L. Sprague de Camp might be present, so that I could ask about an early reference he'd made to Seabrook, but he had become too frail to journey from his Plano home. Likewise, I was more than curious about Jerry Pournelle's recollections of H. Beam Piper's claim to have been born on another timeline. It seemed that Jerry was a no-show as well.

Of course, I'd been aware that the old writers I'd grown up on were all gone—but had not confronted the fact that the subsequent generation, like Larry Niven and Dr. Gregory Benford, whose coffee klatches I attended, would all be men my age or older. The truly new writers, particularly the women, were doing some exceptional stuff of which I'd been entirely unaware.

I valiantly endeavored to comprehend Dr. Catherine Asaro's exposition of super-relativistic speeds without being completely distracted by its brilliant author being, unimpeachably, the Babe of Physics as well. Asaro had it all: a scientist and novelist with the kind of leg musculature maintained only by accomplished dancers. That thought, of course, could only make me think of my wife Linda, and the big nothing of a life I would be returning to in a couple of days.

Joe, down from his home in Dallas–Fort Worth, had been helping to man the convention suite in one of the hotels, so I spent a lot of time there, having mildly interesting conversations. While I still looked forward to hearing Dr. John Cramer on Monday and, more immediately, John Norman on Sunday afternoon, the WorldCon would soon be over.

As typical, I was gravitating more often to the bar. "I'm wondering what I'm doing here with all these 'geeks,' anyway," I responded to a query from Joe. Culturally, I was a fish out of water with most of the crowd. "Am I just trying to get next to old guys like Benford and Cramer because I wanted to write sci-fi and couldn't?"

Joe, whose appetite for the personal lives of his friends is normally limited, had made an exception in my case. "I'd hoped to do a little redirect on your obsession," he confessed. "I began to notice that this story you're fixated on has an uncomfortable abundance of suicides." I was surprised and secretly gratified by the concern. Lately, I'd thought that I could drive off into a ditch and no one would notice. It was true that I wondered if the good times were not all in the past—of a world where I was only marking a time that had become my enemy.

Still, I did get slightly hot. I regarded myself as a most unlikely candidate for outright self-annihilation.

I told him that I was too fearful of death and too little at peace with myself. "I'd just like to be sure I'm going to get laid again before I die!"

Overall, I'd found the Con an at least acceptable expenditure of time and money. While it had held no particularly great revelations for me, it beat the alternative. Gritting my teeth and coughing up the substantial late registration fee, I'd reminded myself how miserable long weekends always were. Couldn't get any business done, everything being closed, and most people I knew would be involved with family. My only human contacts would be the odd page from workers ticked off that they'd been tapped out to work the Labor Day holiday.

Candidly, another consideration in my decision to attend the WorldCon was the presence of John Norman, author of an infamous male-dominant fantasy series. Linda and I had found light escape in the *Gor* books for years. Were she still living, she would have given me no peace had John Norman been in town and we'd failed to attend. The success of his novels in the seventies had resulted in his later suffering years of blacklisting. You see, the *Gor* stories feature female sex slavery. Now, you have to understand the way this worked in late-century America, forever pining for the comforts of rigid dogma, which it is too pluralistic to be capable of enforcing.

The recent catechism held that male submission for sexual pleasure fell, along with homosexuality, within the parameters of politically correct orthodoxy. Whereas female submission, like adolescent sexuality, was tantamount to rape, anathema to the thought police who monitor social discourse as well as behavior. Even portions of the generally libertarian science fiction community had conspired to silence Norman.

He had turned out to be a pleasant, distinguished gentleman with silver hair, who looked every inch the philosophy professor that he was in actual fact. I remarked to Joe, who had known Linda well, how sorry I was that she wasn't here to meet him. When we were introduced to Norman's wife, I mused whether she trusted her husband around the coterie of chain-bedecked young women who flocked to his appearances. There were always at least a few whose affects ran toward tight black clothing and body jewelry.

Joe had laughed, "Probably, but she knows very well not to trust the Lindas of the world."

On Sunday, Norman was doing a panel entitled, "Are There Any Taboos Left?" Just one or two, surely . . . It was a bit late convening, and I was standing outside the meeting room, well, brooding—actually—upon the assembling crowd, roughly divided between "geeks" and "mundanes," with a few unattached women.

---

IN THE STRANGE LIGHT of what was about to fall on me during the coming days, it would be easy enough to look back and decide that I sensed something untoward at that very moment. But such was not the case.

She was standing by the door, looking at the program posted for the John Norman panel with a severe expression, insofar as could be discerned through the exaggerated makeup that turned her eye sockets into black pits. My quick glance about seemed to verify that the other lone males did not yet have the scent. They were probably intimidated by her social mask and armor.

Goth. An entire subgenre of the literature aimed at this rather nihilistic ethos. While they were not really that rowdy, Con dynamics had them and the other gamers more or less quarantined in a computer arcade. Frequent sadomasochistic drag notwithstanding, it was unusual to meet one at any function apart from their specific fascinations.

Her appearance did challenge all comers. The jeans nicely displaying the curves of her bottom looked actually worn through, as opposed to strategically ripped. Boots, tightly laced leather vest exposing her pierced navel, small silver Visigoth ax dangling from an ear, and the silver band molded about the lobe of a pierced nostril—I supposed she must have something stuck through her tongue as well. Any who were tempted to confront all this likely expected a surly rejection.

Her only visible colors were her elaborately done nails with what appeared to be star bursts worked on electric blue, and brilliant, though remarkably natural-looking red hair, drawn back into a tail. Long red hair always exerts a gravitational tug on me, even after half the women in America had rediscovered henna.

I would otherwise have been no more likely than the next middle-aged guy to get it up for initial moves in the face of all that. Yet, I felt an unaccustomed arousal as I fantasized what other piercings or scarifications might be among the mysteries of the strong, sturdy young body.

I had stepped on past her into the doorway when I thought, *What the hell?* I stopped and looked back into her raised eyes, green enough to confirm her natural hair tone, though its highlights were likely cosmetic. She did not react to my nodded greeting for long moments. She had a wide face, JJ's type of face, but with prominent cheekbones and lips that would be full and sensual even without the contemporary outlining. The burning pale green eyes within the black mask had a disturbing intensity. They were the kind that could demand answers, while yielding nothing of what lay behind them.

"Hey," she finally responded in a low monotone, her full lips barely parted. Her name tag, only grudgingly worn for admission, I estimated, labeled her with the conceit of a single name, Leiris. It brought to mind Michel Leiris, who had written an essay accompanying a photograph of William Seabrook's red-leather discipline hood for one of the Trocadero museums.

If she displayed the slightest interest in the sexual proclivity inherent in Norman's work, this remote association might make a useful gambit. The panel was starting up, obliging us to move inside. I was still standing between her and the room with my back to the doorjamb. On impulse, I offered my hand to her. What I might accompany the sideways handshake with, I'd no idea, something lame I would imagine. She looked at my hand, then up at me, and her lower lip seemed to quiver. *Whatever does she think she's seeing,* I wondered. *Do we have drugs involved here?* Abruptly, she clasped my hand, but with her left palm downward onto my right, and didn't release it.

Without a clue of what passed for social protocol among such creatures, I drew her beside me into the meeting room, still holding her hand. Enjoying cheap gratification at various curious looks, I stopped beside an empty row near the front. She stepped past me and seated herself with another puzzling gesture, hands sweeping upward just before her butt connected with the seat. It was slight, but noticeable, like the quick shake of her head, as if clearing a fog.

Slouching insolently down, she spread her elbows on the backs of the chairs and rested a booted ankle on her other knee. *Is this baby stoned out of her mind?* I wondered again. *Am I trying to connect with a flake?* She evidenced no uneasiness sitting beside me, elbow against my shoulder. Couldn't possibly be an older man buff, could she? I couldn't get that lucky!

Norman quickly dominated, as it were, the discussion, though the chair, a writer heavily into e-games named Sonia Lyris, made very good points. The women of science fiction are generally not slaves to political fashion. Sensing that Sonia didn't want to tie it on with Norman, I mused as to whether she might catch hell from some self-appointed sisterhood if perceived soft on pigs.

I seemed to surprise my companion by remarking on the chair sharing her name, rendered with an alternate spelling. She'd been looking at me when I turned to her, giving up a startled, flustered smile. Her posture had morphed again. She'd gradually drawn herself up from her slouch and was sitting with her knees together and hands clasped demurely in her lap.

The panel concluding, she approached the chairwoman. I heard her say that she had read Sonia's Web page. Maybe she hadn't been attracted to the panel by Norman at all. I chatted with Norman and Lyris about the contradiction posed by Anne Rice. Female authors were allowed to explore erotic slavery, of both genders in every conceivable combination, without being subjected to ideological commentary. The girl just stood and listened—listened to *me* with seemingly rapt attention. She was certainly looking intrigued by *something*, so before she could escape, I quickly invited her for a drink.

"Aw-hunh," she leisurely drawled, "Marriott bar in an hour." The punker persona was back in full bloom, and the decisiveness was startling. There are dangerous pitfalls in being my age and alone again. If a woman even so much as smiles at you, you may immediately conclude that you have something going!

"You're sure?"

"You can be way sure when I say aw-hunh," she

threw over her shoulder, as she left me checking out a threadbare spot on the butt of her jeans. I'll admit it, I was thrilled, try as I might to harness my imagination. I puttered around, understandably antsy. Checking the message board in the arcade, I found that my carefully printed notice, soliciting information regarding the life and work of William Seabrook, with my 800 number attached, had gone missing.

As I'd not been unduly optimistic about obtaining fresh leads on the Seabrook source, I thought little about it. Even the older participants would be unlikely to recall a Lost Generation journalist whose writings had been of adventure and social concerns, with just a bit of the occult. Finally I'd killed enough time to walk the two blocks to the Marriott through the blazing Texas afternoon, calculating that a preliminary drink to loosen my tongue might be in order.

In the bar, I sipped my Scotch and surveyed the bottom of the huge atrium, which the next two floors overlooked from tiers. I'd been noticing how the curved ramps and stairs, even the two flights of escalators, worked into a general spiral motif. It all reminded me of one of the dreamscapes I'd often visited while keeping a dream journal. The bar was semi-open, only partially partitioned from the lobby, where she was chatting with a clique who looked presentable for the hospitality suite of *Forever Knight* or something else in the vampire venue.

She'd seen me enter, and a girl with spiked hair beside her had scowled at me as I had passed them. Well, the peer group was a dream come true. I had begun to toy with the notion that the social conditions of our New Rome, limited job market, end of conscription and wars of attrition, et cetera, were even further extending adolescence.

Should I infer bisexuality from the way the girls crawled on each other; "oh my God, I've not, like, seen you for an entire hour"? Who knew? I was playing farther out of my yard than usual here.

Eventually she detached herself and came in to surprise me with her choice of a martini, which hardly seemed to fit with the display I'd just been watching. We commenced the awkward ritual of initial encounters. Though she presently lived near Atlanta, she'd grown up in San Antonio.

As it was for myself, attendance at the Con had been a matter of convenience for her, since she would not be out for accommodations with family and friends in town. She'd been seeking escape in science fiction since she was a kid; a time that I'd been reminded was not far behind her.

Maybe not so bad. She could talk about new work of which I was ignorant, and I could turn her on to the classics. I bounced a few of the older writers off her, being sure to mention Phil Dick. Likely he'd been spacey enough to appeal to the younger set. She retaliated with a barrage of names I'd only heard of, if at all—William Gibson, Neal Stephenson, Pat Cadigan. I parried with Dr. Gregory Benford's coffee klatch where I'd been able to squeeze a few questions concerning the shadowy history of Hugh Everett in among the demands on his attention. She'd read more of his work than I, but was unfamiliar with his early triumph *Timescape*.

"A fascinating read, though Benford's paradoxes are exactly that."

---

"ALLOW FOR ANY FORM OF TIME TRAVEL to the past and it requires an alternate world for self-consistency, a world in which the proposed transit, message, or mere observation from a possible future did occur," I offered, shamelessly showing off. "This would be the case from the tiny time loops of Feynman's backward particles, all the way to fishing a wormhole up from the quantum foam and expanding it to transfer macrocosmic bodies. Which seems to be the notion behind that television show . . ."

"*Sliders*! Pathetic, much? Every week, they're cramming their morality up the portal of another universe. Wouldn't even watch it if Kari Wurher weren't so totally hot."

Well, *that* sounded interesting. I omitted mentioning that Linda and I had been deep into the early *Sliders*, watching it weekly. In that connection, I was still able to work in a reference to my late wife—to tap any mileage emergent from widower status, though I'd no personal evidence of any properties that are so damned much fun. Against all my efforts to heighten interest, she was absently bobbing her shoulders to the bar's background music and giving the distinct impression that time was at a premium. I was feeling hopelessly awkward and despairing of pulling this thing out, fundamentally clueless as to what sort of creature I was trying to connect *with*!

Yet, all I could think to do was to reference back to *Sliders*, bringing up Fred Alan Wolf. In numerous books, he'd searched for alternate-world observations in everything from high-energy physics to artificial intelligence to dreams to shamanism. Without surrendering physical discipline, he seemed to understand that science is not the totality of the life of the mind, or of life in general.

"These tunes are so very tubular, they really are. So, that dude Wolf, what he said?" The vernacular, in addition to her distracted effort at continuing conversation, tended to bring the expression "space cadet" to mind. Nevertheless, I expressed my fondness for Wolf.

"Wolf makes no secret of his subjective motivation. He lost a young son who, after many reversals, had only begun to realize his potential. No mystery there, Fred just wants to see his boy again, to see him smile and hear him laugh. Do I hear social workers out there declaring him delusional? You know what they can kiss?"

She looked up abruptly at the unexpected vehemence with which I'd surprised and confused even myself, but I couldn't interpret what briefly sparked behind the dark band across her eyes. What the hell? I just went on about Wolf, quoting his remarkable insight on the "complex-conjugate" waves, undulating back and forth across space-time:

"'Without any discernment between the details of

future events, without any attempt to clarify where, what, when, et cetera, these events occur, the feedback . . . is from all of the future events. This results in the sense of destiny.'"[2] While she had seemed to turn and listen closer, I was still afraid of losing her. Switching gears, I resolved upon another conversational gambit.

I still didn't know whether Leiris was a given name or surname. "Do you know you have the name of a famous French poet?" She looked up with that curious, startled smile again, seemingly her mode with certain questions about her personal self.

"Mother's birth name. I've reapplied it." The explanation of her appropriation of a traditional name derailed her further, dismissing a despised stepfather with a string of choice obscenities. "Dead matrilineal, yea?" she snickered.

Once initiated, her patter was nervous, nonstop, and only quasi-comprehensible. I wanted to get a word in edgewise, to tell her about the connection with Seabrook, hoping to segue from there into bondage. My attention wandered from a description of a prior encounter:

". . . so it's a thing where I'm like from outta town, and this dude was like, 'yea, cool,' and I was like, *'kewl,'* and he was like, 'yea.' So, we gotta put a wrap on this." I was roused from a benumbed trance by her hand on my wrist. "Hey, so I'm outta here," she announced

2. Wolf, Fred Alan, *Star Wave*, NY: Macmillan, 1984, p. 96.

directly. "Like, your digits? As if, we could hang later?"

We agreed that we would both be at Dr. John Cramer's panel the next day, but as she was leaving town a few hours later, there would be precious little time to "hang." I held up my end, giving her my card with its 800 number, but my heart was sinking as she left.

I sighed as I watched her stop in the lobby to talk with a sinewy blond kid who appeared to have been waiting. I say kid; he really looked a bit older than the rest of her group. At least he wasn't the type you often see with a drop-dead babe; some skinny little ratlike thing in oversize clothes, turned-around cap, scraggly whiskers, and eyes slightly less intelligent than my malamute's. I reined in my thoughts.

All obvious insecurities aside, I'd been to enough conventions, labor, political, et cetera, to know that the chances against a liaison increase geometrically with every day after the opening. Expecting to score off a meeting this late in the game was pretty remote under the best of conditions.

The blow-off was depressing nonetheless. I was irritated at the interruption of my game plan at a critical phase. I kicked myself for babbling my obsessions and delaying initiation of my agenda for too long. I considered leaving, calculating the price of drinks involved in hanging around for nothing. Even before then, I had been familiar with the convenient fantasy of the improbable pickup—a choice rationale for continuing to drink in bars.

---

BUT I KEPT ON SITTING THERE,watching her as she rode up the first long flight of the escalator. She turned slightly and looked back down at the bar, but the black eye mask hid her expression. Moving slowly away from me, as someone on the deck of a departing ship recedes from a lonely watcher on the shore, she held her clasped fingers to her lips in an attitude that looked like, well, like *longing*. On the second flight, she turned away and folded her arms about her middle, head lowered. I watched her until she was out of sight.

Man, I grieved after she'd disappeared, that's so desperate, it's pathetic! I knew nothing whatsoever about her, whose room she was going to, or anything at all about her situation. I ordered another Scotch and moped further.

I didn't think I looked too bad for a half century, enough thinning hair to presentably wear long, tied back in the fashion of the courthouse lawyers I dealt with. I'd arrived at an all-purpose costume, sport jacket with collarless shirt and boots, which served for most meetings and after hours as well. My well-trimmed beard could pass muster for business in informal South Texas, and I fancied myself interesting, inclusive of mixing with younger people.

Reviewing my conversation, around the panel and afterward, I was satisfied that I had come off exquisitely boring. And face it. Unless that young a girl has a proclivity for older men to begin with, nothing is going to be enough. Unless it's a money deal, a thing I never had to rely on when younger and refused to do now, even on the rare occasions that I had it to spend. I thought about the blond boy and just couldn't find the probabilities to see this thing other than as a blow-off.

But I couldn't bear to murder hope when I was startled to recognize her coming back down. It took a second because she'd lost the black eye mask, and her makeup generally seemed more conventional. You could hardly say her appearance was muted, though. She'd changed into one of those two-piece suit-things with padded shoulders, otherwise closely molded to her alluring little shape. Her skirt was very short, and bare legs had deliciously come into fashion that summer.

On her left thigh, like a garter, she wore some sort of dark band. Her half-open jacket suggested that the heavy-looking silver chain she had coiled around her neck draped across her breasts inside it. The chain had a barbaric look, which complemented her silver bracelets and contrasted with the modern suit. All that, crowned with the pyrotechnic hair now brushed out and spilling in waves over her shoulders, turned out stunning. Heads began to turn while she was still a story and a half above.

Blond Muscles, who was still waiting, scurried for her as she reached floor level. He appeared to comment uncertainly on her outfit, sickening me as always with those of my gender who are so fearfully insecure as to actively resist a woman looking her best. Her back to my view, her shape was further accentuated as she planted her high heels apart and gestured, palm upward, clearly explaining herself. *Oh babe,* I thought, *any male who doesn't like* that *is due no explanation.*

They were far too distant for me to hear anything, yet I was glued to the tableau, chiefly to the curves of her ass and the fierce cut of her leg muscles. The back of her other hand lay, elbow crooked, against her hip, fingers spread to accentuate still another odd pose. Her posture was reminiscent of something that eluded me, and I wondered at her eclectic combination of mannerisms.

She ceased gesturing and laid her hand placatingly on the young man's chest. Yes, it's true; I'd reached the point that it built my ego when I could so much as get a girl like her to sit down with me! The blond's broad shoulders seemed to sag, as with disappointment, and the girl with the spiked hair entered the scene, taking her arm, and drawing her toward the clique of young Goths.

She recoiled into a rigid stance, ankles together, clenched fists against her hips, in obvious anger. What I saw next I could hardly believe, when she actually stamped her foot. Then, as if in unbelievably slow motion, she turned and strode purposefully, high heels clicking, toward the bar.

The young man had turned red in the face, but it was Spiked Hair who ran after, catching her at the entrance to the bar area. I still couldn't hear what was being said, but her annoyed dismissal was audible to the whole room, "Bite me, twice!" The other woman stared with disbelief as she came ahead, tossing her hair, and perched on the stool she had vacated earlier, next to *me* at the corner of the bar.

---

EVEN THE CLOCK STOPPED FOR A MOMENT.

I don't mind telling you that this pumped me up like nothing I'd experienced for a long time. Breaking a date is one thing, but a young woman blowing off peer-group demands is quite another. Even so, the green eyes that seemed lit by a pale fire from within were intensely appraising me. Heads up! Somehow I'd been teleported to first base, but it was a long way to home. Like a drink "mark" in a hustle bar, I already had my wallet out, ordering her another martini.

Seen close-up, the chain and bracelets were as captivating as the woman they adorned. They were real silver; old, old hand-beaten stuff—no doubt hammered over some base metal. With a smirk, she crossed her bare legs in a blatant tease. She was showing off the thigh band to be of braided leather thongs, twisted so tightly that they must have bitten painfully into her smooth flesh. *So that's the deal,* I thought. *She really is into Norman's slave mystique.*

Joe and I had recently laughed over a West Coast sex posting on the Net that hilariously proclaimed, "Once you've experienced true Gorean slavery, nothing else will suffice." Well, I could do this, so I promptly set into a discussion of Norman's books and how an erotic publishing house was bringing his suppressed series back out. I was trying to waste no more time, yet come off as both intellectual and titillating.

Become a master of the art of dominance and submission; not to sound frightening were she a novice, nor boring if she were heavily involved. A thin line, but I knew how to do it, I hoped.

Something was still not connecting. While my conversation didn't seem to be repelling her, her interest was tepid. If I had read this wrong, what were the chain and thong signals all about? Without the punker mask her features would have been almost sweet—were it not for the whiff of something primeval, as if her heritage led back to some wild, remote place that couldn't be defined by geography.

From books to film. No surprise that she was a fan of the work of Tarantino and Rodriguez, still . . . Reality smirked at me when I mentioned Bogart and she volunteered her preferred "old dude" to be Mickey Rourke. Her full lips grew petulant, almost pouting. As I felt slipping from my grasp possibly the hottest chance I'd had with womanhood in years, she grew openly distracted and fished in her purse. She unfolded a sheet of paper and, as the card I'd given her tumbled from within, I recognized the paper as my notice that I'd posted on the message board.

"This is you," she stated, rather than asked, with abrasive flatness. "You down with cyberpsycho shit, or what?"

There are moments when you know your life is about to change. Ordinarily, we know these divergent and convergent junctions only in hindsight. Sometimes, the path of destiny divides in full view, and you know that nothing is ever going to be quite the same again. Even as I framed the query, "You know Seabrook?" her earnest gaze told me that I might well be having one of those strange moments. "And, what's cyberpsycho?"

"There were some books I was s'pose to get, but they got lost," she answered cryptically. "He's all over the gamers' Web sites, but his work is like, a little hard to find?" She went on to educate me that another subspecies of the cyberreality had woven Gothic sadomasochism together with various schools of dark mysticism. The fantasy scenarios of this virtual cult, including some based on the work of writers I'd mentioned to her earlier, even incorporated bits of Seabrook.

I simply abandoned my intended come-on altogether; began to tell her the story of William Seabrook that I had thus far reconstructed. I gave her a synopsis of how the path of the branching worlds in fiction led back indisputably to Seabrook, weirdly paralleling developments in physics, which would ultimately confirm the literary notion. I observed how it was therefore ironic that some of the most fascinating and frustrating things about Seabrook were the temporal inconsistencies in his record.

She watched me and listened intently as I went on and on for over an hour. Regarding his boyhood through postadolescence, if indeed that phase ever ended, his account was virtually the only source.

"Seabrook was raised in Maryland's spooky Pennsylvania Dutch country. One day his *fey* and maybe slightly demented grandmother, with possible assistance from a delightful little bottle, led the sad little boy into a clearing in a new wood he'd never seen before. There he saw beautiful bright-plumaged roosters, as tall as houses. He described their legs as like the pillars of cathedral aisles. Willie's only happy escape was into that 'other dreamworld' until his grandfather smashed Grandmother Piny's laudanum bottle. But it was too late to stop the hypnotic effects of her drugged mind on young William.

"His earliest boyhood pleasures had included gazing at pictures of women in chains. One day Piny had shown him a throne on which sat a girl, robed in green, with her ankles bound by shining metal circlets joined by a gleaming chain. Willie remembered pressing his hands against her ankles until his own hands held and drew the chains tighter. From that time on, he had two ambitions—to be a writer like his grandfather, the editor of the *American Sentinel*—and to chain women. Growing up, he moved from lassoing little girls to spending his earnings on complicated gold and silver chains with which he fastened women to pillars and ceilings. Most of the women seemed to enjoy it, even went to dances with him, tightly chained."

Seabrook did not believe that he had ever ingested laudanum while in his "fairy godmother's" care at age five. He was convinced that the visions were a form of telepathic communion presented by that numinous figure's drugged mind. In his autobiography, he had chronicled his obsession with his girl-mother Myra and his guilty, ambivalent feelings for Charlie, his ill-fated younger brother. During the family's exile to the Midwestern plains, in tow of his Lutheran minister father, his escape was by way of dreams of visiting fabled Samarkand or Timbuktu.

---

HE'D BEEN INVOLVED WITH "BLACK MAGIC" since "early manhood," Seabrook would write later. What that life-stage designation might have connoted in his times was unclear. He had held a bachelor's degree by nineteen, and completed his master's a year later. Speculating that his dark fascinations may have been "in the blood," he cited family lore holding his ancestor Peter Boehler, an old Moravian missionary and mentor to John Wesley, to have been deeply involved in the black arts.

The bondage motif to which Piny had introduced him, by whatever means, became a permanent fixture, influencing more than his sexual nonconformity alone. The writing on his foreign adventures, his forays into the occult and psychic phenomena, all were shaped by that early template. After becoming city editor of the *Augusta Chronicle* at twenty-one, he took off for a year in Europe, 1907 into 1908. Far from being out of character in itself, this first great escape presaged a lifelong pattern.

I wondered, too, if Willie had been actualizing "somebody else's dream" during the following seven years. In 1909, he broke into serious journalism on the *Atlanta Journal*, where he met Ward Greene. He married Katie Edmondson, the daughter of a Coca-

Cola executive in 1912—in the days when the drink was still laced with cocaine. That was a year after he'd established a successful advertising agency. In his fiction based on Seabrook, Greene would have the ad agency doing the promotional work for the silent film classic *Birth of a Nation*.

By late 1915, however, his pathological ennui was only partially relieved by a series of mildly scandalous affairs. Breaking his connection with the agency, to the horror of his wife, father-in-law, and acquaintances, he made for New York to attempt enlistment in the Lafayette Escadrille. Failing the vision test for the Lafayette Squadron, he had instead entered the American Field Ambulance Service.

"Now that AFS has evolved into a student exchange program—my cousin went to Germany with them—it's pretty much been forgotten that it was originally a unit of the French Army. It might, however, have had a kinship with scholars even then. That unit, in which Seabrook enlisted along with Dos Passos, Hemingway, and other future literary lights, has been described as college-extension courses for a generation of writers. The ambulance corps was a volunteer unit in the old sense. The enlistee had great discretion over his term of service. Seabrook was mustered out, after being gassed at Verdun, though he was never discharged. He returned to the United States after several months' recovery.

"That may well have been when he met Aleister Crowley, as he claimed. However, I found that Crowley did not occupy the Washington Square apartment that Willie described until a year later. Likewise, Willie indicated that he met there forthwith Crowley's *protégée*, Leah Hirsig, 'naked as a jaybird,' although Crowley didn't meet the Hirsig woman until late 1918, and she wasn't in residence at Washington Square until early the next year . . ."

We had moved to a table as the bar buzzed around us, but the noise seemed to recede as though we were in a world of our own making. The late sunlight through the louvered windows painted her with alternating bands of light and shadow. She shifted her chair around to avoid the sunset directly in her eyes, and I had a moment's *déjà vu* of something far away. Had I been less deadened by life, I felt as though I might have been able to grasp and hold it.

"As if, the 'two-slit' thing, like in high school?" she commented on the light. The incongruous association reminded me of Dr. David Deutsch. Without thinking, I immediately went off and started expounding.

In Deutsch's view, "the case that was already unanswerable" inhered in his very commonsense interpretation of this most elementary of quantum experiments. The two-slit (or more) experiment, in which an interference pattern creates dark bands across the target screen, used to be thought of as demonstrating the "wave nature of light." But the results are the same even when the photons are released one at a time and clearly impact, particle fashion, on the target.

Taking stock, Deutsch had found that when a photon passes through one of the slits, something then interferes with it, deflecting it in a way dependent on which other slits are open. The interfering entities apparently have passed through some of the other slits, behaving exactly like photons—except that they can't be seen.

His bottom line was that the "interfering entities" are photons, which exist in a huge number of adjacent universes, similar in composition to the tangible one. Each obeys the same laws of physics, differing only in that the particles are in slightly different positions in each alternate reality.

Were the worlds truly noninterfering, as had been supposed during most of the forty years following Everett? Deutsch had thought not, and given birth to quantum computing.

> . . . If the complex motions of the shadow photons in an interference experiment were mere possibilities that did not in fact take place, then the interference phenomena we see would not, in fact, take place . . . In practice this means that interference is strong enough to be detected only between universes that are very alike.[3]

The ring of truth was there. The proof was shown by an experiment conductible by schoolchildren in a darkened bedroom. It had been studied at various lev-

---

3. Deutsch, David, *The Fabric of Reality*, NY: Penguin Putnam, 1997, p. 49.

els of sophistication for the entire duration of modern science. Proof had become indisputable with the technology to release the photons one at a time. I had been astonished by the simplicity.

"It's not been the many-worlders, but the scientific establishment that's wasted decades, taking excursions through every form of mysticism rather than confront the obvious. Being an old radical, my amazement has its limits; just more of management's crap!" I joked. "Richard Feynman had explained the iridescence on birds' feathers, or even the beautiful colors on ugly oil slicks. They're all merely complex combinations of interference patterns . . ."

"Wait," she interrupted. "Back in the day, I dug up this cool old Coke bottle from my grandmother's yard." I had to call time, for temporal-translation purposes. It seemed she was drifting into musings from her childhood.

"Just substitute your 'the day' expression for 'my day,' and what once was old, is then new again." I smiled indulgently, preparing to make one of those real long reaches that might contrive an illusion of relevance.

*"Du-uh?"* The green eyes flared, coming right back at my condescension. "As if, *'patina'*? The iridescent colors? All those years underground, the glass exchanged particles with the minerals in the earth. Particulate interactions over years 'n years, and its composition morphed—filtering light, like a demonstration of the interference among space-times you said the dude was talking about?"

I was chagrined. Far from drifting while I talked over her head, her feedback had been metaphorical, even poetic. She had consolidated my ramblings into images from her own experience—and carried the analogies a step further.

---

THE BAR, IN THAT DIFFERENT LIGHT, seemed indeed another reality. Her hair fanning out over her shoulders, she looked like a woman of another time, perhaps one of those remarkably neurosis-free *femmes fatales* of the forties. She finally lit a cigarette she had been long holding between her lips and held it in the European fashion, with her small finger extended affectedly. By God, I felt as if I were sitting in *Rick's Café Americain*, or maybe on the quay at Toulon! I didn't know what decade I was in, but it surely didn't feel like century's end.

Returning to the safer and more promising ground of Seabrook, I feared that I had to be doing the man a further injury as I summarized his life, careful and comprehensive as I tried to be. The energy level was palpable. From time to time, her eyes would widen in the shadows, but she said little more—just asking me to specify a source or clarify the chronology.

I ordered another round and began to explain the problems with the time frames, in terms of the composite character Justine, who appeared to be the only major figure in the whole combined saga who was purely fictional; or, more likely, a broad composite of a number of women Seabrook had known. Unlike the solid historical personages of Willie and his friends and lovers, even those whose identities he lightly concealed, identifying Justine was like chasing the grin on the Cheshire Cat.

I came straight up about there being no question that the predilection of my partners and me for mildly sadomasochistic amusements, over the years, had led to my enchantment with Justine, alongside of the desire to resolve her kaleidoscopic reflections into the real-world personas on whom she was based.

"I had wondered," I was going on, "Willie had described a cool Greenwich Village sophisticate, who had made no appearance after 1931, though he had designated her a friend for life. Might she have been his Justine? Later, there was the business in what he called his 'barn' . . ." I saw her hands distinctly shaking as she tried to light another cigarette.

The time for artfulness had ended, and I wanted what was hovering between us to be made known. "Why did you take my notice?" I questioned. I had gradually put together the reason she was there with me. It must have involved some happenstance upstairs, when she'd noticed that the posting's phone number was the same as on my card.

She answered so softly I could barely hear, holding herself tightly, as if grasping for an elusive sense of control. "What are the chances?" she whispered half to herself, darting a glance at me before breaking off and turning her face away. She shivered visibly, though it was quite warm in the crowded bar, her chain tinkling like little bells. I was surprised by the track of a tear in the bar of light across her cheek, and her voice cracked slightly as she struggled for coherence, "I don't . . . I can't believe I'm doing this."

Yes, it's true, I'm a pig. I moved to press whatever advantage her internal confusion had opened and hated myself for using the most elderly lines in the book. I placed my hand on her knee and recited, "It's not an accident that we met here."

But the uncommonly growing sense of familiarity seemed to let her find comfort in the moss-encrusted move. I felt ashamed. "Let's back off from Mr. Seabrook for a bit. Let's talk about Ms. Leiris. I don't know, I feel a need to address you a bit more personally?"

There was another long pause while she studied me, as though *I* were the puzzle. It has to be rare for it to be that difficult for someone to say her own name, and never so incredible for another to hear it. Abruptly, she laughed, just a bit hopelessly—giving a little shrug that said everything had become just too overwhelming, anyway. "As if you'd believe—Justine?"

Moving right along . . . I would make no more journal entries attempting to tabulate synchronistic events. Even had the twists and turns not followed upon each other in such hot succession as to make it impossible to keep up, at that point I had already hit synchronicity overload.

Justine had attended the University of Texas at Austin, as had I many years earlier. I've always found it amusing to hear the Legend of the Sixties as interpreted by the students of "Generation X." Given what I'd just heard, I was only mildly surprised to discover that she had met my young cousin, who was currently in attendance there. By that point, my only reaction was: sure, of course, why not? Beneath the Goth affectations was an educated young woman. She'd followed up a psych degree with some graduate study, then briefly worked for an airline before moving to Atlanta only a few months earlier.

The move had been to take possession of properties bequeathed to her by a great-grandmother who had died before Justine was born. As per the will, the inheritance had been held in trust for decades. Suggesting that some unspecified aspects of the estate had proven trying, she'd decided to take a break and come home for the science fiction convention. Of the details that she did choose to confide at this early stage, two stood forth, one being that the bequest included Seabrook memorabilia, notably an item that sounded like a notorious painting from the Seabrook story.

Early in 1940, the novelist Marjorie Worthington, a woman who became one of Willie's great loves, had painted an elaborate wall panel on wood, limning John Donne's "Hymn to God the Father" and illustrating the chapters in Seabrook's life, including the outré ones. Unsuspecting that the mural would ever be seen publicly, Marjorie let go of her typical inhibitions and included nudes, girls peeking out of cages, and a hanging figure in a red-leather mask. Could the naked woman in the mask have been the elusive "Justine"?

Willie had rather cynically described the final segment, which featured his immortal soul absurdly rendered as a toy-sized white woolly lamb, scampering away toward a field of daisies. I supposed that I might once have reacted similarly. Remarkable enough to locate objects of my quest in this fashion. More bizarre was that, in the Seabrook saga I'd capsulated for her, my companion suspected that she could identify her ancestress as none other than a historical Justine!

It seemed that I was reaching under the table to touch flesh and blood engendered by the one figure in the story whom I had taken to be fictional, or at least an elaborate composite. Around the time this child had been born, Kris Kristofferson had brought out a song whose refrain laughingly wafted through my mind: ". . . A WALKIN' CONTRADICTION, PARTLY TRUTH AND PARTLY FICTION."

---

I did not let go of her knee. Soon wonder reawakened libido, and I reached higher to touch the twisted leather thongs. I pushed the band a bit from where it had cruelly bitten into her thigh. She flinched as I gently kneaded the line that appeared, a comfort that only increased the localized pain as the circulation returned. Leaning forward, she grasped my other forearm and pressed my hand inside her jacket between her naked breasts. I fingered the chain, marveling that it might well have been one acquired by Seabrook on his fabled trip into the old Arabian domain. I drew its links slowly across a nipple and felt it harden.

She gasped slightly and spoke again in the near whisper. "I'm thinking that I'm not welcome, much, to use my friend's room." Beyond the obvious, I felt a crucial decision being made, slipping between us like the passing of a spirit. At that moment, I could have no clue as to the consequences.

No problem, I lived alone, just the dog and me. We left the bar and descended some stairs off the lobby to a glass door that opened on San Antonio's famous Riverwalk. We passed a couple of the young people from her group and she pointedly drew my arm around her, but they barely looked at us as we went by.

I was reminded of a time, back in "the day," when I had thrown my books at the principal and dropped out of high school. On my way out, defiantly lighting a cigarette, I had paused to cuss out some old antagonists. As they had comprehended the situation, their eyes sort of glazed over and they'd walked away. I had been no longer a part of their reality; I'd ceased to exist in their world. I remembered wishing that someone had told me that it could be that easy! While my parents had shortly pressed me into entering another school to finish up, the small bit of bravado had constituted a rite of passage. I wondered whether Justine might be feeling something of the same nature.

We paused on the Riverwalk, regarded as highly romantic by tourists, though less so to locals. Until an evening such as this, one which seemed "the goal in sight again." I could almost believe the proposition that we are able to choose among our possible futures, that I had somehow found my way to that moment. Yes, I was indeed basking in the envious glances of men, as well as those of outright hatred from some women—we all have our little agendas. But I did feel that I had to exorcise one last demon of sanity before giving myself over, altogether, to midlife crisis.

I used to joke with my late wife about her "Three Faces of Linda": the exotic dancer seen on the stage, the flirtatious courtesan who was her clubroom persona, and, of course, the "real" Linda, predictably a bit shy and withdrawn. Those personalities had generally occupied discrete blocs of time. This creature, on the other hand . . . I had watched the tough young punker waver into something indefinable within spans of seconds, then morph into a being as kittenish as Seabrook had drawn her "composite" predecessor. I looked down into those pale green panther's eyes, which again seemed as primordial as her Arabian jewelry.

"Who are you, really?" I wondered rhetorically then, in all hopeless honesty, just blurted out, "And what in the world do you want with me?"

The enigmatic eyes moistened, as they seemed to divine all my shades of meaning. "Where is it written that same is good?" Thus dismissing ages, acculturations, et cetera, she snuggled tighter under my arm. "Something wonderful is happening," and that was all she would say as we drove to my house—in a neighborhood where it's best not to be after dark unless both the cops *and* the gangs know you.

In my defense, I will tell you that the childlike joy in that expression resonated with a *hope* long absent from my heart. I do possess some sense of responsibility, beyond simply not wanting to deal with the guilt later, but this was of a different order. If I had banished the demon from one shoulder, an angel on the other was still being troublesome. The old folks would have said it was warning me, *If you don't live up to that, if you let her down, it's the sort of thing for which you will surely be damned.* Please don't laugh at me; I'm as serious as death.

Still, I gave myself over—what did you really expect? Uncharted territory it would be, then. In my experience, when you notice something magical, something the poets would sing as evidence a union is meant to be, it's best not to tell Girlfriend about it. Women generally don't appreciate anything that far outside their control, inclusive even of acts of God Almighty. So here was one who just seemed to say to go with it? I had no more questions. Right then at least. Questions would soon multiply like a mutated virus.

---

IT WOULD BE ABSURDLY COY to refrain from the most intimate details of what was happening to me. From what I was to learn of the viewpoint of Justine's exhibitionistic little soul, it would be flatly disingenuous.

Someone wanting you that bad can raise the dead. While I had not yet been disposed to just go on out to the cemetery and lie down, I'd been emotionally and sexually shut off for a long time. Even my bedroom had certain tomblike qualities. Due to curiosities of old house construction and expansion, it was a fully enclosed inside room, without outside walls. No sound or vibration disturbed its silence. Hidden away in decaying south San Antonio, the place must have seemed to her like the dark side of the moon.

Drawing a deep breath, she stepped to the center of the room and stood looking at the bed, as though caressing the image of what we were about to do on it. She then loosened her skirt and let it fall to reveal that she had worn nothing beneath it.

Turning about slowly, displaying herself for me, she shed her jacket and lifted a questioning eyebrow. Wearing only her body jewelry and heels, she was easily as sensational as any showgirl I'd ever had a lech on. Still, I responded that I wanted her to be as naked as possible. Dropping her eyes, she breathed a soft, "I understand," unwinding the heavy chain and taking off her bracelets. She also relinquished a tiny chain that draped about her hips. Her nipples were unpierced, as I'd learned when I caressed them at the bar. But, as she lifted her leg to remove the painful thong band, I saw the glint of metal below her reddish pelt of pubic hair.

"No tattoos?" I wondered, as she kicked off her shoes and moved to the bed. She sprawled across it on her belly and propped herself up on her elbows with her chin held by her fingers, regarding herself in the full-length mirrors on my closet. Fixing me with her eyes in the reflection, she pointedly spread her thighs.

"The only dead-on work is done in Europe," she explained, assessing me in return. "I'd have to get *way* up on something, to let it be put on me." I took off my coat and moved around the bed to mute the lights, hoping to give myself every possible edge in comparison to her hard young body. As I reached for the lamp on the nightstand, she grabbed my butt with both hands, pulling herself to her knees. She loosened my belt and aggressively shoved down my trousers. Pressing my hands behind my back, she began to demonstrate the utility of the ornament on her pierced tongue.

I was erect in a matter of seconds and, not wanting to risk losing it, hastily pinned her back against the bed, losing more clothes as I could. I cursed under my breath as I remembered to reach for the condom, which, hope springing eternal, I kept on the nightstand. But she seized my wrist and nipped at my pectoral with her teeth. "Nay, please! I don't want that," she hissed.

While I hated the thought of trying to keep it up to get the damned thing on, I felt obliged to protest, "Unfortunately, I know that it's perfectly safe, Justine, but you don't know me, now do you?" God, I felt so responsible, it made me sick.

"A good time at a party? Not. This is some kinda real, and I wanna feel you come inside me," she breathed, smothering any further discussion with her mouth. I didn't recall ever being kissed quite like that before. She was a starving succubus, gnawing and sucking on sustenance long denied, squirming against me, as if trying to claw open and crawl inside my skin.

Handling Justine's sweet, firm flesh alone would have impacted, not to mention the way she held the rungs on the headboard in a facsimile of bondage. She moaned and writhed as I ate her pussy, lapping up her abundant lubrication. This was perhaps less a product of any expertise on my part, than of her labial ring's configuration. A thick protrusion on one side was designed to remain in more or less constant contact with her clitoris.

When I did grab some neckties, strategically left (like the condom) on the headboard since I rarely wear them, and bound her hands, she gasped in the semblance of innocent anticipation, "Are you gonna hurt me now?" This set me on fire and, when I told her no, not then, she teasingly purred, "But you will, sometime? Tell!"

As I whispered to her fantasies of sufferings to come, she rolled over on her belly again, flexing her buttocks irresistibly. When I spread her and touched the tender flesh, she whimpered and involuntarily flinched away, but I seized her hips and dragged her back. The long muscles in her back quivered and she sobbed uncontrollably into the pillow as I penetrated her anus.

"Dead right! Make me feel it, make me feel every motherfuckin' second of it!" She screamed and cried and cursed, bucking furiously as I reached under her to manipulate the cunning little ring against her clit. She came repeatedly and violently and I was astonished to sense at least two of the "Faces of Justine," the tough punker and the playlike victim, momentarily merge.

It was like having two women simultaneously, superimposed on one another. Her spasms subsiding, she turned on her back, easing me out of her before I could come and looked up at me, eyes wet and lips parted in an expression of absolute surrender. In that moment, I knew I could do anything whatsoever to her. She looped her bound wrists around my neck and sought my mouth, lifting her hips for me to enter her vaginally.

Her demeanor neutralized any residual performance anxiety, and I discovered with delight that another labial ring, located farther down, performed for me the same function as the clit ring did for her. The contractions of her vaginal muscles gently nursed me toward climax. She kept her eyes open, their pale green fire burning into my soul as her slow undulations became unendurable. When she brought me off, she stretched all her muscles and came again with a long luxuriant moan.

Directly she was drifting off, oblivious to the tickle and stickiness of the fluids we had generated. The sequence of choice left me more bemused at her apparent indifference to hygiene, but it was not something I was going to struggle with. As I pulled her on top of me, so that she might go to sleep without the burden of my weight on her, something happened that went beyond sex. Some more etheric fluid filled my heart.

Holding her, just holding her was like . . . like coming home after a long trip. Yes, like coming home is all I can call it. I don't mean that she was like my wife, or JJ, or others I've been with. The piercing and her other exotica, her morphing personas, all made her far different. But the greatest difference was the quiet conviction: Yes, this is what I'm used to. This is familiar, and safe, and . . . home.

# II
# Circumstance

Wrapped in Justine's arms and legs, my thoughts *did* finally drift back to JJ, nonetheless. Unworthy as it might be seen, I'm afraid that it was rather along the lines of gloating at her probable disbelief, could she but have seen me then! I'm talking serious disbelief here, hard-core denial. JJ's truths, her sense of reality, seemed to reside in whatever notions were most comfortable and convenient for the parochial minds of the moment. Truthfully, she had turned out to be not so different from the way I'd previously remembered her—from the portentous year of 1963, that single long storm of synchronicity, in personal lives as much as world affairs.

In our later era, I first became uneasy when dragged to view a popular film that left the screen awash with passivity. My perception was that the male lead wussied out after claiming cosmic certainty that comes only once. What was supposed to be attractive about failure to embrace his lover's confession of compliance?

Not me, surely, but my JJ was careful to make no such confession. It became obvious that she would not leave her husband. Her basic conservatism reasserted itself, her discomfort with stirring things up, a pastime in which I take positive delight.

To my credit, I refrained from making the acquaintance of more bartenders over these issues. For the first time in my life, I caved and sought counseling. Those of us, and this is not at all gender-specific, who spend our lives pretending to be tough guys may ultimately determine that we have maintained our image at a terrible price.

The counselor, a Pakistani Sufi woman skilled in regression techniques, taught me much about the frailties of memory. Unexpectedly, I discovered a dark arc into which I could never see to resolve its contents. I'd not denied the reality of repression for other people, but finding its trail within myself was disconcerting.

In deep hypnosis, I discovered how I'd "consolidated" some temporal facts. If asked before how many times, as a teen, I'd run over to JJ's house on foot, I'd have answered maybe a dozen. Standing on her lawn in the hypnotic re-creation of the breakup, her dropping her chin when I tried to kiss her, I realized that I had been there scores of times not including all the lonely "drive-bys" of later years. However, when the counselor gave me an exercise of writing a chronology of my early romance with JJ, I found that some sequences and juxtapositions made no sense at all.

There was a lucid recollection of sitting at a downtown shoeshine stand—Fort Worth, Texas, having no "uptown." Built into an unused doorway no larger than a closet, it was wallpapered with an eclectic collection of scripture, joke-shop obscenities, and magazine cheesecake. It was situated in a zone of derelict hotels, which would later be abolished when it was deemed that the emotional stability of the city's middle class demanded prettification.

My mission had been to pay the outrageous sum of two whole dollars for a shine. Included in the fee would be directions to any contraband about which I might inquire, specifically, more persuasive identification than my doctored driver's license.

All this had all been preparatory to a proposed venture in underage marriage with JJ. I had been in a delinquent frame of mind, mild by today's standards—the proverbial teenager in leather jacket . . . although, in my defense, I did have an old Harley-Davidson to go with it! When she became pregnant late in 1963, presumably by my successor, who briefly balked at marriage, a grand gesture had seemed indicated.

The problem was that the timing made such a version of the enterprise thoroughly implausible. The vision seemed to incorporate elements from a full year before the pregnancy that had supposedly triggered my derring-do. I could not so much as recall whether I had succeeded in obtaining the items sought or not. Still, the vivid memory remained, and could not be denied. Perched on the high shoeshine chair, I had been happily inspecting a brand-new book, acquired only just before I'd arrived at the shine stand.

It was the copy of the *I Ching* that I have to this day: the Bollingen single-volume edition with a foreword by Carl Jung. Intrigued by Philip K. Dick's use of the book in his classic of that year, *The Man in the High Castle*, I'd been determined to possess it. Knowing full well that my life would end without JJ, I suppose I'd hoped that it might open for me the gate to another reality, as it had for the characters in Dick's fiction. Failing that, perhaps its oracular powers might enlighten me as to how to win her back against all odds.

I had gotten downtown early in order to search it out, combining the physical and metaphysical in my quest as I was to do again—more years later than I could have conceived of at the time. Entering at the side door of old Barber's Bookstore, a local institution nearly unto today, I had an experience of the synchronicity upon which the ancient Chinese tome was allegedly based. High on a shelf just inside the door, I had spied the object of my search.

I must claim that it most plaintively called out to me, because I promptly tucked it beneath my leather jacket and stepped back onto the sidewalk before the door even had time to close. Continuing on my mission, I had passed a newsstand. The papers left no doubt of this vision's date. Their headlines had been full of the missiles of October.

---

THE OLD *I CHING*, rebound a couple of times, lay on my nightstand even then. It had been my quiet friend throughout the years. More recently, it had acquired a cherished companion—not a book that I sought out, but one that had *found me*. The night-light painted this other friend's faded dust cover with new life, while Justine stirred softly against me—and I remembered my times with JJ.

JJ *never* would have carried on in bed like this little babe! In the nearer time, the fault was partially of the environment. The logistics of my job and house being inconvenient for nooners, we often had been reduced to a downtown whore-motel. The concierges, a couple fresh from the Indian subcontinent, kept it clean enough in spite of its chronic limitations. One rainy afternoon, we had been making love "Southern style"; that is to say, as befit a man of my age—slow and *deliberately*.

"How do you imagine they arrive at the particular figure of thirteen dollars for two hours?" I had wondered at this finer point of pandering for some time.

"However they do it, you get what you pay for," she'd griped. "The carpets are soaked whenever it rains."

"Your feet are never on the floor, anyway," I teased. "No more inconvenient than playing with each other in your parents' living room." I recalled to her one of my fonder memories from our adolescent romance. When she couldn't get out of the house, we would sit in front of the television in the darkened living area and "mess around," as we'd called it back then. At that age reaching inside her clothes, running my hand down her belly to touch her forbidden parts, had been as near acute a thrill as the sex act itself. "We would get in a serious lip-lock," I described, leading her through the motions, "then I would *slowly* slide your panties off . . ." I was remembering the way her toes would curl when I stroked her smooth, bared flanks.

"And sit on them!" Flushing, she was starting to squirm in response to the fantasized revisitation. "It was usually my shorts, and you would *hide* them, so there I'd be, bare-assed—what if my stepparents had ever walked in?"

"I imagine they had at least some idea of what was going on. Besides, that very thought was what gave you a gigantic orgasm every time"—I'd laughed, playing with her pussy—"just about like the way you're going to come right now if you'll let yourself go!" The prediction had been directly fulfilled, which hadn't kept her from chiding me.

"You're *bad*, you know it? You're having simply too much fun with all this." That sort of remark would bother me. Something in her tone told me it wasn't really a joke, so much as recognition that I appealed to a part of her that she'd never truly allowed to be free. I could only immediately remember one occasion that JJ had ever departed from a sort of sedate resignation—a capitulation dressed up as sardonic, but not really.

Near the end of our farther yesteryear, she'd attempted to poison my love with a lurid recitation of having done her intended, along with two of his friends, at a church youth outing—the location being plausible enough for the time and place. However, I would later realize that it had to have been a fantasy. There was no way those boys had it up for pulling a train. Not a matter of scruples. Their cowboy image notwithstanding, such indulgence was far too *country* for Texas city kids of that era. Having to get naked and perform in each other's presence, and thereby kicking in the boys' ubiquitous homophobia, pretty much rendered group sex implausible.

My reaction to the purported ravishment was, at the time, "inappropriate" even to me, not to mention probably providing her with horrified confirmation that I could be regarded as a wrong person. Inexplicably aroused, I found myself loving her even more. Now I had to wonder—might that early expression of voyeurism, with a discernible masochistic edge, have tightened a kink that would finally help bend my attention after Seabrook's strange devices? In any event, I did love her yet. Read my story and tell me how could I not.

In our adult era, I had begun to press for additional dimensions to our renewed relationship, to get it out of the bedroom alone. So, we had begun taking lunch, almost daily, in a park on the San Antonio River where we could talk and feed the ducks. Middle-aged love is different. It can be calmer and more thoughtful. Still, it was there that I argued with the preposterous concern of distress to her grown children, of whom I knew only vaguely, never having been allowed to meet them. My take was that adults who owed her their lives should damned well put up with *her*. I knew that the end was near when, at our usual parting kiss, she dropped her chin.

I would learn so much more about JJ, and our world, and myself that it would strain the limits of credulity. Suffice it to say that you now possess the constellation of events that sparked the inception of my quest. If you are inclined, as was my little love, to serve the gods of the mundane at all costs, you may then regard what followed as obsession going over into dementia. If so, then seek other reading material. For you will surely abhor the circumstances that followed from my determination to conclude the unfinished story of William Seabrook.

Driven by the subjective need to unravel the mysteries of the aberrant memories with their twists and warps of chronology, of just what the hell had happened to me then and later, I turned a different eye to my youthful fantasies of other worlds, other realities. Increasingly, I no longer cared about very much apart from this single eccentric interest. My life winding down, only an elderly dog left dependent on me—it takes no deep psychology to comprehend such a solitary obsession.

I'd found that almost all authorities agreed that Murray Leinster had published the oldest and wildest explicitly branching-worlds story as far back as 1934. Many later authors took inspiration from this original piece. Greg Benford, a physicist and science fiction writer, would ultimately speculate whether Everett himself might not have drawn his original notion from Leinster. A daring concept for a physicist, to suggest that a scientist might have been inspired by a science fiction writer rather than the other way around!

---

A MYSTERY MAN OF PHYSICS, Hugh Everett III devised the "relative state" formulation of quantum mechanics around 1956. Given its bizarre and supposedly counterintuitive properties, his vision of a cosmos with essentially infinite numbers of branching realities received scant credence when published the following year.[4] Even rendered into more popularly accessible form in the seventies, it was ridiculed as pure science fantasy until theoretical work late in the century suggested that bases for practical experimentation existed. To be coldly realistic, you might say, until the invisible government perceived such benefits as unbreakable cryptography in it.

The viewpoint of another generation ruled in that earlier world. Our old redbrick school building would never have survived a good earthquake. Nevertheless,

4. Everett, Hugh III, *The Theory of the Universal Wavefunction*, Princeton thesis, 1956, 138 pages (publication in DeWitt, Bryce and Neill Graham, *The Many-Worlds Interpretation of Quantum Mechanics*, Princeton, NJ: Princeton University Press, 1973. The collection of all pertinent documents).

when the siren sounded, we were required to crawl under our desks and pathetically hide our eyes with our little hands against the imaginary blast. As an eleven-year-old looking up at the arched tops of the high windows, still opaque with the blackout paint from the last war, I had known only that I was regularly made afraid. Forget *Happy Days* and similar tripe. On the whole, the children of the fifties did not dream, for to dream was only to ride the nightmare.

I found it depressingly easy to sum up in a few sentences everything that was publicly known about "the late Hugh Everett," as he was commonly referenced. It was not easy to locate even so much as an exact date of death. For a while, I wondered if he might not have been a suicide, as had Seabrook and a number of other principals in this strange saga. Eventually, I concluded that his relationship to the Cold War defense establishment had at least some bearing on the dearth of information.

I'd grown exasperated with intriguing but vague descriptions such as "maverick physicist," "unaffiliated with institutions," et cetera. With some amusement, I noted that, in physical science's own political paraworld, one unaffiliated with any *academic* institution is deemed to have left the field. What a naughty boy Everett must have been to follow the Cold War example set by Teller and numerous other Dr. Strangeloves.

It was painful to learn of a lecture trip Everett made during the late seventies to the University of Texas at Austin, careening about the campus in a

Cadillac with steer horns. In those years I'd owned a successful nightclub in the North Texas Metroplex. I'd possessed the liberty and interest to attend his lecture, had I known about it. With renewed popular interest, Everett had planned to do more work, but died of a heart attack in 1982. Sadly, I knew that the earlier collaborators had distanced themselves, to greater or lesser degrees, from his theory.

During my research, I realized that there had never been much imperative toward democratization of scientific information in the West. Quite the contrary. Before the Second World War, only a handful of scientists and science writers, principally in Britain, undertook to explain to the people what science was all about. This "Invisible College," primarily of leftist political persuasion, included J.B.S. Haldane and J.D. Bernal. On the literary side, they were linked with Aldous Huxley and Olaf Stapledon. In science, their tradition led back to the great Paul Dirac.

In the pivotal years of 1938–41, their efforts grew frenetic. Through the cold British rain, they could watch across the Channel the rampage of a beast that made the monsters of our own societies look benign by comparison. In the fall of 1939, the war machine began to roll. On the Continent, Werner Heisenberg, Erwin Schrödinger, and the other great physicists who did not have to run for their lives were forced into a lackadaisical abstractedness by the preposterous tenets of "Aryan science."

During the war, state security consumed all the powers, and the Cold War came hard on its heels.

Thanks largely to the influx of German and Jewish scientists, America had come up to speed in physics. *Scientific American* was no longer, as it had been earlier in the century, on a par with *Popular Mechanics*. While we ate off Formica and watched *Ozzie and Harriet* struggle with chrome toasters, there came a move in government actively to suppress the dissemination of most scientific information. Speeches in the *Congressional Record* tended not so much toward hysteria about Communist agents as to ridiculous propositions that high-school students might build atomic bombs in the bathtub. Fear of the people themselves! Ideology lapsed into an elitist mode. You were supposed to "trust" those who "knew more."

As with a rumor in 1938 that the Nazis had split the atom, a certain moderation of this stratification of society into initiates and morons became necessary during panic over Soviet space successes. Still, this would remain the atmosphere Hugh Everett came up against when, by the year of Sputnik, he extracted from quantum mechanics a truly rationalist interpretation. I mean to say, the one that would allow even a single universe to exist without some subjective observer to magically "collapse the wave function."

---

BY THE DARK DECEMBER OF 1941, as the world's empires locked in a struggle to the death, the great Richard Feynman had visualized a physical entity whose very existence was defined by reciprocal interaction with its own past. He had already developed an approach that many regard as the precursor of the many-worlds interpretation. Feynman had broken with convention to present the novel image of a particle "turning a corner" in time. I didn't believe that he could have arrived at a concept of converging pasts without some preconceived notion of the branching worlds.[5]

Simultaneously, in England, the little engineer J.W. Dunne was nearing the end of his life. Before "turning the corner," he'd been feverishly trying to explain, to a war-haunted world, the implications for human immortality of the physics of time. Fiction writers close to the sciences spun fantasies that would sometimes spookily illustrate those notions. The collective mind at work, or something else? I wondered what the good Catholic boy Hugh Everett had begun to read by age eleven.

A movement caught out of the corner of my eye had interrupted my musings. When I glanced about, nothing was there. The dog was outside, and my living room was silent, empty. It had been too large for a mouse, and there had not been a cat around for years. Trying to return to my work, I found myself

5. Feynman won the 1965 Nobel Prize for his work in quantum electrodynamics (QED) and was among the earliest to speculate on the possibilities of quantum computing. Matthew Broderick's sentimental film treatment, *Infinity* (Overseas Filmgroup, 1996), a story of Feynman's early life (including the death of Arline Greenbaum, his young wife), might suggest additional motivation for his refusal to join in the conspiracy of silence against Everett's concepts of time and reality.

confused by one of those uncanny moments when the arrangement of materials on my desk seemed quite unlike I had thought I'd left it. I could not refrain from processing the momentary episode in terms of my fascinations.

Driving against fatigue on the Laredo highway, I'd once or twice swerved to avoid a figure suddenly glimpsed on the shoulder. Looking back, there would be no one in sight. If we live that near to a hallucinatory state—if just a tiny biochemical change can induce visions, then why cannot we conjure, almost at will, those beloved images we would most desire to see?

I wondered at such episodes, which all experience with some regularity. Might they not be fleeting perceptions of moments in other worlds, where the cat *was* on patrol and there was indeed a hitchhiker by the roadside? Might not we appear as ghosts in their worlds, as they in ours?

Could such seemingly random sightings constitute "observations" more sweeping than the alternate paths of single particles? Might communication among world-branches, "calls" made over an "Everett phone," be more readily received than visualized in all the elaborate setups of "hard" science fiction? Might not the technological foo-foo be but metaphor for a faculty more accessible than our ordinary sense of sanity finds comfortable? If so, what signposts might guide observations along and across a network of branching time-highways? Did more recent science suggest any kind of grid lines that might be discernible to a perception extended across a branching cosmos?

My admittedly subjective obsession could focus on at least one demonstrable concern. One thing that I could get my hands on was the anomaly of the preconception, the notion, of the branching worlds having worked itself out in literature decades before Everett's formalism of 1956–57. I addressed myself to this evolution of ideas, from the presumed completion of quantum formalism in the twenties to the more recent interpretations.

I then recalled an article I'd read some years before by David Deutsch, then a young physicist at the University of Texas at Austin. Speculating about the future possibilities of quantum computing, he'd convinced me from a philosophical standpoint that the many-worlds interpretation constituted the only truly rationalist, materialist resolution of the quantum impasse.[6]

I found a few recent articles by and about Deutsch, who'd become a major theoretician of quantum computing. I was elated to learn that a new book had just been released. In it, he described the use of an algorithm developed by Peter Shor of Bell Labs, among the earliest mathematical processes for quantum computer setups, that seemed to necessitate the employment of computation resources in many worlds simultaneously. Arguing that the classical idea

6. Deutsch, David, in *The Ghost in the Atom*, editors P.C.W. Davies and J.R. Brown, Cambridge University Press, 1986.

that there is only one universe was thus destroyed, Deutsch threw down the gauntlet to those still clinging to a single-universe worldview. He challenged them to explain how Shor's algorithm works. In fact, that question had been addressed years before the work of Deutsch—or Shor—had posed it.

---

"THERE EXISTS A FASCINATING THEORY that two worlds branch from every bit of destiny action,"[7] wrote the science fiction author Andre Norton, who had begun her writing in "another world," where it was years before her readers could be allowed to know she was a woman.

Conducting a systematic search for the specific inputs that had framed my notions, memory returned of hours spent fishing worn covers from high, dark bookshelves in an old library as spooky and exciting to a boy's eye as anything dreamed by Ray Bradbury. Also, the garish covers of old paperbacks and pulp magazines, purchased for a few cents in used bookshops, logically had to have been from even earlier decades than the hardbounds I recalled. As I recovered bit after bit, the old Halloween thrill returned to quicken my fifty-year-old heart.

In *The Door into Summer*, Robert Heinlein entertained, then dismissed, the "old" notion of branching time streams. The trick was in the word "old." A *notion*

7. Norton, Andre, *Star Gate*, NY: Harcourt Brace, 1958. Quotation is from the prologue.

might well be old, as old as the fairies in their paraworld beyond the hollow hills, but Heinlein gave one to believe that he was arguing against a scientific theory. His story was in print months *before* the publication of the theory he had referenced. That was among the mildest of the contradictions.

I had soon begun to go well beyond my own personal time in the pursuit of the research. I didn't know what my associates thought of my lowered productivity, as I would sign out into the field, then bury myself in more modern libraries. I'd turned out to be a really very good labor representative, in spite of burnout from watching unjust spectacles, such as lifetime employees being sacked while dull and impotent union organizations did nothing. For what little good I'd accomplished, I did not want to be considered as having gone over the top.

A rep may function quite well being thought of as a playlike lawyer, corrupter of public morals, or even as a goon, but "airhead" is *not* an appropriate image. That simply would not do! However, as with many of the workers I'd helped with problems on the job, my position had "downsizing" clearly scrawled all over it. I knew the job wouldn't last much longer, so I seized the opportunity to plunge bodily into the questions raised by the developing "temporal anomaly" I was uncovering among writers' memoirs and publication dates.

Not alone economic struggle, but life itself seems to decree against discovering that anything our secret hearts long to believe just might turn out to be the case. We teach our children the "hard facts of life"—not facts unless they kick you back, right? There is no Easter Bunny or Tooth Fairy and, along these lines, your narrator hardly had opportunity to so fantasize.

What I'd expected and hoped to find was that, "somewhere in time," an esoteric tradition embracing the plurality of worlds had existed in the physical community, as physicists refer to their collective self. I thought that its notions might have been processed through the literati until science fiction writers rendered them into print. This had seemed highly possible in Britain, where the genre was not ghettoized, set apart from literature, as in America.

---

"READING HARD SCIENCE FICTION IS A POOR WAY TO LEARN SCIENCE. . . . The reader of science fiction . . . may 'know' many things that are not so, if only through the process of osmosis."[8]

From a standpoint of rigorously proven experimental facts, this caveat should be well taken. However, science fiction fandom has never really shared this perception. Much as they may deny it, the fans have always wished to believe that science fiction has presented them with deeper, profounder truths than it was possible to access otherwise. This was even more the case for those of us who grew up on the old science fiction twenty-five to fifty years ago.

8. Cramer, John, *Twistor*, NY: Morrow, 1989.

In my quest for information on the many-worlds, I'd turned often to Joe's resources. A research chemist at a prestigious foundation, he also happens to be a lifelong science fiction fan. His broad literacy includes the cybernetic, unlike your low-tech narrator, and he also possesses near photographic recall of anything he's ever read. The data retrievable from his encyclopedic mind was invaluable to me, not to mention his ability to encompass the bulk of my personal madness without wincing.

As Joe sees it, while American science fiction today may not be wholly out of the closet, the young reader, unarguably, is deprived of our earlier thrill. We experienced the reading of science fiction as something of a dirty little masturbatory secret, hence charged with all the lure of the forbidden. Maybe the effect derived from frequently reading it under the covers with a flashlight.

For months, I'd been scouring the libraries and bookshops, digging up the old science fiction I recalled from pre-Everett times that clearly presaged the many-worlds. In the process, I'd identified other, more mainstream literary works predominantly by British authors, which were clearly germane.

*That stormy evening* . . . sorry about that, but it really was, you see. The gusting torrents and ball lightning had reminded me too intensely of a night years before. That night Richard, my closest teenage comrade, had entered upon a path of disappointments, on the darker side of love, which would take his life by his midthirties. It had been a common enough story, rejection by a pregnant girlfriend in favor of a rival whom an ignorant community deemed a "better catch." But, from that night forth, Richard had seemed damned to repeatedly re-create the same failures.

Joe had been in town, and we were at my house reviewing the above-mentioned works. His phenomenal memory aside, neither had Joe actually read these materials for many years. We were both astonished at how precisely the early authors had represented a theory not yet formally constructed.

Across the Atlantic, I'd found another pregnant hint from the neglected British giant Olaf Stapledon. He was subsequently as much despised, by the American literary establishment, for the fact that he indisputably produced literature as for his leftist politics. I was hardly innocent of the ominous imperatives that had framed official intellectual bigotry in the United States since at least the late thirties.

America could not admit quality to exist in the genre in which Stapledon wrote in 1937:

> In one inconceivably complex cosmos, whenever a creature was faced with several possible courses of action, it took them all, thereby creating many distinct temporal dimensions and distinct histories of the cosmos. Since in every evolutionary sequence of the cosmos there were very many creatures, and each was faced with many possible courses, and the combinations of all their courses were innumerable, an

> infinity of distinct universes exfoliated from every moment of every temporal sequence in this cosmos.[9]

Stapledon had written in praise of the work of J.W. Dunne, an engineer, whom I have characterized "a scientist." That inclusion will no doubt antagonize a few idiots with sheepskins. Tough shit. Dunne and his great admirer, the author and playwright J.B. Priestley, were vital cross-links within those British intellectual circles of the thirties noted earlier—links that not only affected this sort of literature, but also were major conduits through which the ideas of the great physicists were popularized. Those early writers, attuned to the cutting-edge science of their time, crafted a vision of motion in additional dimensions for a public having difficulty just getting behind relativity.

---

JORGE LUIS BORGES'S "THE GARDEN OF FORKING PATHS" presented a labyrinthine analogy for the vision following upon Dunne's intuition. The great Latin American scholar produced, in "Garden," possibly the most eerie of the anticipations of the many-worlds. Annotators have remarked that Borges read everything, especially what no one else read anymore. Small wonder that he credited Dunne.

He described a "work within the work," a fic-

9. Stapledon, (William) Olaf, *Star Maker*, London: Methune, 1937.

tional book by a Chinese author involving an ". . . ever spreading network of diverging, converging, and parallel times. This web of time—the strands of which approach one another, bifurcate, intersect or ignore each other through the centuries—embraces every possibility."[10] Set in life-and-death intrigues during the First World War, Borges's images were so compelling that Bryce DeWitt used them for the frontispiece in the 1973 exposition of the Everett theory.

Borges wrote those words in 1941, while brilliant young physicist Richard Feynman was putting the finishing touches on his "many-histories," proposing to explain the path of a particle in time and space, and was being romanced by a shadowy government nuclear program. By September of that year, a new story appeared by Robert A. Heinlein, already gone into war work.

This was the story of which I had retained the most compelling recollection from my early reading. For months, a fragment had plagued the corners of my mind about a professor's escape from a disastrous future back to his college days. What was that, I had wondered? Where had I read it? Did it not have to have been written before Everett? When I located the item, it was in a 1953 collection. Heinlein's Dr. Frost likened time to a rolling, hilly surface rather than a line:

---

10. Borges, Jorge Luis, "The Garden of Forking Paths," in *Labyrinths: Selected Stories and Other Writings*, editors Donald Yates and James Irby, NY: New Directions 1964, Modern Library 1983 (written 1941).

> Think of this track we follow over the surface of time as a winding road cut through hills. Every little way the road branches and the branches follow side canyons. At these branches the crucial decisions of your life take place.[11]

Beyond the right or left turns to different futures, he visualized other possibilities, typically missed through tunnel vision. By means of such shortcuts, one could presumably strike out across all possible time or even take paths that looped backward. Heinlein went on to illustrate all the possible departures from "the road of maximum probability."

Joe objected, "Couldn't you say that this is what science fiction writers are *supposed* to do, predict future developments in theory? One role of the genre, I think, has been to bring the collective consciousness to bear on legitimate thought experiments." Very much a scientist and not at all airy, I wondered at how he put up with my flights of fancy.

"Language in these pieces is uncomfortably precise for a thought experiment that hadn't even been framed yet," I argued. "Substitute a particle for a person as the subject, and these quotations give you a damned good layman's description of the many-worlds. Precision like that decades in advance of the

---

11. Heinlein, Robert A., "Elsewhen" (originally "Elsewhere") in *Astounding*, Sep. 1941. Subsequently published in the collection *Assignment in Eternity*, pp. 69–70.

theory would not be prediction but prescience."

I had paused for thought. "Even if Feynman may have worked out his math during 1941, his famous lectures from which writers have extrapolated were still in the future." I would soon be reading hauntingly similar passages that lay not ahead of Heinlein's work, but a decade behind him.

We'd continued while the wind whipped the trees against the house. In the morning, I would discover that one of my ancient mesquites had been uprooted. Perhaps that was one small portent of the wrenching discoveries I was to make about my own life and motivations. Neither did we ignore the evidence of argument *against* branching worlds. As with *The Door into Summer,* Ward Moore's classic *Bring the Jubilee* argued contrary to a theory that had yet to be articulated.

It had become evident that the most persuasive pieces of the old literature had a couple of other things in common besides their representation of the branching paths. One was the consistent use of a "psychic" means of contact, instead of a technological motif. It was the choice even of writers who were otherwise heavily into gadgetry.

The means employed would involve focusing the attention on a set of symbols, be they magical, geometric, or symbolic logic. Sometimes the mind would simply be attuned to accept the possibility of such a transit, through exercises like regressive hypnosis. It struck me that this approach had greater compatibility with a mathematical artifact, which suggested a "weak connection" between the branches, than did most recent popular fare on the subject.

The other commonality was that, again in the majority of cases, the contact was not accomplished by a search for wealth, fame, pleasure, and was certainly not the result of any dispassionate search for scientific truth. The motivation was ordinarily a matter of something painful: fear, grief, loneliness, outrage—the deepest yearnings of the human heart, base or noble. It seemed as though the writers imagined you had to turn up the psychological heat.

That night had been disturbed by dreams. My proposed manuscript had become a "work-within-the-work" in the drama of my own life. That life, in turn, was somebody else's "work." It was the sort of dream known as "lucid," wherein one is aware of being in a dream, though I didn't feel it was exactly a dream—simply a different frame of reference. As I fixed up with caffeine and nicotine the next morning (*you must have a good breakfast*), I took time to get it down in my journal.

The scene had been a small yet two-storied brick building on the Left Bank in Paris, to which I'd never been closer than a layover at Orly. It had arches and a courtyard, with an open stairway leading up to . . . a place where I lived? There was a cafe with a bit of old neon in the windows on the ground floor, and I started to go in but didn't want to eat alone. I turned back toward the river. All sensory input was present, even to a cool, gentle breeze. I could even hear the wavelets lapping against the cement.

---

ON THE QUAY stood a girl in gaudy peasant dress, like the "Gypsy act" Linda used to perform. Red curls were done up under a bandanna, and she wore heavy silver bracelets and chains. I knew that I'd been there many times, never before remembering upon waking—been there looking for her. Then I was terrified that this would be like those dreams where you run, and reach, and reach, but fail to grasp.

I fell to my knees, thinking, *Oh God, she must forgive me,* though I'd no idea for what. But then she was holding me, and rocking me, whispering in my ear over and over, "It's me, it's me . . ." She was smiling and brushing away my tears. I awoke, clutching the thought that I'd never felt so comforted or known anyone as beautiful.

As per the instructions of J.W. Dunne, I'd been keeping a dream journal for months. I dutifully recorded this one, with no clue as to what it might symbolize. I had begun to have the precognitive results he predicted, encountering a sight or hearing a snatch of conversation dreamed previously, though nothing like my heavy-duty experiences of postpuberty. One of those had been a predictable fantasy of sex with two girls, but quite specific, as to location and the details of the clothing I helped them out of. Imagine my happy surprise when that had come true in every detail only a few years later. The emotional impact of the one just experienced had been, however, a bogey-bear. As though I'd been lost in a hell of loneliness and the woman was a saint come to get me out.

Were my gnarled feelings for and about my late wife an issue? Without a doubt. I am no "yuppie" to mask my pain with pop-psych garbage and persuade myself I had no responsibility. I *must* have been able to do something more! Could I not have been there one more time for Big Richard, the loyal comrade of my youth, or been a more reasonable influence earlier? And what of a man I'd loved and admired in college, cut down by an assassin's bullet at the age of twenty-three? Those two other tragedies had ended with discrete events in space and time, the slightest mechanical pressure on a trigger at a given moment.

I was no simple-minded "born-again," to take solace in any "grand design," either. The world of their god is a hideous game of dungeons and dragons; one false step and even the most worthy are lost forever. Not least my little red-haired angel, JJ—was there not a time when another path could have been taken, a wholly different kind of life that could have saved us all? In the bright, empty morning light, I prayed more fervently than I had since boyhood. To whom or what, I was clueless as any modern man.

I could sense nothing about me but the soulless surfaces of my kitchen. In the abandonment of the material world, I longed for the comfort of my dream-angel. Of what value were my silly bits of precognition if they had done nothing for the lost ones, the gone ones? Was such a weak faculty anything more than just an ironic footnote to a cruel cosmos?

Other nights of lucid dreams and synchronistic events pertaining to my past had marked the route leading to my sleepy ruminations, lying beside this decidedly out-of-the-ordinary babe. The strangest had been of a ritual dance around a glyph drawn on the ground. Later, I couldn't remember the symbol, but did recall drums in some far-off jungle. I do not find it in my journal. As happens with unrecorded dreams, while recalling the content, I've lost track of exactly when I experienced it.

The dance, moving around points on the circumference, seemed like life-and-death struggles in linear time, but was revealed as simply a ritual when time was seen as "collapsed" into the design. It reminded me of Dunne's explanation of the formula, based on the square root of minus one, for collapsing the temporal into a spatial dimension. I knew that the ritual applied to a variety of immortal beings and human families who were under their charge—and something about the relationships among those entities. Might I have revisited that dance, which seemed to have begun from before always, when I would finally drift off to sleep there beside Justine?

It is possible. Certain impressions attending events, as well as my studies of the science and the literary anomaly, took place concurrently—though you will be reading about them sequentially. I might believe that what was coming, with measured, inexorable steps, had all the definitude of that ritual dance. However, the next discoveries, when experienced, had been perceived in a quite linear history as major revelations.

At the far end of the history, there had remained no decisive additional source between 1927, when Dunne had offered a partial but useful theoretical context to which the branching paths might be grafted, and Leinster's first fictional exposition of their function in 1934. Leinster's treatment required something more, and the same might be said for all—on down to that of Borges, the most elegant of them all, and beyond. What was the essential ingredient added between 1927 and 1934?

During 1940, the writers L. Sprague de Camp and Fletcher Pratt had their collaboration, "The Incomplete Enchanter," serialized. De Camp would soon be working, together with Heinlein, at an experimental facility in the Philadelphia Naval Yards for the duration of the war.

Along with another coworker, Isaac Asimov, they would establish a "problem-solving group" that submitted suggestions to the Navy on classified matters. I would soon learn that this "Philadelphia experiment" included the informal participation of Murray Leinster. I'd wondered at how we could only speculate as to what might have been going on there, or how it may have related to the "real" Philadelphia Experiment of 1943. De Camp and Pratt wrote:

> . . . there is an infinity of possible worlds, and if the senses can be attuned to receive a different set of impressions, we should infallibly find

> ourselves living in a different world . . . In a world where everyone firmly believed in these laws, that is, in one where all minds were attuned to receive the proper impressions, the laws of magic would conceivably work, as one hears of witch-doctors' spells working in Africa today. *Frazer and Seabrook have worked out some of these magical laws.*[12]

---

IN THE SPRING OF 1947, a pulp magazine had published the first story by Horace Beam Piper, a self-educated forty-three year-old employee at the Altoona Yards of the Pennsylvania Railroad. This commenced a career obsessed with alternate worlds that, sadly, was largely distinguished posthumously. Like Seabrook—the source to whom, as far as I know, only Piper and a very few others ever had the courtesy to tip their hats—he would take his own life at about age sixty.

Some held that Piper believed in the transmigration of souls, more precisely rendered in Greek as *metempsychosis*, and believed that he knew where he was destined to go. What is a known fact is that, at a science fiction convention in the early sixties, he told writer Jerry Pournelle that another of his alternate-world tales was a true story. Pournelle affirmed that

12. de Camp, L. Sprague and Fletcher Pratt, "The Incomplete Enchanter," in *Unknown*, May and Aug. 1940. *Unknown* was the other classic "pulp." It perished in the World War II paper shortage.

Piper told him, in utter seriousness, that he knew because he had been born on another timeline.[13]

With a reverence that you will later understand, I quote H. Beam Piper, "The Last Cavalier,"[14] from his first story, "Time and Time Again." A casualty of a future war had awakened in his twelve-year-old body. With the help of books by Dunne, among others, he was trying to work out a theory:

"If somebody has real knowledge of the future, then the future must be available to the present mind." Piper followed through with the questions that Dunne had posed. If there had ever been so much as one actual instance of precognition, then "every moment must be perpetually coexistent with every other moment."

He went on to ruminate as to whether some part of the self might not be free of temporal limitations, able to access perceptions from those coexisting instants. He speculated on their generally limited nature and why few provable cases were observed. But suppose one could act on such perceptions, to change an outcome? Would not then some minds, by definition, have observed alternate, actually existing, realities?

Piper, writing in 1947, knew nothing of communication among the branches of a wave function, much

---

13. Jerry Pournelle attests to this in his introduction to *Piper's Federation*, NY: Ace Books, 1981.

14. Annotator John F. Carr respectfully appropriated Pournelle's sobriquet for Piper in a bio for *Analog* (the successor of *Astounding*) in Jan. 1988.

less about notions of counterpart "qubits," from universes nearly the same, entering into some kind of shared, "covalent"-like relationships. Yet, following Dunne's logic, he had gone further:

"There must be additional dimensions of time; lines of alternate probabilities. *Something like William Seabrook's witch-doctor friend's Fan-Shaped Destiny.*"[15]

Within days, I'd believed that I had confirmation of my source from publication dates alone. Separating the apples and oranges, it's true that generic alternate realities had a long tradition in mythology and folk-tales. Their general use in science fiction went as far back as Edgar Rice Burroughs and Arthur Merritt. But the quest for the specific concept of the branching paths, which so eerily presaged the theory that Everett would formalize only by the year of Sputnik, had channeled down to one question: What was the Fan-Shaped Destiny?

15. Piper, Horace Beam, "Time and Time Again," in *Astounding Science Fiction*, Apr. 1947.

# III
# Seabrook

BY LATE IN THE REMAINING WEEKS OF THAT BLAZING Texas summer, I had believed that I was becoming well acquainted with Mr. William Seabrook. Possibly the oddest component had been added in late July, when I happened across his autobiography in an antiquarian bookstore. Its tall shelves and musty stacks returned nostalgic recollection of the store in Fort Worth, where I had purloined my *I Ching* so many years before. The dealer, distinctively enough for a younger man, was familiar with Seabrook's name, but assured me that none of his books had come through the store for some time.

Browsing a closed case inside the front door, my first impulse was to be somewhat irked to discover nothing other than Seabrook's *No Hiding Place* peeking back at me. I purchased the first, and only, edition for thirteen dollars. The bookseller was as well aware as I that no one else was likely to want the book anytime soon, and I questioned him as to the apparently recent acquisition. I seemed to note in him a particular confusion as to his demonstrated possession of the book.

As I left my card, requesting to be notified should any more Seabrook material magically appear, the dealer had only been able to lamely comment, "That must have arrived here just for you," a most unnecessary pitch. I would have cause in only a few weeks to reflect on how unspeakably pregnant his surprised excuse was to prove. At that moment, though, I only supposed that he might have smoked some really good dope that afternoon, and thought no more about it.

There were a number of other small oddities about this particular find, the first being the good repair of a 1942 volume that had been in circulation. Preserved under plastic was the original dust cover, especially striking in that rubber stamps branded it as having done time in the library of a small college in Oklahoma. The eerie rapport I developed with its content was portended by the sentimentality of a little newspaper clipping that I found to have survived so many years of handling.

Taped inside the back cover, it was a brief obituary of the author. Examining it in hopes of determining its newspaper of origin, I found that someone had penciled on the reverse, in a very nice hand, "This belongs in the book." Finding it, amidst trying to profile Seabrook's innermost self and reading the outpouring of his deepest feelings, evoked whispers of nameless sentiments from—I knew not where.

There was a curious passage in which he described

an afternoon in the autumn of 1908, when he'd been sitting on a park bench at Lausanne by Lake Geneva. By age twenty-two, he'd tramped about Europe for over a year and done a stint of philosophical research at the University of Geneva. In the cool of that fall afternoon, his reverie on Mont Blanc and the High Alps had been disturbed by the arrival of a young couple in an expensive Darracq.

He'd studied them as they strolled about the park and sat on a bench next to his, the young man of about Willie's age holding the golden-haired girl possessively. With less than five francs in his pocket, Seabrook had watched them, in their velvet-and-fur-lined clothing, pondering whether he would ever want a car and a girl like that. In his book, he would recall a foreboding of awakening years later and finding that he had indeed wanted those things. He feared the thought of facing himself as he might have become by then.

During the next five years, he decisively broke into journalism, married a Southern belle, Katherine Edmondson, and established a successful advertising agency. He then had for himself the girl, the car and chauffeur to boot, the club memberships, et cetera. At that time, he'd taken Katie and his friend Ed, who'd been one of Katie's beaux, to a small lake by Grant Park in Atlanta. There he had them act out for him the scene he recalled from Lausanne.

> . . . I knew that unless I could make myself know and feel in some way that the thing was

> real, I might go through my whole life in it as a sort of exteriorized dream—somebody else's dream again . . .[16]

Though I suspected the exercise masked the voyeuristic thrill of watching his young wife in the arms of a man she might have belonged to in another life, the expressed levels were real enough. The "somebody else" references were nominally to a strange hobo he'd met on the Savannah River. But they resonated in an eerily disparate way with me.

I continued to prowl the bookstores and libraries, accumulating his books and retrieving what magazine and newspaper articles I could from microfilm. I moved from fascination with Seabrook as the probable source of the branching worlds to involvement with the total person. As I read his adventure stories, I was frustrated in the effort to nail down their compelling quality. He had been a good writer, sometimes superior though never great. The early lifestyle parallels might suggest a comparison to Hemingway, still . . .

While I had inexplicably managed to miss Seabrook in my younger reading, I saw clearly that various writers whose works I'd devoured had not. Images wafted up from forty years before, of summer afternoons sitting cross-legged on the floor before my schoolteacher-mother's bookshelves. The musty dankness of an old evaporative cooler had seemed the very essence of the dying fifties. It had provided the

---

16. Seabrook, William, *No Hiding Place*, NY: Lippincott, 1942, p. 127.

only circulation as I'd fingered the already-aging pages of books with funny old covers like those I was holding now.

How could Seabrook's *Adventures in Arabia*, or *The Magic Island*, or at least the big-seller *Asylum* have failed to be among those books? I saw evidence that he'd been a pivotal figure in New York and in the Paris of the Lost Generation. Later, the effects of his pioneering work had reverberated down the decades even to the present moment, almost always without credit. It was as if, with his suicide in 1945, he had become an Orwellian nonperson.

While his name had been expunged, open season had been declared on his work, and everyone and their cousins had shamelessly plagiarized his concepts. His later works catalyzed those convictions. The oddest impact began in late July, when his autobiography presented itself to me. Apart from a distinctive mode of acquisition, the content had an unexpectedly personal effect when examined in conjunction with existing biographical materials.

Reviews of his autobiography, *No Hiding Place*, in 1942 had ranged from prudish revulsion to sardonic "Seabrook the Semi-Sinister" to praise.[17] I found it poignantly wistful. I was becoming enthralled with another man's life story, both its upside and downside. Through all the episodes that I literally could not read with a clear eye, was the sense of his life work

17. Fadiman, C., reviewing *No Hiding Place* in *The New Yorker*, 31 Oct. 1942.

and activities being *driven*. In spite of his obvious efforts to be bluntly honest, even brutally frank on the deepest personal levels, the suspicion lingered that he was goaded—by imperatives remaining nameless.

I was resolved to learn as much about this man as I possibly could. Some commentators had characterized both his autobiography and the biographical work *The Strange World of Willie Seabrook*, by his second wife, the novelist Marjorie Worthington, as factually unreliable. Well, if such work by anyone has ever avoided becoming somewhat self-serving, I have yet to see it. But I quickly discovered what the critics and reviewers were talking about.

Both Marjorie's and Willie's senses of chronology sometimes seemed to be nonexistent. I set about to reconstruct for myself when the reported events of certain periods of his life would have to have occurred. And what was more important, in what sequence. There were times when I would survey my notes and it would seem that the "card decks" visualized by Deutsch, composed of alternative snapshots of moments in entropic order, had been scattered randomly across my carpet. Some felt almost like my hypnotic regression vision, like a moment in a shoeshine stand where 1962 and 1963 had seemed impossibly coeval.

I endeavored to collate the sources and resolve the anomalies in chronology, which seemed to grow even as I studied them. I found that, contrary to my first impressions, Willie and his work had not entirely disappeared after his 1945 suicide. Various writers and publishers, with even more varied motives, had raised the more titillating and scandalous aspects of his saga at least once per decade since his death.

For some reason, these recurrent revelations never seemed to attract the attention of a mass audience. A 1968 paperback of *Witchcraft* had gone largely unnoticed, and Seabrook had remained a footnote in the literature of the occult during a decade when it was all the rage.

The silence on the erotic front was, to me, even more puzzling. The late century had seen an increased popularity of sadomasochism. I would have thought that further commentary would have been begged by the sensational value of testimonials from respected figures, like George Seldes and Man Ray, concerning the kinky sex lives of the Lost Generation.

Most of all, I was drawn toward those extraordinary women who appeared to have loved Willie Seabrook all his life, and beyond. In reality according to his detractors, they should, by all rights, have despised him.

Marjorie Worthington would find herself, in her late years, appalled by her own history. She tried to cover up having willingly borne the marks of Willie's whip and proudly wearing his collar to parties in Paris and New York, one in 1933 celebrating the publication of her own work.[18]

At the same time, her continuing adoration would force even the hateful "politically correct" commenta-

18. Man Ray, op. cit., p. 156.

tors of our own petty era to concede that she had continued to believe for the rest of her life that he would eventually be rediscovered and live forever through his work.

She'd written a book in that hope, that prayer, and I hoped that Katie had lived long enough to read it. Katie and her second husband (who had formerly been Marjorie's) had disappeared from public life after their marriage early in 1935. I had gotten no leads on their later history.

I had developed a sense of morbid kinship with those lost souls of a lost generation, most of them dead before I was barely a man. Most haunting of all was the fascinating and elusive composite figure whom Willie had called Justine.

Willie spent most of the late teens and early 1920s in New York City, where he and Katie became major figures in Greenwich Village Bohemian society. Katie opened the first Greenwich Village coffeehouse at 156 Waverly Place—that is, the first not to become a speakeasy. It quickly became the in-place for Village society, belonging to the remarkable Katie. How many women in modern times have done such a thing as follow their men to war?

He was ten to fifteen years older than the bulk of the Lost Generation. I had the notion that many were predisposed to sit at his knee owing to that, absorbing, then imitating things that he had already said or done. It was probably impossible to establish that Willie had inspired the life choices of those literati, however.

But in my imagination, I beheld paths leading

from the mystique of the Gothic South, tramping across Europe into the Great War, debauching in the literary life of Paris and the Village, to safaris into Africa. I knew that it must be true; the sands of time and the heavy footprints of the later immortals had obscured those of the lone adventurer.

Willie was reluctant to admit, when writing for publication, to any more than the bondage component of his sadomasochistic games. He wrote that he had confessed all about the Justine of *Witchcraft* to his friend Dr. A.A. Brill, the dean of Freudians in America, but I found no indication that Brill had ever documented the fact. I had to turn to the memoirs of others to find the obvious spelled out.

---

"JUSTINE" WAS HANGING FROM HER WRISTS with her toes on a stack of phone directories that she could kick away if so inclined. Willie explicitly stipulated that the exercise, conducted in a darkened room, was to assist her into a trance state. I was unconvinced that the episode had begun for largely research purposes. The whole setup, letting the submissive regulate her own misery, was too typical of a pure sex game. At least, my personal experience suggested that.

From the adjacent room, Willie became concerned with the tone of her mumbling. Checking on her, he found that she had kicked away all support and had been hanging free for longer than was safe. He got her down and revived her from the trance state against her protests. She recounted being enthralled by an elaborate and amusing series of events, involving a lion, at a street circus in what sounded to be a small European city.

Wanting to see more, she'd chastised Willie for lacking the courage of his convictions. It had, after all, been a matter of *her* pain! That defining occurrence early in their relationship was to become central to the book *Witchcraft*, and would supply Willie with a public rationale for the ongoing practice of his sexual proclivity.

The upshot was that he took her on "her first trip to Europe," some six months later. In the ancient Papal city of Avignon, they'd happened upon the circus with all the details she'd described, down to the cranky old lion pissing on the spectators in the front row.

They could never fully re-create that precognitive effect, though "research" involving Justine went on over a period of years. She failed to foresee the Armistice, boom, depression, the death of the Pope, though Willie remained overheated by the possibilities. He had made for her a leather mask, allegedly for sensory deprivation effects, under circumstances that suggested the project took place after his African expedition of 1929.

I began to visualize the enigmatic Justine, with her features obscured by the leather mask, as though in one of the surrealist productions presented by Willie's friends at the *Château d'Noailles*. At the same time, she had grown as real to me as any of the old celebrities whose names both Willie and Marjorie dropped with frequency. The "diabolical" leather helmet in no way "dehumanized," but marked her guise as an icon of mystery. The flesh beneath grew as familiar in my imagination as any I'd known or touched.

Around the year 1923, a distinct chronology appeared, for a while, in step with Willie's career of writing books about his travels and adventures in exotic lands. Also in 1923, Seabrook had sought to write Aleister Crowley's story for syndication. Then, at Katie's *156* coffeehouse, they connected with a young *Bedou* nobleman from Lebanon, who provided them with an entrée to the desert sheiks. They embarked in the spring for fifteen months among the Arabs, *Druse*, and *Yezidi* "devil-worshippers."

Decades in the future, a brilliant old carney, Anton LaVey, would bid to fill the late-century shoes of Aleister Crowley, publishing his *Satanic Bible* and companion *Satanic Rituals*. A cursory examination revealed that Seabrook was not simply a source but, concerning some matters, LaVey's *only* source. Ironically, that latter-day "most evil man in the world" proved another of the few with the moral rectitude to credit derivation from the lost author.[19]

Over the following several years, Willie and Katie would go on to make a couple of extended visits to Haiti, but he would never receive credit due for his

19. LaVey, Anton Szandor, *The Satanic Rituals*, NY: Avon, 1972, p. 155. In "Pilgrims of the Age of Fire," the preface to a ritual derivative of Seabrook's account of the Yezidis, LaVey stipulates to Seabrook's early-1920s pilgrimage into the desert to Mount Lalesh, recording the journey in Adventures in Arabia with a brave and compassionate objectivity. He likens Seabrook to Bierce, Shaw, Twain, or Wells.

impacts on anthropological and archaeological studies. I knew that every beginning anthro student is conditioned to hold a grand contempt for the adventurer-explorers who preceded them. No "Indiana Jones" allowed. If, by chance, a conclusion of an adventurer should prove out, these "scientists" of our time bury the evidence in the back-dirt and mum's the word.

The Seabrooks were reported to have landed at Grand Bassam, on the Ivory Coast of French West Africa in November of 1929.[20] Wamba, the sexy young witch of the *Yafouba* tribe, was truly an alluring figure. Known throughout the forest for her power, Wamba seemed to wear as little as was plausible, except for her red-leather hat decorated with a feather plume—which turned out to be an early-century French fire helmet. She would sit cross-legged, fanning herself with a silver-handled cow's tail, surveying all before her with a bland, disturbing smile.

Sensual and pleasure-loving, she could be spoiled, high-handed, and an impudent comedian, when not on the job and in communion with primordial, nameless things! Toward the end of her story, I felt that Willie had been sorely tempted to continue to share his sleeping bag with her. Maybe he would have, had he not returned to play house with Marjorie in

---

20. *The New York Times*, 17 Nov. 1930. References events supposedly only one year earlier. Typical of a number of newsprint idiosyncrasies. Their actual arrival in Africa would probably have fallen another year before that, in late 1928.

Toulon. But I'll let him speak for himself, as this constituted the revelation of the original source of the branching worlds' theme.

---

> WAMBA BELIEVES THAT ALL POSSIBLE FUTURE EVENTS EXIST IN EMBRYO. . . . She believes that fate, though written, projects itself into the future not as a straight line, but fan-shaped, in myriad alternate paths multiplying to infinity.
>
> I am walking in an unknown forest. There are as many directions to walk as there are points of the compass. I know nothing of what awaits me in any direction, but in all directions fate awaits me, things already written in the sense that they exist already, and are therefore inevitable, but alternate, depending on the path I take . . .[21]

He reflected upon the impotence of logical process to supply foresight as to which way to turn. In the labyrinth of variables, no choice was trivial—any moment of destiny might change the future. In light of my consternation over chronologies, Willie's example turned disturbingly personal:

> . . . if you look back you will discover just as fatally a hundred cases in which seemingly pointless hazards or decisions changed your

21. Seabrook, *Jungle Ways*, NY: Harcourt Brace, 1930–1931, p. 82.

> life. Will you come over and make a fourth at bridge this evening? . . . a girl drops in . . . you find yourself married to her . . . Fate, providence, blind luck, or Wamba's fan-shaped future.[22]

Thus wrote Seabrook in 1930, serialized in *Ladies' Home Journal*, of all places, before the book was published in April of the following year. That was four years before Murray Leinster would publish the first branching-worlds science fiction story and over a quarter century before Everett's scientific explanation!

> . . . but with all her wisdom she could not help me further. She said that if I consented to remain there always, and give up everything, including my white ways of asking, she might eventually make me understand, but that it would be a road from which there could be no returning.
>
> Her words were painful to me, and familiar. But they were the words which only saints or madmen, the very wise or the very simple, have ever truly dared to follow.[23]

Willie's continuing life would evolve from a splendid decadence in the early thirties, to a quiet

22. Ibid., p. 83.

23. Ibid., p. 125.

respectability, to a restive renewal of his earlier interests. I continued to pore over every source I could locate. I hoped also that I might get a handle on the untoward "retrocognitive" sensation that I had about the man and his loved ones, their times and work.

I was no nostalgia buff, focused on any of the decades through which Seabrook had lived. I knew that my regrets and yearnings lay all within my life span. Yet, the essence, the atmosphere of those long-ago moments, every so often, would seem as real to me as the moisture on Justine's bare breasts.

Not a believer in reincarnation or anything of the sort, I rationalized. My parents had been contemporaries of Willie's friends and lovers, if a bit younger than the man himself. Absorption of their views and recollections might explain the recurrent *déjà vu* that emanated from every new bit of information I uncovered.

---

THERE REMAINED THE ODDNESS OF THE CHRONOLOGY. It was true that the disparate perceptions and recollections of various observers could seem like altogether different worlds. But the written record was seldom aberrant to this degree. When he had returned from the World War in 1917, Seabrook had worked first for *The New York Times*, then for Hearst's King Features Syndicate, to whom he may have introduced Ward Greene, a comrade from his Atlanta days—which Greene then made into a life's career as editor and general manager. Greene's *Ride the Nightmare,* a fiction based on Willie's earlier life, often dovetailed with some known facts better than did the supposedly factual chronicles of Marjorie and other participants.

As I began to compose a rough draft from my piles of outlines and notes, I wrote in my journal:

> Further research continues to alter the chronology. New bits of data serve to exacerbate the contradictions among others. Just have to accept that the perceived reality will continue to shift during the course of the project.

In 1930, Willie had decisively parted company with Katie and returned to France to write. Though he claimed to have spent a year writing *Jungle Ways*, his agent had made big advance money available early. Willie and Marjorie expanded and upgraded their loft above the quay at Toulon and, by the end of April, had leased the *Château d'Evenos*. For whatever personal motive, Willie had been determined to hold control of that ruined fortress of ancient Var, even as he could not afford to improve it, nor was much inclined to do so.

About that time, Aldous and Maria Huxley took a house at nearby La Gorguette. Then began Willie's days of wine and roses . . . or perhaps gin and poppies would be more apropos. Anyway, Marjorie's chronicle came into play, debatably more reliable than his own account for the next several years.

Those were the heady days of the Lost Generation. George Seldes named Seabrook among the outstanding Riviera personages of the time, along with D.H. Lawrence, Frank Harris, H.G. Wells, and Angelica Balabanoff, former secretary of the Comintern. Lawrence died that summer. Huxley was at the small, depressing funeral and likely Willie also.

The accounts of other observers to this period began to "flesh out" the story of his sadomasochism, whereas he himself denied any interest in pain per se, other than for its role in his psychic experimentation. Willie's writing had focused on classical images of Grecian slave-girls bound to pillars. His approach made me think back to the columns of a private sex club that had once existed in the Deep South, where Willie would have made himself right at home. I certainly did, when Linda and I had encountered it many years before. The columns had flanked the rear of the stage and the club girls, attired as classical slaves, were especially fetching when they were occasionally bound to them naked.

Ward Greene, when writing through the viewpoint of a character hopelessly in love with "Beth" (Katie), handled the public bondage with prim disdain.[24] Marjorie, writing at age sixty-five, had put it all off on Willie and his "research girls," distancing herself from the whole enterprise and denying any personal participation.

24. Greene, Ward, *Ride the Nightmare*, New York and London: Cape and Smith, 1930, p. 158.

However, the Marquis de Sade was very *in* among the surrealist crowd, as was primitive art (so that Willie's collections were much admired). The wife of arts patron Charles de Noailles was most proud to be a descendant of "the divine Marquis."

Propelling me into more and more extensive research was a growing empathy, no longer with Willie alone, but with all the characters of his drama: Walter and Jeannot Duranty, Aldous and Maria Huxley, Man Ray, and Lee Miller. Now there was a babe in any time! Her lips adorned *Observatory Time—The Lovers*, arguably the ultimate surrealist painting, and her gorgeous blonde body was immortalized in her mentor's photographs.

The 1988 republication of Man Ray's memoirs contained never before seen photos from the Man Ray Trust. Shot at Seabrook's Paris apartment in 1930, they would have been perfectly in place in a modern bondage and discipline magazine. It was difficult to believe they were almost seventy years old. Each new revelation engorged my fascination further.

A curly-haired woman, trussed up on the carpet in leather straps, brought me up short. I enlarged it as much as possible to get a better look at her face . . . as well as for the fact that it was a damned erotic picture! Highly stylized twenties makeup constituted far too much of a mask to make out her features, though she seemed pretty. I found that I had to sit back and remind myself that all those people were *dead*, and had been for years.

---

MAN RAY DESCRIBED A SILVER DISCIPLINE COLLAR he designed at Seabrook's behest and had executed for Marjorie. It created a sensation at social functions. In his *Self Portrait*, he wrote,

> He (Seabrook) made her wear the collar thereafter whenever they went out to dinner and took a certain pleasure in watching her at the table eating and drinking with difficulty.[25]

Marjorie's account included none of that. Her "winter of 1930" appeared to really be that of 1930–31. I was gradually recalling and becoming used to an older and more precise usage in which the winter was named for the year of the solstice at which it began. In the company of one Natasha, "a playmate of Marjorie's," they had sailed on the *Berengaria*, Willie's old tub of choice, to be in New York for the publication of *Jungle Ways*.

Constant name-droppers, Willie and Marjorie spiced the stories of their interludes with the likes of Theodore Dreiser, Dashiell Hammett, Sinclair Lewis, and Upton Sinclair. In April, after a flap over his treatment of cannibalism had assured the book a roaring success with a scandalized and therefore titillated public, they returned to Europe. Their stateroom party before departure was the first point where

---

25. Man Ray, op. cit., p. 156.

their respective chronologies came fully into sync.

Back in France, the saturnalia continued. The Seabrooks were visiting with Jeannot Duranty at her home in St. Tropez. The former Jane Cheron had, in earlier years, been engaged in a *ménage à trois* with her husband and Aleister Crowley.[26]

George Seldes, whom Mussolini had kicked out of Italy in retaliation for his book, *Sawdust Caesar*, got into the act. I will give Seldes the last word on these matters. Willie had demonstrated for Seldes and his companion the equipment in his Toulon loft overlooking the Mediterranean, musing that sadomasochism was too noisy a business for apartments anywhere.

> Willie showed us what he called his lion's cage—and all sorts of riggings from the wooden ceiling, chains and pulleys. He said he preferred to hang his women by their feet when he whipped them . . . He now asked the beautiful blonde from . . . Texas, whom I had brought along, if she would be willing to spend some time in the lion's cage and be treated like a wild animal—and to my amazement Miss Texas agreed.[27]

It seemed that Willie had himself spent some five days being whipped and chained within the cage.

26. Taylor, S.J., *Stalin's Apologist*, NY: Oxford University Press, 1990, p. 32.

27. Seldes, George, *Witness to a Century*, NY: Ballantine, 1987, p. 270.

Maintaining that his search for psychic transcendence was not mere pretension, he told Seldes, "I wanted to walk along the borderland of genius and insanity, the dividing line, the crest. I wanted to look at the other side, I wanted to see the face of God, and yet return."[28]

"His first wife (Katie), who could have been typecast for the role of 'beautiful Southern aristocrat,' which she was, divorced him. She grew tired of being whipped."[29] After twenty years? Right.

> His second wife (Marjorie), who years later wrote a biography in which she called Willie "a fine, intelligent and lovable man with a touch of genius as well as madness," ran away from the loft several times and stayed at the apartment of my friends nearby. Once she showed us the welts made on her back by Willie's whips. But she always went back.[30]

I've quoted Seldes's final word in full. He had not understood what those people were about. When Willie and Katie, whose full control over her own life no one ever doubted, ended their relationship—the reasons were patently far more complex.

While Marjorie's views and feelings were always conflicted, there could be no doubt that he had meant everything to her. She, an independent woman and

28. Seldes, ibid., p. 270.

29. Seldes, ibid., p. 270.

30. Seldes, ibid., p. 270.

successful author in her own right, struggled for years to save Willie from alcohol and his own demons. Self-sacrifice for another having yet to be redefined as "codependency," she only left him after he had gone over altogether into the masochistic end of the equation, in an irretrievably self-destructive fashion. No, Seldes and maybe even Man Ray did not fully understand, but they were honest and sympathetic friends.

---

SOMETIMES, WITHIN THE SWAMP OF LITERARY CRAP, may be found a spark of humanity so genuine that it softens the heart of even the most opportunist critic. I digressed to contemplate the continuing affection of Willie's comrade Walter Duranty for the aging dancer Isadora Duncan in her fading, dissolute years:

> I knew that she was fat and lazy and drank to excess and did not care whether she was ill-kempt or sloppy, but I knew also that she had a hole in her heart which excused everything. In all human experience there is nothing so devastating as a hole in the heart, no matter what it comes from.[31]

That I might well have said the same of Linda toward the end, that struck the spark. Willie, and Katie, and Marjorie, and all those around them became even more real to me. No longer was it

31. Taylor, op. cit., p. 123, quoting Duranty.

merely a matter of empathy. Somehow, what they had created, what they *were*, was for me still tangibly alive.

Hardly literary immortals, these had been lost in obscurity. Their books were flaking into dust and gathering cobwebs on the shelves—unread, unloved, forgotten. No, this was more real than such a vapid immortality. It was as solid as ornate iron lampposts and the infrastructure of old bridges, glimpses of which would, more and more often, call me back, back to bygone times—*to their times.*

During 1931, Willie prepared for a return trip to the Sahara to expand upon the story of Père Yakouba, *The White Monk of Timbuctoo*. His friend and patron Paul Morand was away in the Far East, but Seabrook eventually prevailed upon other contacts with the Trocadero museums to lend assistance to the proposed expedition. He and Marjorie left on the first leg of their air adventure on January 13, 1932. Winding down a drinking bout of heroic proportions with Yakouba, he would include an odd reminiscence of a night when he retired "in a jumbled time-sequence," unable clearly to distinguish the moment from a time decades past.[32]

It's possible that he hoped the door between Katie and him was not entirely closed. During the course of writing that year, he chose to thoroughly dissemble as

32. Seabrook, William, *The White Monk of Timbuctoo*, NY: Harcourt Brace, 1934. A new French edition of his story of the life of Auguste Dupuis-Yakouba was issued in 1996 (D'ailleurs, Phébus, Paris).

to the status of his relationships: "Katie, for once, was even further away than Paul Morand; she was already heading, on an adventure of her own, for the high mountains of Mexico."[33]

Oh, by the way, ". . . Marjorie Worthington, young American novelist who had collaborated with me on former work, and who chanced to be in Paris. She had promised tentatively to join the expedition."[34] One would hope so; after living together for nearly two years . . .

Conversely, in *Air Adventure*, he even exhibited very controlled jealousy at Marjorie's flirtation with a young French officer. This supported Marjorie's later position that Willie would always manage to tell the truth, in his fashion.

The Timbuktu trip was of relatively short duration, and by April they were moved into the *Villa Les Roseaux*. It shared a beach with the Huxleys, no doubt enjoyed by nude bather Max Eastman with his beautiful Russian wife, en route to visit Trotsky at Prinkipo.

In *Witchcraft*, Seabrook described how, with Marjorie working on a novel, he met a sinister "Abbé Penhoël," through a clerical friend.[35] The story went that the Abbé threw a spell on Marjorie that threatened her life.

---

33. Seabrook, William, *Air Adventure*, NY: Harcourt Brace, 1933, p. 4.

34. Seabrook, ibid., p. 4.

35. Perhaps the model for the love interest in Worthington's next novel, *Come, My Coach*, NY: Knopf, 1935, about a woman who fell in love with a priest.

Willie claimed that he came to her aid with psychological and magical skills, principally directed at terrorizing the offender, including a threat based on the Fan-Shaped Destiny. She was recovered by October and referenced none of that in her book. She did recall the visit that summer of Willie's oldest friends, Max and Ward Greene, mentioning her resentment of *Ride the Nightmare.*[36]

*Witchcraft* contained a number of anecdotes from that time frame, including an encounter with a wanna-be vampiress on the beach, and smashing a St. Remy sorceress's "witch's cradle" setup. This was presumably because Willie objected to her torturing her nubile granddaughter—on the narrow platform an apprentice would straddle for hours, supposedly learning to ride on a broomstick. Perhaps her technique was offensive?

Willie wrote with official skepticism about all these matters, even as he pursued them with verve. His drinking was rapidly becoming debilitating, and much of *Air Adventure* had to be ghostwritten.

Nonetheless, his mystique was intact. On November 5, Aldous Huxley wrote to the Vicomte de Noailles about their neighborhood at Sarnay:

---

36. Worthington, Marjorie, *The Strange World of Willie Seabrook*, NY: Harcourt Brace, 1966, pp. 123–124. Willie and Max had been blood brothers from their teens at Mercersberg Academy. Greene's work has also fallen into obscurity. Some was moderately groundbreaking, such as a play, *Death in the Deep South*. Compatible with his image, however, he is best remembered for his script writing of Disney's *Lady and the Tramp*.

> Sarnay is full of the usual Lesbian baronesses—all of them in a flutter of excitement to know Mr. Seabrook, because the rumor has gone around the village that he beats his lady friend. One is reminded of the hysterical excitement of cows when they see a bull in the next field coupling with another cow![37]

---

THE LAST TIME SEABROOK SAW ALEISTER CROWLEY was in Paris sometime in 1933. Crowley was far into a downhill slide himself by that time. Making a meager living off an astrology scam, he had approached Man Ray with a proposition. He would demand that wealthy women who came to him for horoscopes provide him with a Man Ray photograph. Man Ray would reciprocate by requiring a Crowley forecast from his clients. The proposition was not adopted.

By mid-1933, Willie was doing nothing but drinking. At last he realized that drink was going to take him out if he didn't do something. He wrote his publisher, Alfred Harcourt, who provided helpful assistance with getting him incarcerated for treatment, the arrangement of simple detox situations being highly problematical in those days.

He sailed for New York on the *Europa* in October, Marjorie taking another ship a few days later. After a

37. *Letters of Aldous Huxley*, editor Grover Smith, NY: Harper and Row, 1970. Letter from Huxley to Noailles dated 5 Nov. 1932. (See also *Between the Wars*, essays and letters, Chicago: IR Dee, 1994.)

brief dry-out at Doctors' Hospital, he took a penthouse studio, with Marjorie in separate lodgings nearby. For the next couple of months, he indulged in his favorite games with various "research girls" and "secretaries." Man Ray observed a bit of this when he came over on assignment,[38] and probably chasing Lee Miller. Lee had ditched Man Ray, and then set up her own studio in New York.

Just before Christmas, drinking more heavily than ever, he gave it up and entered the Bloomingdale Sanitarium, where he was treated for seven months. Released in July of 1934, Willie entered upon four years at their new home in Rhinebeck, New York, perhaps closer to a state of contentment than he had ever known. I would come to wonder at whether, when the evening shadows of the haunted Catskills reached across the Hudson, had he ever reflected on his friend Crowley canoeing along those same banks twenty years before? Had he been able to remain mercifully oblivious to the undertow that was destined to pull him down?

In April of 1937, the Huxleys arrived in the U.S. The Seabrooks helped them obtain the old Astor estate where they stayed near their friends late in the year. Aldous became friends with J.B. Rhine. That giant of parapsychology had managed, for a time, to beat back the establishment and force the recognition of paranormal studies by mainstream science. Evidently Huxley had plugged Willie in with Rhine. By

38. Man Ray, op. cit., p. 156.

the summer of 1938, Seabrook was growing restive, and drove down to Duke University to observe some of Rhine's famous ESP experiments.

> What took me down to visit professor Rhine and have a look at what he was doing, was neither clean, clear nor cold. It was a private obsession of mine that went a whole lot further back and a whole lot deeper than any taste for the esoteric picked up by living with voodoo priests in Haiti and witch-doctors in Africa. It went so deep indeed and so far back, and had entangled me in so many complications—paralleling the other tangles and complications I've confessed—that instead of trying to deal with it chronologically I have held it all until what happens in this chapter brought it to a head.[39]

Though he congratulated Rhine and others for lifting the study of the paranormal into a cold and clear scientific light, his response was to convert his barn studio into a "medieval *hexen-küche*."[40] Detailing his view in *Witchcraft*, he held that Rhine and his associates might learn something from the alchemists of old, to turn up the heat under the crucibles of science. He complained of cold and sterile methods wanting of the psychological heat and stress necessary to ignite dormant psychic powers.

39. Seabrook, *No Hiding Place*, p. 386.

40. Seabrook, ibid., p. 370.

---

> THIS SUPERNORMAL STUFF IS ALL IN THE SAME BAG, you know, whether you split it into telepathy, clairvoyance, mystical vision, fourth-dimensional excursions, or the metaphysical corollaries of the Einstein theory in which space if not time curves round and back on itself like a serpent swallowing its tail. Dr. Rhine is not merely experimenting, you know, with telepathy and clairvoyance confined to the immediate instant, to the "nick" of time. He is experimenting also with precognition, previsionary clairvoyance, seeing into the future. Also with retrocognition, i.e., seeing back into the past clairvoyantly.[41]

More than once I had seemed to discern implied interest in an underlying theory that remained forever unstated—a "final theory" of the paranormal, which had some sort of involvement with the nature of time. Thus, when he converted the studio into his magician's workshop-cum-dungeon, approaching the study of the paranormal through systematic torment of his "research girls," the enterprise was not as facetious as it might initially sound. As seen by her centrality in *Witchcraft*, all hearkened back to the wonder of Justine in Avignon. I had no doubt that he was, by

41. Seabrook, *Witchcraft: Its Power in the World Today*, NY: Harcourt Brace, 1940, p. 188.

that time at least, seriously attempting to unlock the gate to alternate realities.

Since his earlier days, he had garnished his sexually generated proclivity with valuable tips accumulated in Haiti, Africa, and from the *Rufai* Dervishes in the Middle East, who practiced torture as a path to spiritual enlightenment. In a sense, that would give *Witchcraft* some problems as a factual document.

Accounts of his adventures in the teens and twenties tended to be overlaid with elements that were generated at the barn in 1938 and 1939. Those, in turn, were embellished with data gleaned from the *Rufai*, and other things that had happened years before. On the other hand, this amalgam of composite pictures provided some interesting insights. But it was probable that ultimate success eluded him. In frustration, he began to drink again.

Marjorie worried, both about his drinking, and in fear that the sadomasochistic activities would go too far. The neighborhood was amused and tolerant, the cab driver calling up with, "Got another 'research girl' for you, Bill, and she's a lallapaloosa."[42] Willie and the girls even did a photo shoot for *Life* magazine in a Virginia swamp entitled "*Life* Goes to a Hexing Party." Behind the hoopla and the sex, however, was something deadly serious.

Willie attested that he wrote over a hundred thousand words of observations on what seemed to happen in the barn with the girls, some volunteers and

42. Seabrook, *No Hiding Place*, p. 372.

others paid retainers, who suffered in the cage, the witch's cradle, and other devices.

> What they voluntarily endured and saw mystically and described, would constitute, stripped down . . . a document, beside some of the so-called mystical revelations of the religious ecstatics of the Middle Ages.[43]

The Huxleys returned from California to observe, which Seabrook implied to be partial inspiration for Aldous's *After Many a Summer Dies the Swan*, a spoof on the quest for immortality.[44] Other observers and possible participants included Walter Duranty. The young scholar Maya Deren, who subsequently became an authority on Voudon herself, was definitely there. During 1939, he did a series of lecture tours, some on the occult, spent a few months in New York, then back to the doings at the barn.

The text for *Witchcraft* was finished by the beginning of 1940. In May, he began work on a biography of Dr. Robert Wood, the maverick physicist of Johns-Hopkins and an early science fiction writer. The going was slow, and his drinking accelerated. He also seemed to be growing highly superstitious. His hysterical reaction to the gift of a Haitian *ouanga* bag sent by Hal Smith impugned an already tenuous stability. His disagreements with Smith and Jonathan Cape,

43. Seabrook, ibid., pp. 372–375.

44. Seabrook, ibid., p. 373.

whatever those might have amounted to, were a decade in the past.

In January 1941, he went to a friend's place behind Woodstock to finish the book. There he met Constance Kuhr, one of the few female journalists to have been on the ground for the Nazi invasion of Poland. She'd then been through Dunkirk and the crack-up of France. Also, Kuhr was apparently a thoroughgoing sadist. Perhaps Willie's psychological coin had completely flipped over from dominant to submissive.[45]

Little more was known. Kuhr's methods for dealing with his alcoholism were extreme, having him scald his elbows so he couldn't lift a glass. After he moved Constance in, Marjorie moved out. She'd been able to swallow a lot of things, but not that. When even their doctor at Rhinebeck advised her not to come back, she got a divorce.

Walter Duranty, long an admirer of Marjorie's, was not slow on the uptake. He was moving on her within a month and, in his fashion, followed up over a long period of time. Walter provided a merciful diversion from what was coming, even though she was rapidly becoming obese and never really getting over Willie.

She would occasionally see Willie for lunch in New York. After Constance bore his son in February of 1943, he became focused on getting to England and the Continent as a war correspondent. I was a bit unconvinced by the patriotic protestations as motiva-

45. Seabrook, ibid., pp. 387–394.

tion, for this old guy with a pickled liver, to want to run off to war again.

He didn't make it. From that time on, he was in and out of hospitals for further psychiatric treatment. By contrast, continuing his sadomasochistic interests, he made a serious effort to interest Dali in the project of a ballet based on them, showing Helen Montague some "very beautiful" photographs.[46]

---

RHINEBECK, NY, SEPT. 20 (AP)

> William B. Seabrook, 59-year-old author and explorer, was found dead today from what Dr. Samuel E. Appel, Dutchess County Medical Examiner, said was an overdose of sleeping pills. Dr. Appel listed the death as a suicide . . . investigation showed that the author had "made threats" to take his life.[47]

Thus, Marjorie's little "lamb of God," as she'd called him, was finally released—but I couldn't believe it was to rest in peace. I felt that he might have listened more closely to his friend Walter, and thought about holes left in people's hearts. By God, those women had loved him so much! Devotion like theirs *must* count for something. Irrespective of the reasons, the depth of my identification had become profound.

46. Worthington, op. cit., p. 248.

47. *The New York Times*, 21 Sep. 1945.

It hardly seemed credible that I could have missed him. That none of his best-selling books had been on my mother's shelves seemed impossible. Her interests had been broad beyond the seemly for a Texas schoolteacher in the fifties. Yet had I read even one, I felt a certain conviction that I would have inexorably been led to a copy of *Witchcraft*. Had that occurred, I knew that the figure of Justine would have become an icon in my precocious and happily perverted young mind.

I felt cheated of being shaped by this influence. How might it have changed my life? Had I read his adventure stories at fourteen, I would have wanted to *be* him, to follow in his dangerous footsteps. So much that I continued to ignore all other aspects of my original quest as I chased down every available source on Seabrook.

His treatment of Wamba's Fan-Shaped Destiny was, arguably, the precursor of the many-worlds interpretation as applied to literature—twenty-seven years before the formalism was elaborated by Hugh Everett and forty-three years before it was popularized by Bryce DeWitt. He had been to the mountain and seen the promised land, and became obsessed with getting back. I believed that his obsession went, indeed, "a whole lot further back and a whole lot deeper" than to Africa in 1929.

Seabrook had been searching for something very specific since at least 1907, when he had gone to Geneva. I thought he had found it in Africa, and that returning to Europe had likely been an error. He thought he had good reason to anticipate the fun and games awaiting him back in our world. By the time they became no fun and all games, it had been too late.

Certainly I felt that the blackout, the *blacklisting*, of his diverse impacts on literature and culture should not be allowed to stand. Most especially the real possibility that the branching-worlds thesis in literature might well have influenced the scientific interpretation, rather than the reverse.

Likewise, his influence on the occult, and his early public proclamation of sadomasochism. That last was possibly at the behest of none other than A.A. Brill. William Pepperell Montague had seen in Seabrook a champion of his proposition that a materialism sufficiently radical would lead on to a new idealism, in which matter was not denied but transfigured.

My friend Richard used to claim that he could hear the "laughter of the gods." At the end of Willie's story, inside and aside was always the mischievous laughter of the sprightly composite Justine. Whenever the anomalies ganged up, she was always nearby, as "Deborah," possibly Crowley's consort "Leah," or simply the figure in the red-leather mask. Maybe composed of pieces of Willie's wives and anonymous "research girls," possibly with a pinch of Lee Miller, but more.

Seabrook had described Justine's presumed Leah Hirsig component thus: ". . . that was her name in the phone book, and in the cold world outside." Referencing her nudity, he noted "the one thing she did wear.

She couldn't very well avoid wearing it, because it had been branded into her fair hide with the red-hot point of a Chinese sword: on her breast she wore a Star . . ."[48] Even before I had found Ward Greene's strange book, *Ride the Nightmare*, and read of a Justine kneeling in the same position as Leah at Washington Square, I had somehow sensed that composite literary device was at least one key to the enigma.

---

AMONG THE SYNCHRONISTIC CURIOSITIES that had been accumulating in my journal, two more had been waiting to set the stage for what was about to happen. These took place when a trip on union business took me back to my hometown of Fort Worth, just before the WorldCon in late August.

The first was to be the weirdness of my acquisition of a 1949 paperback version of Ward Greene's lightly fictionalized early life of Seabrook, *Ride the Nightmare*. I'll describe the circumstance of its finding later; suffice it to say that it originally appeared to rival the appearance of the autobiography. The next offering of the "Library Angel," however, had been so involved with the circumstances of my own life as to freak me.

I'd made my obligatory pilgrimage to the shelter house at Lake Arlington, bathing in treasured misery over my lost JJ, that gracious source of tears for worlds that might have been. I resolved to reestablish contact with my boyhood friend Charles, whom I'd

48. Seabrook, *Witchcraft*, pp. 217–218.

not seen for ten years. Thus sensitized, and dreading telling him of Linda's death, I was wholly unprepared for having the wounds so unexpectedly salted.

Charles for some years had two wives, not sequentially. You will have likely gathered my total indifference whether the circumstances constituted de facto, if not legal, bigamy. I will mention that our beloved Marilyn, a Native American, was his wife in the eyes of the *Lakota* religion. The rest is no one else's business and too precious to all concerned to debate.

Our lives had been intimately, if not bizarrely, entangled when our inseparable friend Big Richard had met a violent death typical to bikers. Neither are the details of that tragedy germane, except that the emotional complications had left me with guilt, which had generated an estrangement from Charles and Marilyn for many years. It was my burden, not theirs.

Perhaps I should say it was not germane, *as far as I know*, a caveat that I would soon learn to apply to many observations. In any event, what I had to deal with was the news that Marilyn had died, due to complications resulting from multiple sclerosis, less than a year before. I'd not even known she was ill, and now the loose ends would never be tied up. Like the big hole where Big Richard used to stand, like the emptiness left by Linda, it would never be filled.

I'd spent forty-eight hours in near-continuous conversation with Charles, rehashing what had happened, not happened, might have happened, and should have happened. Near the conclusion of that masochistic marathon, I was stunned by an event that drew fresh consideration to my bookseller's behavior, and perhaps to a perceptual abnormality I'd experienced when discovering Ward Greene's book.

Charles is a pack rat who seems to have nearly everything he's ever owned. In itself, the fact of him dredging up a copy of the 1968 reprint of *Witchcraft* out of a box of books, lost among a decades-long accumulation of auto and motorcycle parts, might not seem all that strange. Still, Charles can remember the exact location of nuts and bolts he removed decades past. That he found no recollection of ever having possessed such a book *was* somewhat singular. As youths, we'd had a passing interest in the esoteric, after all.

For some hours I'd compared the paperback to a photocopy I'd made—only weeks before the book had inexplicably vanished from the library's reference shelves. I deduced that what Charles had found could only be the 1968 reprint. Deduction being indicated, in that the odd paperback's flyleaf contained only the original 1940 publication data.

I could not resist associating the conditions of the find with the blank I continued to draw about prior contacts with Seabrook's work, the light of my recent obsessions coloring it very personally. It felt as if these things had always stood near to me, surrounding me, waiting for me.

Driving back to San Antonio in a simmering emotional soup, I came face-to-face with what I was engaging in. Psychological pabulum could not replace those who had been the meaning of my life. I thought of boyhood experiments when we had tried to send our consciousness into our futures; the marginal evidence that, sometimes, we had apparently succeeded. Through a glass darkly, too weak a connection to do any greater good . . . If it were mental illness, should I go madder than Phil Dick, so what? What did I have left to lose? In truth, I questioned whether my life had been worth the living at all, if catastrophic errors always outweighed the good. Near the end of my tether, one more thread had frayed.

I couldn't shake the stuff boiling up in me. There were thoughts of my mother, and a world changed beyond recognition in just my lifetime. There was regret at finding myself childless late in life and fear of facing myself as the lonely old man I was already becoming. I experienced a dark nostalgia that was far from comforting, as if an irrational belief that I might have lived better had it been in other times. Behind and around it all was a heartbreaking *homesickness*, for the places and people lost every time another door had closed.

As I gained the San Antonio city limits, intent on either a stiff drink or a happy pill, the radio had been babbling about *El Niño* kicking up, generating a flurry of storms in the Caribbean and the Gulf. In earlier years I had a strong interest in climatic change and would have paid more attention. Apart from the possibility of some welcome relief from the oppressive heat wave, it seemed small potatoes compared with the storm within my own soul.

I watched a lone seagull in the evening twilight, flapping along above and beyond the branching interstates, which I knew he used, like the rivers, as a map. Would that the "paths of probability" I'd been studying were so clearly defined! Those might rather resemble a topographical map of a steep gorge or mountain—"bundles" of lines of very similar paths. Worse, the nonlinear terms might signify a constant crossing and recrossing, loops in which every convergence might be seen as the other end of a divergence.

Looking back, there is a thrilling chill in remembering what could have been the synchronistic moment, when the quantum membrane between metaphor and reality became strained to its limit. The bird seemed to dive right at my car but, just as I thought it would smash into the windshield, it had turned and risen again. I continued to watch with bewilderment until, again leisurely, it disappeared into the dusk. For the bird no longer seemed to be escaping, but running *toward* the gathering storms.

# IV
# The Justines

WAKING TO VERIFY THAT I HAD SURVIVED MY NIGHT of passion with Justine, I lay in bed thinking about what all this was possibly going to mean. I could smell coffee brewing and hear her talking to my dog. I knew this much—a sadly forgotten joy had been returned to my life. If there was any way on God's green earth to keep this improbable encounter going, even if for only a little while longer, I would do anything and everything necessary. I looked for my robe, then spotted Justine's clothes scattered about the bedroom floor and concluded that she must be wearing it. Good sign.

I paused by the mirror for a reality check. Not really overweight, but gravity definitely in evidence: belly sagging a bit; butt okay; muscle tone mediocre. It was obvious I was no fan of the sun, and looked as white as the belly of a toad. The upside of that was that my skin looked about as it always had, with little wrinkling. But my grayed hair and beard struck me as looking old, old, old.

I hit the shower, scrubbed and deodorized everything I could reach, trimmed wild hairs, and prayed that I had farted all I was capable. As I dressed, I was keenly aware of the regimen being utterly unlike anything I ever did in the morning. The thought of her looking at me, and wondering what she possibly could have been thinking the preceding night, sickened me.

I slipped quietly into my main living area and stood watching her as she sat behind my desk. The growing lump in my throat should have clued me right off that I was over the top. An encounter, which should have been some fun before both went our separate ways, had become something I wanted to keep forever. Wisdom would be that I could all too easily kill it by clutching too hard, but I didn't want to let go.

My malamute lay at her feet, happy, protective, and content for there to be a woman in the house again, maybe vaguely hoping that he wouldn't be left alone so much anymore. Justine was absorbed in reading my Seabrook files, her toes caressing Kong's big furry neck. She had one knee drawn up, foot beautifully arched against the edge of the seat. The robe spilled open to display the muscular cut of those legs that had been so unbelievably wrapped around mine just a few hours before.

She was reading from my file of hard copies, shot from microfilmed book reviews and bio items on Seabrook, from the thirties and forties. She'd hardly had to search, as my materials were spread all over the room, but it was apparent that she had been flagrantly prowling through them.

On my desk was a rough draft from which portions of this present account were later transcribed. It was incomplete, particularly as regards the Seabrook background—much of it no more than glorified notes. My copy of *Adventures in Arabia* lay open to the drawing of a silver "bride's girdle" or belt, of the *Yezidi*, so obviously related to her own barbaric jewelry.

*Adventures in Arabia*, arguably, was second only to T.E. Lawrence in establishing the popular literary and film image of life among the desert tribes. Willie used the name of "Arabia" in the old fashion to denote the entire Arab domain; he did not visit the Arabian Peninsula. The book had secured his position as an authority on the *Druse*. He and Katie were on the ground in the Syrian puppet states of "Greater Lebanon" when a *Druse* rebellion against the French Mandate broke out in the summer of 1925.

Marjorie Worthington asserted later that he had fought with the *Druse* against the French. This was not impossible. Willie, still technically attached to the French Army and a frequent visitor to France, would have been inhibited against using such an adventure for self-promotion. In any event, he was in demand from newspapers and foreign-policy clubs back in New York in late 1925.[49]

---

49. "Proud Druse Race Enraged at French," *The New York Times*, 2 Nov. 1925. Also, "Foreign Policy Association at Dinner in Astor, Discuss Mandate in Near East; Wm. B. Seabrook, here from war zone, says they hate French more than Turks," *The New York Times*, 20 Dec. 1925.

It took nothing away from the validity of our mutual interest to presume that I had one real chance with Justine. Her involvement with the Seabrook saga was clearly intense and personal. If I could contrive to remain an integral part of her quest, there might be a remote chance of molding this thing closer to my heart's desire.

She looked up, "Hey. Prompt me why you aren't, like, a college professor or something?" She gestured to my piles of research materials, and I laughed. It was not as though I hadn't been asked that before. Things just had not fallen that way in this life. On an impulse, I told her about the bikers and strippers with whom I had spent my youth. "Professor" had, in fact, been the biker name the dancers had given me.

She nodded understanding. "I can see why you're so up on Willie." She turned back to the copy of a 1936 *American Magazine* article, "Green Hills Far Away," in which Seabrook rationalized not finally returning to his life as an expatriate. Directly, she leaned back and sighed, looking at the pictures on my desk. Speaking carefully, as though trying to stay on top of something inexplicable, "Sentimental, much?"

Unclear whether she was referring to Willie or me, I tried to balance between both. "He tried to understate the sentimentality in his writing, but he couldn't conceal it. You know, I think there's something of that nature at the core of most tough guys."

She snapped back from the pictures. "Take long for you to learn that?" she demanded, in an interesting twist.

"Lifetimes, babe,"—I laughed—"many incarnations."

She picked at the edges of my draft pages. "Cool with me scanning this?" I nodded assent. Of course, it served my purpose to show her anything she wanted to see.

I asked what impressions she'd gathered from the chapter roughs. "It's all—about convergence," she mused. "Things, like, come together around your own story." I didn't quite see that last part, and wondered at her psychological "take" on what I might be saying about myself.

"I'm not sure that I want to let a psych grad know the full extent of my madness, yet." I knew full well what impossible convergence I'd sought. Poor Linda had summed it up not long before she died. She'd said that what heaven must be is a second chance.

The green eyes were again burning disconcertingly far into me. "It's much cheaper to call ideas insane than process them." So, I talked some more about my writing project with her, how I had, in fact, been tempted to represent myself as a professional writer or an academic researcher. But it somehow seemed important for all of it to be the truth. I supposed that might have been a reaction to years of writing political propaganda and legal arguments.

I decided to go some distance into Linda and our mutual history. Our shared sexual proclivities and social views had, in the years when we'd started out, been sufficiently radical as to make us voluntary outcasts from most parts of society. We'd lived in an "us against the world" mode for so long that, finally and in extremity, there was no help to be had from anyone who hadn't walked in our shoes.

Carneys, scooter-trash, radicals, sadomasochists—when you live outside the prescribed limits, the truth about our loving society is a simple one. It would just as soon see you dead, encouraging the nihilism that feeds self-destruction. In the case of Linda's gentle soul, it had succeeded.

I feared that I might go so far as to antagonize Justine when I got wound up and began to express my contempt for the "helping professions," with their narrow little judgments. Kong, the malamute, reacted as he typically did to my tension or anger by setting up a melancholy complaint in his amusing "ahroo-har" malamute-talk. I laughingly welcomed the interruption to my habitual pontification, and we stopped to play with him.

I told her Kong's history, how this huge dog had been able to ride about South Texas on a platform on the back of a Harley-Davidson, behind an equally big guy. How Big Richard had left him with me years before, when he had gone out to get himself killed. Kong had turned out to be the best dog I ever had, and had been Linda's constant companion in the years while she helped society annihilate her.

I stroked his huge old head and remarked fondly, "This doggie goes to heaven."

I heard Justine stifle a sob and was dismayed to find her eyes brimming with tears. Sitting there semi-clad, the tough little punker dissolved as she clutched her knuckles to her lips, looking again toward the picture of Linda in her better days. She had been beautiful in the costume from her slave girl act, based on a belly-dance outfit but with a lot of leather and chains. "What's up with that—not loving you?" she blurted out. I was nonplussed. How had I given that misconception?

"I was the love of Linda's life," I said quietly. "Insofar as I failed her, I bear the karma." Why I chose to voice those misgivings, I'd no idea. It seemed that another face of Justine had cut in. Drawing herself up, she looked *stately*, even in her effective nudity. She gently touched Linda's picture, as if in benediction.

"Not her, bless her heart," she said softly, then her voice changed, "Her!" She nodded to the adjacent frame, holding an old high-school picture of JJ and the touching little verses I'd given her when we'd parted for the second time. "She's the one in the beginning of your story, yea?"

I confirmed the likeness of JJ, some thirty years earlier. Now, an emotional expression like Justine's can be taken in a very ego-enhancing light, and I confess to interpreting it just that way. Graciousness being indicated, I offered the first event as being in the nature of the times, before the youth upsurge of the sixties. Conformity had been the iron rule and "good girls" were supposed to regiment their conduct to what "everybody thinks."

Moving right along past the actual facts: Texas girls back then having a major streak of healthy old country promiscuity; "everybody" referencing only the toadies, who could be counted on for knee-jerk bigotry while the rest remained silent; "thinking" being anomalous in Texas . . . I passed on any commentary I might have otherwise issued on JJ's weakness of character. Much as I had loved her all my life, naturally I had some mixed feelings.

I moved to embrace Justine as she stood up from behind the desk. The oversize robe was falling off her, and she let it drop. She clung to my neck, pressing herself against me. Dared I hope? But finally, she wrote off her emotionality to a sugar drop and decided that she was craving an omelet. I didn't have everything necessary, so we drove a few blocks through the decomposing south side to a Denny's on I-35.

I talked of my working-class family, of the old Stockyards district in Fort Worth. Now a tourist trap like the Riverwalk, back then it had been a little piece of Chicago dropped deep in the heart of Texas. Like JJ's folks, my parents had moved up, after World War II, but remained attuned to their roots. My white hide denotes no bleeding-heart champion of the underdog. I simply would have been no more at home among the aging white yuppies and "High-spanics" of San Antonio's northern suburbs than would most of my *Tejano* neighbors.

---

SHE WAS A SENSATION to the morning people in the restaurant, wearing her suit from the previous evening. The barbaric jewelry again brought out that whiff of indeterminate origins. It reminded me of the early-century notion that the Irish and Finns were the same red-haired warriors known as far away as Mongolia.

She put my regular waitress, Criselda, at a loss, too. Cris, a personal friend as well, was accustomed to seeing me either alone, or with *Tejanas* in my own age bracket. She served me a leer with the coffee. "*¿Eh, cabrón?*" She shrugged suggestively toward Justine, who then addressed her politely *en Español* and turned out to be a good deal more bilingual than I am. You should understand; that, in itself, continued to be uncommon among Anglos in San Antonio. More so than in, say, Laredo.

We talked more of the possible origins of the branching worlds. Many of the s-f geeks wanted to see Murray Leinster as a lone genius in 1934. He'd illustrated, in pretty much Einsteinian terms, a scenario in which a space-time catastrophe fractured the continuum.

A mathematics professor and his students were brought into contact with fragments of worlds where they found, among others: a triumphant Confederacy; Norsemen colonizing America; a still-flourishing Roman Empire. Leinster's Professor Minott had instructed his students that the future is only a coordinate—that imagining a unitary destination would be as silly as denying spatial directions other than the cardinal points. An indefinite number of futures await, dependent on which forks in time are taken. I recalled, for Justine, how language from certain passages had turned out remindful of Seabrook's accounts of Wamba:

> . . . between the forks of the road I choose not only between two sets of landmarks I could encounter, but between two sets of events . . . so those paths in the future may lead to two entirely different fates . . . with more or less absence of deliberation we choose among them.[50]

"Now, that smells even stronger of Seabrook than Heinlein's piece, especially considering that Willie had laid down the same thing, only four years before, in *Jungle Ways*. Leinster went on to argue that the roads not taken being equally real, and similar choices being confronted at every *past* moment, then we must of necessity be surrounded by an overabundance of alternate realities.

"After exploring the titillating possibilities of the temporarily accessible worlds, Leinster gave Minott's nauseatingly conformist kiddos the opportunity to return home. He had the good doctor greet the very idea of going back to being a mathematics professor with savage laughter!

"At the end, an unprepossessing young lass named Lucy turned out to be the only one of the brats who had the right stuff. She failed to see the homely wisdom of continuing to be a wallflower for her class-

---

50. Leinster, Murray, op. cit., pp. 19–21.

mates, who'd established their ability to carry their postadolescent social strictures with them, even unto carboniferous jungles! She wound up dashing back across the closing time fracture to join Minott, hopeful of becoming an empress in a new world."

"Lucy, you go, girl!" Justine snickered.

Eventually, I had to arrive at the always-curious Philip K. Dick.

She raised an eyebrow. "As if adjectivally too mild?" Yes, it's true; Phil Dick was as crazy as the proverbial dog. But he was a genius nonetheless, and I had no confidence that I could, any longer, afford any sense of sane superiority.

"*The Man in The High Castle* was post-Everett, but the texture kind of hearkened back to the earlier writers. More, the unique use of the *I Ching* as a method of transit between worlds brought Borges's Chinese book to mind.

"There was something else that I couldn't put my finger on at the time—something with the same quality as Norton's phrase 'every bit of destiny action.'" Dick, like H. Beam Piper, had claimed to have experienced alternate realities himself. My own reading, of his later work and history, did not dispose me to argue against his distinction as one of the more unbalanced minds of recent literature.

"Meds, which facilitated his penchant for the little brown girls on the streets of L.A., *would* tend to alternate your realities! Out there, yea, but don't dis him." It seemed she had read about a prescient emergency diagnosis that Dick performed on his own child, which went far to support his claim that something untoward had happened to him. "No sicker than Poe, I'm sure."

"You just can't get away from the fact of the literary anomaly," I contended, returning to my central obsession. "Everett's interpretation of '56–'57 wasn't widely popularized until the early seventies. Should we choose to see a possible progenitor, in Feynman's 'many-histories,' to explain the body of fiction during the fifties and sixties—Feynman only formalized his work in 1940 . . ."

I digressed, as I'm prone to do. I had found commentary expressing surprise that Everett seemed to have developed his theory entirely from the Schrödinger viewpoint, without detectable influence from Feynman's work. This despite both Feynman and Everett having John Wheeler for their thesis supervisor at Princeton, and did Wheeler contribute very much . . . Justine was looking irritated, so I got back on track.

"Much of the key material was being presented during the years 1938 to 1941, while Seabrook was concluding his studies of the paranormal. Leinster had presented the earliest branching-paths story back in 1934. Then I found that Piper, de Camp, and Pratt had credited Seabrook's African material published in 1930 and 1931.

"These science fiction writers led me to Willie's association with Wamba as the hidden literary source of the branching worlds. Later, in 1940, Willie repeated the story of the Fan-Shaped Destiny in

*Witchcraft*. A reviewer mentioned Wamba, the 'handsome African priestess' who believed that the future already exists in space-time, shaped like a palm-leaf fan. He put it this way, '*Except for the fan,* by the way, this resembles the theory advanced by J.W. Dunne, the British scientist in *An Experiment with Time*.'[51]

"Not to eviscerate a dead horse, but just how is it that, while a book reviewer of the forties could get the scientific facts straight, supposed literary scholars of our time can't? I remember another quotation, from Wamba's mentor, whom Seabrook called 'the Ogoun':

---

> THERE WAS AN OLDER MAGIC by which time is twisted backward, so that the forward magic becomes as if it had never been . . . as if it had all been a dream, or a thing done by shadows, which are as if they had never been, and leave no trace when light appears.[52]

She gave a careless smile. "A lost magic by means of which you could go back and delete, so that a bad destiny would like, become not? That is so totally *kewl!*"

"One way to put it. I don't know if Seabrook would have shared my opinion that he reached his pinnacle there at that moment. I even fancifully considered finding a way to get to Africa, to follow the trail of

51. McHugh, Vincent, *The New York Times*, 7 Sep. 1940.

52. Seabrook, *Witchcraft*, p. 34.

such a tradition. Later I read some recent magazine articles on Côte d'Ivoire, ravaged by plague and growing civil strife. It sounds as though there is little left of Wamba's land other than ugliness and death."

Then I moved on to aspects of his life and career, and to the temporal curiosities that had emerged during my reconstruction. There were the frequent time displacements where the various sources, including Seabrook himself, couldn't seem to remain consistent. I told her of 1908, when Seabrook had left off tramping through Europe to study philosophy at the University of Geneva. He never expanded on that, beyond one mention in his writings, despite being a sometimes-shameless self-promoter.

The stint at the Geneva campus was anomalous, utterly unlike Willie, a decided nonacademic. Given his degrees in philosophy, a study of Kant was not odd in itself. But his production of a graduate paper on time, space, and causality was at variance with a life not at all oriented toward scholarship. In the same breath, he spoke darkly of learning from the work of Jules Michelet and other books, not in the curriculum at the University of Geneva. This image of the melding of the lore of ancient and forbidden tomes with more recent science is, in American literature, almost solely the creation of H.P. Lovecraft. I wondered if Seabrook, a Machen fan, might have also been into Lovecraft.

"I got to thinking about what else might have been going on in Geneva in 1908 and did some digging. Minkowski had just expounded the implications of

Einstein's relativity for the first time: the 'block universe,' lifelines in four dimensions, and other concepts that J.W. Dunne would employ later.

"Why, even Lenin was there. He wrote a philosophical treatise touching on what amounted to early quantum notions. In a small intellectual community, where everyone knew each other, it would have been odd had Seabrook not come across him. More inexplicable that he wouldn't have commented on it later."

"Hey, Willie was a Republican," she laughed.

Well, what do you know about that? I wondered. But I grinned back. "The Lost Generation rarely let any political litmus test get in the way of their fun. I'm not sure that Willie even *had* politics that early, but most of his friends would have been socialists of some flavor."

"If he were all, y'know, about weird sex? Check it out. Weren't the commies prudes, muchly?"

"Another product of modern education," I sighed facetiously. "Even ten years later, the Sovnarcom regime, the pre-Stalin government—those were also the days of Alexandra Kollontai and Isadora Duncan, opium and free love. Why, even Lenin's lover, Inessa Armand, was somebody we could have talked to. Maybe played with," I added, feeling out what all she was up for.

"One of Willie's partners in crime in the thirties was Walter Duranty, whom Roosevelt credited with bringing about the recognition of the Soviet Union." I was knowledgeable about Russia, from an antiestablishment point of view, had even visited the old

U.S.S.R. once, so I hoped I was scoring points with my scholarship.

"Duranty," she mused. "Hey, academe? Believe me when I say to slack off the attitude. I'm not liking that. It makes you sound, like—someone I don't *even* want you to remind me of!"

I was appalled at the trap into which I'd been stepping. The point of my game was to ridicule vacuous elitism. But, it was not amusing to a kid whose experience, of growing up surrounded by stupid rednecks, was more freshly painful than my own. But she held a different view.

"Clueless that it sounds wanna-be, with you getting all pedantic on my ass at the same time?" She put down my attempted explanation and got up, absently wiping her fingers along the seam of her skirt. "Don't go there."

While she was in the rest room, I sat and agonized over how much damage control was indicated. Cris freshened our coffee. "Where is she from?" When I told her San Antonio, as far as I knew, Cris looked skeptical. I asked about the girl's Spanish.

"*Bueno, mijo,* but different, it's like she speaks Spanish with a New Orleans accent. And her English is different, too," decided Cris, whose profession is people. "Don't you hear it?" When I admitted that I had not, she maintained that Justine sounded a bit like some of the "snowbirds," the part-time residents from the North.

Watching Justine return to the table, as did almost everyone else in the restaurant, I wondered at how careful I needed to be in handling this charming mystery. She sat down looking thoughtful. I started to apologize, but she waved it off and changed the subject, with no trace of the bitchy flare.

"You have this expert thing going, on people and histories I need to know about. You've been studying all that for months." Momentarily, I thought I'd identified what Cris had been hearing. Not so much an accent, as a certain *elegance*, which crept into her speech when she dropped the punker affectations.

"Would you, could you," she asked shyly, looking at her lap, "come with me to Atlanta and bring your research? Hey, you would be wanting to see the mural and the other things?" She looked up hopefully, "You were right, I'm way sure this is not an accident." Well, I couldn't believe it. Phase Two in, I looked at my watch, eighteen hours.

It was true that I was set up for sudden out-of-town trips, with a bag always packed. All I had to do was ask Cris to look in on the dog, and scrape the books and papers together. It was Labor Day morning. No one would even be wondering where I was for another twenty-four hours. When they did, well, you don't work long as a rep without being able to bullshit.

What if this really was something more? In my wildest fantasies, I could not have imagined how much more. It was difficult to trust the ease with which this thing was happening. No promises of correspondence; no major project of getting her back to San Antonio, or creating excuses to get me to Atlanta? Just the prospect of waking up looking into those eyes, my arms around that body. Had I ever been the sort of man who would pass on Justine because he was afraid he might lose his job? I don't think so!

I looked at her evenly, "If I blow off everything to come be with you, do not imagine that your interesting family background is the reason." *Certainty like this comes but once . . .*

She blushed, I swear she did. "It's all that," she whispered, and tentatively held out her hand. When I responded, she seized mine with an unexpected painful grip. "Check it out," she said earnestly. "We'll go hear Dr. Cramer. Then I gotta say good-bye to my mother, so you come home and pack, and I'll pick you up after two o'clock. Not to come off butch, but I wanna be outta here soon. All kinds of traffic tonight, yea?" I agreed, and she squirmed like a happy child getting out of the booth. I marveled at yet another face of Justine.

---

"QUANTUM WEIRDNESS, THE BEST GAME IN TOWN," Cramer's panel discussion, was held to a packed room. There were only two panelists, one being a mechanical engineer who wrote short stories with some interesting observations concerning the use of quantum mechanical principles in fiction. But the crowd had come to hear Dr. John Cramer, the physics professor from the University of Washington, who had published a couple of best-selling science fiction novels and wrote a column for *Analog*.

More importantly, Cramer had originated the

Transactional Interpretation of Quantum Mechanics. It was being ballyhooed as the "third interpretation," opposed to both the traditional view of wave function collapse on the one hand, and the many-worlds on the other. While Cramer laid the groundwork, enumerating Einstein's bill of particulars against the spookiness of quantum mechanics, I offered Justine my thoughts on the politics of the scientific establishment.

"When it began to seem that the results of quantum computing experiments could be explained only by the many-worlds, a virtual cottage industry appeared in the physical community. There was a purely ideological mandate to supply an alternative interpretation, any interpretation to let them escape the branching worlds as a model of reality."

"Are we thinking that Cramer plays to that?" I was impressed that her degree in psychology did not prohibit a sound comprehension of the politics of actual life.

"Not really." I clarified that I had the highest respect for Cramer's work. "But when popularizers choose to believe that promoting his interpretation as one of the majors will serve their ideological imperatives, he'd be a fool not to go along with the process." Cramer educated the audience as to how Steven Weinberg, the discoverer of the electroweak force, had explored a loophole of adding a small "nonlinear" term to the quantum equations. He mentioned that a colleague of Weinberg's, at the University of Texas, had found that cobbling nonlinearity onto the many-worlds interpretation would allow for a communication between various branch universes.

"That's Joseph Polchinski's 'weak connection' between alternate worlds," I whispered to Justine. In my research, I would turn to the deeper journals such as *Physical Review* or *Annals of Physics* only when necessary and always with perturbation. Doing so would require that I impose on someone with a hard-science background to translate most of the content. But I had read of this modified interpretation.

---

THE BRANCHES MIGHT RETAIN A "WEAK CONNECTION." The introductory line of Polchinski's paper had stated flatly, "I show that Weinberg's nonlinear quantum mechanics leads either to communication via EPR correlations or to communication between branches of the wave function." My mathematically minded friends assured me that he lived up to his claim, which presented the physical establishment with a hellish choice:

> . . . thought experiments described herein would seem to be simple enough to carry out in practice, thereby determining which of EPR communication (across time) and Everett communication (between worlds) is actually realized.[53]

---

53. Polchinski, Joseph, "Weinberg's Nonlinear Quantum Mechanics and the Einstein-Podolsky-Rosen Paradox," in *Physical Review Letters*, 28 Jan. 1991, p. 400.

It appeared that Weinberg had hoped to wed quantum mechanics to relativity, but feared that the nonlinear mathematics would violate Einstein's laws. Polchinski had carried the contradiction further. He demonstrated that the only way to preclude communication across time, with its consequent violation of special relativity, would be to allow for the possibility of an "Everett phone" amongst the branches.

There the matter seemed to have languished for the remainder of the decade. As I had learned with the writers, so it was with the scientists. Whether we are in an "ignore it" phase or an "explain it away" phase, the mandate to the chroniclers is always the same—obscure the fact that a mystery or a contradiction even exists. *Or*, raise the fact of its existence to hallowed heights of almost religious inscrutability, like a form of faith.

Cramer credited Heisenberg and Schrödinger with the creation of quantum mathematical formalism, "completed" about 1927. He expounded the orthodox view that quantum mechanics were unique as a scientific theory, not having arisen, like most, from a preconceived notion of how the cosmos operates.

Quantum mechanics was supposedly an exclusive product of the math created to accommodate observed experimental results. Regarding the many-worlds interpretation, at least, I believed there was proof that this was partly a fiction. Far from springing full-blown from the head of Zeus, just such a preconception had propagated upward. It had come from strata of our human brother- and sisterhood that the scientific establishment will not credit for anything, beyond being potential guinea pigs for experimentation.

Justine began to exhibit intense interest as Dr. Cramer described how Eugene Wigner had shown how to make a quantum system run backward. By complex-conjugating it, the waves were shown running from the future to the past. As he proposed his transactional view of nonlocality, I saw her note down a quotation, "Backward in time to the source," and underline it.

Cramer then bitched for a while about National Security Administration monies funding IBM's quantum computing research. I'd already suspected that security interests in quantum cryptography were responsible for the dearth of information as to what was being brought on-line at Los Alamos and other sites. I wondered what research agendas Cramer thought were being shorted.

He was taking a purely utilitarian argument, emphasizing the relative value of the admitted probability of factoring large prime numbers without touching the question of where the gargantuan computing power comes from. Much less recognizing that the algorithms necessary to solve the problems implied that the results were achieved by collating information from computing resources in many universes working in tandem.

He offered comic relief with a story of how his second novel, *Einstein's Bridge*, had been based on the assumption that the Superconducting Supercollider would be brought on-line in Waxahachie, Texas. When the project had been canceled, he hadn't been able to look at the manuscript for a year and a half. Then he had a bright idea in the shower in Munich to embroider the story with a voyage in time to change history, so as to have the SSC really built.

To the charge of science fiction promulgating "junk science," he penetratingly responded that, in his view, an "unholy graft" between science and Eastern religion was the *real* junk science. On that, Justine turned to me, "What are we thinking?"

"I tend to agree." I shook my head. "I just don't understand why Cramer and others can't see many-worlds as the rational resolution of the quantum interpretation problem."

Cramer was bragging that he troubled to attach appendices to his books distinguishing the real scientific roots from the literary fictions and speculations grafted on top. Justine smiled, "Like what was the branching paths grafted on top of?"

She began waving her hand as Cramer was responding to a query on micro-reversibility. He was explaining that the real practitioners of the many-worlds extend the formalism so that two universes that become physically identical may converge as well. He then touched on the notion that nonlinear effects might be experimentally sought at the highest energies and energy densities, and that the SSC would certainly have been helpful, before getting to her.

"Can you use these interpretations jointly, or any two of them together?" she cut to the chase. I rather glowed as the room turned to look at this extraordinary little being beside me.[54]

"I think they're mutually exclusive, actually." Then he looked at her, and added, "Conceivably, you could have Everett-Wheeler joined at the hip to one of the other ones, but I don't think anybody likes to do that because it violates Occam's Razor . . ." He went on to talk of the metaphysical baggage that burdened each of the theories and how one wouldn't look to acquire two such sets of baggage.

She looked to me again, and I felt enormously flattered at being allowed to annotate Dr. Cramer. I hoped that the life of the mind always got her this excited. It might stand in for irregular or lackluster sexual performance. As the panel wound up, I explained how a fourteenth-century *ecclesiastical doctrine*, purportedly the search for the least complicated solution, had come to amount to an article of faith. "It was invoked against Galileo because the mere implications of a starry night sky were too 'uneconomical' to be believable to the medieval mind. Many processes in nature violate Occam's Razor. Besides, why should metaphysical simplicity be a consideration of science, anyway? As our friend Willie said, 'To simplify that which is not simple, is simply to falsify.'"

---

54. The audiotape of this panel discussion, conducted at the Fifty-fifth World Convention Of Science Fiction, San Antonio, Texas, 1 Sep. 1997—featuring John Cramer and Ron Collins—is available from The Sound of Knowledge, San Diego, CA. It confirms that a female participant put this question to Cramer, as it does the rest of the synopsis herein.

JUSTINE WAS INSISTENT on strolling the Riverwalk one more time from the convention center back to the Marriott. Secretly, I was elated as she held my hand and demonstrated to downtown San Antonio that we were a unit. I was only sorry that there wouldn't be an opportunity for her to knock their socks off at the Cadillac Bar. In the lobby we met Joe coming down from the convention suite, so at least he had a chance to meet Justine in all her splendor. When she kissed me and ran upstairs to retrieve her belongings, his eyes were properly wide.

"What have you done did?"

"Don't ask, because I don't know," I told him, admitting to my growing supposition that I could claim no credit for mechanicking any of this situation. I explained that I was going to have Cris see to Kong while I took off to Atlanta with this young babe. I gave him a quick outline of our meeting and the presumed connection with Seabrook and an original Justine.

"No shit! She has the mural?" Since we'd first learned of it, Joe had been beguiled by the notion of Marjorie's painting. I told him that was the presumption, though I could honestly care less should she turn out to be thoroughly delusional. I mentioned the various faces of Justine, and how she'd seemed when I'd first encountered her. "Goth, huh?" Joe mused. "She doesn't look like one now; don't know how to characterize her. She sort of defies description, doesn't she?"

"Well, yesterday, about all she was lacking was a Mohawk."

"I don't know about you," Joe ruminated, "but the

thought of that red hair in a Mohawk makes me hot." He offered me a high five. If you are very lucky in life, you get to meet a few people who honestly wish you well, without secret agendas or personal designs.

Justine drove an electric blue Honda Del Sol. Seeing her off from the parking garage, I noted her fingernails were painted to match her car. I had the distinct feeling that the swatches of gaudiness about her were not in the way of a fashion statement, like Joe's fantasy of a red Mohawk. The affects bespoke a fundamental personality template, as did the absolutely frightening way she hit the exit ramps going down.

Who knew what this girl might do? Heading for the house, I lectured myself to the effect that, if this were a chimera, I would know soon enough. Though a comedown would be a hard fall, either she would come for me or she wouldn't; it was that simple.

I looked about my house, at the pathetic remnants of my life, as I had known it. If I let myself think, if I began to pick up the little mementos about me, the old hurts would begin all over. Was it my imagination, or had I just failed to notice, as everything had grown so dark and shabby? How long had it been since I had ceased opening the curtains? There was nothing left here but memories that burned like the bite of a whip. There was nothing to be lost that compared to what I might sustain if I let myself hesitate at this crucial moment.

I got food and water prepared for Kong, then came back in to find him sitting hopefully by my prepacked bag at the front door. Seeing that hurt, too—remembering how he used to go everywhere with Linda and me. I assured him that he would see me again, hopefully soon, and got a bit emotional thinking how he was the last part of my life, as it had been, about which I still cared.

Then I began to gather my essential materials into a large leather file-folder case I'd gotten off one of the lawyers with whom I worked. This included my basic Seabrook file, the photocopy I'd made of the library's reference copy of *Witchcraft*, and disks with my rough draft and additional notes on such as DeWitt and the works of J.W. Dunne. The case being legal-length, there was some space at the end, where I carefully packed the copy of Willie's autobiography and Marjorie's book as well.

Had the kid been up prowling about longer than I'd thought? Apart from the *Witchcraft* file and the books, it seemed as though there was nothing I could readily lay hands on. It was one of those moments when nothing seems to be as you left it.

As an afterthought, I went back and added a copy of Borges's "Garden," and other loose sheets with obits and bios that I really should have gotten scanned so it could all go in my pocket. Union work was far behind the corporate side, and I didn't have easy access to the new technology yet. Then I dressed more comfortably in jeans and a blue work shirt and pulled out a corduroy jacket. The professorial thing seemed to sell real well.

I tried to settle down and wait, but the silence in

the house made me antsy. I made sure everything was turned off, pausing in the bedroom to remember the night before, which already seemed like a dream. There, too, something seemed different. Endeavoring to isolate the numinous effect, my scrutiny abruptly leapt back to the headboard of the bed. The old ties I had used to bind Justine's wrists were nowhere to be seen. What the hell? Had she taken them with her, as trophies? The thought disturbed me. Treasuring mementos in place of the actual person struck me as too reminiscent of JJ's approach to things.

I went back and sat down once more, then remembered to get my copy of Ward Greene's book. There being no more room in the legal case, I put it in my coat pocket along with my stash of Valium (as much security blanket as necessary medication) and sat down yet again. The hour had elapsed. I pulled out the Greene book and studied the garish cover inside the protective plastic wrap. It was nothing less than *Ride the Nightmare* reprinted as a paperback in 1949. While tediously trying to locate the original, I'd been unaware of this version, due in part to its having been retitled: *THE LIFE AND LOVES OF A MODERN MISTER BLUEBEARD!*[55]

---

What popular fascinations of 1949 the screaming association with Gilles de Rais had served, I had no clue. The lurid cover illustration presented Greene's fic-

55. Greene, Ward (original title *Ride the Nightmare*), NY: Avon, 1949.

tionalized Seabrook, in overalls, as an artist instead of a writer. He was seated on an ottoman with a drawing pad on his knees. Apparently secured to an easel, rather than a canvas, was the model herself, with her wrists crossed above her head. To all appearances unconscious, she was stripped to the waist, though a lock of long blonde hair strategically covered her breasts and the implied bonds were not visible. All this at "the amazing pre-War price of twenty-five cents," the back cover touted.

Just before visiting Charles in Fort Worth, I'd gotten together with Joe and his wife Diane. Since it was near my birthday, they wanted to visit an interesting bookshop where Di had seen an item she wanted to get for me. Having about an hour to prowl before the store closed, Di went to find my present, Joe was about to go off to the science fiction, and I was headed for the erotica downstairs. Joe first pointed out a section of locked cases containing first edition science fiction, old occult, and other interesting items.

I'd noticed a job lot of old paperbacks on some open shelves below the cases and had begun perusing them, amused by the campy covers. "God, look at this," I'd said, showing a book to Joe. Only as I had been about to return it to the shelf, did I notice the author and subtitle. After I'd despaired of owning Greene's book, my friends had inadvertently led me to an unknown edition, of which probably only a few copies still existed.

Even before the event at Charles's house involving

*Witchcraft*, this had gone into my record of synchronistic events. There had been, however, an anomaly that I'd dismissed as inconsequential until that further find obliged me to rethink all these matters. For long moments, as I'd knelt beside the bookcases, I'd seemed to deny the reality of what I held in my hand. I'd even entertained the irrational supposition that the very evident original title must refer to *another* book by the same author. Later, I'd taken hours before carefully examining it, even actually forgetting a few times during the evening about the remarkable item, which seemed as if it had been waiting for me.

Were aberrations of perception and memory common to instances of synchronicity generally? Did some censorial function in the brain dictate, "Now, here's how it *must* have happened," and, failing that, blank it out if possible? Certainly, anyone experiencing such would not be prone to report that aspect. If you're making a point that something untoward has occurred, you don't cast aspersions on your own memory in the same breath. Or, might this observed behavior, repeated by the bookseller, Charles, and me be linked instead to the peculiar "forgettability" of Seabrook's historical record?

I leafed through this other present from the "Library Angel," a semifacetious concept of the physicist Wolfgang Pauli. Collaborator with Jung in the study of synchronicity, Pauli had been renowned for such events in his personal and professional life. Justine would get a kick out of the parts about her namesake character, whom Greene had devised a full ten years before Seabrook had ever written of his Justine. Another hour had passed, and there was a heavy weight on my chest. Did it end like this, a flash in the pan that never went anywhere? Another "what if?" to torture me into old age? My experiences in bouncing off young women, even in my youth, did not inspire hope. How long before I heard the predictable "I just can't right now?"

Maybe an old boyfriend calling, while she was at her mother's, with a revelation of cosmic significance that she had somehow overlooked? All that crap that they go through as they flail about without a clue as to what they want. "Didn't know I needed you, baby, till you left town." A bitter lampoon of self-serving young male bullshit ran through my mind as I paced the floor. "Well hell, I almost got off my dead butt to find you. Now that somebody else wants you, I'll have to kill you or myself if I can't have you." Or worse, her addressing me with *". . . if only you weren't so much older."*

In my nervous stalking about, I'd wandered back into the bedroom. Idly inspecting the closet, I spied the errant ties hanging on a rack with other unused items. Now, why in hell would she have troubled to hang those up? I wondered, in the suddenly oppressive silence of the enclosed room, as I fingered the neckties. Then came an eerie perception that their material was to no degree crumpled or creased, as though they had been hanging there for years, like their fellows—untouched, unused.

An irrational fear gripped me. Momentarily, it

seemed as though I might have stepped briefly into a universe that had housed such a magical little being, then been transported back—back here. Here, to a sad and lonely place where she did not exist at all, where my memories of her were sheer dementia. Oh no, oh please God . . .

I snapped to as a revelation nullified my gloom. I was not going to let it happen! If she didn't show, I'd call Joe before the convention offices were boxed up, get her address and other registration information, and catch a few hours' sleep. One way or another, night would find me on the causeway across the Atchafalaya swamps, on my way to Atlanta.

By God, I would *make* it happen! Between her sexual tastes and involvement with the Seabrook saga, there was enough for me to work with. There were levels here, true enough. Part of it was the old Halloween thrill again, but there was something so much more—that would move me at any cost.

Was it significant that I confronted the fact of having fallen hopelessly in love with her at the very moment she pulled into my driveway?

I watched through the window as she got out of her car. In tight blue jeans, studded denim jacket over a halter top, she was as exquisite as she had been the night before. Relief was tempered as I saw her dab her eyes under her dark glasses. Not out of the woods yet, I thought; but unlike minutes before, I felt ready to deal with anything. Inside the door, she laid her head against my chest. I asked her what was wrong, hoping I exuded the confidence I'd acquired by taking a fundamental decision.

"Y'know the thing where you can't remember ever being called a 'child' till after you're age of consent? *Then*, we wanna get all parental . . ." she answered, gesturing with an upturned palm. "Believe me when I say, if some people don't have a thing in their lives, they're all—about how nobody else should."

"The bad news is, babe, that's the great majority around us."

"I never know what's up, with Mother and me. She's not too stoked by me on the road alone. Hey, I really thought she would fret less with someone 'looking after me.' I am such a *retard*. I flipped her off, was way harsh on her to deal with my going. Now I feel all gnarly."

"Well, you're of age and have your own means," I spoke carefully, surmising that the means were precisely the issue.

She mockingly slapped her forehead. "I forgot!" She grabbed up the heavy leather case with an air of urgency, "We're outta here." We'd just started out the door when the phone rang. I cursed under my breath and began to put down my bag. "Nay, please, let it go." There was alarm in her voice, and I looked at her curiously. She tugged on my wrist in a childlike gesture I was coming to recognize. Something about taking the hand was important to her. "I'm way sure it's her," she explained. "She was going off about calling you and 'taking care of this.'"

It's true. I've become a cranky old man, especially

on issues of sex and politics. "Justine, nobody is going to put any paternalistic threats over on me. I grew up around all that trailer-trash behavior, too. But, after fifty years, I've been around too many blocks to take it." Yes, I did take it personally. It brought back thoughts of JJ and everything that had gone into tearing us apart.

---

"WE'RE SO NEW AND BEAUTIFUL." The strange cadence had returned to her speech, a stress thing? "It's about not wanting her to even touch us right now." Her voice begged, "I don't want anything to touch us!" I shook my head, not because I wasn't impressed.

The telephone continued to demand attention to whomever was trying to reach me from my world. My wonderful world of tears and hopeless prayers at the kitchen table, where even my dreams had become tableaux of remorse. After ten rings it ceased, as the Caller ID picked up the plea of whatever urgency from my reality. I could return it later, if it mattered more than the rest of this painful void.

And you know what? I didn't want anything to touch us either. In fact, I wouldn't have it. I suppose now that something must have broken inside me, when I judged that reality was to be simply a place that didn't hurt. Looking back, I honestly don't know whether I could then have coped with a wider understanding of the inevitability that had already touched us.

We drove out on Interstate 10, the afternoon's photonic inferno blasting us toward Houston. She'd handed me the keys and said we could switch later. Of course, she immediately tuned the radio to something loud and strident. I imagined that she was still shaken from the confrontation with her mother. She fished in her purse and came up with an old half-pint metal flask. While she took only a small sip, the evidence of maintenance drinking made me uneasy.

Hardly new, and not so beautiful, it was a disturbing reminder of Linda's habits at the onset of her decline. Loosening up, she began to read some computer pages she had in her bag. With luck, we could make the state line by dark. Which was good, for we'd then have to slow down the bright colored, sporty-looking car through Louisiana, over what had become known as Drug Highway.

I glanced at the sheets she'd been absorbed in and asked her what she was reading.

"Off the Net, slash fiction."

"I'm almost afraid to ask."

She snickered and explained this cybernetic genre. It seemed that the "slash" denoted the mark between two names, like "Kirk/Spock" or "Mulder/Krycek." These titles originally identified mainly gay knockoffs on popular television series, e.g., Mulder *on* Krycek. In time, this "fan-fiction" venue had expanded into broader kinky fantasies.

She had been reading "A Woman's Touch," which featured Agent Scully and a young female intern working under her, as it were, at the FBI—and about to pull in Mulder for a threesome . . . I strained to hear her rendition over the radio. It was blaring a music vaguely reminiscent of my young cousin's noise of choice. According to her, it had been christened after factories, idled for retooling, where the style had originally been performed.

"Some of the writing is kick-ass," she enthused, "I've got one at home you'll get up on; Scully gets tortured in an 'S 'n M' club installation. Is that lascivious, or what?" I reached into my coat pocket and handed her the paperback, with a caution that she might find it too tame.

"Can we turn down the industrial?" I rather had to shout.

"*Post*industrial," she corrected, "rules!" Though complying with my request, laughing eyes challenged me to follow up. She knew very well that the name would be the full extent of my familiarity.

The story of how the paperback had come to me got her attention, and we began to discuss it as she searched the contents. She focused, as expected, on the Justine portions. I pointed out how Greene's early "Justine" resembled Crowley's Leah Hirsig more than did the Justine rendered by Seabrook. In the process, she was insistent that I tell her what I knew about Aleister Crowley.

Willie's interest in the occult was a given, and he certainly had the money and leisure to travel. Despite all that, there was absolutely nothing to support occasional assertions that Seabrook had known Crowley in his Paris years, during the time of the "Paris workings."

His friend Walter Duranty had been, in fact, a participant in Crowley's famous series of magical rituals performed in Paris during early 1914, but many years before Duranty had met Seabrook. Crowley had arrived in New York near Halloween of 1914, a time when Willie had been fully consumed with success in Atlanta.

Marjorie Worthington had written:

> In some way—and I believe it dated from his earlier association with Aleister Crowley during the Greenwich Village period in both their lives—Willie's witchcraft and magic were tied in with his sexual sadism.[56]

There was no doubt that the period she was referencing began with a first meeting with Crowley in 1917, after Willie's return from the First World War.

Whether or not Willie had been introduced to Aleister Crowley over lunch in 1917, by the journalist Frank Harris, there was little doubt that was about the time he met the woman he styled Deborah Luris. "Deborah," like Leah Hirsig, an apparent part of the Justine composite, stuck in Willie's libidinous imagination. Retiring to Georgia to try out the life of a gentleman farmer at his father-in-law's expense, he continued to visualize her tied to trees or pillars.

Confessing his fantasy to Katie, he was astonished, though highly gratified, when she encouraged him to

56. Worthington, op. cit., pp. 193–194.

follow up. He promptly went to visit "Deborah" in New York for a week of passion that he alleged was his first actual practice of bondage. This evidently so impressed him that he and Katie moved to New York.

While both Willie and his biographers suggested a break with Katie's family upon the relocation, there must have been some back-and-forth to the Georgia farm for several years. For one thing, Crowley visited with them there in the late summer or early fall of 1919, just before returning to the Continent. Crowley, never burdened with the conceit of humility, would comment on the visit in his "autohagiography":

> In the autumn I accepted an invitation to visit my friends William and Kate Seabrook on their farm in Georgia to which they had retired. He had held an important position on the Hearst papers, and his sanity and decency had revolted against so despicably disgusting a job. He knew he was a genius and the effect of knowing me was to make him ashamed of himself. Alas, not long after my influence was removed, he became a backslider.[57]

While *No Hiding Place* and *Witchcraft* contained many anecdotes of Village life in the late teens and early twenties, no chronology of that period was in

57. Crowley, op. cit., p. 794. See also Seabrook, "Wow!" in *Golden Book*, summer 1935, pp. 313–316; reprinted in *Worlds Beyond*, ed. Damon Knight, NY: Hillman Periodicals, Dec. 1950.

any sort of evidence. I had found I could refer somewhat to Greene's fictionalized treatment, *Ride the Nightmare*, for at least the flavor and some of the sequence. Greene had "Jake," his fictional Willie, meet "Justine" in 1919 after returning from service with the U.S. Army—rather than 1917 following Willie's actual release from the Field Service.

This divergence was in marked contrast to his treatment of the features syndicate where "Jake" was employed; the characters there being almost one for one with the personalities of Hearst's old King Features Syndicate, where Willie had worked in those years. Greene had also clearly filled in with fiction a near-total ignorance of Seabrook's life before they worked on the *Atlanta Journal*, beginning in 1908. He even seemed doubtful that Willie had ever been to Europe before the war.

Near its conclusion, "Jake" was considering departing for France with "Beth" (Katie) and "Justine," presented as a shy and beaten-down creature whom he had inherited from a figure representing Crowley. Like Leah Hirsig, this repressed character was a former schoolteacher. The contrast with the Justine Willie would draw ten years later in *Witchcraft* was striking.

There, Seabrook would describe a happy and vivacious, almost kittenish, young woman with whom he was clearly in love. She, in turn, contrasted with the cool sophisticate of *No Hiding Place*. In fact, "Deborah" more closely resembled the personality of the role-versatile "Santolina Marr," a creation of Greene's fiction.

"Maybe I'm really reaching, but there also exists a discrepancy between Willie's and Marjorie Worthington's accounts of when they met and then cohabited in Europe. She was adamant that it was in the spring of 1926, though she doesn't supply details of their life together until two, maybe three, years later, which is when the other sources indicate they got together.

"It's odd that many of Marjorie's recollections of their early relationship seem to exist in a time frame offset by as much as two years, as are Greene's fictional events. Remember, Seabrook places his meeting with at least part of the Justine composite, Hirsig, in 1917, though the residence and circumstances he describes did not exist for another two years."

First mentioned by Greene, "Justine" would seem to have been initially based on Crowley's consort. But Crowley didn't abandon the Hirsig woman in New York, nor did Seabrook ever acquire her. The sad, timid, and suppressed victim described by Greene was very different from the bouncy, opinionated Justine of Seabrook's 1940 account, his partner for kinky sex games.[58]

His 1942 autobiography, taken alone, supported the model as being the young Village sophisticate of the twenties whom he styled "Deborah Luris." He'd asserted that Marjorie had represented that woman in her mural of his life. Worthington's book made no

58. Seabrook, *Witchcraft*, pp. 264–267 in the chapter "Justine Dervish Dangling"; pp. 273–74 in a lengthier chapter, "Justine in the Mask," which dwells on Justine's personality, the sensory deprivation technique, and gives other examples of her psychic abilities.

specific mention of her, and Marjorie's vague descriptions of Willie's various "research girls" added nothing to this identification.

---

"'LURIS' IS A PERSIAN TITLE FOR THE ROM, OR GYPSIES and appears in arcana involving elves and demons, as well as being the Latin for law. While a known surname, it's rare. I finally concluded it was yet another pseudonym."

Justine leafed through the book, "So what is Greene saying about Willie and Marjorie?"

"He doesn't. In Greene's world 'Jake' and 'Beth,' who is Katie, stay together, preparing to go to Europe sometime in the mid-twenties, possibly with Justine in tow. They're still together through the entire tale, with the writer's omniscient eye, interestingly enough, detesting it as much as does 'Beth' or Katie's admirer in the story. But when Greene published in 1930, Willie was already living with Marjorie on the quay at Toulon."

Chronology had become weirdly distorted amongst the various sources during those years. Ward Greene's fictional story had petered out before the foreign adventures; no help there. Marjorie was emphatic that she had followed Willie to set up housekeeping in Europe in the spring of 1926. But the timing of her meeting Ford Madox Ford, from whose wife they obtained the Toulon loft, suggested 1929.

Marjorie also wrote of meeting the French literary giant Paul Morand at Seabrook's loft above the quay prior to his role in arranging Willie's African adventure. The problem was—when could that have been? Morand had been on a long Southern U.S. itinerary during most of 1927, during the bulk of which Willie had been in Haiti with Katie.

More decisively, Morand's own time in Africa, which had prompted him to bring a project to Seabrook, had been in 1928, while Willie was still in Connecticut writing *Magic Island*. Still, Marjorie remained committed to the notion that she had been with Willie in France at least two years before it appeared possible, including that proposition in her biographics.

Dating had to be considered tentative for yet another two years. This was unfortunate, for those years enveloped the trip to Africa during which Willie had discovered the Fan-Shaped Destiny, my central focus. Morand was convinced that an author other than himself, due to his sensitive diplomatic position, simply had to undertake a special mission to Africa. The purpose was to live with a tribe practicing ritual cannibalism, of which little was known in the West beyond gross comic-strip stereotypes of savages dining on missionaries.

Willie's account of this in *Jungle Ways* generated sensational controversy. I explained to Justine that whether he sampled human meat in the jungle with the *Gueré*, obtained some later from a medical school in Paris, or ate it in a Black Mass with Satanists was of total indifference to me. The writers of all my Seabrook sources had, of course, doted on it. It sufficed to say that he initiated such a decades-long popular fascination that Anton LaVey would be inspired to employ the same publicity-generating formula in the sixties.

Seabrook's account had him meeting Paul Morand after the publication of *Magic Island* and going into the Ivory Coast in the winter of twenty-nine. Both Willie and Marjorie placed their first meeting at a bridge party, which he set on an October evening. According to Willie, that was just before he and Katie had embarked to connect with Morand in Paris and initiate the African adventure.

Other chroniclers went along with those assumptions, but placed their meeting in 1929. The problem was that the documented events of their lives in France during 1930 would leave no time for the trip to Africa. It made far more sense for that sequence, the meeting with Morand, meeting Marjorie, and then leaving with Katie for France and Africa, to have started in the fall of 1928.

Willie and Katie had determined to soon part, but they remained close companions and made the Africa trip together. When they embarked on the *Berengaria*, it was not Katie, but Deborah Luris ("Justine") who was throwing an absolute fit over his proposed liaison with Marjorie.

"As if Willie was too drunk to remember?" Justine studied, no doubt getting as confused with all the bits of data as had I. "Some kinda shit, about how long he and Marjorie had been shacked up?"

How had she arrived at that on the few details she

had so far? "There are indications in some of his other writings that do support that. At first, I thought it was because they'd lived together before he and Katie were known to be separated, and was still leaving their future status open. But it doesn't explain Marjorie's lack of supporting detail for over two years. And there is something I can't put my finger on which gives this the same texture as the two-year discrepancy as to when he came home from the war and met Justine."

"Desperately seeking Justine," she laughed. "What's going on with troubling to hook up the time sequence of a fiction? Why'd you wanna retrieve her so badly? You knew all about his wives, about Katie and Marjorie—why the obsessing with this lost love? Me, I'd be into Wamba; more interesting, much?"

This was not to be the last time that I would have to dodge the shrapnel of my own words. "There's another rub. It just doesn't *read* like fiction! Reviewers questioned the believability of the characters, even though the cast of this *roman à clef* had to be well-known to many of them. And Seabrook's description of meeting Leah Hirsig is closely compatible with Greene's introduction of a 'Justine.' These are the kinds of reasons that led me to conclude she was a composite character." I hoped I had sneaked around any discussion of lost loves.

"*Roman à clef*? Key to the romance?"

"The joke being that those critics should not have needed any key."

"Composite characters can't do this!" she teased,

grabbing my crotch not so gently. I was promptly distracted from further literary education across the breadth of Texas. What the fuck? Maybe I should hold further detail of the other Justine's psychic experiences, particularly the fascinating points of the street circus, as a zinger for later, if needed. I had no qualms about manipulation when it involved a matter of such importance.

# V

# Crossing the Styx

EVENTUALLY, EVEN JUSTINE'S PASSION FOR THE SAGA abated. The holiday traffic didn't get too bad until Beaumont, from where we could begin to see a line of thunderclouds hanging weirdly just above the state line.

"Texas," I sighed as we got out to eat in Louisiana and smelled the ozone of the storm ahead. "How can drought be that specific?"

I discovered that she loved Cajun food as much as I did and established that she at least understood French on a menu. Still in disbelief at what had entered my life, I watched her marauding through a huge platter of crawfish and asked if that thing through her tongue got in the way of her eating.

"It does leave a dent in the ice cream," she snickered, and began a lurid description of the swelling when it had been clamped down for the first few days. God, I thought; part of her really is still such a kid!

"Do you think you can eat everything on your plate?" I teased back at her wicked grin.

"Do *you?*"

On the dimly lit parking lot, I unlocked the car and handed her back the keys. I was somewhat slowed and fatigued after the meal. More, I suspected that hogging the wheel might come off as tedious chauvinism. She was hugging and squirming against me as the thunder rolled off in the dark Louisiana night.

"The *quai* at Toulon," she breathed in my ear, "it sounds so romantic and exotic, just the sound of the words; I wish *I'd* been there . . ." She was morphing again, and in the strangeness of her speech I fancied that I might hear the taste of New Orleans that Cris had alleged. Beyond the kitten, the happy and excited little girl, there was something else.

"Do you speak French?" I asked.

"Nay," she whispered, "but I'd like to learn."

"Maybe we can go there someday," I offered. Was it my overheated imagination, or was there something fundamentally unquestioning in her green eyes, something one might legitimately interpret as love? If so, I could not imagine why. Look, the truth was that I had just gotten by in bed the previous night. Yes, I'd pulled it off, but not so as to make a young girl see stars. True enough that I was tickled shitless about it, if only because I'd stayed hard enough to do anal.

Still, instead of mounting up, Justine seemed more inclined to mount *me*. The spicy food, I mused; the ozone in the air? Clinging to my neck, thrusting her tongue between my lips, the exhibitionistic display seemed to arouse her punker persona, among other things. If I ignored the clicking of her silver post against my teeth, I could find myself being carried back to a time when grubbing on gravel parking lots had ranked with major sexual encounters.

However, the attention we attracted was from a pair of rough-looking Cajun boys in work clothes with colorful bandannas. Getting out of a beat-up pickup on the other side of the Del Sol, they halted by our front fender and began to hassle. "Old dudes with hot young babes," one snotted off. "Sorta makes you wanna puke, don't it?" I tried ignoring them, but he had propped his muddy boot on our bumper, studiedly violating the comfort zone. "Yo, hoochie-mama! Mine gez harder and staz up for-ev-er."

I felt Justine begin to tense up. "Get in the car and open my bag," I whispered to her, then growled, "Why don't you walk away before you're having to explain how you let an old man kick your ass?" As we commenced this ritual of male violence, I did have some worries. Out of state, my Texas carry permit was only an arguing point, but, more importantly, my gun was stupidly packed in my bag. Instead of doing as I told her, Justine turned and stepped between the aggressors and me.

"What he said. So let's have a react now, shall we?" She moved slowly toward them, hands in the pockets of her studded jacket. The loudmouth straightened up in surprise as she spread open her jacket to display her haltered breasts. "So, you're all that? Wanna try some things?" she inquired huskily. I seized the moment to reach in and quickly unzip my bag, wondering if she were buying time or was she maybe heavier than even I wanted to get?

"You like this?" she teased. Closing on the loudmouth, she showed him her pierced tongue, and his mouth cracked in a leer. "You can have one dead like it." Her hand slipped out of her pocket with a sinister metallic click, and the young punk dropped back in shock at the flash of the ancient stiletto knife. "Don't you wanna play?" she purred in a voice that conveyed a rather appalling confusion of sexual stimulation with something like a craving to wallow in carrion.

Her tone then changed into an eerily haughty chastisement, "You are so *insipid*! If you had been nice, we could've played. I don't *like* people who aren't *nice* to us." The weird scene, laced with its twisted sexuality, had allowed me plenty of time to free up my revolver. I'd held it but had not brought it up and, fortunately, a Louisiana State Police car pulled into the lot before we might have been obliged to press the advantage.

"Bummer"—she sighed—"you'd of *liked* it." When they didn't move she continued, "So what are we thinking, as if they're gonna believe *you*?" Her voice returned to kittenish innocence, "I am so sure, when I wiggle my butt, tell how you were gonna throw down on poor little me and my daddy . . . last chance now, before I do help-screamage here."

They glanced nervously at the troopers, who had parked and were looking our way, and began to back off. "Goddamn sick pervs," the loudmouth spat with disgust. "Bitch!" Justine snickered with evil delight.

"Intense. *That,*" she emphasized, "was *Gothic*!" She would not have been the first violence-prone personality I had met that could exercise total control, until nominally justified in an outburst out of all proportion to the injury. As we pulled back onto the interstate, I interrupted her giggling to ask about the knife.

"Aren't those antiques still highly illegal in most states?"

"Moot," she answered, stretching herself with an isometric push against the wheel, visibly coming off an adrenaline rush. "This hot young babe has always been able to rely on the kindness of Southern policemen." She threw me a wicked glance, "And I've only had to give it up once." When I didn't bite, she added, "Like, fun?"

Straight-faced I asked, "Referencing putting out, or only once?"

"Busted," with a guilty grin. "Uniforms do push my buttons."

Apparently pleased that I neither overreacted to the incident, nor compensated with machismo, she coaxed me over beside her, becoming in seconds a happy little girl again. Why worry about my virility, I reflected? There was some part of her that had enough testosterone for both of us. What part of the things that came out of her mouth represented the real Justine? Ahead of us, the lightning performed a violent ritual of its own.

The storm had a fortuitous dimension, for I was soon to learn that Justine does not slow down unless she's forced to—regarding anything. When, between the storm and our bladders, we had to pull over at a rest area, I temporarily finessed back the wheel.

Being eastbound, it was well that we didn't have Texas plates. Texas cars are primary drug-search targets on the presumption of being a conduit of drugs to the casinos, and who needs the hassle? This topic opened a channel for me to inquire into her tastes in chemicals, presuming that she had smoked some grass, anyway. Having taken the plunge into this thing, I might at least start educating myself to that with which I was going to have to deal. I found out.

---

JUSTINE PRODUCED A SMALL, ORNATE SNUFFBOX from her purse and snapped open the stiletto. Thrusting its tip into the box, she offered innocently, "Nose candy?" This on the heels of the display on the parking lot, with legal intervention hovering in the wings. Oh shit, I thought. What did we have here? I *hoped* the powder *was* cocaine. I'd heard that pharmaceutical-grade meth had returned for the first time since the Vietnam War. Please don't let her be all cranked up! She glanced up. "That's right, we're doing crime here."

While she fixed her nose, I was doing a quick reevaluation of her recent performance. Then she shook her hair and informed me, "It's sort of an *apéritif*, like speedball?" She misread, in part, my silence and laughed nervously. "So, it's like that. *This* really surprises me, it really does . . ."

Oh yeah. Tight-assed old fart. How many more stereotypical traps was I bound to fall into? Of course, I immediately went to work on making matters worse by trying to explain myself, but she seized the moment. "My bad. You don't gotta go there. I know it's about Linda. And this was special—that's why, with the snort? It goes away. Reefer is cool, yea?"

I let matters lie, agreeing to the part of my disconcertion that she had seen through. I would study on the rest. I was not up to speed on the new youth, and certainly not about the drug culture. But I was willing to bet that the cocaine and heroin "cocktail" she had snorted was as uncommon today as in the opium days of the early century. Then it had been the chic poison of choice in the circle around Aleister Crowley, and among a few fashionable Parisians.

"At least baby's not a big stoner, yea?" she pressed, seemingly concerned that she might have alienated me. She went on about drugs, and I found myself intrigued by her view that a society might be analyzed through its drug habits. The recurrent return of amphetamines, for example, presumably presaged warfare. She opined at length on the unpublicized renewal of interest in acid.

Given my generation, it was *she* who expected extensive drug experience on *my* part, and I had little to tell her beyond some good peyote stories from my college days. Before long, I realized that she had smoothly led me into the story of my life. I was even unsure whether, for her part, the drug interlude might not have been a calculated distraction.

Willing to go with it, I then told her some more of JJ, of memories, and anomalies. One noteworthy feature following from the magical night at the lake had been the archetype of The Ring that I had given to JJ when we were fresh and new. The reappearance of a cherished gift often figures in testimonials of rekindling, but mine had a little extra twist.

Long years before, I'd searched diligently but vainly for a ring with two symbolic pearls. I'd not told JJ I'd had to settle for one with but a single pearl for fear of degrading the gift. After she had sadly returned it, amidst the rest of our adolescent tragedy, I'd bickered with a pawnbroker over the value of a single cultured pearl. How little could he have known we haggled over the value of a piece of my soul.

"Well, this was big business for me back then, and I'd clearly recalled it all those years. When we got back together, she wanted a ring like I'd given her before, even bringing me a catalog page with an illustration. I tell you, I just about shit when I recognized exactly what I had *sought* for her, but failed to find, all those years ago—*a ring with two pearls*!"

"You mean . . ."

"The ring she *remembered* receiving and *wearing* had two pearls. But, the ring *I* remembered purchasing, giving, and finally selling had only one.

"The circumstances of our first breakup are nothing special. They involved peer pressure, the cruelty of an ignorant and insular community, possibly an odd but pervasive rumor that we were somehow related. Not that it would have been any large thing to me; in my family, one's first sexual experience was more than likely to have been with a cousin . . .

"With the aid of the regression techniques, I was satisfied that there had been no confabulation, on my part, of the memory of the ring. *But* I had no reason to doubt her either. More than one writer has styled amorous convergence as the spilling of realities into one another. You have to wonder."

Finding significance, Justine pressed me for details of a memory I had touched upon, which both JJ and I clearly held. We were sitting in a car on a parking lot near my old family home in east Fort Worth. I had offered to marry her because she was pregnant, a grand gesture, you see, because the child was not mine. But the memory as we recalled it was impossible, for when she had conceived her first child, we were entirely out of touch.

By that time, I was off on my Harley-Davidson, dating cocktail waitresses in Dallas. An active plan to marry a pregnant high-school girl was rather implausible, especially since she, herself, clearly had not been heavily invested in it.

A glimpse into an alternate world? Very tantalizing, considered in conjunction with the matter of the ring. I described possible paranormal experiences, during that same era, when my hormones had been running at full tilt. My friends and I used to sit up in my room and play with hypnosis, focusing on candle flames to try to see the future, or regress to a remote past. It was during those years that I had the intensely lucid, often precognitive, dreams that I'd remembered all my life. I reflected on the relevant theories of J.W. Dunne, arrived at decades before.

Like Oppenheimer and too many others who had followed him, the old engineer had been broken-hearted at the reality of his patriotic work raining death on innocent people. Watching the approach of yet another world war, he had sought answers to fundamental questions. Believing that he had established a physical basis for precognition, he perceived the consciousness capable of focusing on any of the multitude of equally existing moments. During sleep or unusual mental states, the consciousness might drift in time—inclusive of observing the future.

"I've seen the name, several times. Didn't he have the alternate-worlds thing going on? Time tracks that branch out every time a decision can be taken?" she asked, raising a common misconception of origins.

"Many writers credit Dunne for their inspiration, often without troubling to read him." I smiled. "He didn't really advance branching time in his books. His enormous contribution lay in subjecting the common perception of time to hard relativistic influence. This is an example of how sloppy scholarship papers over the issue, with the result of discouraging further delving into the literary anomaly—when it's not simply ignored altogether.

"Dunne wrestled with how Einstein's scenario would allow a future to be observed, and then changed. If the 'replacement' future was then experienced, how could the one previously observed have been *real*? His great admirer, J.B. Priestley, employed

Dunne's theories in plays during the late thirties. He struggled with this conundrum for decades. Haunted by a case history in which a woman had saved her child from death by drowning, Priestley remained troubled by the question, 'What about the dead baby?'"

Justine was having fun, as if listening to ghost stories, while I proposed that the many-worlds alone would resolve this contradiction. The precognitive mind had touched one of many similar but alternate realities. Acceptance of proactive precognition would seem to demand that at least some marginal interaction continued among the branches.

"I can tell you about a dream that embodied the principles of Dunne's experiments exactly, though it took thirty years to be realized." As the Gulf War blazed on the television in my living room in San Antonio, I had remembered the dream. I was living somewhere in South Texas with a large wolflike dog; there was a "war in the gulf," which I had taken to be the Gulf of Mexico. I had seen the explosions in a lowering green sky amidst talk of "new weapons." As I watched, along with the rest of the world, the night-vision attacks on Baghdad, I realized that, in my dream, I had seen it on television! Just as I would learn that Dunne had precognitive dreams of things that he later read about in his newspaper.

---

AMBER FIRES AND REFINERY LIGHTS made an otherworldly juxtaposition with lasers and neon. "So why aren't we believing the future is fixed?" she asked, as we approached the temples of chance, the casinos on the shores of Lake Charles.

I drew a breath, "Because of another dream that was part of the series, one that can't come true anymore." There was a major lump in my throat. "I went to my house—it was in a blue twilight—and knocked on the door. A young woman with red hair answered. In the study off the foyer, I could see my father with his paper. He looked slenderer than I knew him; had a kind of scholarly look, smoking a pipe. I think he was wearing a small beard."

I still remembered it all too clearly. I lit up, to get the lump under control, and plunged ahead—too late to stop then. "For a long time, I thought it was a Jungian kind of thing, my anima and all that. But one day a few years ago, I shaved off my beard and saw in the mirror something that the adolescent boy who had the dream could never imagine. It was the face of my father on a thinner man who smokes a pipe sometimes."

"You see," I told her, trying to keep my voice even and still be heard over the thunder that was crashing around us, "I believe I saw myself in a later time, when I still lived in that house, and was the father of a young woman—who can never now be born in this world." Justine, hearing my voice betray the emotions, gripped my wrist.

"Mightn't it all be, some way, about me?" she asked brightly, near-endearing in her typically postadolescent conceit. "You do know that you could be taken for my father, dearest, in a young boy's dream, I mean? This is coming out all wrong, before I even finish. As if you weren't my lover, I'm way sure I wouldn't mind you being my father, *ooh!* I did say that, I really did, but . . . hey, what's up with the redheads?"

Unseen in the darkness, I smiled wanly at the evidence that I was not alone—in letting my mouth overload my ass. "Oh, it's JJ of course. After Linda and I were married, I described JJ to her, when she asked about other women I'd been with. She said, 'now I know who the little redheaded girl is.'

"I had no idea what she meant, until she explained that she'd noticed I was never amused by that character in *Peanuts*. She said that when the little red-haired girl hurt Charlie Brown's feelings, I always got mad. It hit me between the eyes that she was right. I'd never had any conscious recognition of the identification."

This had gone far enough. I had been venturing too near to exposing my motivation for following the trail of the branching-worlds theory. Did all this sound crazy or what? I tried to shift the conversation onto her, but she had another track in mind.

Taking off from my mention of Linda, she wanted to know all about my wife. I found this acceptable, for it might open the door to discussion of sex and bondage games. I could demonstrate how she would be less limited in her sexual expression with me, than with some young asshole who cherished the typical passion for the practice of monogamy—on the part of women.

Linda had become a very successful stripper, belly

dancer, and all-round showgirl working the national circuits out of Dallas. You might have heard of her, if you're at least a little older than Justine. Her stage name was Deva Dasi, from a Sanskrit word meaning "slave-girl of the god," connoting the temple prostitutes of antiquity.[59]

Justine was enthralled by the image. When the storm forced us to stop a while longer at Lafayette, she was laughing happily, over a grisly snack of alligator boudin, at Linda's exploits as a stripper. By then I understood that any strategy based on the bias of young women for talking about themselves would come to naught. This babe was a whole different smoke, first determined to hear all about me. Several times I had seen her psych training play in, and had to accept that I was being consciously worked.

I did not gloss over the downside, but I refused to take any phony rap. Linda's folks had been old carneys, hard people from a hard place. While they had sent her to private schools and tried to groom her for a better life, they were incapable of shielding the girl from the nihilism of life on the midway. Long before I'd ever met her, she'd been a teenage alcoholic.

If it were exacerbated by our lifestyle, I'll take that blame. I would never have considered steering her away from the dancing or the promiscuity that gave her the only joys she had in her too brief life. It was

59. Deva Dasi is documented in local Texas media, particularly *Dallas Morning News*, *Scene Magazine* cover story, Sun., 27 Nov. 1977. Also *Texas Monthly* magazine, Jan. 1979, feature story by J. Bloom, p. 50.

precisely when she could no longer dance or play that the illness had become acute. Any regrets I harbored on this count were of fantasies left *unexplored*. Perhaps it's true that the candle that burns twice as brightly burns half as long. For in her day, before the sickness took her down, Linda had blazed.

Beautiful and desired by many, men and women, she seemed unable to abide the protective barrier established by the edge of a stage. Her paramount fantasy was of being given to anyone who wanted her. Now, contrary to the swill of idiotic screenwriters, acting this out had limited practicality, even in the days before the epidemic.

She would try, though, wherever it was to any degree feasible. Her passion for bondage ran as deep as that for the freedom of the dance and, in an odd way, they were intertwined. I didn't altogether discount the neo-Freudian suggestions that Justine would offer. The influence of a mother, who had for years systematically crushed Linda's will into a submission of which others might take advantage, couldn't be ignored.

Still, I believed that Sigmund, the stuffy bourgeois, had to be discounted after a point. Like most of us, she had no whips and restraints around her childhood home at which to sneak nasty little peeks. Yet such fascinations lurk in the collective unconscious of us all.

Linda had been booked by one of the old-time burlesque agencies on a Southern tour. In Printer's Alley in Nashville, she'd played half of a girl-on-girl act.

Years later, when we had our own club, we would adapt it to a bondage theme. Then she'd done her first entirely nude work in Panama City. She was pretty keyed-up by the time we had worked our way back to Atlanta to end the run with a three-week booking on Peachtree.

The gig had begun typically enough with three twenty-minute sets per night; there were fewer dancers in those days, and they performed longer at a stretch. They were fully professional; elaborate wardrobe, props, and effects, including special lighting, were expected to be provided by the performer. A dancer on the road needed a partner for help with lift-and-carry alone. Pay was high, minimal drink hustle or other scams, nothing by commission. They kept all tips and were not expected to support other club personnel.

"Get outta here!" when I told her the pay to which Linda had been accustomed. "No clue it was so involved."

"Why should you? All you're shown on TV or in the movies are images of cops strolling into lowlife joints like they're too good to be there. When Hollywood admits the existence of the professionals, they serve up single-moms-supporting-their-children who 'just-want-to-have-a-normal-life.' The fact is that most professional strips are in the business to escape from 'normalcy.' They're into it because they get off on it as much as for the money, and that's the long and the short of it."

It would have been four sets a night except, being

a feature, Linda did some spots with the comic and was cut in half by a magician's sword instead. The highly erotic, sacrificial aspect of that role had been simply made for her! Her basic function had been to be distractive.

All she really had to do was to lie on a black-draped, altar-looking platform, wearing a gown that fastened behind her neck. The magician would loosen it and push it far down on her hips, baring her torso. Her split skirt would fall open to display a lot of leg as well. From that point no one would notice what was going on with the fake blood and other stuff I was passing to the magician, or much of anything other than her.

Justine had taken the wheel at Lafayette. As we cruised the causeway above the fifty miles of interconnected bayous, swamps, and waterways, the moon came out to illuminate eerily the sinuous, twisting passages below us. The storm had not yet reached there. Far off, I spied lights moving among the reeds and stumps in the water and pointed them out to her.

---

THE "BAD JUJU" was probably swamp gas, but this sighting digressed us for a while onto Seabrook's history with voodoo. The material he had gathered in Haiti comprised the book *Magic Island*, which would introduce the idea of Voudon as a religion to a mass audience. It included the first use in American literature of the "zombie." Beginning with the 1932 horror film classic *White Zombie*, B-movie producers would flourish for decades off what he had initiated. While he was admittedly a sensationalist, sedate academic authorities failed repeatedly to debunk the content of his exposés. Impatiently, Justine pulled me back to my long-ago trip with Linda over this same route.

Decades later, I had to admit lacking a clear visual of the Peachtree club owner, but that wasn't altogether a matter of memory. As at that first meeting, she would always be sitting rather back in the shadows and wore a long wig, a variation on "big hair," which largely covered her face. Her mystery had enthralled me, though I was uneasy about the fashion in which Linda took to her, in a way that she seldom did with any other women.

I remembered Linda's turn of phrase, after they'd been to breakfast together one night after closing. Linda had told me that the darkness was not about concealment. She'd said that the old woman wore the darkness like a protective shawl, helping to keep her warm. That in the darkness, her dreams still lived. Two nights later, she'd asked us to accompany her to another location, a roadhouse she'd opened a few years earlier.

"Hey, roadhouse?" Justine queried.

"Old name for a highway bar, usually a honky-tonk. This was actually a private club, but it was out on a highway and so she called it a roadhouse." She'd driven us out in an old black Cadillac, one of those long old boats. No sign identified the large, two-story stone structure, with sealed shutters on its windows, as the club called *The Château*, but it looked the part.

The interior had been lavishly appointed. The rear entrance to the stage had been flanked by Grecian columns that rose far up above a second-floor balcony, to a ceiling with a painted moon and stars. Plush drapery framed wall murals, featuring idealized coastal scenes, with what appeared to be medieval ruins.

There had been service bars on both floors and, when we had been seated at her reserved table at the corner of the balcony, we could observe the entire operation. We beheld a staff of dancer-waitresses, a practice on which we had not been too keen back then, outfitted in short tunics. They worked the tables, kneeling slave-fashion, and danced barefoot on the carpeted stage. The carpet prohibited real dance as we knew it, and the performance in progress was more a posed classical vignette, portraying some mythological theme.

Aside from the fanciful aspects, the decor had been distinctly early-century. There had even been glass fruit on the tables! The entire ambiance had been something one would have imagined from some exclusive underground establishment forty years earlier. I'd no idea that something such as that existed, but none of it equaled the most unusual aspect of the place.

It was after hours, and many of the patrons were leaving when I had visited the rest room on the lower level, amused to meet an attendant attired, like the other male personnel, in formal evening dress. I would not see that affectation again until the advent of "gentlemen's clubs" of the later century. Returning to the clubroom, noting that the inner security door had been closed, I'd almost bumped up against a completely naked girl—hanging by her wrists from chains that dropped from the railing of the balcony above.

The very young, peaches-and-cream blonde, with a soft-looking but nicely shaped body, evidenced understandable discomfiture. She could only just reach the floor with her toes, so that her straining legs and feet could only partially support her weight. Though a small spotlight illuminated her plight, her trembling muscles and face reflecting her pain, the staff had continued about their business around her as though she were merely part of the decor.

For long minutes, we had drunk in the exhibition. Our hostess had been explaining to Linda that the hapless blonde, who was fully visible from where we were seated on the opposite balcony, had been accepted to work at the club. She would be "initiated" that night with a gratuitous experience of the corporal penalties meted out for infractions of policy.

"It's a game we play sometimes to thrill the supporting patrons," she'd shrugged. "And, as you observe, it keeps the girls on their toes," she had punned with a gravelly laugh. "It's all understood." Though we might find it strange, she'd told us, the girls performing the roles of slaves held veto power, in many affairs of the club, over the members who supported it.

Not so strange, I'd thought as I had begun, with some excitement, to surmise what additional diversions *The Château* might offer. That way, no one could claim that she had been victimized.

The old woman had gone on to clarify that the girl had been brought around by her husband, a young Army officer who was also present that night. There had been a noticeable component of military couples involved with the club, and our hostess had educated us on that point. She told us that she had a strong affinity with Réage's erotic classic, which had been released in the States a few years earlier.

I'd read it then, and had turned Linda on to it, but our hostess had the distinction of having read the original *Histoire d'O* just after it had mysteriously appeared before the French Academy in 1952. She'd advised us that one could only grasp its full meaning by appreciating its extraordinary use of the French language. The British edition had been widely circulated among the armed services for years before the American publication.

It had found a ready audience among the young marrieds in base housing, she'd explained. There, "wife swapping" and other late-century variations on the old free-love theme had been popular throughout the Cold War. Only much later would they catch on within a campus counterculture, many of its constituents military brats themselves.

"Again the lie was given to the conceit that the Baby Boomers discovered everything," I remarked, then began to digress onto these practices in relation to Seabrook, hoping to tie all this to Justine's immediate interests.

"I wanna hear what happened to the blonde! *Tell!*" I told her, as I will tell all, so just have patience. I would soon have more occasions to recall the sadomasochistic rituals, which I had found meaningful beyond the obvious. Linda and I had both believed that there was something more to it than an erotic display alone. It had been as though the old woman had hoped something specific to be evoked in that temple she had built to her erotic preoccupations. I did tell all, with what I was to fear might be a calamitous result.

I broke off as I realized that Justine had been silently weeping. *Oh man,* I thought, *I've done it now,* and thinking I was on the right track, too! I carefully touched her hand on the wheel. "Is this freaking you out?"

She gripped my wrist and drew a labored breath, "I'm good." She wiped her eyes, "That was intense. You never went back?" I relaxed a bit. Maybe I'd chanced the gauntlet and gotten away with it again. I didn't want to get into my misgivings about the effects our experiences might have been having on Linda.

"We had to go fulfill other contracts back in Texas. Then the agency closed and the old Southern circuit broke up. We wrote them the next year when we saw they had actually advertised for 'slave-girl dancers' in one of the big 'swinger' magazines that were around back then. I think it was a matter of management changing and the club closing down before we could get back there."

The way things had gone for Linda in the end, I'd often wondered if I had made a terrible mistake by not simply staying there. Yet another might-have-been, on which I withheld commentary. I didn't know how deeply I might be getting in with Justine as things were. I could read nothing in her face in the dim lights of the dash.

"Of course, that was another time," I tried to back water. "Today, with all the crazies, the disease, and everything, I'm not sure how far I'd want to push something like that anyway." Still nothing. The rain was growing heavier again. "Are you ready to stop for the night? We can get some sleep anytime."

"I *said* I'm good!" The green eyes flashed a sideways rebuff. *"Damn!"* She harnessed the attitude, and continued, "We'll pack it in soon. You're saying you talked much with the old woman about your lives? What was that like? Who was she?"

"We only knew her as something like Madeline, some name like that. Remember, it's been nearly thirty years. As to being pumped, couldn't avoid it. She could read me as clearly as you can," I said sardonically, though the equivalence wasn't the truth. Many of the memories had been painfully fresh then, and much easier for the old woman to elicit.

"You talked with her about JJ? That's a lovely poem you have with her picture, by the way; it would've made me give it up." There was the strangeness creeping into her voice again, and the sudden shift did not bode well. There is some limit on how much a young woman wants to learn about her predecessors, especially one still living. They certainly don't want comparisons, even favorable ones.

I did not trust this a bit, but as if reading my mind, she commanded, "Excuse me? You must have affection for the past, muchly, to revisit like you do. I wanna know about it all—what you are looking back at that makes life seem so wrong and horrid. Why does a man who's done such interesting things wanna, like rewind and start over?"

"It's not JJ alone, babe," I protested lamely.

"But that's where it begins, yea?" I was in the deep shit then. It seemed that I'd run my mouth and exposed myself to the point that there was no way out. The damned little psych grad had me trapped. After starting neatly to confess everything, there would be no way to explore the issues that bound us together—without admitting to the obsession that had led me to discover Seabrook's influence. I began to tell the rest of the story, and not just of JJ, but my lost ones as well—all the sadly truncated lives with which I could not, would not, come to terms.

---

WE'D CROSSED THE "STYX RIVER," as a road sign in the Mississippi darkness had demarcated some whimsical place-name. I felt that Charon's barge was indeed bearing me into the land of the dead. About me were the ghosts that I could no longer hear "in the whispers that had followed me since we were lost to each other."[60] The past had caught up with the present, and I could feel all those years coming for me now.

When we finally had exited the interstate and dropped down to Gulfport, checking into a motel near the shore, we were both so run through that sex was not an issue. Justine had peeled off her jeans and burrowed directly into one of the beds. I'd hit the other one and turned out the lights. I'd lain there watching the white line continuing to roll behind my eyelids, wanting to say, *good night, I love you,* but not speaking. I had said more than enough that night. My life had spiraled wholly out of control.

Now, it was the classic anonymous motel morning with gray light through Venetian blinds. Uh-oh, the morning after; just delayed by twenty-four hours and several hundred miles. I was alone in the room, but Justine's bag reassured me that I'd not been ditched outright, not yet at least. "On the pier," a sheet of motel stationery advised me. While I smelled like a skunk and thought about washing up, I had to know where her head was at before my heart dropped through my bowels.

What in God's name was I doing in a motel room in Gulfport, with a girl half my age, whom I'd found myself called upon to torture with my reminiscences? Soon, I'd likely be hitting my bank account for a ticket back to San Antonio, having blown everything.

Outside, the sky was slate gray, welcome relief

---

60. Davis, Lynn, "Lost Child." The verses accompanying JJ's photograph.

from the Texas inferno. I walked to a gazebo in a beachfront park across the street. Down the beach, the skeletons of new casinos were stark against the gray sky. I squinted at tiny figures out on a long fishing pier. Flaming red hair whipped about one beneath the sheltering eaves of the roof at the far end.

As I trudged out along the pier, the rain was approaching like a gray wall across the water. The fishermen were packing up and heading in. Even if we started back at once, we'd never make it before the squall hit. Rather, I wouldn't, I thought morosely. With her body, so different from mine, still able to run and play like a child, she would have no trouble at all.

I could see her clearly in profile, shoulders hunched with elbows on the railing, pensively watching the approaching storm. Barefoot in her jeans, spray from sea and sky soaking the halter top against her breasts, she looked so damned *young*!

Approaching her, I registered the tension in the taut muscles of her back, my eyes following where they ran down enticingly below the beltless top of her jeans. I wanted to touch her once more, one last time before hearing what I had to hear. What could I have been thinking, fantasizing possession of a creature like her? I could hear it already, "This was a big-assed mistake; how can we get you home?" then running downstream from there. Might as well just throw myself into the Gulf.

I placed my hand on the small of her back, appalled at my skin, which looked to me like crepe paper against the smoothness of hers. She turned her head, creases in her tawny, resilient flesh disappearing without a trace, but her tendons were like steel cables. She looked up with a haunted expression, her eyes changed to some nameless color by the gray light. "The scary thing is that I almost wish you had been my father," she began without preamble.

All right, at least *this* was original. But her wistful tone seemed to confirm my fears and bore me down, as if the lowering sky was falling on us. "I suppose you know how that resonates?"

"Believe me when I say aw-hunh!" She almost spat the words as her tension snapped, her voice filled with pain and anger. "As if, walking home from school, I would daydream of somehow finding my real daddy there. Of being so extreme happy that I would've done anything to please him?"

She wiped at her eyes. "This is so *hard*. Way sure I'm still that little girl and being an adult is just for pretend. I have a psych degree, but I'm still afraid of the dark." I started to respond, but checked myself. Of course I knew that I'd been flying on father-issues, and those are double-edged swords. Pop-psych is like arguments of faith; both are no-win games, which is why people are fond of throwing them at you. I waited to see where this was going, and she pushed ahead.

"What was wiggin' me was knowing how it felt, even before I knew it was you looking for Seabrook and all. Dead on that I had met something I couldn't walk away from. I already knew you were all that.

Believe that I never would've said a thing, till you had already had me and it was too late to go back! I do go way too far teasing and provoking, I really do, but I don't want you to believe I drop my pants for every random hookup."

This sounded as though it had an internal logic, but there were pieces missing. Clearly, I'd walked into the midst of a lot of things she'd been mulling over. I remained silent, but kept my body language open and accepting. Maybe what had risen between us the night before had been simply the first predictable emotional crisis and, just possibly, I might run the gauntlet once again. She relaxed a bit with a little rueful grin.

---

"FUCKIN' MY DADDY, the concept did work on my head. I'll own that. Totally Gothic!"

*O-kay,* I thought, *now I really don't have a clue.* "Drop back, there?"

She shrugged impatiently, as though I should have already put her outpouring all together. "Yesterday morning, JJ's picture on your desk," she scolded me. "As if I'm to believe you never knew her middle name?"

I frowned in confusion at the unexpected twist. "Why, her name is Jeanette . . ." I may be slow sometimes, but then the roaring surf was beginning to be drowned out by a roaring in my head. "Justine, what am I about to hear?"

"What you said," she laughed at the irony, "her

name is Jeanette Justine. Dearest, you loved my mother!"

I feverishly reviewed JJ's descriptions of the children she'd never let me meet. There were two daughters, the older a stewardess with children of her own who was thirty-three; the other . . . No! Jesus, Justine couldn't possibly be that seventeen-year-old, could she?

There, laughing so kiddish in front of me—for a moment I was having visions of a Mann Act prosecution. And on this other issue, "Justine, I swear, I did not even know where JJ was for thirty years. God, I don't believe this is happening. We're having a conversation out of a goddamned soap opera!"

She laid her hand on my chest, "No surprise she didn't prompt you about me. Mother has trouble copping to a lot of things; she calls it 'keeping things in their little boxes,' and it looks like each of us has our own cache." She then embraced me, plastering her wet front against me and gripping the back of my neck. I needed that, for the little homily of JJ's was one with which I had become all too contemptuously familiar, during our brief adult affair.

"Seeing her picture on your desk, reading what you'd written, I had to know, much. I went and got all confrontational. I'm way sure that, if it hadn't been something so totally weird, she would've denied even knowing you. But I was all, y'know, had I fucked my birth-father, and she was like, you not in her life for years, and I was like, cool, but then she put on an attitude, about like I *had* been doing incest."

"The scariest part was knowing I would've been all—about being with you some way—dump it off, get you to run away with me to Mexico, or wherever, and live in serious sin . . ." She finally paused for breath and held me even tighter, were it possible. I felt as if she were looking for a marsupial pouch into which to crawl.

"Dread this, wondering if it will make things better. Or not. She like, slipped, that if you'd been my father, she thought . . ." she choked the rest through sudden tears, "you would've always been there." We both just stood there, holding each other through the most curious blend of emotions that I believe either had yet known.

The storm had struck, and the rain poured in torrents, so we sat on the benches of the deserted pier, trying to sort it all out. Memory of JJ's middle name must have been buried for years, and I was sure I'd never had knowledge of the restored Leiris surname at all. With the details of Justine's confrontation with her mother, I could have no lingering doubts as to whether this was for real. I recalled her fixation on JJ the previous night.

Justine was the product of what JJ called her "promiscuous period," during a separation from her husband. When she had found me again later, I'd beaten myself up a lot for not having kept track of her, thus missing that opportunity when I could, conceivably, still have made JJ mine. Justine having been born a good nine years before JJ's youngest . . . A sudden insight perplexed me. In a world of choices not made, paths not taken, I might well have been Justine's father!

I got hung up in that for a few minutes, thinking of that prospect correlated with my obsessions, which had placed my feet on the branching path leading me to this moment. Thunder rolled and lightning crashed out in the Gulf as another storm cell approached. For the first, but not the last time in this adventure, I became frightened. What in God's name was happening?

I felt a poignant sense of loss that, more than once in lives that might have been, I had missed her. In this one as well, for that matter. I anguished that I could have known Justine for up to ten years in San Antonio, had paths ever crossed. Two at least, had her mother not hidden her family from me as though I were a monster who might harm them. Again, I don't "move on" very well. "What-Ifs" had been, for a long time, my breakfast cereal.

I was drawn back to her continuing story of a misbegotten reconciliation between JJ and her husband. Justine had grown up feeling singled out from her half siblings and despised by her stepfather. She'd returned the favor, and it seemed as though our mutual hatred of that man constituted another common bond between us. The isolation from family and friends that he had demanded, even as a youth, had graduated into the predictable pattern of the abuser. It's a cultural paradigm that good old gawd-fearin' redneck Texas condones even today.

In her psych-major fashion, she saw her extreme

independence as derivative of being left to her own devices. She suggested that she'd forced her own amputation from a dysfunctional family unit as promptly as possible. When her bequest came due, she had been more than happy to move to Atlanta.

Only months before, the implications of JJ's remark, on me always being there for Justine, would have saddened me, though perhaps raised my hopes. But then I was more bemused than ever by the woman's refusal to leave a man she didn't love for me. At what price had she maintained the notion of a life lived in Leibniz's "best of all possible worlds"? Still, any resentments I'd ever directed at her were being redressed royally, were they not? And didn't I kind of have my hands full here, anyway?

Unless I grossly misunderstood, this youngster had been blatantly announcing that I was the object of her twisted father issues, but behaving for all the world as if she loved me woman-on-man nonetheless. On my part, I found myself agonizing as with the discovery of a lost daughter I had never known. Should I stay away from those thoughts?

My long-held contempt for psychology to the contrary, I wondered if I needed a shrink, though I doubted that *Doktors* Freud and Jung in collaboration could have fully unraveled this one! I recalled Richard saying that the trick was learning to laugh *with* the gods. Certainly it must be them now, I thought, roaring in the swirling storm at this cosmic joke.

Justine was describing with unabashedly fiendish glee her confrontation with JJ. Her mother had gone into a snit and threatened to take the issue up with me. I was grateful Justine had persuaded me not to answer that phone call as we'd been leaving, because I could understand and sympathize with both women. JJ's shock and confusion probably had equaled what I was going through, and Justine had yielded to an irresistible temptation to exact payback on a cosmic scale.

"Give it a rest, babe," I admonished. "You have no idea. Your generation looks on sex and any consequent choices as your right—which is as it should be. Your mother . . ."

"The prevailing mores blew her shit away? Her childhood again? That is such a *crock*!" Maybe I'm a wuss, but I don't think you would have challenged the cold steel in those eyes and voice either.

"Over halfway to Atlanta, and when you're finally willing to talk about yourself, out comes something incredible." I sighed heavily. "Please tell me that there isn't some other little item that you haven't mentioned yet."

The long pause suggested to me that there might well be something else to be known, but she spoke before I could question further. "I hope you'll be down for all there is to know about me. I did want us far away from *her*, because I didn't know if you would be all right with this. Believe that this was a mind-fuck for me, too, and when things went *way* weird in the car last night . . ." Her voice trailed off.

"My history puts you off?" I misread her.

"Not like you mean." She glanced at me with the haunted expression. "Guess I gotta go there."

Again in psych-major mode, she sought the roots of her personal masochism in her childhood. Flogging herself as a wrong person, she craved expiation from guilt, real or imaginary. A daughter named Justine was to be the recipient of a bequest from JJ's grandmother, and JJ had doubtlessly seen this as an advantageous position for the girl. But her apparent strategy to level the playing field for her love child had backfired.

The stepfather had been all too willing to punish her, but she had only responded to him with the same resentment he felt for her. He had no right, you see. Only the emotional equivalent of the father she had never known would she endow with the authority to punish her and thus let her be free.

While his behavior had to be deemed irrational, considering the pending bequest, it was easy enough to imagine the man's sodden brain marrying a lust for control with his resentment of her origins. From early on, his cruelty toward Justine went far beyond anything exacted on his own children.

Probably in sync with the deterioration of the man himself, the mistreatment had degenerated into sexual abuse. He was not a pedophile, but by the time she was becoming nubile, it was clear that he had *some* use for her in spite of his contempt. It's an old and common story, one that seldom if ever encompasses the complexities of any given situation.

"What did he do to you?" I reluctantly asked, as she shivered against me on the bench. The paternal issue was one thing; her quest for the father was likely what had made her liaison with me possible, But *this*? God, how I'd always hated spending my life cleaning up other men's messes!

"All that." She shrugged. "He had this whole *droit de seigneur* thing going on." She met my eyes, but misread the focus of my curiosity. "Hey, I'd wanted to clue you on this later. No, wait. As if you wanna hear it described? First time he went 'twixt my legs, the attitude was all, y'know, an alternative to being whipped, a special punishment he had prepared for me.

"He was a real piece of work. Something would be my bad, yea? Always when we were alone. He'd make me go lie full-on across the bed, like when I was little, waiting to get a spanking." She described all this utterly without expression. "I'm way sure that was to torture me, too—lying there and feeling all gnarly and exposed."

---

"WILLIE, WHAT HE SAID? NO HIDING PLACE? That was me, back in the day. Believe me when I say I even learned how to enjoy it. Sometimes I'd get naked and lie there, but not spread, like I was s'pose to? If I couldn't handle him fucking me, I could make him go soft; he was usually drunk. But he wouldn't be too stoked. I knew I was gonna get a whipping when I did that." She looked at me coldly, and I wondered if I were being instructed on what *not* to do. "He used one of those old, thin yardsticks."

I was astonished by her brutally matter-of-fact

account. Due to causes buried deep within her, Justine had arrived at a method of coping that the compulsively socially correct will deny even exists. While she had hated the offender all the more, she had learned to embrace the things that happened to her, taking a strange and complex satisfaction. I am sexually sadistic, true, but not such a bastard as to inflict myself on a helpless kid. I hated even more the whim of fate that had left her to endure it alone, had kept me from being there for her.

"Conventional explanation would be low self-esteem, and so forth," I offered uneasily, unsure as to how to tread carefully.

"Yadda, yadda, yadda."

"You reversed the roles, taking him out of the picture by making him as faceless an object as possible, experiencing it as being all about yourself?"

*"What-ev-er."* She shrugged again. "So now I don't really like sex and, some way or other, don't know it? Changes I'm getting put through are, like, fragmentation? Check it out, as if 'dissociative identity disorder'? I've been through every drill psych has to offer, till I could hurl. Got diagnostic stats manual criteria coming out my ass!"

"I'd as rather think of you 'owning it,' like you would say. Justine, I need to know if I put us at risk the other night?" Her revelations, delivered so deadpan, made the format of our wonderful sexual encounter become alarming.

She was silent for long minutes. "Let's not overidentify, shall we?" I started to speak, but she shushed me. "He couldn't get it done for me; I wouldn't let him. He would usually buttfuck me. No knocked-up baby, yea? Wet his fingers in my pussy and put them to my lips; said that proved what a slut I was. Dead right, there! Later, when I'd be horny, I'd think about that while I got it done for myself. Like denying him my orgasm was cheating him?"

With time, she had become aware of changes in the world around her. An increasingly intrusive society had lost tolerance for offenses within the family. An older Justine, sophisticated beyond her years, found that she could inspire fear in her cowardly oppressor. By sixteen, she'd begun to carry a knife.

"Not exactly Daddy's little princess?"

"Hardly. No, wait. Princess did start getting whatever she wanted. As if, extortion?" Of course, my lame oxymoron had to founder against so decidedly "incorrect" an ear. Would there be a test afterward?

The man was not so demented as to fail to grasp the situation into which he'd placed himself. Namely, that he could end up getting cut and going to the joint as well. In forcing him to back off, Justine had empowered herself. Finding that she was not inclined to disrupt what her mother pathetically regarded as a life, she just wanted to get away. Her stepfather agreed.

"Am I twisted? I've been a big ho'. I really have, but I've been careful about disease and not getting hooked up with flakes. *Believe* that I've gotten the education and made the payments to own who I am. When I say I'm livin' large, no one can tell me I'm too far out there." She dismissed society's "protective" functions with remarkable insight.

"I spent years being *his* victim. As if I should spend more years being *their* victim? I don't think so." Genuine emotion had been returning to her speech. "But you can be so sure that, for ten years, I never let anyone hit me in the butt. Not once, till you." She heaved a shuddering sigh, but it was visibly expressing an unspeakable relief. Then she made a confession the like of which you seldom hear from woman or man.

"Nothing has ever taken so much ass, as walking outta that bar, away from you. Going upstairs was like trying to escape a gravity well. Then it was all—about seeing the number on your card and the message from the board, and realizing I'd seen postings from you on the Net but like, fucked around? And there you were in front of me, like all kinds of inevitable.

"It was totally over. I was dressing up like I thought you'd wanna have me, and knowing that if you left, I'd be all, paging you to come back. I could not *even* believe what I was doing, getting ready to offer myself to you, body and soul. Have a clue what that was like?"

Actually, I was running breathlessly to keep up. Then I registered the hopeless little laugh when she had confessed her name. I saw her dressing herself, posturing herself to please, she had to have relived . . .

"When you pulled me back and wouldn't let me get away, you made me feel it all again, but not the same. Then you reached down and, *touched* me, and I came for you—right then, not once-removed! When you turned me over, oh, I loved your eyes! I saw you accepted that I had given it all up, and it was as if I weren't alone anymore."

That hit me like a whiplash and my composure faltered. Pulling myself back together, it occurred to me how all of this combined still failed to address the mysteries that had interwoven our paths. I suspected that she was aware of this. Her analysis was the means by which she had been educated to rationalize her own feelings and circumstance.

In the face of what was happening to us, the thing that was coming to us on that pier, in a sea storming with primal forces that could snuff out our little lives in a heartbeat, then more than ever she needed some parts of her life to make sense. I could only wish that *mine* might. I turned my eyes to the boiling clouds. "The kinkiest thing about this may be me having sex with a psychology graduate . . ."

The attempt at levity was lost. She wrapped up her end without breaking stride, "When you were describing your experiences, you didn't pick up on my shock of recognition? I'm so up on you that I don't think anything could turn me off."

Recalling her thoughts about incest in Mexico, I laughed uncertainly, "Yes, I guess we could say that has been pretty well established." While the atmosphere was not lightening, the rain had slowed, and she stood up. Her tension had returned.

"Prompt me right now if you really want me." She stared out into the Gulf, as if afraid to meet my eyes. "If you do, I believe we'll always be together, no matter what. But I must know now if you wanna throw me over and go back, after JJ or whatever . . . Nay, please don't make me go on alone." Her voice quavered. Somewhere in all this, the strangeness had returned and become pronounced. "Please, if you want this, take me right now!"

She waited for my answer, and I couldn't imagine why I hesitated. A fatal attraction is only a problem if you don't want it. I was knocked out that all this had been going on in her while I had wallowed in my silly insecurities. Never would she have to fear abandonment. Logically, I could not live long enough. It would be me who would age and sicken while she was yet young. She would never have to plead with me that it was still her inside, never know how shamefully shallow I could be . . .

From what depths was *this stuff* coming? I had abandoned no one; my record was clear. What I had traditionally thought of as sanity gave one last, feeble protest before it expired. "Do I want you?" The very question seemed as preposterous as her mother's "Do you remember me?"

"Of course I want you. But, my God, girl, look at you—look at me . . ."

I'll never be able to describe or express this, no matter how hard I try. The heartrending girl-cry that sounded as though it echoed down the halls of eternity did not even resemble her voice or speech. She gripped her fists under her chin and I wondered that one young lifetime could contain that much pain, and consequent release.

"Don't go there, don't *even* go there! Can't you see that I never wanna have to stop looking at you, ever again?" As though the enormity of it all caught up with her at once, she sank to her knees on the deck, her tears dissolving into the rain and the waters of the Gulf.

Somehow, I couldn't abide her like that right then. Seeing her on her knees before me aroused a strange, sickening sense of shame. I gathered her up and she lay against me like a sleeping child as I carried her back down the rain-slick planks. If she had somehow found her father and lover in one, I was going to buy into it. *Come hernia, come coronary,* I thought, *there is no way I'm going to let this girl down.* I would not allow the slightest indication that I might ever let her go.

The newly washed greens of the trees, bright paint on the antique houses facing the storming Gulf, the ozone in the air—all things seemed fresh and new. I was breathing in the air of a brand-new world and knowing I was never going back to the old one. As I felt my lifelong obsession with her mother pale into an ambivalent footnote, I knew that *now* I had seen it all! Of course, I was wrong again.

# VI
# The Testament

I TOOK HER WITH ME INTO A HOT SHOWER, WHICH relieved the chill of our soaking in the morning storm. Lathering each other up, it developed that my body hang-ups of the preceding day were missing. How not, when she watched me, slightly blushing, as I gently scrubbed the contours of her young flesh? It is not distasteful work to stroke under full, firm breasts and down along a well-muscled abdomen. No, I should have been the one to feel embarrassment when, rinsing off, she began to compulsively use her lips on my aging chest. Working down my belly, she went to her knees again and, this time, I felt no shame, quite the contrary.

The shower had one of those adjustable heads on a flexible tube, which she pulled down with her. "Spread your legs," she commanded with a wicked glance. *Oh, really?* The needle-spray was stimulating enough before she reached back and began to gradually turn up the heat. The treatment began to get intense, but damned if I were going to cry uncle! In wonder, I watched her implicitly worshiping my aging flesh, apparently desiring nothing other than to fill herself with me.

I tried to reach down for her, but she pulled back from my cock just long enough to gasp, "I don't care about that right now. I wanna get it done for you; I want you to come." When she dropped the nozzle and dug her electric blue nails into my butt, there was no difficulty on that count. I was staggered, but I could no longer discount the obvious; for some reason, in some fashion, she genuinely did want me!

After a great seafood lunch in a glass-walled restaurant overlooking the still-churning Gulf, we set out for Atlanta. By the time I swung the Del Sol northward at Mobile, the sun had come out and the day was fine. Contrasting with our weird drive through the Southern night, there was little conversation while we cruised through the forested Georgia hills. I drove, and she nestled against me.

Justine was apparently content, though I'd made little enough verbal commitment to her when she'd poured out her soul. Still, a crucial something had passed between us. This I could not have denied, even had I been so inclined. My mind full with trying to get a handle on what was happening to me, I surmised that she felt much the same. In my own internal quest, I'd remained vigilant for synchronies as a sort of barometer. I'd prayed that the fabric of reality might be worked, to worry loose a few threads of what my life might have been, or maybe had been and lost.

But what was happening was outrageous! Synchronicity appeared to overwhelm causality in a nexus of uncertainty, of which the wild weather presented an objective metaphor. Justine had said she saw convergence, but I feared the chaos of delusion. Could I persuade myself that my mad fantasy to return to the lake and the young JJ had been, all along, linked with a destiny leading me to her child instead? The implications of this possible outcome to my life were extraordinary as anything I'd been consciously exploring.

If that was the case, how did the strange saga of the life and work of William Seabrook fit into all of this? Or did it, I wondered, as we skirted Columbus, beyond serving simply as the point at which we touched? I had a most unsettling moment as I glanced at her, dozing with her head on my thigh, hair red as the Georgia clay on the embankments streaming past us.

That association of her with the environment evoked something from my unconscious. I could but partially call the reminiscence up to awareness, a sentiment of grief so inexpressible as to be stanched only by oblivion. That notion being something I was unaccustomed to, it sent my mind spiraling again into a bizarre domain in which Justine did not exist at all.

I fished in my pocket for a Valium. Could I have gone utterly mad? Might I be on this wild odyssey all by myself, this being resting on my thigh a nymph by the strictest definition? A Gaia? Might the eerie sense of familiarity devolve from her being a hallucinatory manifestation of a reality that I failed to cope with and railed against?

I settled down as the tranq cut in, reasonably sure that I could confirm the reality of our meeting. Unlikely as it might seem, this young woman was quite real. There were receipts in my pocket establishing that two had lodged and dined. No, the ugly thought that I was avoiding in the real world was the prospect that I might be nothing more than a casual circumstance in realizing her destiny. I had to face, after all, the probability that she had substantially more to offer the world than I yet did.

The colors of the natural beauty without exacerbated the foreboding of mortality. How often I had ignored the simple joy of life, and how little time was left! Could she recall for me youth's brave illusion of feeling like an immortal being? Or would she make me old by punctuating the pointlessness of all existence confronting extinction?

We reached Atlanta late in the afternoon but, with the modern loop around the city, were able to avoid most of its traffic as well. Old Atlanta had been forced even farther underground, like the great Texas cities, with big chunks of Los Angeles dropped on top of that which I remembered. To the north, the hills still grew rougher, and deciduous forest blended with the softwood of the tree farms. Along the American autobahns, we made our way to the little town of Buford, now a suburb of Greater Atlanta.

The mills and factories of an earlier era called

Progress had marked the road from Chattanooga I had traveled with Linda so long before. They had given way to the usual generic collection of discount gas stations, Wally Worlds, and Pizza Huts.

Above the main artery, then lighting up for the evening, a few vagrant houses of vanishing yesteryears held on to the rocky hillsides, among newer bricks and mobile-home developments. In second gear, we climbed a winding street pitted with potholes that were real axle-breakers. Justine directed me to a gate in a rusted iron fence. It sported a statue of a deer that would have been life-size had the representation been of a Texas whitetail.

Inside, concealed by trees and overgrown shrubbery from the encroaching residential district, a Victorian monstrosity to quicken the dead heart of Tennessee Williams clung to the side of the hill. An odd location, I thought, for a cosmopolitan woman of the "smart set" to finish out her years. What could have moved her to bury herself in these Southern hills, what reasons beyond the obvious? Atlanta had been Katie's place, after all, and other pieces of Willie's roots had been nearby.

A quiet wistfulness wafted about its weathered sides and sagging balustrades. A casemented corner rose in a false tower to support an octagonal "birdcage" turret beside the tin roof. Disintegrating wooden shake awnings shaded the windows that surveyed the darkening hollows below. Those lengthening shadows were baleful as the broken relief of Ollioules Gorge, in a picture I'd seen of that menacing ravine when I found Evenos on an Internet tourism site. An elaborate lightning rod, with curlicues and lateral rings, asserted the old house's defiance as it hung on for dear life against time and change.

---

"LET ME GO TURN ON THE LIGHTS."

While dusk was about to settle, I observed there was still plenty of illumination. "Nay, I totally want you to see this!" I watched her butt as she bounced up the porch steps and unlocked the door. As she stepped inside, the old screen crashing behind her, her youthful vitality became a welcome relief from unbidden thoughts that the house inspired. Maybe I'd overdone the Valium?

Momentarily, the entire house was lit against the coming twilight by a little electric lamp in each of its windows, even those in the tower and gables up above. Looking closer, I could see that they were tiny glass lamps in a wild variety of shapes and colors, most resembling old oil lamps. She skipped back down the creaking steps, and proudly announced, "I'm way happy they came on. If even one bulb is out, none of them will work."

"Wired in series," I thought aloud, somewhat cheered from my reverie on the house where her ancestress had grown old. "Well, they do kind of make you think of old-time Christmas lights, don't they?"

The pride in her voice subtly changed as she gazed at her fancifully lighted windows. "I'm sure she found them one at a time, and added them so that there would be a light in each and every window." In that strange light, her features were preternaturally *real*. It seemed to me that I was seeing the pretty spirit within this young thing shining through her skin. I wallowed in the luxury of a guilty question as to my right to inflict myself upon her, whether she thought she wanted it or not. But I conceded that to be luxurious speculation, indeed. Of course I would. Anyway, why presume that I would do harm?

The larger part of the house turned out to be sparsely furnished and unused. Justine had moved her bed, a large four-poster of course, into what had been the library-study and camped out there, among the remaining treasured possessions of her great-grandmother. Certain touches caught my eye immediately, relating to descriptions I'd read of Seabrook's quarters in New York: a faded cashmere shawl on one wall; a Chinese lamp above the antique roll-top desk in the corner; a long Adam mirror.

My eyes swung back to a print framed above the desk, and I went over to study it with mild disbelief. Reclining, along the length of a stone bridge with multiple arches, lay the figure of a naked girl. She reached an arm above and behind her to grasp the roof of a tower on the bridge's superstructure. Serenely dozing, the peaceful giantess's long tresses descended beneath the surface of a river below. Justine shared in my admiration of the old drawing.

"I love old bridges so." She glanced at me and giggled. "Yes, dearest, even the ones in 'Madison County.' I'm afraid I'm like JJ that way!" She looked back at the reproduction. "I was charmed by that when I saw it in school, but I hadn't remembered whose work it was." She pointed to the signature, *Man Ray, 1917*. "Behold my surprise when I found it here."

*Behold mine,* I thought, the gooseflesh rising on my skin. On the edge of having to confront the reality of this part of her heritage, as well as the stunning revelations of the morning, I said, "Its name is *The Bridge at Avignon.*" I almost whispered, as if something might overhear. My generation had been into Man Ray and the surrealists, but Justine, the "Gen-Xer," had not recognized him, nor known the history. If this anomalous thing were as real as it was beginning to seem, I had to quit playing games and tell her about the "composite" Justine's vision of the street circus. In the face of what was happening, her ancestress's alleged psychic ability might likely be more than an incidental factor.

The study furnishings, plus Justine's bed and some Persian rugs, made the room cozy, almost overstuffed in comparison to the rest of the virtually empty house. Along with a kitchen and bath down the hall, this was all that she'd needed. She'd been spending her recent days and hours reading her great-grandmother's papers and books, with which the shelves along two walls were still amply supplied. After we had brought in our things, she took my hand and led me to a staircase to the upper rooms.

"I'm afraid it looks like your estate was pretty well pilfered," I remarked, and she nodded silently, turning on a light in the second-story hall that was as yellowed as the wallpaper. I paused to look at some large prints that still hung on the walls. Two were of street scenes, one of a boulevard in Paris, the other appearing to be early-century New York in winter.

I laughed at some others, "Babe, these pictures look like those *swamps* we were driving over last night!" She just motioned me toward a narrow stair that I calculated led to the turret room. We stopped for her to unlock a heavy door that would have been a formidable obstacle in any era. The blue twilight from without called me back to the darkened upper hall of my boyhood home. Had its whispering shadows followed behind me?

I guessed that Justine might be feeling a similar spookiness as she took my hand, this time very like the little girl afraid of the dark, drawing me into the dimly lit room. There were windows on half of the octagon, the remaining sections abutting the roof. Each window had its little light, silhouetting a New England rocker that sat facing them. The dim illumination had already revealed to me that something much like the fabled mural was truly there, covering two sections of the wall.

It was evident that all this room had ever been for was to simply sit and watch the painting and the windows with their little lamps. There was the ghostly feeling that the old chair might, ever so slightly, begin to rock. Might I walk around it to find the ancient Justine sitting there still? I reached to lift its tidy with incredulous anticipation, when Justine turned on an old-fashioned pole lamp to disclose the faded, checkered upholstery beneath. Ward Greene had described just such a piece of furniture, belonging to his character "Justine," sometime before 1930. Was that the moment when I recognized the living legacy of an actual human being? Oh yes. All doubt was extinguished that the original Justine, by whatever name she had been known, had been a discrete entity, a living woman of flesh and blood, not a composite or a fiction.

I stepped over to examine the loving mural with its prayer by John Donne. By this point, I knew its little characters and vignettes as I knew the figures and episodes from my life which had been haunting my dreams more often of late. This was again like visiting another man's dreamscape, and I felt the same hushed reverence that Justine was demonstrating. More, viewing its magnificent reality confirmed Marjorie's disclaimer, that it had not been painted with a promotion in mind, that she'd never intended for it to endure public display.

---

THE WHOLE PAINTING WAS A PRAYER, not Donne's lines alone—a heartfelt prayer for the immortal soul of its subject. Curious though it remained that a woman of Marjorie's sensibilities had been attracted to Willie Seabrook to begin with, the touching sincerity of her work of art, that she had believed lost, was undeniable. I was humbled and shamed by remembrance of my worldly scorn at its creator, as well as for having doubted its caretaker.

It was with a feeling akin to fear that my fingertips lightly brushed the figure of a tiny nude spread-eagled on a doorway, face locked within a helmet of red leather. I could imagine that, rather than the expected texture of paint and wood, my touch might somehow intrude upon the trembling, sweating flesh of the masked icon within whose home I now stood. I was moved to verify what I could see of the figure's naked chest. Whoever's features the mask concealed, they were not those of Leah Hirsig. Upon her breast there was no Star.

I turned quietly to see Justine kneeling by an old cedar chest under the windows, gently removing its contents. A pretty party dress from the flapper era, a couple of beautiful little beaded handbags, a box of cigarettes of a vanished brand, bundles of letters tied with faded ribbons, and other keepsakes. The precious memories of a lifetime were stored in that chest.

She then began laying out items of the same barbaric silver as the jewelry she'd worn in the Marriott bar. One pair of bracelets was in reality manacles—with locking clasps and rings attached. When she spread out the belt, with its uncut stones and little chains, my last skepticism dissolved. By description and illustration, it could be none other than the *Yezidi* marriage belt acquired during Seabrook's Arabian adventure.

Justine handed me an African mask, one that he might have received from the very hands of Wamba, she of the Fan-Shaped Destiny. Justine stayed on her knees, hands between her thighs and looking expectantly at me, as for approval. Seeking to lighten things up, I smiled, and said, "Thank you for looking after all this. Uncle Willie would be proud." For a moment she seemed oddly surprised, then giggled with delight.

We gathered up the Seabrook articles by unspoken consent, Justine carefully replacing her predecessor's other treasures in the chest, and took the memorabilia back down to her living area. She then spoke of how the estate had been picked over, in spite of its owner's careful planning. I agreed it significant that most items explicitly named in the will had not been taken. In this situation, the theft was likely connected to someone who had been with the law firm, or an earlier executor. A quarter century having elapsed, something of this nature was to have been expected.

In the study, she pointed out how there were no first editions of anything left on the shelves. The only works of Seabrook that remained were *Asylum* and *White Monk*, neither of which could have given her a complete picture of the man or his work. There were, however, many old books. She watched me as I browsed their titles.

I knew my growing astonishment must have shown, for there were Charles Hinton and J.W. Dunne, books about Einstein and Minkowski, the Michelson-Morley experiment, the third volume of the Feynman lectures—all the classics that I had read in pursuit of my own quest. There were philosophical works on the ancient idea of the plurality of worlds, and more recent science magazines. I examined an old copy of *Physics Today* lying above the roll-top.

"Justine," I gasped, "do you know what this is, the edition for September of 1970?"

"It was inside the top of her desk, and that was the month she wrote her will. As if she'd been reading it at that time?"

"This contains the first popularization of Everett's theory by Bryce DeWitt," I told her. I shook my head as the old copy still readily fell open to the well-thumbed pages of the DeWitt article, its paradoxes illustrated by little drawings of the predicament of Schrödinger's kitty-cat.

The hard science ended, naturally, with the classics. Priestley was there, alongside Lawrence Durrell and other time-haunted writers of literature. There was Michelet in French, and other French sources that Seabrook might have perused in the library at Geneva. Also in French were Paul Morand, Anaïs Nin, and Pauline Réage.

There were Aldous Huxley and Gertrude Stein, Hecht, Van Vechten, and others dear to the heart of a Lost Generation New Yorker. I was given pause by a little book on puppets by one Tony Sarg. More when I touched the spine of Thomas Wolfe's *Of Time and the River*, written just down the road from Seabrook's residence at Rhinebeck.

Thunder rumbled outside, startling me back from . . . somewhere. It seemed the storm had caught up to us. There before me were Eleanora Deren's *Divine Horsemen*, and a number of other books on Voudon in Haiti and America, as well as its African origins. I pulled down *The White King of La Gonave*, and pointed out to

Justine its introduction by Seabrook, which she hadn't yet noticed. So many things of my own obsessions—why, I'd just found de Sade, then Borges. Might Borges, who was close to the poet Valéry, have not also known his friend Paul Morand? Maybe he had been influenced by Seabrook more directly than by merely reading things everyone else had forgotten . . .

The wind rattled old shutters. "It's time," Justine expressed in her same hushed tone, as if something momentous was at hand. As, oh God, it surely was. She unlocked the roll-top and turned on the Chinese lamp, motioning me to sit at the desk, and placed in front of me a document. It was a long letter on some twenty sheets of yellowed bond paper, their age implicit in the typewriting of an Underwood Standard. I discovered the old typewriter still in its desk well; maybe untouched since that other Justine had last replaced it all those years before.

Justine merely told me that the letter had been attached to the will, then moved away to let me read. She cleared off a large table in the middle of the room. I glanced at her with sexy thoughts, once or twice at most, absorbed in her project of carefully arranging the memorabilia on the table. Thus had Seabrook displayed his trophies in the barn studio—he *would* have been proud. Perhaps a spirit could rest a bit easier.

The rain had begun again, high up on the tin roof and reverberating through the empty house. I remembered my trip through the South years before with Linda, thinking how every night seemed to be a rainy night in Georgia. But there, in Justine's library-bedroom, all was warm and cozy, and I began to read. Even when I would later read Willie's lost manuscript and wonder at its incredible message, even that would not have the devastatingly personal impact of this first introduction to his true mystery.

I was soon engrossed. There was additional information, clarification, and provocatively leading hints that I'd sought in vain through the resources I had available. Lighting my pipe, I was drawn into the love and pain of that other Justine, first as she'd laboriously typed her final defiance of time and death. Then, perhaps because I'd read so much of them and their world, back to early century New York, to Toulon and Avignon, and Rhinebeck. Even now, a maelstrom of emotion renders it indescribable for me. I simply include, in its entirety:

## THE TESTAMENT OF MADELEINE LEIRIS

September 20, 1970

My Dearest Justine,

Having not much longer in this life, I address this personal communication to my great-granddaughter. By the time you are reading this, you have become heir to the lion's share of the properties enumerated in my legal will, to which this document is attached. Doubtless, my act of leaving a substantial bequest to a person not as yet conceived, as of this writing, will be viewed as but another whimsy of an eccentric old woman.

I have the assurance of my attorney that it will stand as long as proper legal niceties are observed, to wit, securing of a pittance to other potential claimants and, my soundness of mind not be held in question. To the first issue, I have selected a firm that is old and highly respected in Atlanta, positively stodgy, with whose founding family I have maintained very close association. Other agents are prepared to ensure the process should there be any breach in my charted path, so I have complete confidence that all will go as intended.

As our countrymen are scandalous among the great powers for their remarkable narrowness, I am constrained to circumspection regarding certain matters. At the same time, I must needs supply adequate direction that you may receive your true bequest with all deliberate haste. Some women of our blood-line have been known for particular forms of intuition and for uncommon recall. Therefore, I advise you to search your recollections for memories that may serve you in the search I know you will now undertake.

There are interesting matters for you to explore among the histories of our progenitors. The information in the formal documents attached will enable you to unearth that heritage. Such pursuits are something for which your mother, bless her heart, and my niece who reared her have little use. They summarily dismiss anything they consider to be of the "dead past." That has come to give me a chuckle, the dead past; what an idea! The tip I can give is only that you not become <u>unduly</u> involved with the minutiae of genealogy. The succession of historical personages who gave you your physical being is important, but not paramount.

A score of years and more will have elapsed. High damned time, I would say, for your mother to have seen fit to divulge your grandmother's tragedy. My only child ended her brief life in sorrow, in illness, not long after she gave birth to your mother. I was given to great deliberation by that catastrophe. Be mindful of how very wrong it is to belittle young love, its joys and its sorrows. So many lives have been ruined. Should you ever feel yourself in like fashion loosely connected to this life, remember me. I have lived long, thanks in large measure to always finding umpteen other things that needed doing.

Those days of the late Forties were a hellish time for a girl to bear a child out of wedlock. Her "shame" was visible to all of a foolish society bent on turning back the clock to a time that had never been. Some died, by the butcher's hand, most in the living death of shotgun weddings. Public policy had become secret adoption, an illegal practice that should never have been countenanced. At best a racket, at worst an abominable experiment, I would not have any of it in our family. Dreading that the contingencies of my life may have had a detrimental effect on my poor child, though she had materially wanted for nothing, I would not risk a re-enactment.

I arranged for my barren niece, together with her husband in Texas, to adopt and rear your mother. I would help from time to time, but generally kept my thousand-mile distance. I might have erred; should have kept her with me. I hope that you will not be put off when I express my certitude that your mother's eventual marriage was a gross mistake. You may understand my reasons by and by. I would hope, by the time you are of age, that union will have ended.

This practice, of passing on the name Justine, began as a little gesture of hope for the immortality of my lost daughter. It was I who made it a part of your mother's name and, as the tradition has not been observed with your sister, I am confident that you will have become the latest Justine. For one thing, your mother will not jeopardize this bequest by failing to oblige me.

Please do not misconstrue me. I love your mother dearly, but my niece proved out to be a little prig who reared a child tolerably banal, so much as to eschew her birthright and her probable destiny. Though I pity her, all is not lost. The identity of your grandfather is of no moment. The dimwit to whom your mother bound herself may or not turn out to be your sire. No matter, the maternal line alone is important to us. I, myself, have had two marriages and various lovers. One alone will I trouble to chronicle.

---

In an early fall twilight, in the twilight of my life, my heart goes back, as I suppose it does with all women, to the very first. Dark and brooding, brash, counter-poised, guilt haunted, even twisted, but so magnetic and powerful! Dear, dear Willie. I suppose I would of always loved the bad boys; and not I alone. Also my darling Katie, who kept the years after Willie's passing from being unbearable. Even prissy little Marjorie, who would ask you to believe she was a damned saint, someway wading through all of Willie's queer leavings without getting any of them on her.

How Willie could make me hate him! Not for what I chose to endure willingly at his hands. I will stand by his affirmation of my role in all that. I had better ought to censor myself here pursuant to my attorney's advice. While it appears that a broader ethic regarding personal beliefs and practices is in place, he cautions that, decades hence, prudish minds may yet again dominate psychological definitions. As I said, a stodgy firm. No, I would hate Willie for the cavalier fashion in which he treated the women who loved and adored him.

Only after he was gone, when I read the collection of notes from the barn experiments, was it impressed upon me what he had believed himself about. So painful to embrace the solitary nightmare he had ridden all the years I had known him. I ask you though, had he fully shared his secret with any of us, would we truly have believed him? Only after close study of his books and letters could I no longer deny the bitter and yet wondrous truth. In all our incarnations, we are yet part of the human condition. For all our wit, how often has the prayer gone up in contrition, in remorse; for one last chance, one more moment to say I am sorry, or thank you, or even just good-bye?

Your true inheritance, my child, is that which he called The Fan-Shaped Destiny. Of imponderably greater value than the material bequest, you must find the reasons that I have obliged you to come to Atlanta to collect it, and will send you farther yet down time's dark river. You are wondering, I will warrant, if something uncanny is not afoot. This is a deliberate puzzlement for you to solve. Trace our lifelines, my child, and find yourself in the course of it. In this epistle, I will treat only with singular moments of my enduring life with Willie Seabrook. With these missing pieces, you will find the rest for yourself.

If you have been told that I was the first Justine, you may be surprised to learn that I was not born with the name. It was my dearest Willie who christened my sojourn in this life with the character of the divine Marquis. My birth name was Madeleine and I was born around the turn of the century in

New York City. Back in my day, ladies had the luxury of obscuring our exact dates.

I well recall that first meeting, early in the year of 1917. I was working in the studio of Tony Sarg, the former German Army officer who had decamped and eventually immigrated to the United States. His popular marionette theater brought him instant celebrity in Greenwich Village. Ten years later, Tony would design the first giant balloons for the Macy's Parade. Like my Willie, he is not muchly remembered, either.

I was too young and green to understand Tony's politics, though back in that day, most of the *avant-garde* were Socialists of some denomination. In the studio girls' eyes, he was well schooled in Prussian authoritarianism, but he had some kind of conflict with the growing might of High Germany. One day he had attended a luncheon given by the proprietor of the Brevoort, a man named Orteig, who was a sponsor of the Lafayette Escadrille and the Field Service. He had brought some of the returned veterans back to show off the studio where we made the puppets.

Willie was then thirtyish, a tad older than his comrades. He cut a someway sinister appearance with his dark tousled hair and mustache. He was big and brooding and scary-looking as he stalked about the studio with his shoulders hunched. He made a splendid figure in his Field Service uniform, his Croix de Guerre on its red and green ribbon adding a Napoleonic touch. Should history anymore be taught when you are educated, remember that the German ambassador had just then been expelled. It was no longer the sophisticates alone who understood that American entry into the "War to End All Wars" was imminent. By then, those early volunteers were cast as visionaries and heroes, to have tasted the horrors of war before being called.

Near the end of his life, he would hurt my feelings for a while by maintaining that I had made as little impression on him as I had dreaded. I could not construe his claim that he had scarcely spoken to me, as I had so wanted to entice him in my tiresome studio smock. After all, I would chide myself for months; this hero was married to the incredible Katie, who had become a nurse to follow him off to war.

Her family was, reputedly, from big Southern money. I was but a callow dilettante, whereas she was a belle. My parents had means sufficient to keep me comfortable, though they wished I would marry. With the changes being wrought by the Great War in the offing, I could have become part of the new elite of educated professional ladies. I was more taken with the arts and the bewitching characters who hung about with the likes of Tony Sarg.

Willie _had_ talked with me and, to my bewilderment, flirted. He had then bowled me over with uncanny knowledge of my life and personality. He knew how I so loved to wear weighty bracelets and chains and _toc_ like that, back before "costume jewelry" became fashionable. More dreadful was his hint that he knew what that affectation signified for me. Never, in all my enduring life, had I told anyone about being "kidnapped" and tied to trees by the little boys, or how delightfully far those childhood games had gone!

Willie wrote that he had dreamed about me and wanted to visit. When he taxed me with a harrowingly explicit vision of what he wanted, there was positively no question about it. I went to meet him wearing so much leather and metal that climbing the stairs, to the studio I had borrowed for our play, I must of looked a scream. Wishing that he would be less solemn about it all, I did as best my shaking knees would allow to play the _blasee connaisseuse_ of everything we were about to do. I soon discovered that Willie was as nervous as I.

The rest is history. I was still floored that Katie had encouraged him in all that, when he then moved her up to New York and did not leave for six years. Willie was my first love, my greatest love, and Katie became my best friend for life. As mad as he could sometimes make me, I had sensed early on that my debt to the both of them was colossal.

---

One of the exotic denizens of the Village who frequented Tony's studio was the infamous Aleister Crowley, who billed himself as a black magician and was suspected of being a German operative. Willie had early warned me against Crowley, which was passing strange. For one thing, I was almost surc that had been before he had in fact met Crowley himself. Also, Willie was a Republican and had no interest in the political charges against the man.

Moreover, after Frank Harris had introduced them over lunch at Mouquon's, Willie had become quite taken with Crowley. Learning that Crowley was reputed to employ sadistic rituals in his magic, I was absolutely sizzling when Willie refused to take me around. As if Mrs. Seabrook did not socialize with Crowley? In truth, Katie was one of singularly few ladies that the "Great Beast" seemed genuinely to respect. Everyone loved and respected Katie, not least of all myself.

Another peculiarity in this puzzlement was Jimmy, Willie's friend from his newspaper days in Atlanta. Jimmy, a pious, bespectacled man with thinning hair, would have looked right at home, as Damon Runyon described him, passing the collection plate in a Baptist congregation. Destined to head a national news syndicate, Jimmy wanted only to be regarded as a good reporter. He and Willie, the flamboyant bad boy, made quite an odd pair. They would always be friends, even after Jimmy published a weird little book based obviously on Willie. The scandal sheets, in the know as to the personalities, found it juicy and near enough to libelous for their tastes.

That book would later magnify my unease concerning the entire Crowley matter, but I enjoyed it, in large measure because Marjorie hated it. When I first met Jimmy during an autumn visit to the City, he watched me so queerly, as though here was <u>another</u> man who knew absolutely everything about me. He inveighed against Crowley, but only piqued my shameless, catlike curiosity with his urging that I observe Willie's cautions.

I was young and impetuous; even my worship of Willie would side-track me for only so long. At a venture, I pestered Sarg for an introduction. Finally, in the late summer of 1918, Tony's own nefarious purposes were served by recommending me as a "companion" to A.C., as we called Crowley, on a river trip up the Hudson. I up and went! We started upriver from Hyde Park, in a damned canoe of all things. Before long, it began to turn into one of those hideously uncomfortable, insect infested, out-of-doors "experiences." Moreover, I found A.C. a pompous ass and physically repellent. At length, my crawling skin reduced me to spinning tales and throwing tantrums like the petulant child I probably was. I succeeded in making myself tedious enough for him to send me home.

On my way back down to the City, I was desolate enough, without having to suffer a growing terror that felt akin to deja vu. Passing through Dutchess County, I began to wonder if the Catskills really were haunted; or what if Crowley really and truly was a magician and did something unmentionable? Glimpsing the lights of the River mansions near Rhinebeck in the twilight, I was overcome with the most horrid foreboding. What if I lost him, what if I lost Willie? For no apparent reason, I was squalling up a storm. The River, twisting into its Stygian darkness, seemed bound for a hell of wailing loneliness. Then it was that I made a crucial decision.

Willie, who had something to do with financing A.C.'s excursion, was most put out. Coming from Willie, I was shocked to find him so beside himself. Persuaded how repulsive I had found A.C., he relaxed only a tad. While I idolized him and was therefore biased, I positively could not construe why he would remain so touchious. Katie had become a star of Village life, planning to open up a smart coffeehouse. She held me forth as her <u>protegee</u> and A.C. never would of dared antagonize her. Try as I might, he would not be gainsaid and, when he did slacken, it was the strangest thing.

He never broached the subject to A.C., but I was not tempted to regard that as weakness or hypocrisy. I think he fathomed A.C. as the sort of dog who would only be encouraged by marked territory. The Seabrooks socialized with A.C. till he left the country the following year, but I had no desire ever again to go near him. Whatever had occasioned all that hellblackness in the Catskills, I would do nothing that might invite the dreadful thing to return. Some months after the river trip, A.C. invited Willie to his rooms on Washington Square. Willie met and, I would presume, played with A.C.'s new <u>protegee</u>, a woman called Leah, who became a fixture of A.C.'s career. Willie would later write of A.C. and Leah with awe and intrigue, but what I remember is this:

Later that night, he came to my apartment with a bottle of gin as if to celebrate. Then things turned strange, nice, but strange. He made love to me with a tenderness unlike I would of expected from Willie. Then he held me in his arms painfully tight, as tightly as he had ever fettered me. Then he cried till he went to sleep.

Not for decades, till the end of another great war, when I myself wept over the revelations of his last written words, would I understand that his tears had been of the most infinite relief. Neither could I have known, nor would I have believed, what Willie had at last convinced himself that he had spared me. I would check onto this strangeness again, at Avignon, and in Paris, and anytime Paul Morand's friend was around. This "Pauline" was somebody among the French literati, who looked at me in a disturbing way that reminded me of Jimmy. I learned little, as Willie tended to run me around France like a naif tourist, while I was more fluent in the language than he. That would peeve me doubly, as my distant cousin was a well-known French poet and a friend of Willie's.

---

The years went by and with them came change, as is the way of things. It was the spring of 1931, when Willie had wintered in New York for the publication of his African book, introducing Wamba and The Fan-Shaped Destiny. By that time, he was totally involved with Marjorie Worthington, and I was livid. The very idea that he could throw Katie up was an abomination! Though she had been seeing Marjorie's future former husband, I knew that in her secret heart, the dreadful word "nevermore" beat darkly as the wings of Poe's raven. It was as if the dark shadows of my ride through the Catskills were being visited on darling Katie, who deserved them least of all. There was going to be some kind of accounting, for I resolved to execute my long standing decision. I had gone that winter, with Katie and Lyman Worthington, to greet their arrival from Europe on the old Berengaria. When I saw Willie grandly helloing us from the deck, with Marjorie and some pretty little Russian countess, where I used to stand beside Katie, I knew what I had to do.

From that day, I inveigled Willie into bed at every opportunity. While I was over thirty, late for a woman in those days, I succeeded in becoming pregnant. Oh, I was seeing other men. Already, seeing the carnage of youthful lives had turned me someway sexually predacious. I saw myself as taking revenge, for those who should have been free, for other times when they would have been appreciated.

I had no interest in establishing paternity. When Willie returned to France, Katie and I went to the stateroom party. That little frump Marjorie was bawling her eyes out across the corridor because we were even there, when it was she who would be leaving with him! The mutual antipathy that had grown betwixt her and me was a personal matter, and everything I tell about her will be, of course, prejudiced. I hugged my belly and gloated with sadistic glee, at owning a part of him that I suspicioned she would never know. It was only being wise, cruelly saying I hoped the ship would sink. He would always be my dashing, dominating hero, however much a little boy he was. And I am his Justine forever.

Dearest child, I am not able to tell who your grandfather was, nor foresee who your father may be. You may pour the two together and I will warrant that they could not add up to one William Buehler Seabrook. Those who have belittled him are loathsome hypocrites who, hiding the skeletons in their own closets, attack with his own honesty a man big enough to tell the truth about himself. Critics in the main, social and literary, are full of hooey. If any of those "defenders of womanhood," who savaged his sexual practices, gave a hoot for the opinions of the real women who lived and loved with him, you could not have proven it by me. I am here to testify that it was so, so sweet. After he was dead, they erased him, instead of having to own up to his effects, his power. I have got to collect myself, for I have yet to get through the awfulest part of the story, its ending.

---

He and Marjorie took the place at Rhinebeck in the fall of 1934, after his first bout with dipsomania. When I first saw the house, I feared that I had experienced there, a long time past, a vision not unlike Lowell Thomas's friend in those same haunted hills. I knew that Willie's best years were behind him. However long it might take, I dreaded that he never would leave there alive. As his trusted friend, I truthfully wished him contentment, of which Willie had ever known so little. I felt then that he was lost to me, the chapter ended, the book closed. I had a child to rear and the Great Depression to get through. Quite practical, commonsensical. Later, I could only torture myself over how things might have gone, had I taken another view.

You will have learned about the business I established in Atlanta, with the help of old friends of Willie's who remembered me fondly, especially the lady Jimmy had called Santolina. You will not have trouble identifying her; prominent in the Social Register, even as she was unmistakably, to the naked eye, a mulatta. In the way of the old Southerners, the country-club set around her simply failed to notice. Her family had been, still are, twentieth century barons, with irons in every fire, from banking and politics to the symphony. It was positively not permitted that money as old as hers should be tainted with color! In the neighborhood, she was known as "pure Creole," whatever the hell that was suppose to mean. Expending vast amounts of energy on a myriad of tangled activities, it was as little surprising when society overlooked her patronage and protection of me.

During the next decade, she would introduce me to some "witchy women" from the Southern bayous who would help me keep my sanity through what was coming. For my money, she was very muchly a witch in her own right. She always regarded Willie with something like amusement but, with the familiarity of years, I learned that it was not contemptuous and not at all mean.

The craft of the likes of Santolina was an advantage you will likely have to do without. M. Mitchell's winds of change are now blowing with ferocity across the old Southland, as across the world. The pains taken to hold back histories are again, as always, to no avail. With the inevitability of entropy, the value of our time fades, together with its evil. The first cold Mistral seemed churned up by a hot cloud over Hiroshima. Willie's telegram arrived the next week, only hours after the radio had announced the surrender of Imperial Japan, and sounded like he had that on his mind. When he wired me to come be with him, there was a phrase I took as a typographical error, whose depths I would only later begin to suspect, ". . . it seems we live in yet an otherworld." Even as a by-the-by, those words conveyed such a strange presentiment that I was to remember them.

Riding the trains up to Rhinebeck, I had no inkling that I was on a mission to collect our legacy. With the South receding behind the curved windows of the observation car, I twitted salesmen in flashy suits and lollygagged about in utterly girlish fantasies. Might the dark shadows not close over us; might my hour come 'round at last? I knew little or nothing about Willie's third wife. She had served as a war correspondent during the early Nazi onslaught and looked a bit like Katharine Hepburn. The guess-gossip held her as what, today, they are calling a dominatrix. I was unsurprised that Marjorie had left him. Little regard as I had held for her, I knew that Willie had been her masterful hero as well. No more than I, would she have wanted to see him brought to his knees. It may be I was a product of my times, but had Willie wanted or needed to explore the other side . . . no, wait. Betwixt us, child, there can only be the strictest truth! I will not pretend I was glad that someone else was there for him. I would of done anything at all, even that.

As hell would have it, I arrived in the evening. The lone cab driver, Bob, was waiting for me at the station. Even so, I knew we must pass those malignant, squatting River mansions in the twilight. With Bob making leading conversation, openly titillated that I was back again in the presumed role of a "research girl," I watched the mansions as though they were monsters that might leap on us. In truth, they were gracious old homes, and it was the loveliest time of the day to me - anywhere but there.

Which were the more horrid, darkened windows like the eye sockets of skulls, as if the dreadful thing might enter by them, or the lighted ones that called out to dead drummer boys and suicided girls, to the dead crewmen of Henry Hudson, to all the forlorn spirits and lost souls of the Catskills? I was tempted to invite Bob into the back seat to exorcise the ghosts, but I was glad I was there for Willie. The thought of him needful and alone was so hateful to me.

Someone once said that the secret of life is that it gets harder as it goes along. My childish moonings turned into dust. The wife was away for a few days with their little son, and Willie wanted me in and out before she returned. He always inquired after my daughter whom, at that moment, I believed doing quite nicely. Why, I was actually proud that I had managed to rear such a lovely innocent. It did not occur to me that I had in no way readied her for the world. Neither had we discussed her paternity. Willie did not ask, and I had never said. He knew. I think he was ashamed that he could not bring himself to ask.

When Willie took me up to the barn, I vainly hoped that he would ravish me, or chain and whip me, anything. Just let me have him back again! I should explain that the "barn" was a much larger habitation than the cottage in which he had lived with Marjorie, then Constance. He had remodeled it with bedrooms, kitchen, and banquet hall on the ground floor and his studio "dungeon" above. Up there he kept the cages and some altogether nasty gadgets, illumined in the ruby glow from leaded stained glass windows.

I was well versed in his experiments at the barn, having supplied him with a number of his "research girls" during the foregoing seven or eight years. I, myself, had been a participant in several episodes, once for the edification of the Aldous Huxleys, no less. I would so love to have been with Willie on the Riviera, sharing a beach and mysterious adventures with the Huxleys and other exotic friends!

As I saw it then, ignorant as to why he never would permit me to tarry long in France, all that had been wasted on Marjorie. During the sessions in the barn, she had always hidden in the cottage and fretted. I would choose the girls for their sexual bent. On that basis, they enjoyed themselves thoroughly, the rough stuff included. While I had no doubt that Willie thought he was gaining insight into mysteries, nothing I saw there held the sensation of destiny. Nothing as when Willie had taken me to the little circus in Avignon, the one that I had "previewed" while hanging naked in a trance for hours.

Over the later years, Willie had compiled notes detailing the results of the barn experiments. They were a hodgepodge of typed sheets, handwritten pages, some loose notes on napkins, and other scraps of paper. I would discover the fragments called The Fan-Shaped Destiny scattered among them, their narrative thread weaving like a serpent throughout. He expressed his desire that I take it with me when I left.

He had also prepared for shipping the mural Marjorie had painted, which he knew I loved, irrespective of its source. In its case, Marjorie's guilty obsessions paralleled Willie's own, so it was very forceful. We were all there: heroic "Willie of Arabia," drunk Willie, Piny, his girl-mother Myra, our darling Katie, Marjorie, and even little me, dangling from a doorway wearing only my red leather mask. I was not even dismayed that I came off looking incongruously _cute_!

He also had me select what I wanted from among the memorabilia. I chose the _Yezidee_ bridal belt from Mount Lalesh, to go and stay with the Arabian bracelets and chains he had given me twenty years beforehand; also some of the African demon masks from Wamba's tribe. Another of my regrets was not meeting her, about whom Katie had spoken much.

It must have been the most unadulterated denial that blinded me from seeing him disposing of his affairs. Willie could scarcely be accused of having been a quiet man, and I had assuredly learned enough of psychology to appreciate what his rare peaceful demeanor might portend. Did a similar blindness prevent me from being helpful to my daughter, or could that have been as Willie hinted in the manuscript? When you read it, you must determine the measure of my guilt, which I cannot escape bequeathing to you as well.

Whatever the case, I chose instead to credit some notions that I would have dismissed at another time. Even as I wonder today at the broad sweep of Willie's imaginative brush, I would not be inclined to test it. Willie did have some prominent friends, numbering among them some of the leading scientists of the day. More recently he had struck up acquaintance with some of those writers of scientific romance, as he called it, after the English fashion. They had been privy to government projects during the war years. He fumed that those contacts had been severed because he had been deemed, for no apparent reason, a security risk.

It never would have occurred to Willie that they might have merely taken him as a loon! If his ramblings about a past, not even as ever popularly perceived to have been, sounded impracticable, his transitional elements were natural enough. When he spoke of Walter Duranty's intimations of a blanket of secrecy and a frightening passion for control coming down over our country, it sounded not so far-fetched, even less so in retrospect.

Young people of today, many so like our own "lost generation," rebel against the sophistry of society. I ponder how sad it is that they have not been permitted the truth about us. Be on the qui vive for this, my child, because it is personally important to you: history as we know it is so often a lie. I believe that the prevarication begins at home and percolates upward, not the reverse. Your mother's ill fortune was being reared in a place where the children were regularly lied to, about every last thing that had framed their reality. Confronting adulthood, she cannot imagine a life on terms other than copy-book twaddle.

While I doubted that the most demented of Federal employees would regard Willie's psychic experiments as aught but an alibi for outlandish sexual games, he was working off some disturbing facts. I was reminded of confidences gleaned from my clientele in the course of business. Something dreadful had, I knew, been swept under the rug in Philadelphia, two years past, and I was mindful of other pieces of "non-history." The cold-blooded murder of lovely little Dresden is only now being owned up to. There are other things that will never become a part of your reality. Was it a phantasm, that hot summer night in New Orleans, when I lay awake listening to the explosions as U-boats torpedoed barges in the Mississippi? Lie would pile upon lie. In the depths of the stagnant decade that followed, Aldous and Willie's nightmares of a universal banality would seem to have come true.

My Lord in heaven, Justine! I meander because it is so difficult to write, even now. I agreed to take the big portfolio with the entire collection of notes, professedly for safekeeping. Then we slept in each other's arms one last time. I remember that there was a terrible storm, and I awoke from some grisly nightmare that I could not later remember. Then I went away. It was the following week before I found convenience to look through the material and begin to impose some semblance of order upon the grotesque calendar embedded in it. Then I began to read with captivation and an increasing urgency.

The Fan-Shaped Destiny described a world much like our own, but not; the histories and fates of people I had known so well, myself included, so distorted. Parts bore an uncanny resemblance to Jimmy's fiction, and I recalled Willie's frequent hospital stays in recent years. Might there have been good reason? Could he no longer separate real memory from I knew not what? His narrative gave mad, literal twists to otherwise common enough metaphors. Willie ever had trouble with time, but while he might exercise artistic license, he would always end by telling the truth. By the time I found the buried fragments that contained a personal message, making myself construe their suicidal intent as not fictional; oh dear, it was already too late.

I was in a stew about what to do. Should I try to telephone, dash up? I did not want to have speech with Constance. I had already begun to make arrangements, though I had never been on an aeroplane and still do not much relish the idea of flying. Then Santolina came to my door. Not expecting to find me at home, she had written a note. When I looked at her face, then down to what she held in her hand, I knew, even before I read the heartbreaking little news clipping that was attached. "Rhinebeck, N.Y. Sept. 20, William B. Seabrook, 59, American author and explorer, was found dead Thursday at his Dutchess County farm home . . ." "Oh Willie, Willie, don't go without me again," my heart screamed. "Put me in your pocket and take me with you. Please, can't you?"

Santolina had written on the back in pencil, "This belongs in the book," meaning Willie's autobiography. So, I taped it inside the back cover of No Hiding Place, where it is to this day. When I closed the cover and placed it back on the bookshelf, as though admitting our story had ended, it seemed I must surely lose my mind. Sometimes, just knowing someone is there is enough, even if you cannot be together. Knowing that they are out there and happy, or even out there and miserable, but that you may someway get home and make things better . . . but this, this "no more forevermore forever," as Willie used to say. The thought of the years ahead without him was unbearable.

I had to call Marjorie, for he had been the love of her life, too. When I had to speak the unmentionable words to her, to tell her he was gone, was the first time I totally broke down. Finally I had stopped hating her for coming betwixt Willie and Katie. I took time to leave a message for Walter, begging him to go to Marjorie. Then I packed and went to be with Katie. Thank God for Katie, en or massif, as good as gold. His child would have pulled me through this utterly wrong, hateful world, in which William Seabrook did not exist. So soon was I to lose her as well, like her father, dead by her own hand. For long after that, it was Katie's love that stayed my hand from joining me with my lost ones.

---

The task of assembling the scattered fragments of The Fan-Shaped Destiny became another salve to my grief. As I read the narrative woven serpentine through Willie's last effort, the proposal that he had hoped the barn experiments would support was revealed to me, and my sadness was diluted with wonder. Could such things be? Again, I must be circumspect, but I studied for myself the queer reckoning of time in Willie's books. I have first editions of them all; I leave them to you as well. I had taken these peculiarities to represent artistic liberty and, though rarely, self-serving distortion. Then his explanation led me to compare them with Jimmy's story; and later, with Marjorie's book as well.

Instead of the ravings of a madman, I began to perceive a weave. To Santolina alone was I comfortable voicing my suspicions. She took me to meet more friends and cousins from the darker side of her family, not referring to the color of their skin, in Mississippi and Louisiana. They taught me of ideas undreamed-of and produced facts to back them up. I learned how the lives we think we know, in the words of a greater writer than my darling Willie, "fork and swirl and run parallel, unaware of each other for long, and may eventually converge." Also I learned a discipline, largely from the manuscript, but partially from those ladies, mambos, as they called themselves. In that they may no longer be there in your time, I will not further direct your attention to them.

What is required of you, my child, is to journey to Rhinebeck, for which I am so sorry, but it must be done. The manuscript and its allied material are being held for you by a law firm in Kingston, across the River from Rhinebeck. It came there during my efforts to have it published. Despite the assistance of the Montagues and other influential friends of Willie's, I could never overcome legal difficulties with his estate. Conceivably, there were larger reasons as well. After Marjorie's attempt to revive interest in his work failed, something else happened, which inspired my determination to oblige you to go and collect it.

My Willie had left me a map that I have been resolved to one day follow. Last year, something else occurred that showed me how scantily we appreciate the rich tapestry of our existences. I had opened up a private club, out toward Stone Mountain. That property will also come to you, though I am doubtful that the club itself will much survive me. Santolina is gone now, as well, and naught but we could maintain the always tenuous relations with authority.

We had booked in a young dancer whose husband was traveling with her. I talked long with them both, about which I will say little, lest you think me mad as my favorite author. Only that in his early youth, the young man had loved your mother. What I learned from them made me mindful of how lifelines destined to converge may not do so to our liking, but tentatively approach each other, then draw apart. This may go on, like a teasing mating dance, till they finally intersect. Should you cross his path again, remember me to him, the strange old woman from another lost generation whose destiny touched his for a brief interval.

At last, an old lady is very tired. Yet there burns a spark as bright as the constellations of those magical nights betwixt the wars. Perchance it will flame up again. So I will to bed and you, soon to Rhinebeck, to "time and the River." There you will read The Fan-Shaped Destiny and remember me. Should you, in that dark place, feel something so very close to your heart, dread not, for I will be with you. We are separated only by time; and believe me when I tell you that love is not diminished by death.

*Madeleine Beiris, "Justine"*

---

THE GODS LAUGHED as my mind recoiled from the brief horror revealed on the final page of the old woman's *Testament*. It left me no more shaken than did her account of the news of Willie's death, and the little news clipping that had broken her heart. The clipping that had now returned to its home in my black-leather lawyer's case. The proof was inside a book cover, written in pencil in the hand of another woman. I had not even questioned that "Santolina" was other than a pure work of fiction contrived by Ward, or "Jimmy" Greene. That page had so many typos and strikeovers, mute testimony that she could barely see to write it. It still bore evidence of having been moistened, and I knew that she had wept again when she read it over, twenty-five years after his death.

Maybe I was practicing my own avoidance as I touched the little depressions and smudges and thought, *this is the real reason that suicide is wrong.* He might have lived less than another decade, but he had made her grieve for him the rest of her life. So many extraordinary women had loved Seabrook. Why wasn't that alone enough to make him want to stay alive? I stared at the corner of the ceiling, much as I had stared at the treetops outside my home long years before, trying to send my mind into the infinite. Had the infinite now come for me? As at several times in my reading, a wintry sharpness prickled over me.

Justine was standing in the doorway, returned from the kitchen with a bottle of gin, tonic water, and two glasses. Smart girl to bring the bottle, I thought. Though a Scotch drinker, I accepted a strong pour gratefully. At that point I wouldn't even have declined a snort of that powder in her little box.

I was thinking of a tragedy in the sixties, when my friend George was the victim of a political killing. It was the worst thing that had yet happened in the young lives of most of his friends, but paradoxically, seemed also the confirmation of all we believed about the malevolence of the state. Conversely, the words just read, which I might take as confirmation or at least strong suggestion of a paranormal dimension to our existence, could and did scare the shit out of me.

"So there was something else you had forgotten to mention," I stated the fact without rancor.

"Identify, much?" she raised her eyebrow.

"She's not descriptive about the young couple, but I have the horrible feeling that it can't be anyone else." I looked at my leather case and dreaded the further revelation. "And you waited until now to tell me because . . . ?"

"Do you get it now—why I was so wigged?" she pressed. "Believe me when I say it was not *even* the extreme coincidence of you and my mother? Hey, I really thought you had to live it for yourself, I really did."

I gestured my understanding. No, I could not have believed it until I'd seen it for myself. I went to my case, screwing up my courage for grudging admission to the still less plausible, and handed her the book where she perched on the edge of the tall bed. "It doesn't end there, Justine. Here is Seabrook . . ." I recalled another stunning disclosure that might go far to explain her empathy with my obsession. At least a few things were becoming clearer! "Here is your, your great-grandfather's autobiography." I turned away and stood at the window, watching the lightning bursts above the dark hills. I wanted to cry, and couldn't keep my voice steady, "Look inside the back cover."

Behind me, there was an indeterminate silence, then an incredulous "Get outta here!" When I turned back to her, she hardly seemed frightened like me. Rather, her eyes were wide like a child's on Christmas morning, and she held the book clasped against her breasts with both hands, as if it were the most wonderful gift.

"I think it's time we left off talking about 'coincidence.' This feels more as though we've fallen into the hands of the living God! That book"—I pointed an unsteady finger—"lay on these shelves for thirty years, then disappeared after the old woman was gone. It spent other decades in a library, of all things. The clipping stayed taped right there, Santolina's note to Madeleine identifying it.

"It's the very book she wrote of to you, Justine, *intended* for you. It passed from hand to hand, until it was sold again to my San Antonio book dealer. It's like it went out *looking* for you, babe—finally coming to me, shortly before I was to meet you and bring it back here! What is this thing, what is my connection, and how long has it been going on, for God's sake?" This had all gotten too heavy to put up any kind of a front.

"What Carl Jung said? An event is not, like 'synchronicity,' till it's consciously perceived as meaningful. Delaying that recognition by twenty, thirty years, *is* pushing the envelope!"

I looked at her earnestly, "For two years, I agonized over every revelation of possible close encounters with your mother, when, arguably, I still might have been able to alter our history. Those thoughts would make me want to scream every time another instance was revealed." I shook my head. "Had I known what's in your letter, that I was so close to her grandmother only five years after I'd lost JJ, I think I most certainly would have gone mad!"

"*What-ev-er.* Coinkydinks, then." At my look, she playfully expanded. "Co-ink-ee-deenks—like, synchronicity?" I expressed dismay if the future of psychology was being represented, and she smiled just a bit sadly, "Better oughta drop a chill pill, dearest. If you had known . . . hey, then you could've been my father. *Au contraire,* I might've never been born."

---

RICHARD, I THOUGHT, I'M STILL NOT LAUGHING! After a while, the rain was slowing, and I assured her that the last thing I could sanely want was a world with no Justine. We concluded that, in spite of everything, we were hungry. She hadn't much food in the house, and Buford was a predictable redneck heaven as regards cuisine. Justine was thinking more like French or Greek, so we drove into Atlanta.

She filled me in on the elder Justine's business history, as she'd gathered it from lawyers and locals. The old woman had owned what sounded to have been the classic brothel with exclusive clientele. It had flourished through the Depression, the war years, and well into the fifties, fine old decadent Atlanta being what it was. Around 1957, she'd made all the money she wanted and retired, but amused herself in her late years with the burlesque club and *The Château*. Its bizarre sidelines were evidently a product of having the money and influence to do as she wanted, profitable or no.

I couldn't complain about the meal. Justine's choices were excellent though often strange—but my steak *au poivre* cost a small fortune. Among the things about the girl that I rarely saw change, even in four-star restaurants, were her eating habits. Maybe a slightly hyperactive twenty-six-year-old metabolism was involved, but Justine ate like a pig at the trough.

Let me clarify this as a comment more on manners than quantity. They were less pronounced against her punker slouch than amidst the moments of weirdly poised elegance. Her command of the correct forks came off as a virtual *abuse* of etiquette. Watching her almost literally *wading* through her plate of escargot was an appalling sight. I asked if she were enjoying the blue sauce, which looked like it might be effervescing radon gas.

"Scrumptious," she grinned, the expression leaving me a bit bemused. I wondered if that, like "big eyes" for ambition, was something *else* that Gen-X imagined they'd invented. With our wine, we pored over the questions raised by the surviving library, and dissected various aspects of the *Testament*.

"While I was looking for more data on Willie's relations with Aleister Crowley, I was scanning the index of Crowley's *Confessions* for Seabrook's name. Back up the list, I spied Tony Sarg, whom I recognized from *No Hiding Place* as having employed 'Deborah Luris.' The reference took me to a detailed description of the tantrums and general fussiness of a woman named 'Madeleine,' procured by Sarg as a companion for Crowley's trip. Crowley remembered her like this:"

> . . . wonderful hair—orange-red curls, calculated to produce delirium tremens at a moment's notice . . . a short sturdy figure trimly tailored, with a round smiling face, and an ivory complexion framed in that pyrotechnic display of hair. Sarg's eloquence failed to do her justice.[61]

"Later, I noticed that Marjorie had referred to a Madeleine, supposedly their Gypsy cook at Les Roseaux." I handed her Worthington's book, which I'd brought along with us. "On page 150, she also describes a visit with Willie at a hospital, in the fall of 1933 when he was trying to detox. Seems like there was often a red-haired woman about."

Justine found the place where Marjorie had walked in to find Willie talking with Ward Greene, and another friend, an unidentified attractive redhead. The joking and laughing had ended in a sudden awkward silence, as if Marjorie were someone who had arrived late at a cocktail party. She had reflected that these people had been part of Willie's life before she had known him, sharing old jokes, secrets, and adventures.

"For a moment she felt a strange relief," I pointed out. "She imagined that Willie could somehow *slide*

---

61. Crowley, *Confessions*, pp. 784–787.

*back in time*, become well again. Then the eerie mood broke. Almost as though to convince herself, she then asserts that none of them could be the same as they were a minute or years before."

"*That* sounds like a twisted sister. You s'pose Marjorie was all—about a french fry short of a Happy Meal? Ooh, look here . . ." Justine continued reading, "'Ward Greene, *whom everyone called Jimmy*, said something funny . . .' That's dead on!"

I nodded. "There's not the slightest question of the people Madeleine wrote about." I told her of a photo section in the back of *Jungle Ways*, depicting Seabrook and Wamba heading up their party, also a rare photo of Katie Seabrook in Africa. Justine continued to leaf through the book as I talked. "The lesser-known legend about dead drummer boys and suicided girls sounds like something I read in a piece called 'Gregory's Drum' . . ."[62]

Justine waved interruption, reading from late in Marjorie's account, "And one evening my telephone rang, and at the other end was a woman who had loved Willie, too. She told me he had been found in his bed . . ."[63] She broke off and, when she looked up her eyes had moistened and her lip trembled. "We know who called her, don't we? You feel it, too; I know you do. Don't ask me to believe other."

I did not ask. I knew exactly what she meant. I

62. Higgins, Susan, "Gregory's Drum," *Taler's Tales Publications*, Fall 1995.

63. Worthington, *Strange World*, p. 248.

had felt it at least since we had entered the octagonal room, where a poignancy nothing less than tangible clung to every possession—of a woman who had worshiped the memory of a lost love. Justine, of course, was fixated on the personality of William Seabrook.

"Hey, I'm way sure he's the only father figure I'm ever gonna have." Well, I decided to let that one go right by, noting she could find that ancestry in the autobiography, including his contention that black magic was in the blood. He had written of his ancestor Peter Boehler, of the Moravians, associate of Count Zinzendorf and John Wesley. Upon being accused of witchcraft in his later years, the old churchman had contended that he had only been fighting fire with fire.

I also noted that Madeleine's Lowell Thomas reference was to be found under the heading "Possibility of Precognition" in Seabrook's book on witchcraft. I still didn't "spoil" the two chapters on the other Justine by going too far into that material. In a bit of surly perversity, I think I was then feeling that she was falling too far behind on the shock quotient, and should get to share more impact of all this fun! There is a standing joke that the nice thing about being a guy is not having to deal in feelings. After the emotional overload of the recent days, I was perfectly happy to engage in some well-earned denial.

"What's up with the place where my mother, and all the children, were always lied to?" she asked.

I sighed. "She couldn't have been more right about *that*. A substantial percentage of the respectable matrons of postwar east Fort Worth had formerly been on staff at a fine old establishment called Top-O-The-Hill. It was near where Lake Arlington was built in 1957. 'What did you do in the war, Mommy?' was not a question to be countenanced on the pious east side.

"Babe, I see 'sluts,' like apparently your entire maternal lineage, your *gens*, as partisans in a revolution whose benefits you are reaping. There was a sexual revolution and the 'bad girls' won! Some were victims, like your mother and, evidently, her mother." The steely armor did not reappear, so I pressed ahead. "The 'morality' those girls were taught was a monstrous obscenity, that they would burn in hell for loving. In reality, the only rule was not to get caught. When she did, JJ believed that, despite the ring on her finger, she was an unlucky loser—damned to control by a vicious animal she had to try to please."

Justine looked askance. "Was there some kinda law that she had to marry him? She could've been with you."

---

"SHE BELIEVED HER PERSONAL LIFE ENDED RIGHT THERE. Even had she been able to make that choice, the fact that she got knocked up forced her to ally herself with *some* man." I thought of the young JJ as she had been before. "She was such a good little poet. Did you know that? Maybe it helped her hold on to some semblance of self-esteem. It was as near a tragedy as her mother . . ." My emotions were in a horrible tangle. Reaction to the uncanny events and the hurts and regrets of the past bled into each other. Somehow, I had to draw back from all this for a while.

Justine nodded and spoke softly, "I love you for that, I really do. But you can't go there, 'twixt Mother and me—big issues! I gotta tell you that I agree with the *Testament*. These big 'differences' are muchly a matter of one generation always lying to the next. Hey, other than JJ, please?"

"There's something to that. I truly loved all that part about nonhistory," I complied. "In the time and place where JJ and I were trying to grow up, no thought was allowed unless it suggested the desirable social and political conclusions. I guess that's why I despise concepts like 'politically correct,' and I imagine that the old woman regarded it as a hideous little hellhole."

I speculated that you could extend that proposition, as Seabrook had apparently begun to do. The postwar reaction had not been exclusively against political ideas—also sexual nonconformity. A largely successful campaign had been launched to convince the entire "Boomer" generation that personal liberties had never been broader than they, themselves, were experiencing. The Orwellian madness then spread like an oil slick. The most bizarre censorship had been directed at obscuring the nature and implications of scientific knowledge—especially, though not solely, as it had related to the recent war.

"Even today, we only get tidbits on such anomalies as the occasional V-One rocket bomb found unexploded on American soil. Back when JJ and I were in grade school, the public-school buildings still had the residue of blackout paint on the windows. Suppose that wasn't an unnecessary precaution?"

"Back in the day, there was this totally weird buzz on, about an explosion at Medina Base." Justine named the San Antonio depot where nukes were still stored.

I confirmed her childhood memory of a dark rumor, "Except that it was long before you were born, back in the fifties. There was damage throughout the city, and it's still classified. Babe, if you could visit the past, I think you'd find it a very different place than we assume, almost an alternate world in itself, just due to the lies that have become 'common knowledge.'

"Mark Twain was only a bit more fanciful when he visualized a time traveler initiating an industrial society centuries before a social and economic base existed to sustain it. He was realistic to have it disappear, except for tiny 'anomalies,' not dissimilar to the sorts of things archaeologists really find."

"What are we thinking here? Please, where are you trying to go?" I was aware that I'd been bouncing off the walls, using peripheral conjectures to avoid the troubling central revelations. My implausibly "happenstance" involvement with no less than two previous generations of her family had been revealed as only the beginning. My quest to reconcile my personal issues had culminated in both an "inadvertent" return to the presumed source of that line and, "coincidentally," an open-ended involvement with yet a third generation! I wasn't ready to deal with it all, and she'd been willing to tolerate my digressions.

"Visualize this, as if you were reading a science fiction novel. American scientific magazines become embroiled in the burning question of communication with the dead, while a decadent intelligentsia waffles among fascinations from sentimental belief in guardian angels to embrace of sexual sadomasochism. In the heartland, fascistic movements obsessed with ancestral heritage battle with working-class communists. A dread of alien invaders provokes panic while the real powers arm for Armageddon with everything from high technology to black magic, and virtual secret societies seize control of national security and communications. An alternate world?"

"Hate rhetorical questions, *hate* them!" She slurped at her *étouffé*. "What? A near-future scenario?"

"The autumn of 1938. My only point with this is that we are not, in any sense, highly knowledgeable about a 'real' past. For argument's sake, postulate an alternate past in which the 'problem-solving group' at the Philadelphia Naval Yards was very high-powered.[64] They and their colleagues had written science fiction in much the same way as former intelligence personnel have written spy fiction.

"Assume further that the so-called Philadelphia Experiment did involve tinkering with space-time, as has been represented in some fiction. There would have been heavy security on this, to be sure, just as

64. Isaac Asimov, Robert A. Heinlein, and L. Sprague de Camp. Murray Leinster (Will F. Jenkins) told Michael Swanwick that he had been an informal consultant to the Group. (Comments from Swanwick at the Fifty-fifth WorldCon.)

around the Manhattan Project." I was reminded of the story of the 1944 raid on the office of *Astounding Science Fiction*. "Greg Benford wrote that the Manhattan Project was so afraid of imagination, disciplined with facts and numbers, that it feared science fiction itself.

"Willie could, with at least a marginal interest in 'scientific romance,' have been aware of some of this. Other science fiction writers, in particular Murray Leinster, who, you'll remember, had written the first branching-worlds story in 1934, were picking up on things. Maybe Willie knew Leinster. Continue this chain of remote associations to the physicists he knew, like Bayard Rodman. Or his friend Robert Wood, who, having written some of the earliest science fiction, was part of that community.

"Willie's published work in the forties leaves no doubt of his obsession with space-time. The barn experiments were about seeing across time and realities, as well as tickling his pickled libido. But all that aside, I must believe Seabrook's alleged late obsession with government was not much more than that. While the Feds may have cast a wide net for anything they paranoically imagined a threat to U.S. scientific hegemony, Willie was not engaged in anything that remotely approached hard science.

"I think it's safe to assume that, nearing the end, he was not the most stable personality of whom you've ever read," I concluded. "I relate to him too well for that! I'm only stressing that in the 'real' era of the Second World War, as opposed to the conventional assumptions we hold about those times, it was probably easy enough to imagine anything.

"Fun conjecture somewhere has to run up against bedrock science, and some of the more colorful propositions of science fiction must be discounted. None of the rationales that may have affected Willie's thinking do a thing to increase the probability of fantasies such as, say, security considerations of secret government projects to alter history."

"So like, not incredible to direct a far-reaching paranoia?"

I nodded. "Regarding Duranty, I would have thought that it would have taken some more years' decay of his career before he lapsed into paranoia.[65] But it's likely that *any* speculations from his nefarious buddy might have set Willie off." Of course, I was prepared to pontificate further, to edify this babe with an area wherein I could at least pretend to be in command of what was going on.

"At the same time, you're way sure his work was suppressed? For why, because of the S 'n M?" Before I could answer, she shifted gears and her speech changed even more perceptibly. "What about choosing among futures? Did my great-grandmother manipulate things that have happened to you now? As if some kinda witchy thing?"

"Maybe the old woman cast a spell, that's still

65. Taylor, op. cit., p. 351. "Even during these years of extreme paranoia, when the 'Red Scare' was reaching its peak, the FBI made the decision not to investigate Duranty . . . Duranty had ceased to be of interest to the Bureau after January, 1951."

working itself out? If not manipulated, I must believe that it has been something in the nature of her precognition. The 'coinkydinks' are just too weird. But what else does it insinuate if I take her at her word that Linda and I only *happened* to book into her club?"

Justine gazed into her wine. "Dearest, she had only then become aware of you, years after you broke off with JJ," she reminded me softly. "How not take her word? Oliver Stone couldn't write the conspiracy theory that has your entire life manipulated!"

"It's true, babe. Even as I talk, I hear myself spiraling into the same paranoia wherein I classified Willie. Indulge an old man. Before Oliver Stone, we had Ian Fleming." I instructed her as to the old James Bond epigram, "One time is happenstance, two times is circumstance—three times is enemy action." I threw up my hands. "And what of the goddamned book that seems to have always been waiting for me to bring it back to you, which sought me out as though it was sentient?"

There was a smaller point that was troubling me more and more. "By her admission, she hints at as least as much as she says. So, what are we to do with, 'Should you cross his path again,' rather than 'as well'? Did I meet you before now, and she had foreseen it? I did live in the same city with you for ten years. Or did she just mean . . . oh hell, I don't know!"

A thousand other questions plagued my mind as avoidance of the central issues began to break down. I poured the last of the wine to slow the wheels in my head. I then began to confess my misapprehensions that I might be solely a vehicle for the realization of her destiny, or recovery of her heritage.

She grinned impishly, "Disturbing, much, male egoist?"

"I guess not," I conceded, "only if it did not mean that I ultimately lose you." Now I was giving up the commitment she'd sought on the pier, and I felt my mortality heavier than ever before. "I mean, one day you will have to go on alone, but until then . . ." I looked up and realized I'd blundered as the green eyes clouded and she bit down hard on a knuckle. *God,* I thought, *she can't cope with that at all, and rushed to banish the dark cloud.*

"Look, babe. Priestley believed Dunne's theory as applied to personal survival. Once freed from the linear time we know, you may build up any sort of heaven or hell from the figures in your experience. He wrote that it would be a hell of loneliness if they were merely chimeras for your own gratification, that you have to learn to build to please others.[66] Maybe a good idea to do that in this life?" Did I believe that, I

66. Priestley, *Man and Time*, NY: Doubleday, 1964 (Crescent, 1987) 1964, pp. 260–261—quoting from Dunne's two later books, *The New Immortality*, London: Faber, 1938, and *Nothing Dies*, London: Faber, 1940, ". . . your attention may visit a scene, and you may see again the one you seek. You may hear again the spoken words, you may receive and give the same caresses. But the attention of that other may not be there . . . You can meet again every one you have ever known, at any age you can remember. They will welcome you gladly—if you wish it. They will acknowledge that you had been right, after all, in those little quarrels . . . It will be a terrible moment when you realize that the words are dictated by you . . . You will have what you have always wanted . . . a little heaven of private pleasure—and a hell of utter loneliness. To avoid, or to escape from that, you must be willing to surrender some of your sovereignty."

wondered? Another notion in which I'd lost faith years before—that unselfish conduct might constitute survival behavior?

"*Kewl*, I win!" Justine exulted. "If you really wanna build to please me, I want you to take me to the *Wild Orchid*."

# VII
# The Châteaux

*WILD ORCHID* WAS THE PRESENT-DAY NAME OF WHAT had been the elder Justine's Peachtree Street burlesque club. Though still freaked, I was intrigued with the prospect of verifying that I had been there before, "in another life," so to speak. Coming on it cold, I would never have been able to recognize it. The classy, if campy, place I'd remembered on a seedy street had become, thirty years later, a rather shabby place on a restored street. A modest lounge, which featured a band, had attached to an oyster bar on the street floor. The burlesque showroom with its small theatrical stage had been upstairs.

The present-day outfit also operated lounge style, with an occasional go-go girl, but their real business was a nude joint on the second floor. At first, I wondered to Justine if it indeed was the same place. While the lounge room looked familiar, there was no oyster bar, nor did it seem there was any space for one. The upstairs seemed smaller, as well, despite being absent the stage where Linda had performed with the magician. I doubted that the enclosure in the center, which had the character more of a pit than a stage, would occupy equivalent space.

Only when we were passed by the door charge did I recall that I was accompanying this property's landlady. The operator would have been naturally solicitous anyway, even had the weeknight business not been slow. With some amusement, I found it relaxing to be back in an arena where having a woman half my age on my arm was worth no extra looks! The operator confirmed that the building had once been larger. Fire had wasted the oyster bar, long before, and that entire half of the building had been sold.

"Where did you first meet her?" Justine had become quite taken with the recognition that I possessed some small living memory of her predecessor. "You said she was sitting back in the dark."

"Gone." I gestured to the wall beyond which the other half of the room had been lost to fire. "The office as well." Since hearing about Linda's desire to work at the roadhouse, the setting of the "interview" had fascinated her.

After witnessing the activities out there, Linda had so wanted those experiences for herself that she could taste them. Another featured dancer had been obtained from the agency, to the magician's distress, and Linda had been "interviewed" in the office late on a Friday night. In an effective ritual, she had been stripped and probed with questions about her sexuality. She'd then been driven, still naked, out to *The Château* to assume the position in which we'd observed the young blonde. It occurred to me that the girls hanging from the balcony had been reminiscent of the "living decor" that had edified visitors to Seabrook's apartments in Paris and New York.

I'd described to Justine the way her great-grandmother had appraised me when she handed me the bundle of Linda's clothing, declaring offhandedly that it was a good night for an initiation, the patrons more aggressive. She had told me that we would go out and watch. I could have helped do the honors if I'd wished, but, in that the other girls tended to be more implacable, she recommended that I leave Linda to them. The high erotic charge of the situation, as thus described, had not been lost on one such as Justine.

I was reviewing these memories while Justine, maybe just a bit aroused, blatantly flirted with the operator. "The studly says they do hot-oil wrestling on Thursdays," she whispered with a giggle. I glanced at "studly." No slimier than he ought to be, I concluded. *What-ev-er.* She then began regaling us with tales of an adventure in mud wrestling during her college days. I reflected on how big an ass I might have sounded the previous night—declaiming, as though to an innocent, on the history of the skin trade!

Watching the operation, a typical nude joint running a drink hustle, amused her. A tall girl, who reminded me of Linda in her younger days, was working a customer in a booth. Their backs to us, her gown straps were loose on her bare shoulders, hinting that it was unfastened down the front. Their postures in the dim light, plus her sporadic twitches and small sounds, insinuated that mutual masturbation was in progress.

I studied Justine, her eyes shining and nostrils a bit flared. Indubitably the progeny of old Justine, I thought, and a girl after my own heart.

"In the technical jargon of your professional staff, 'heavy mix,'" I joked.

I've had it supposed that, because my general politics are far to the left, I somehow forfeit the right to enjoy such crass "exploitation." Allow me to clarify: I did not spend a life fighting the system, at great personal cost, to further advance institutional intrusiveness. I believe the right of individuals to "exploit" themselves and their endowments, inclusive of the sale of sex, to be undeniable. Finally, I resist any cadre presuming to monitor public morals, whether self-appointed or state-sponsored. Any questions? Told you I'm a cranky old man.

---

"DUDE, I WANNA DANCE." Justine grinned mischievously. "Gimme tunes!" The operator registered surprise, then started looking for opportunity. He was thirtysomething, clean-shaven with ponytail and earring, in a good suit with dark shirt buttoned to collar without tie; official hard-guy uniform of the nineties. A kind of younger version of me, in fact, and could grow a better tail. Should I be concerned? I cautioned under my breath that she had a business relationship to consider.

"My bad, tonight." She waved me off with a grand indifference. "You can punish me later." Again, be perfectly clear that I had no basic problem with any of this. I'd once spent enough years around that business as to be jaded to things that most seem to find highly kinky. While I wasn't sure whether her playing about sexually would be the same rush for me, as in my younger years, I knew for certain that inhibition would be counterproductive.

If I were serious about keeping a youngster like Justine, I'd best be prepared to let her play. Our emotional bond appeared to be a given. Hell, no potential contender had any outside chance of touching the convoluted thing going on between us. My unnatural advantage appeared to be absolute.

Why did it not surprise me when he generously offered her some costume from his office downstairs? She gave me a teasing kiss before running off to change. When she returned, she was adorned deliciously sluttish in a black, thigh-length cover-up, which opened down the front to display her pierced navel and provide a glimpse of the front of her panties. I marveled again at those legs, "You should wear high heels just as much as you can stand."

Waiting for the music to be cued up, she snuggled beside me. "He sat on the couch in the office, checking me out, while I changed," she whispered, "so I stripped bare before I put anything back on. Thinks he's all that, he really does. He's gonna be all over me. Are *we* thinking he should get lucky?"

"Justine," I asked in good humor, "what are you doing?"

Her full lips parted sensuously. "Playing the whore," she breathed, and playfully grasped my crotch. "Hey, this gets you up, I know it does!" I could hardly deny that, and it had been years since I'd been turned on by anything seen or done in a skin joint. While I had no wonder that this display was largely for my benefit, I'd been learning never to be too sure I knew where Justine was going—with anything.

The music came up, and she went onto the low platform in the enclosure. She moved well, working directly to two guys at a stageside table. I appraised her while she got out of the cover-up; she was good for a novice. In another life she would have made a hell of a strip. Was that also what this was about? Was she demonstrating to me that she could do the dancer bit, as I'd described Linda to her?

I'm aware that some cannot imagine pleasure in watching a loved one in such a role. Some may be appalled, some disgusted. If you don't understand, I can't explain it to you; nor would I trouble myself to try. If this seriously repels you, don't look; and spare me meaningless little judgments.

Moving about a pole at center stage, she was grasping it with both hands above her head. Her high heels helped to throw her torso into an "S-curve," showing off her firm bottom. She was peeking at me over her shoulder and revolving slowly, reversing her grip but keeping her hands high up on the pole, pantomiming being tied to it. Then she locked eyes with me, sharply twitching her hips and belly to each beat, as if being struck.

I was getting thoroughly into it. Of course, *then* the operator had to decide to come back and visit with me. One of the very few upsides of age is that date of rank carries the privilege of ignoring idiots and dismissing bullshit. Not father, boyfriend; yes, looks like she's having fun; no, doesn't need the money; no, the rent will not change. Christ, he was likely to get laid out of it; wasn't that enough?

Justine got to her knees and crawled toward the pair at stageside, wagging her butt in cute exaggeration. She sensuously removed her shoes, then, instead of popping her pants, she gradually wiggled them down about her ankles. She left them there as she began the squirming undulations that the girls call "floor work."

She pushed herself up on her hands, jiggling her breasts, and spoke with the men in front of her. They laughed and looked at each other as she lowered her chest back onto the stage and thrust up her hands to them. Each taking a wrist, they held her as she writhed about and flexed her buttocks, again surely in pantomime of bondage and punishment.

The operator was going on about how she could play on his stage anytime. As she would say, I was *way* sure of that! She sat up, lost the panties, and thrust her legs with knees bent over the little tables, a bare foot in each guy's lap. She'd continued to converse, and it was with her clear consent that one reached to play with her labial rings.

When she lifted her hips and positioned herself, the better for him to grasp, I heard a sharp intake of breath from the operator. He was looking furtively about, clearly hoping there were no vice cops in the club. I expected some objection, but supposed he didn't want to piss her off. I laughed as he rushed to dim the lights way down, recalling Seabrook's precious line about the barely pubescent daughter of the *Druse* judge Ali bey Obeyid, ". . . A DANGEROUS AND INFLAMMATORY LITTLE BAGGAGE IF I EVER SAW ONE."

---

Whatever would he have thought, could he have met *this* babe?

Everything is relative to the perspective from which it's observed. Sitting in front of Justine's exhibition would have done less for me than watching her in profile, viewing the attitude of her entire body as she simulated the offering of her most intimate self. Too many years in joints, I guess.

The music winding down, she leaned back on her elbows, breasts and belly quivering, and gave herself up to the stimulation. Then she got up, gathered her things, and acknowledged some tips. In exciting counterpoint to her recent minutes, she posed her nude body with a gracious, almost stately ease. Without looking at me again, she strolled unhurriedly to the stairs.

As expected, she was gone for quite a while. A couple of other girls danced, and I took a sip of the gin she'd left on the table. It was cheap and metallic-tasting—how did she drink that stuff? I ordered another Scotch and reflected. I'd little doubt my earlier account of experiences with her great-grandmother had a role in precipitating this. Just which part had inflamed her to act out? Was it the torment of the blonde or the "slave auction" that had followed?

After watching the blonde's ordeal, I'd known that Linda's flush was not from anger. She'd pressed our hostess, with near urgency, for the detailed conditions of work at *The Château*. When informed that we were about to see a girl auctioned, the high bidder having the use of her until the following afternoon, I had thought Linda was about to faint!

Directly, a young woman had been led to the stage, a big girl with the hard musculature of a professional dancer. She'd stripped off her tunic, with unabashed pride, standing with shoulders back to present her large breasts to the audience. She accepted a collar strapped about her neck with a heavy leash-chain. It was forked, attaching both to the collar and to bands that had been locked on her wrists.

The bidding had been spirited and the girl had beamed as her price rose. Members, some who had clearly purchased her before, had shot jokes to her during the process. When a winning bid had stood, our hostess had laughed that there would be no hotel room for her. As her purchaser had led the girl, naked in her chains, to a table with two other men, she'd explained that they were partners in a tree-farm operation. They would take the girl to a bunkhouse they kept there, where they would get a real bargain and she would get a real workout.

The old woman had expressed doubt, though the girl had been young and strong, that she would make it in to work the next night. After all the years, I still remembered Linda's dazed query whether management took the circumstances into account, and the old woman's wryly melodramatic response. "But darling, you know the poor dear must get a whipping if she misses work." With throaty innuendo, "Suffering isn't nearly as delightful if it's entirely fair, is it? You've always known that, haven't you?"

While young Justine's sacrifice on the altar of lust, symbolic and otherwise, was hardly of that intensity, she was real and immediate. That other had been in "another world." When she eventually returned, hair somewhat disheveled, I eyed her sardonically.

"So, what's real?" She was smirking sexily, but her voice was very serious, again somehow changed. "What would've you preferred to happen? Teased him or gave it up? Hey, as if I went down on him, how 'bout?"

I've been around long enough to know that she was trying to provoke and torment me to her own ends. I didn't want to burst her bubble but, unlike Seabrook, I had no habit of beating myself up over simplistic Freudian jealousy. My guilt runs a lot deeper than that. "Which makes it hurt so good that it confirms my love for you?" I offered.

She considered, sipping her drink. "You down for

that; getting up on me giving it up? Maybe you *do* love me." She glanced at me slyly through strands of mussed hair. "Did I amuse?"

"I enjoy watching you offer yourself to others, if that's what you mean. 'Amusement' connotes an undertone of frivolity or silliness. You looked anything but silly. But, babe, in my mind it raises even higher the improbability of a girl like yourself having no other involvements."

She raised her eyebrow and feigned offense. "There *are* no other girls like me. Still being insecure? Pos we're not guilty about something? Those weren't really my friends at the Marriott, you know. I hired them from an agency!" She giddily threw her arms about me and burrowed into my neck, her mouth working passionately against the side of my head. Once more I felt the sensation that she would open up my skin and crawl inside.

"You'd better believe that tonight, I'll show you how totally *not* are offerings to any others, compared to what I wanna give to you."

While Justine drove very well, she was the bat as if from hell. My determination not to indicate that her speed was well beyond my comfort zone wasn't solely a matter of ego. I wanted to avoid any interference with her expressions of youthful exuberance. If such a policy sounds redundant considering what had just transpired, know that I then perceived so much about her to be of a wholly different order.

To say this young woman was wise beyond her years would be to minimize. For all her postadolescent energy and mannerisms, I could about believe that she could back up her paradoxical affects of jaded sophistication, a posture often ludicrous when struck by many of her young "Goths." Even the psychosexual twists that dovetailed my own with such eerie neatness, even her flagrant wildness seemed quite studied.

*Maybe* I understood the shape of her consuming passion to cast her instincts in a semblance of submission. She had wrested security from a hostile world by means of *"owning"* everything. Successfully bending and twisting all to her devices, there had been nothing left that could dominate her.

Or protect her, either—nothing she could lean on. It might be that her passion to give herself over was hardly that of a victim. Like a senator who seeks out hookers to bind and whip him, it could be testimony to her very power—power that seemed to burn again from her in a preternatural radiance.

I should mention that, having no natural children, I had helped raise some young cousins, a brother and sister, so had some experience with young people. Most young adults are quite inhibited. Even when they regard themselves as great rebels, they're typically quite selective in their nonconformity. Otherwise, they tend to be more blindly obedient to values and authority than supposedly sedate oldsters.

Put simply, Justine's psychology seemed far more complex than her experience should dictate. Her education alone couldn't explain this. In terms of the usual emotional spectrum, Justine was phase-shifted beyond the visible.

I was aware that the entertainment districts of many major cities had become liberally garnished with leather and chains from one end to the other. Nor was I oblivious to the dark sexuality of contemporary film—I was a fan! But the stretch of Justine's journey into darkness was not related to any chic system of alternative values of which I was aware. I could get no read other than her own take, that the emotional vacuum of her childhood had predisposed her to emulate those figures she had lately discovered to be her antecedents.

This intellectualizing was avoidance of yet something else. That was the sweet hurt in my chest, watching her in the dash lights while she raced the blue car down the expressways. During her discourse at the *Wild Orchid*, it had come to me that courtship had gone over into honeymoon. I'd already known that, somewhere in the strange dance of this ritual we'd been performing, in my heart I'd already been joined with her. The only choice I had left was when to confess. I didn't even really *want* to have an option.

---

STONE MOUNTAIN, THE HIGHWAY SIGN DIRECTED US.

*So,* I thought, *the black heart of Dixie.* It seemed that we were going directly on to *The Château*. About ten miles beyond the loop, she took an exit onto an access that seemed a remnant of some older artery. Hardly slowing, she suddenly careened onto the weed-choked remains of a parking lot. The Del Sol slid a bit on the residual gravel, as she spun it around to park behind a dark edifice.

She retrieved a bag and a long Mag-Lite from the backseat, and we made our way round the front of the building. It loomed monolithic, in the rising fog, as the granite hills around us. The stone wall beside us in the Southern night told me nothing; neither did the preframed metal door, with industrial-strength hasps and locks, which Justine was opening.

I held the flashlight, as she bolted and locked up again from the inside, then handed the keys to me as she picked up her bag. We crossed an empty vestibule to a doorway where another metal door stood open on, I sensed rather than saw, a dark cavernous space.

Years before, searching for potential club locations on the north side of Fort Worth, I'd stopped to look at a wooden barnlike building. It had been a long, tall, and narrow structure, someplace around the old stockyards, before the district was restored. Then I could never find that building again. It had drifted, as though out of a dreamscape, retreating back as I had driven away. Should I return to my hometown's streets and happen upon it, it would seem as much an apparition as when Justine turned on the lights in the big room.

Not much was left, but enough. The old bars, the railed balcony above, the broad stage flanked by the Grecian-looking columns. Behind it, the reflective paint of the mirrors had decomposed into a mottled iridescence. In light, at once stark and pale, from a few cleanup bulbs near the high ceiling, the faded murals remained just visible on cracked plaster walls. The real clubroom lighting was gone, of course, as were furnishings, bar equipment, and almost everything else.

"It's so *bare.*" Justine shivered with an indubitably erotic thrill. "It's like a Roman arena. This is it?" She looked to me.

I nodded toward the corner of the balcony. "There is where I sat with her while she elicited my life story. Extraordinary that she could listen to all that, recognizing JJ in it, without giving up a hint of anything."

She had followed my eyes and kept on staring while I spoke, as if straining to make out the old woman. I shared the numinous presentiment, in which the pale light might suddenly warp and twist around the years, tracing a shape of the past.

"Rewind, please. What you did to the blonde girl?" she whispered with a discernible gulp, nearly whimpering.

It had gone down close to where Justine and I were standing. The old woman had invited me to go examine the girl, an exercise most likely marking Linda's reaction. We'd been watching from the balcony, as members would stop by the chained girl and play with her, testing and teasing her displayed flesh. A latecomer, entering from the nippy fall without, had taken the liberty of warming his hands on her body, furthering her discomfiture.

Approaching her, I could see small bruises appearing on her well-handled skin. When I'd slid my hand between her thighs, she had compliantly hastened to spread her legs, stumbling on her toes on the carpeted floor. As I had gently stroked her sex, she'd smiled tearfully at me, though visibly uncertain what I might do to her next.

On an impulse, I had pulled a chair over to her and placed my foot flat on the seat. Then I had reached down and taken her under her knees and bare bottom, lifting her up to balance on my knee and thigh. This temporarily alleviated the strain that had been distributed along her body. She had moaned her surprised thanks, but I'd silenced her mouth with mine, then turned the attention of my lips to her hardening nipples, red and tender from being bitten.

She'd stared at me, wide eyed, as I'd kneaded her clit. I'd understood that her astonishment had been at her own stressed body, beginning to move toward climax under those conditions. I'd worked her harder, holding her on my knee as she had writhed uncontrollably. Finally, she had thrown back her head between her bound arms and screamed, as an extended series of orgasms gripped her.

The members nearby had laughed, some applauding her for giving them a good show. Giving her time to catch her breath, I'd considerately continued to fondle all her intimate areas while her spasms had abated. Her downcast eyes had beaded with fresh tears, as I'd restored her to her hanging posture, and I'd slapped her ass hard before returning to the balcony. Our hostess thought the performance inspired, pointing out that, even from up there, we could visibly see the blonde blushing from hairline to toes in her humiliation.

"The gentleness was an unexpected counterpoint. She was wholly vulnerable when she knew her most intimate responses to pleasure had been made into a spectacle, taken from her." I was working Justine for a reaction, trying to plumb the secret intimated by her demeanor. "When she was carried to have her responses to pain likewise evoked, she went into the agony sexually aroused."

As in a trance, Justine stepped onto the low stage platform and approached the columns. "And this is where it ended for her," she murmured, embracing one of the columns with her arms. It still sported the rings to which chains had attached. "This is where they whipped her," she stated as much as asked. "The other girls beat her till the switches broke." She recalled the way I had recounted it, while driving through the Mississippi darkness. "What if someone didn't wanna do it?"

"If they hadn't wanted to extend her pain, their only option would have been to strike harder, so that the switches would break faster. It wasn't over until all the switches were broken." Justine was flushed, and her eyes were moist, but I wanted to be sure she fully understood the intensity of those long-ago experiences, the differing assumptions of the times. For Gen-X, sadomasochistic sex rituals were more widely practiced; at a minimum, they were known. Now, no kind of sex is ever *approved* in America, but the fact of their popularity was at least acknowledged. In those other times, these had been forbidden pleasures in the extreme.

"Like it's been waiting here all those years, for me. I'm sure I was born for this!" I had, of course, surmised this evening might have been heading this direction, but I had to be very careful.

"Babe, you've known me less than seventy-two hours."

"I was way outta control at the Orchid." She was casting about, seeking what was required of her. "Don't you wanna punish me for that?" she asked, trying to sound light; but this was not a joke. I could feel her quaking as I touched her.

"Remember that I've been playing this game all my life," I told her, massaging the tense muscles in her shoulders. I'd resolved that we would not go off into a trivial, stylized scenario. This was too "up close and personal." "The only distress would have been any suggestion that, having found you, I might lose you, that you might dance off in a different direction."

She stood clutching her little bag in front of her with both hands. She looked, for all the world, like a young girl waiting at a terminal for her first long trip. "Nay, please. When you're finished with me tonight, I hope that thought is no longer possible. I've nowhere else to go, no place to hide." Even the abrasive punker dialect had softened.

She recited the obvious, like a catechism, and I knew it was for the pure thrill of hearing herself say the words. "I do wish I'd been that blonde girl, I really do, with so many watching me hurt. But this may be as if, more appropriate? Three days, for sure; no one knows where I am or whom I'm with. Miles from anyone, dead of night, and I can't get outta here." I remembered her handing me the keys.

---

"IN GEORGIA, NO ONE CAN HEAR YOU SCREAM?" she tried to quip, then went on with effort. "I've been brave so far, haven't I? That's why, in the bag—a whip and other things you might use to hurt me, and I tried not to be sissy when I picked them out. Like, all night if you want; whip me till I lose it. You can do anything you want to me, and I've tried every way I know to ask for it." Her anticipation was laced with a fear that was real enough, but when she concluded, "Hey, bring it *on*! While I've still got the ass for it?" I could sense she wasn't speaking of the pain, exactly.

I then regretted not having fully confessed my love to her, before these demands were put on it, but that would have to wait. The dominant role obliges much in timing and sensitivity. Anyone who thinks it only a matter of doing a number on a helpless person is a fool. Sadly, fools abound. At that moment, the prospect of giving Justine what she'd set herself up for was less appealing than the erotic thought of her in bondage. Most sadomasochistic sex is situational, yet her mind-set demanded that her pain threshold be approached—the very vulnerability that was stimulating her made real.

I took her bag from her and told her, coldly as I could manage, to take off her clothes, turning away to examine what she'd brought. I had to smile at the novice's choice of the Arabian manacles. Most adequate to the task, surely, had we been in the *Rufai* "Hall of Torture," but not if one is concerned with avoiding repeated visits to the hand therapist. There were various clamps, ropes, a whip that was a bundle of long thongs, with one set of ends strapped together to serve as a handle.

The leather was so old and dried as to look like something else she might have found in the house. I doubted that it would survive one good use. I regarded a seriously cruel-looking set of metal pincers. Considering the damage those could inflict, I thought *yes, it's true; she's no "sissy!"* Justine stumbled and nearly fell, awkwardly struggling out of her pants. Vanished, along with her typical speech, was the amateur stripper's grace. Still, this was but another variety of erotic image, and she was turning me on as I held the pincers close to her bare breasts.

"You were not really expecting these to be used?" was my noncommittal inquiry.

All was becoming too real for her easily to maintain a role. "Shit, I hope you don't." She grimaced at the "nasty gadget," looking askance with sincere dismay.

"I do know how to use them," I stated evenly, not intending to do any such thing, but I was getting myself in character. I let her stand there naked, tearfully hugging her belly, while I found some old bar rags to pad the manacles. I was entertaining images of Seabrook's Justine from *Witchcraft*. My plan, such as it was, had been largely to just let her hang by her wrists—until she was exhausted as I was becoming. Problem with younger women is that you always seem to have a tiger by the tail.

I threaded the rope between the old rings on the insides of the columns and dropped the ends. Then I manacled her wrists, which she obediently held out to me, palms together as in prayer. Justine shivered as the squeal of the locking bolts reverberated in the silence of our vault. She watched, with something like enchantment, each small step of what was happening to her. I rigged more rope, which could tauten that running between the columns, and secured the dangling ends to her manacles.

Like every submissive, her gaze had doted on the securing of first one hand, then the other. Her fingers splayed, as if exultant at relief from obligation to effect anything further. I advised her that it would go easier on her arms and shoulders, as long as she was able to hold on to the ropes that I pressed into her palms.

Wide-eyed, she nodded understanding and asked if I were going to tie her ankles. She was so appealing, in her abject exposure, that I kissed her deep and long to feel her quiver against me. When I told her that I wanted her sufficiently free to twist and turn, she moaned and parted her thighs to my touch, her excitement at a fever pitch. She blushed when I touched my fingers to her lips, for her to taste her own wetness, and tried to get her legs around me.

I denied her release. "If you come, it will be when your body betrays you, one more spasm of your flesh surrendering to what's happening to you." I hitched up the rope array, tying off my line to another ring at the base of a column. She gave a little startled cry when she was drawn taut, just barely able to balance on her toes, so that the stress was distributed through her feet and legs as well. I initiated blows to her back, buttocks, and backs of her thighs, snapping the thongs slowly and regularly so that she might anticipate the hits. Her muscles tensed against the blows across her bare skin, which would begin to seem as dull explosions from within.

At first, she stared up fixedly, to where her clenched fingers twisted at the ropes, though she clearly remained aware of my movements reflected in the mirror. The tears that had welled in her reddened eyes began to trickle down her cheeks. In anticipation of each bite of the whip, her eyes closed and brow knitted. At every hit, tremors ran like waves down her musculature to her straining feet. Face flushed, she bit her lip, loath to yield anything easily.

When I moved around to work on her soft front, she goaded me, through the thus far silent tears. "Hey, he did fuck me, and he wasn't very nice about it either!" She threw the club operator at me in a final provocative bid at attitude. "He needs to call me!"

"You enjoyed it?" I suspected this was not dissimilar from the way she used to jerk her stepfather's chain. Trifling with an embrace of the dark side, craving to recognize herself as ravished, defiled—all this stood somehow correlative with . . .

"I was up on you, waiting out there while it went

down," she sobbed the admission. "I played like you had brought me there for that, like it was something you had given to me!" There had been no doubt of her experience with kinky sex. I was reasonably sure that, wherever she wanted to be taken, something more was indicated. I approached her from behind and grabbed her hair, jerking her head painfully back.

"Justine!" I barked. "This isn't just about sex, about how great a little 'slut' you are, or the daddy you missed. You've been stroking the images of this place that I gave you. You were seeing them from outside, through other eyes, confusing your vicarious thrill with the suffering of figures you found attractive. This is about your real pain, about you and the agony of life! If you want fantasy, imagine how ugly the ride would have been had those boys in Louisiana gotten their hands on you."

"They would, would've really hurt me," she whimpered.

"You asked for it, and tonight you're going to get the realities." I shoved her head roughly forward to face the mirror. "Look at yourself. You'll see everything that happens to you, all night long, have to watch what's done to your pretty little bod. I'm going to wear this whip out on you," I threatened, calculating that the old, stiff thongs would not take at all long to disintegrate. "Tonight will be your night in hell, babe, and all you can do is endure it."

There was no way I was going to really mess her up. Neither had I any intention of the session going on nearly that long. That was a head trip, but it had the desired effect. My diatribe left her crying like a terrified child, looking at her crucified reflection with a sort of grief as at loss of self. I believed that wrapped within this was, paradoxically, some hidden hurt against which the very punishment promised release. Even then, the psychological purge had already been accomplished.

Even so, I'd committed to her feeling something in every inch, from chin to toes. I could not hold back, for refusal to deliver is the single perception guaranteed to make a submissive feel rejected. As she involuntarily contorted from the increasing frequency and severity of the lashes, she would only present a fresh part of herself for their burning attentions.

Writhing temptingly about, she would alternately jerk up first one knee then the other, in futile protection of her belly and crotch. But I did not linger on those areas. Such technique betrays a chauvinistic lack of imagination. There is a term for a woman's experience of something beating between her legs. It's called *routine copulation*. When, on the other hand, the thongs would wrap around her body and she felt their tips bite the tender areas of her breasts and flanks, I knew the sensation was like fire. She began to scream uncontrollably.

Grasping with her entire being the hopelessness of her condition, she ceased tensing against the blows. No longer was she straining to contain or localize the pain. Instead, she was feeling and receiving everything, letting it consume her—*becoming* the pain. Acquiescing to its spread and flow through every fiber, her body guilelessly sought the angle from whence the next whiplash would be coming.

It did not take long for her tormented calves and arches to give up, and she sagged from the ropes. I hitched the array still tighter, drawing her feet entirely off the floor. Her screams became frenzied when I mercilessly whipped the soles of her feet. Due to the most basic of instincts, that of running, an assault on the feet elicits a visceral response. It amounts to an invasion of the primal core of one's being.

Nowhere else to go, I sat down to recoup, sweating and with heart pounding. I closely monitored her, hanging there in her longed-for crucifixion. Catastrophic as the final barrage may have felt, I'd actually inflicted no more than small welts and scratches. To my eye, she was even more beautiful, with her head thrown back in a paroxysm that exalted rather than desecrated.

I glanced up at the corner of the balcony. *Was this what you would have wanted to see, old woman? Might you be sitting there now, spectrally watching all this happen to your human flesh and blood? Can you taste her pain?*

My attention returned to Justine. I belatedly considered that this really was not safe. No one knew we were there; what if I had a heart attack right then? It could happen. When I saw the muscles of her arms and shoulders go slack, I sprang to the ropes and slipped their knots. Her unconscious weight sank the array so that she was partially supported by her dragging legs.

I laid her back in my lap, verifying that her breathing was all right. I gently stroked her red welts and without warning she convulsed in my arms. ". . . not hell if you're there," she whimpered. I started to respond, but discerned she was still out. I smiled as she muttered something about "stairway to heaven."

While being worked to the point of unconsciousness is an archetypal fantasy of submissives, I had minimal experience with anyone genuinely passing out on me. Wondering at the scraps of her dreams, I thought that I'd now most certainly have to educate her—as to Seabrook's handling of the original Justine. Also see if she remembered any of the images about which she was complaining. Maybe her ancestress's genetics had conferred on her a similar talent. I fingered her silver manacles, remotely associating them more with the *Druse* than the *Rufai*.

Then she murmured again, and I passed over another threshold of credulity. First I identified that indeterminate something that had marginally tainted her speech from time to time. Now it was distinctive. This Texas girl should not, even rarely, speak with an accent of the old Bronx. They didn't even talk that way up there anymore! Nor, without reading *Witchcraft*, was it explicable for her to whine, like a still younger girl, ". . . oh why'd you do that? I wanted to see the rest of the circus. THE OLD LION WAS SO FUNNY . . ."

---

I didn't move, just sat there and held her for the longest time. But, after that, my eyes never left the corner of the balcony.

Finally, I could no longer endure the silence of the dream-club with its ghosts, Justine's and my own. Getting her to her feet, I half carried her to the car, then went back to lock up. Stuffing her clothes into the bag along with the manacles, I left the whip and pincers behind. As expected, the old leather was frayed and falling apart. Should we happen to be stopped by police on the foggy predawn drive, me toting an out-of-it naked girl with extensive abrasions—let's say I didn't want to spend the rest of the morning being interviewed by social workers?

Happily, the drive turned out uneventful, though spooky. My thoughts ran amongst a matrix of remote associations. Thinking of the old woman living in these foggy Georgia hills had mournful lyrics running around my brain, of a Civil War widow wandering through the Southern mountains. The trick was that you really couldn't say whether it were a madwoman or a ghost, weeping there in the morning rain, who no longer remembered that the war had ended forty years before.

Old Dixie was certainly the place for time-haunted souls. I recalled Seabrook and his advertising agency in the 'teens, which Ward Greene had portrayed setting up a reunion of the elderly Confederate veterans then still living. Someday soon, I wanted to track down what records might still exist in Atlanta to confirm Greene's image of the agency doing the publicity work on *Birth of a Nation*. I'd seen that classic reactionary film in Nashville, during the same long-ago Southern tour that had brought Linda and me to *The Château*.

"I'm hungry!" Justine startled me. Issuing a sleepy litany of complaints on everything *except* her unquestionable discomfort, she then dropped her seat back and turned away. That jogged my stream of consciousness back toward boyhood, to the ruins of a Civil War–era structure, still standing alongside a shunned river-bottom road. My parents would point it out to me during infernally hot automobile trips in a 1952 Dodge. I would kneel in the seat and watch out the back window as it receded into the heat waves billowing off the Texas asphalt. It would seem to me that the mighty conflict had been just over my shoulder, rather than a long lifetime before my birth.

Maybe that cast some light on how I'd been touched by the poignant conclusion of Ward Moore's classic book, *Bring the Jubilee*. Perhaps derivative of Leinster's original, his time traveler had lamented, after more or less accidentally changing the course of the Civil War:

> Are they really gone, irrevocably lost, in a future which never existed, which couldn't exist, once the chain of causation was broken? Or do they exist after all, in a universe in which the South won the battle of Gettysburg . . . I would give so much to believe this, but I cannot . . . Children know about such things. They close their eyes and pray, "Please God, make it didn't happen." Often they open

> their eyes to find it happened anyway, but this does not shake their faith that many times the prayer is granted.
>
> Adults smile, but can any of them be sure the memories they cherish were the same yesterday? Do they know that a past cannot be expunged? Children know it can. And once lost, that particular past can never be regained. Another and another, perhaps, but never the same one. There are no parallel universes—though this one may be sinuous and inconstant.[67]

My reverie on continuities, or the lack of same, was hardly diminished as I eased the Del Sol through the fog-shrouded streets of Buford and up to the house. Justine's disoriented state had morphed into fitful sleep. I was concerned that a healthy young adult should so succumb to the degree of physical stress she had endured. I felt certain that more was going on there.

As I beheld the gay window lights through the trees and fog, something of indeterminate origin twisted in my heart. Shutting down the engine, I contemplated the drowsing girl. Matted hair curled about her face, like the photo I'd seen of a girl Seabrook had trussed up back in 1930. The colors of the lamps across her face brought back lines . . .

". . . the colors and the lines that trace the past will

---

67. Moore, Ward, *Bring the Jubilee*, NY: Del Rey, 1955, Ballantine, 1997, p. 219.

in the semi-darkness form a face, a sleeping face . . ." Where did that come from? How did the rest go?

Remembering her little thought about the old woman wanting to have a light in every window, I shook myself to dispel something cold that had crept in with the fog. Of course she had a connection with the old woman! She was of her flesh and blood. Perhaps of Seabrook's as well, it had been suggested. Of course echoes of those old selves would resonate within her being. Conventional theory be damned, we *do* have a multifaceted connection with those gone before. We feel it in our very flesh.

The rain returned as I steered her inside, mulling her remarks in San Antonio about sugar imbalance. The lassitude and disorientation might well have a physiological basis. Rummaging through her flatly disgusting kitchen, I could come up with only a package of peanut-butter crackers. Justine lazily munched them while I sponged her off. I toweled her dry, salving the more acute abrasions, then crawled into bed beside her. Such a rainy Wednesday morning was good for sleeping in. I roused only a couple of times to the sound of the rain rattling on the tin roof.

---

I LAY THERE IN A KIND OF TWILIGHT, reconstructing what I could of strange dreams and consolidating them into memory. Figures like skydivers, in a snowflake formation, reminded me of my ritual dancers, but I drew back from the association. Permitting such assignments may lead the conscious layers to reinterpret images as stitched-together composites—images that, while unfamiliar, may be quite discrete. I watched them turning and turning until they collapsed into one another like a string of paper dolls.

Another seemed even more the typical sort of mixed-image-fest. I was in the old shelter house at the lake. But rather than JJ, I was talking with Justine, wearing the old party dress from the chest upstairs. She had been offering me a gift, a tray on which, instead of hors d'oeuvres, there was an octagonal icon. As I watched, crystals grew out of it at strange angles, like sections of a hypercube unfolding.

I awoke in the afternoon when I'd thrown my arm about Justine's shoulders and she'd whimpered. I started away, but she reached back for my hand. Turning over with a soft moan, she nuzzled my neck. "Can't find a comfortable position," she murmured.

"Sort of what we had in mind," I ventured, "or didn't you anticipate that going with the territory?" She giggled and hugged me, inquiring whether I wanted to make love. "Yes, it's true that we old men are best right after waking, but you must know that's going to hurt for sure."

She bit my ear. "I'm a wreck, I truly am," she teased sleepily. "Come on, lazybones. We'll do slow-processing." Loving her, I was again home and happy. You have to understand that happy was something I had never expected to know again. Her movements, that time, were slow and deliberate. She liked to talk after penetration, as do I. "Rewind what she said after they were finished with the blonde."

"That the girl would be working the next night; that her fresh marks would make her the favorite. For at least a week, she would get the best tips."

"How did Linda like that?" she sighed.

"She was squirming in her chair. While I'd been playing with the blonde, the old woman had sounded her out about finishing her contract at *The Château*, instead of the strip joint. The drift was that Linda's work with the magician led her to believe we might find all this attractive, so she'd taken us to see the whole deal.

"She'd gone on about Linda's regular acts fitting in but the punch line was that, she would have to be interviewed and initiated like any other slave-girl dancer." I gasped, as Justine reached between my legs and grasped the back of my scrotum, "You are so *not* like your mother."

"I should hope not," she giggled. "Tell more!"

"She told her that, if she thought another girl's punishment too severe, she would be allowed to take her place, that girls sometimes expressed affection for each other that way."

Justine shuddered, gently kneading my balls. "Thinking about that, much, would get me done way too quick-like. How did Linda take to that idea on female bonding?"

Talking about my dead wife could have been just a bit distractive, had not Justine's handling been keeping me aroused. "Linda looked like a deer caught in the headlights, and she asked an odd question. Would the old woman do that herself, do it for her?" Justine slowed our combined motion, looking up expectantly.

"She laughed about her skin being too old and thin; the members wouldn't be particularly entertained by seeing her whipped. Claimed, though, that she'd done such things more recently than we might have believed." I recalled a detail I'd not thought about in years. "She put her hand on Linda's knee, saying that she reminded her of someone, that she might talk a girl into taking her place sometime."

Justine resumed her undulations, closing her eyes. "The blonde?" she sighed.

"Might have been. When Linda was being initiated the next night, I saw the blonde pause while waiting a table and focus on her. Linda stared back at her, their eyes locked. They were thoroughly taken with each other and the reversal of their positions from the previous night."

Justine, building toward climax, yelped as I grasped her tender buttocks. "How, did that make you feel?" she stammered.

"Babe, I'm not still able to call up all this detail because I was so turned off! One night when Linda had been auctioned, I asked the old woman to put the blonde up as well. She accommodated me. I think she even rigged it—there wasn't much bidding against me. The girl was still worked up by what I'd done on her initiation night, and she was just delicious. She knew I was thinking about Linda. She kept me turned on by talking about what was probably happening to her right then."

We had both been withholding climax for indeterminate minutes. As she began rhythmically squeezing me, her juices soaking the sheets, I came almost involuntarily to ejaculation. My extended climax triggered her own shuddering spasms. It was as if the long-ago erotic excitement had melded with our present passion, and through it, lived again. In the afterglow, I wrapped up the story.

"Your great-grandmother blew our young minds. As it happened, Linda was whipped only on the night of the initiation but, during the two weeks, was auctioned several times. I wonder now if that wasn't contrived so Madeleine could spend more time with me? She knew all the buyers and assured me there was nothing to worry about, which turned out to be the case."

Justine sighed once more. "I can see you holding out your hand for the blonde when you bought her, like when you met me," she murmured before dozing off again. "Dead cool."

After we finally got out of bed, Justine expressed an urgent postcoital necessity to go prowl a mall. I first made a run into Buford to get us some burgers and use a phone. The house had only a dedicated line for her computer. Justine explained, "I didn't need Mother spitting in my ear."

I called Cris to see about Kong and Joe to tell him I'd see him when I saw him. Beyond fully understanding the obvious, he was ecstatic to learn that the mural was indeed there, and that this thing was *some kind of real*. Then I talked unpaid leave shit to my boss, feeling guilty for not just telling her that I wasn't coming back. I would need the unemployment when they deleted the position.

I took longer than intended, but it gave me time to think. I concluded that I was *way sure* it was the time to confront the previous night's ghosts. However, in the full light of day, yet another apparition was awaiting me. Climbing the creaking steps I could hear, as during the last night's drive home, another ghostly lyric.

---

"AROUND THE CORNER, AND UNDER THE BRIDGE, a handsome sailor, made love to me. He kissed me once, he kissed me twice, and-ever-since-I've-wanted-to-go . . ." *Déjà vu* bites! Whereas the ghostly lyrics of the night before had been in my head, these were composed of definitely audible material vibrations. Troubling with the sense of familiarity, I identified the tune as a round I could just recall my mother singing when I was a child. It had been a song from her girlhood. My mother had been born in 1904.

"Around the corner, and under the bridge, a handsome soldier made love to me. He kissed me once . . ." Justine was bobbing her shoulders with the old round in her characteristic fashion. In front of the long Adam mirror, she was wearing the party dress from upstairs. She'd also found a long strand of beads and a Grecian-goddess forehead band that looked *art nouveau*. It lay beside her on a small teakwood table, along with containers of the mascara, rouge, and lipstick that she'd applied in a perfect period likeness. "I can't get that tune outta my head."

Riveting me with incredulity was what she had done with her hair. Its decidedly nonperiod crimson length was piled, in an elaborate French wave, on the back of her head. A tube of styling gel, apparently attempted and abandoned, lay on the table. She was using a curling iron and a card of bobby pins to frame her face with little spit-curls, in a mode that I could hardly conceive a modern girl even knew.

"I wonder if they still make Dippety-Doo?" she mused, finishing her curls and placing the classical band on her forehead. "Would you photograph me, tied to one of the columns and looking distressed? Wouldn't I look scrumptious?" She peered at me mischievously in the mirror.

I recalled Willie's fantasies of the chained ladies, which he'd been convinced Grandmother Piny's telepathy had helped generate. "Seabrook would be *gaga*," I answered, "though I'd as rather see both my goddesses and distressed damsels naked."

She giggled and, turning about, curtsied with a slight lift to the tiers of her scalloped satin skirt. She had substituted white panty hose for silk stockings, but the satin slippers were clearly originals matching her dress. She looked a vision out of another age as she donned the flapper beads and beamed. "My heart, you have a most improper imagination. I've been feeling quite all-overish since I woke up, I mean to say!"

She displayed the fact that she'd removed the backing, which would have preserved modesty behind the Georgette inlay over her chest. What the hell had come over her while I'd been away? I wondered at "my heart," which had been delivered like an address rather than an exclamation. The old Bronx accent had become pronounced.

I put our food on the table, moving aside the memorabilia. The African masks grinned at me. Before we sat down, I took a folder from my leather case. "Justine, I have here a copy of Seabrook's *Witchcraft*. I photocopied the reference book in full." As she sat down, looking at the pages with curiosity, I saw her hands sweep up the skirts—with upturned palms!

What the gesture made me remember filled me with awe and consternation. That was becoming a familiar state of mind, ever since a young Goth had seated herself, in identical fashion, beside me at the WorldCon. It was as if a ghost, wrapped in a reality of sweet, young flesh, belittled my wildest conjectures.

Would it have been more easily handled had I believed her demented, victim to multiple personalities, instead of struggling to accept what I suspected might have been happening there? Oh God, this was indeed *some* kind of real!

For once, her typically piggish table habits consoled me, as she savaged the burger and fries with sickening amounts of ketchup. I started reading to her, from the "Justine" chapters, the description of her predecessor passing into a trance during a bondage session and having an elaborate precognitive vision.

I'd reached the point where Willie, upon discovery that she'd long been hanging free of any foot support, had rescued her. She'd been ticked off, because she'd been enjoying her vision of the street circus, the one they were destined to witness the following year in the city of Petrarch's muse Laure, an alleged ancestress of Sade . . .

"In *Avignon*," Justine breathed the name with a melancholy lilt, her perfection of pronunciation discernible to my ear. I just stopped and looked at her. "You're thinking about me complaining last night, which wasn't fair." Her throat trembled, "I'm gonna get to go? Really and truly?"

"Justine, I've procrastinated about telling you this story for *three days*. Avignon was mentioned in the *Testament*, also the fact of the circus, right? Are you pulling my leg? Have you read this story before? It's not in my notes, I know that, but some of the reviewers did, I believe, synopsize it . . ."

Shaking her head with a very slight smile, she seemed to be looking afar off. "Dearest, don't be contrary. Someway or other, it gets read, but not yet." Something in her responses was askew from any sense of immediate reality. She then brought up the red-leather discipline mask; the mask on the little figure in the mural, which the old woman had alleged to be herself. She described it, much as in the pages that I'd been only about to read to her, but made mention of a pair of blue, tightly laced gloves. That rang a disparate bell.

In the mid-sixties, a young writer of Anton LaVey's acquaintance had published a satire on pornography. *The Nightclerk*, like *Candy*, had become an underground classic. A special favorite of my wife's had been a scene in which the female lead, named "Katy," was being hand-fed in a public restaurant. Her arms were immobilized in a pair of blue-leather discipline gloves.[68]

The workmanship of the gloves, among other haunting similarities, had put me in mind of Willie and Justine's restaurant adventure described in *Witchcraft*. That had opened a new portal of conjecture during my research. What else might that author have known? I had wondered whether Katie, Willie's first wife, might have been a component of a composite Justine? Katie had certainly not been a shrinking violet, to be sure, but it was a long reach.

"Someway, this all involves a place called Evenos," Justine was saying, absently running her tongue around the spout of the ketchup bottle before replacing the cap. "Do you know that name? It sounds Greek."

"The *Château d'Evenos*, near Toulon. Seabrook took a long lease, but failed to restore it. The place and its neighborhood are described in detail in Marjorie's book."

"It was certainly all empty and fallen down when we were there last night. The time before, it was full of life. Like you were describing the roadhouse, muchly."

"I'm confused. Which of the 'châteaux' are we talking about?" I tried to laugh, though hairs were rising on the back of my neck. "You've seen it some other

68. Schneck, Stephen, *The Nightclerk*, NY: Grove Press, 1965, pp. 56–64. Compare to the chapter "Justine in the Mask" in *Witchcraft*, p. 274, for similarities, as well as Seabrook's inimitable observation that no one interferes with a girl who's poised and happy, even if her boyfriend is sticking pins in her!

way, perhaps? Babe, it's been like that for decades."

"Not the roadhouse, silly, the castle." Putting down her burger, she studied intently, as though with difficulty pulling something up from long before.

"I dreamed of riding in a huge old open-topped car. Its wheels had wooden spokes, and everything was so bumpy and dusty! Above a dark gorge, there was an old castle with a spiral iron staircase that led nowhere. We laughed about it being the 'stairway to heaven.' It was like *déjà vu*, memories coexistent with their contents. I was dreaming the remembrance of the very dream I was having, but something was all wrong. The other time, the stairs *did* go someplace. I was so glad you were there to hold my hand. I felt like a ghost haunting the ruins."

I remained very still for a while, hoping the fear in me would subside. Trying to follow her dreams resembled my vain quest to correlate the literary sources. They appeared contiguous with histories, even with fictional treatments, of which she possessed no knowledge. More, I felt a less-than-explicable reticence to grapple with an inference of relationship, in some eerie fashion, to our present-day experience.

"No bondage gloves are associated with the mask in any of Willie's writings that I know of. Neither is this 'stairway to heaven,' at least in that form. Where is that coming from?"

---

PLEASE GIRL, I PRAYED, TELL ME YOU READ IT! What I'd said was not totally true. Marjorie had recalled a story of ". . . that strange iron staircase—erected on top of the ruins by that last demented owner, the Count d'Evenos, who wanted to get a little closer to heaven when he prayed . . ."[69]

"Justine, did you see her vision of the street circus?" I burst out, now *needing* to know.

"The lion was in the vein of remembrance of memory. I was here now, long years after those happenings, but knowing I'd not even yet been to Europe. So it was like, remembering things that hadn't yet happened. You'll be taking me soon? Maybe next year?" Her eyes were all starlight and absinthe. Magic was in there, and I could not help but imagine that it formed the face of another Justine—the Justine of *Witchcraft*.

"Speaking of your own dreams," she mused, "we talked all about brain waves, *sans* the spikes needful to earmark a time sequence, and such-like? You opened me up last night, so very wide . . ." My eyes began to burn. ". . . and I feel like, *susceptible*, to dreams that had been waiting for me to have them . . . oh, dearest, not to worry . . ."

I'd drawn back, but I had no clue what she was seeing in my face. Dear God, no! Her perplexing condition was due, in part, to my stupid games. I spilled my guts. "I've suspected that there's no escape from whatever destiny of yours I'm entangled with. I think I can accept that. But babe, you complete my life. I can't live with having found you, just to lose you

69. Worthington, *Strange World*, concluding on pp. 40–41.

again—as I did with your mother. And not to a damned ghost!"

"Oh, pooh!" The green eyes flared. "JJ didn't have the intestinal fortitude to take your hand or to take command of her own life." She thrust her fists against her hips with exasperation. Had she not been seated, I believed she would have stamped her foot.

"So it's like that, after last night? How very boresome your life would of been if you'd married her. There is positively no comparison. If you still think that I could throw you, I'm tapped. I-am-not-JJ! *Damn!*"

Emergent, in her anger, was the persona I'd met on Sunday, and I tried to seize the moment. "That's my point, babe, who are you?" I directed her attention to her elaborate coiffure and makeup, her varying accents and language. "This is something a little more extreme than accessing some scattered memories. Look, I don't doubt the validity of Seabrook's approach to psychic experimentation. I'm not some little narrow-minded shrink"—she raised a disapproving eyebrow, but I pushed ahead—"who would imagine that mere employment of the sexual motif invalidates results . . ."

I recounted Linda's belief that the endorphins released by physical stress often allowed her to leave her body, enjoying watching her plight voyeuristically. Neither had her evidence, that something more was going on, been purely subjective. Once, believing that her back was being arched too far, she panicked. She had thrashed about and freed one ankle, but the cuff that had held her was still closed tight and double-locked. No examination of details could explain what had taken place.

"Now, had this little Houdini stunt occurred in the *Rufai* Hall of Torture, it would be cited as anecdotal evidence of a paranormal occurrence." I groused, "Seabrook was right. The objections to his methods were nothing more than a cultural bias, which exists today in an even more ridiculous form. Were we *Lakota* Sioux, torturing vision-questers at Sundance, we'd be endorsed as spiritual and even religious!"

"Your point being what?" she sighed. "If the Sioux lived close by their neighborhoods, your 'politically correct' would dis them, too."

I admitted that the digression was avoidance. "I can believe that, last night, we did open a gate to something—widened it, anyway. I suspect something's been going on with you in this house for a while. But we can have no control whatsoever over what may be coming through it. Why do I doubt that you've ever said *'oh pooh'* before in your entire life, or even actually heard that expression used?"

I, myself, felt that I was rambling. Still, I was almost angry with her, for laughing at my consternation. Yet her smile was loving and compassionate when she spoke. "Dearest, you have known me for an entire *three days*. If you were now to meet a side of me you'd not yet encountered, then what would be extraordinary about that—from the most commonsensical standpoint? You are only getting to know the woman who belongs to you, the whole little baggage.

"My great-grandmother is *not* a ghost," in a slightly hurt tone, as if I'd insulted the old woman. "Nor do I have an identity disorder." Her brow knitted, but I thought her concern was probably directed at me. "I shan't go away; *it's still me in here*." Her words recalling my thoughts from the pier, I was, once again, deeply chilled.

"If we're thinking I'm possessed, it's a welcome possession. I'm as I've always felt inside." She looked at me imploringly. "Playing dress-up was for fun. Get you stoked up 'cause you're all, y'know, about the past?" She dropped her head, "Or not. Behold my success."

She was trying to pacify and comfort me without really backing off. "Babe, your great-grandmother grieved all her life for a man she'd worshiped, a man whose story I relate to more intensely than that of any other person. But I can't *be* him, Justine, do you understand? If you are turning into your namesake, I can't reciprocate by somehow becoming Willie. In a way, I wish I could; for all his faults, he didn't waste his potential. I only wish I'd done half the things he did.

"See, I think I do believe that maybe you are becoming her, in some sense. I'm afraid because I may not be able to play the role you need from me." I was not moved to further expansion.

Another had once believed me capable of mending everything and held it against me when I couldn't. Neither could I confess the terror that my youthful posturing might have justified Linda's grievance. I drew a deep breath. "If you're thinking reincarnation, it doesn't even begin to explain everything that's been going on, all the connections that have existed and continue to be revealed.

"How was it that I was drawn into this thing, based on a lifetime obsession with your mother? Which I apparently confided to your great-grandmother, when I just *happened* to become involved with her nearly thirty years ago? That, in turn, set something in motion, of which her book finding its way to me, so that I could return it home, may be the most innocent. *Et cetera ad infinitum!* Doesn't all this seem a little bit weird to you?"

"No, wait. Now let me see; compared to *what*?"

"Point conceded." The tension breaking, I laughed as well. "I guess we just have to throw all the laws of probability right out the window on this one!" I thought aloud, "Everything is moving so damned fast, it's dizzying. I fear that as the dominoes keep falling, in a way they never do in ordinary life, it might turn out that a Justine like her will have no interest in me."

She rose and walked behind me, pressing my head back against her young breasts beneath the antique Georgette film. "All I can tell you is that I'm in love, for the first time in my life. Anything other is outta the question."

I took her hand and kissed her palm. "And I'm in love for the last time," I completed the line, though it was hard to voice the finality. I had to wonder at the sweetness of the hurt—in knowing that I meant it.

"I believe," she continued, and I heard the ring of

the old Bronx again, "that whatever is left of her is all—about protecting us, watching over us, and being kind to us." I felt her chest heave, and there was just the slightest break in her voice, but when I looked up, her eyes were dry. "If you think we were manipulated into this," she entreated, "please trust my intuition that we weren't brought here to a bad thing. *Go* with it."

"Go where with it? To Rhinebeck, as she would have had it?"

"We're outta here in the A.M. I'm ready to go to town." Momentarily, I thought I was listening to a weird mix of anachronisms. Then she added, "We can chill today," her accent again at full variance with her costume. "But hey, I still gotta get by the mall!"

# VIII
# Rhinebeck

We caught a morning flight to New York, leaving her Del Sol in a grossly overpriced long-term parking at the Atlanta airport. Justine had begun to pay for everything on plastic, no longer letting me pick up anything. When I'd questioned her, she'd just shrugged it off. She said she believed this was what the money was there for, and brooked no further discussion. I will not deny that it was very comfortable to find us so buffered against the tedious necessities of life, but it was another circumstance to which I was unaccustomed. Our relative ease of movement only contributed to the numinous texture of the events enfolding us.

With every passing hour, Justine seemed more focused on the path before her. She was taking as a given that my appearance in her life, in possession of the details of her recently designated father-figure's saga, was of the nature of an inevitable catalyst.

I gathered there had hitherto been some questioning, some need of regrouping—as with her trip to the WorldCon. Even that mild diversion had spun off objective metaphors of her own eerie catharsis. In that respect, I had to grieve my inadvertent role in her now unhesitating acceptance of the agenda laid down by the long-dead ancestress.

At the mall, she'd scampered about, acting, if anything, a bit younger than her years. So her ultimate selection of a relatively conservative business suit was interesting. True, it fit like that of a young woman attorney out to entice the judge, making one immediately want to put his hand inside it. Perhaps that effect was simply inherent to the wearer.

Once home, however, she'd donned again her period costume and worn it for the rest of the evening. While we'd prepared for the next leg of this dizzying odyssey, she'd puttered about the house, humming more little tunes and handling various relics from the past with an attitude of wonder.

She had been as if looking for memories and occasionally, I sensed, finding them. I could not imagine what might be going on inside her, and watching the process was both charming and frightening. In the morning, she had carefully put away her antique possessions and groomed herself as the modern professional woman. Even as I had marveled at the further transformation, I could see that the dark ghost that accompanied her did not go back into the chest with the pretty dress.

The floral perfume she'd purchased, the elegant

posture, a dozen little nuances marked her as a being of a different order. And I wasn't the only one who noticed. A fellow traveler who had been watching us board the plane addressed her in French, and she responded. Studying her as we settled into our seats, I realized that she'd not consciously registered the glancing contact, sitting quietly with knees together and hands clasped demurely in her lap.

It's not that easy to accept that one's dreams have come true, I reflected while we ascended. Even relatively privileged lives often seem so difficult, so heartbreaking. Life is one complicated bitch! And, of course, you still die. To what end, I asked the empty heavens outside the window? Was I bound for purgatory or oblivion?

Had she been given to me to be just as abruptly stolen away, now that she had fully committed to this course? I feared that, as this metamorphosis continued, the young woman who had transfixed me, sometimes as the tough punker, sometimes a bouncy kitten, would be lost—consumed by a revenant from the dark past.

The morning above twenty thousand feet was all brilliant sunshine. We had soon overrun the swirling weather system making its way along the coastline down below. I would learn that it had been the approach of one of those *El Niño* years that might, more properly, have been dubbed "Rosemary's Baby." For days, we'd been playing tag with this storm, and seemed unable to escape it now. It paced us like an implacable curse, following us as we flew toward Rhinebeck.

Some things had been said the day before, but I knew that more were needed, needed now while there was yet time. I discovered that on some deeper level, I was praying—for help to grasp that moment. Notions and emotions churned, like qubits in a countercurrent, orbiting the far point of the years. I felt as if trapped in that final, Planck-length instant before the end of time.

I sensed Justine tense when the plane bucked some turbulence, and took her hand. Remembering, as she gripped my fingers, how she had declined the window seat, I thought how I'd not have taken the tough little babe for a white-knuckle flyer. Should this plane crash, I thanked God that I'd been granted the feelings of these past days, this moment in time. Yet, a sense of tragedy remained. Whether my own far point, into which I was trying to cram forever, came with a wind shear upon landing, or in bed in ten or twenty years, "all joys want eternity, deep, profound eternity." I wanted Justine for all eternity, and I couldn't even give her a decent lifetime.

A sweet little bitch I'd intended as a mate for the noble Kong had died young a few years before. She had been watching me as I left home one day and, in my conceit, I'd later imagined that she knew she was dying. I had thought I could make out sadness, not in the face of her death, but knowing she wouldn't be seeing me anymore. Then, I'd doubtless been projecting feelings about Linda's impending death, but I was learning genuine empathy for that dog.

For the first time in my life, I found that I feared

the prospect of extinction less than the loss of another. I was called upon for something I'd never really known: *faith*. All I was left to cling to now was faith that the impossible nexus of synchronicity, which had terrorized me only hours before, was somehow there to sustain us. Faith, like Justine's certitude that we were not brought here to an evil fate. If I were indeed powerless to intervene, my life manipulated to lead to this moment, how could I have been so damnably guilty of anything as to make this exceptional adventure the fulfillment of some curse?

I'd also been forced into a thoroughgoing life review, finding its components more elaborately bonded than I could have imagined, bonded even apart from time. Like my dream dancers, my moments had ceased to be perceived as linear, becoming the cardinal points in a cosmic ritual. I could almost see my dream skydivers spiraling away outside the window. As they drifted down into the storm below, they folded up like a chain of paper dolls, collapsing together into unity.

Part of that ritual had been the pledge I'd taken in my heart. But there was more, I knew now, much more was coming. All that I feared, I understood with amazement at myself, *all* that I feared was to be separated from her. Would I not say those things, as I had not spoken them to too many others in my life, until it was again too late?

*God help me,* I lamented silently. *If nothing more, just let me tell her—while she is still as I've known her!* If I could make her understand how I loved her, maybe it would influence whatever was going down. If only I could stay with her, that was what I was about, what my life meant. I suppose that he did help me, for I turned to her and, albeit slowly and haltingly, began to speak.

We landed at Kennedy about noon and collected the car we'd reserved for the drive upstate, a Chevy Lumina with a floor mat already wearing through. *Cheap crap,* I thought, *and it gets worse with every decade.* However, with under 30K on the odometer, it still drove tight and smooth. The trip should have only taken two or three hours had we known what we were doing. Though I hadn't driven in New York for over twenty-five years, the nightmare of getting through the city seemed no worse than I recalled it. I supposed that New York had reached critical mass long before.

When I had spoken my heart to her on the plane, Justine had moved my hand to hold it tight beneath her breasts. It was not lost on me how she bent forward over it, as if shielding something indescribably precious. She had said nothing but, irrespective of an uncomfortable armrest, just melted against me for the rest of the flight.

Once on the ground at Kennedy, though surely relieved of the anxiety of the air travel, she'd lapsed further into her quiet reverie. I had attended to the logistics, infrequently rousing her to proffer her plastic or to sign for something. I had also called ahead to the law office at Kingston to advise them that their longtime client's heir was on her way. A gentleman named Roder, of patently *Québécois* extraction, assured me that the materials would be waiting for Justine to take possession.

As I fought our way through the metropolitan traffic, it was my turn to be largely distracted, calling down the curse of nameless gods on Yankee drivers every few minutes. Justine had declined any thought of driving, for which I was most thankful. Around us swirled the diversity of the great world-city, people from every nation and culture. A group of Hasidic Jews in front of a restaurant operated by Chinese Cubans—all seemed objective metaphors for a chaos of worlds bleeding into one another.

When I studied her during the frequent long delays, I considered how little could be found in her strange recollections to arm her against the enormity of the spectacle surrounding us. I watched her when I could as we skirted the Bronx to link up with US 9, but could make out no heightened discomfiture. If I noted any uneasiness, she'd begun to relax again by the time we were out among the trees and foliage between the commuter towns.

---

APPROACHING THE LARGE HILLS AROUND PEEKSKILL, we stopped for a late lunch. We'd dropped off 9 and driven westward to where we could view the mighty expanse of the Hudson. As we ate, I again followed her eyes out the restaurant window and northward, past West Point. Was she anticipating the approach to Dutchess County, to the places and events that had so troubled the elder Justine a lifetime before?

I asked her how this felt. Was she having flashbacks, as if to that other's life? One reason that I'd never put much stock in accounts of "past life" memories had been their unlikely assumption of a near-total emotional separation from the here-and-now. One's sense of self and appraisal of reality would be highly impacted! I ran these speculations by Justine and momentarily interrupted her eerily quiet vigil.

She'd faintly smiled. "Like in the vein of 'I was the Queen of Sheba. Now I'm not . . . darn?' Nay, there may be a little snippet of something about a county fair—somebody won a ribbon for a pumpkin pie."

The brief respite only accented my pain, as I saw the green gaze withdrawn decidedly *elsewhere*. The speech when hers was softened with a sweet melancholy, to which I could hardly believe Justine, the young hardcase, had ever admitted. I was sure I was losing her. She was slipping away even as I watched her fastidiously separate her meat from the vegetables and eat them one at a time, a European sort of habit. Maybe more significant was Justine, for once, being able to eat without leaving a ring of food around the perimeter of her plate.

Oh my God, what could I do? Beg her to forget all this and return with me to Texas? How could I ask her to give up her bequest and what she believed to be her destiny? It was not like her education left her without theory to throw at a background that contributed little to any sense of self-esteem, successfully compensatory as she might have become. She knew all of that: the search for the father, the overachievement, the supposed pathology of her sexual kinks.

But that "knowledge" was as nothing, goddamn it! I couldn't persuade myself that her distinctive change of affect signified a personality unraveling. From the time of our arrival at Madeleine's house, I had sensed a growing presence that, to my frustration, Justine was inclined to embrace without reflection. She was going to give it up, to give herself over, to let the ghost of that old woman have her, as though she herself was without value. I feared that Willie's Justine, following his dark arts, had indeed succeeded in leaving a door open behind her. But I said nothing. I did not know what else I might say. My throat was gripped with the terror that this was somehow good-bye, a farewell dinner with the Justine I had so briefly loved.

I felt somewhat better when we drove out of sight of the River and the higher Catskills in the distance. Endeavoring to bury my misgivings in the logistical tasks at hand, I could only pray that a continuing cavalcade of improbability might further modify the order of my reality's snapshots.

The route east of the Hudson had been the more scenic, but slowest approach. The sometimes-two-lane asphalt passed through every podunk town jammed with late, stop-every-ten-seconds tourists and early-fall college folk. In other circumstances, I, too, would have wanted to stop and see sites, like the houses with stone walls a couple of feet thick. But the trip was looking more like four than two hours, and Justine complained of feeling "all gnarly." I was afraid that she might be getting sick, the pace of the past several days taking a toll even on her.

We passed through Poughkeepsie, where, in 1907, the wife of the inventor Theodore Miller had given birth to little Lee, the golden goddess of the sun—another background I wished for the time and opportunity to research. Struggling to reconnect with Justine, I tried to tell her the story.

Lee's lover, Man Ray, being easily as egotistical, less voyeuristic, and more hung-up than Willie, it was as likely Lee's independent potential as much as her promiscuity that led to their parting. It was neither so much a matter of her showing off in abbreviated outfits at the parties of Noailles and other patrons nor of running off with other lovers. Jean Cocteau's choice of Lee for a film role led directly to the estrangement.

Lee was destined to have a wonderful life, become an icon of sunlit sensuality for the Western world through very dark decades. For Man Ray, in her absence she became the inspiration that Justine had served for Willie. I had played with the notion that she was somehow another part of a composite erotic synthesis, though it seemed evident that, for Willie as well, Lee had been "the one who got away."

"So, did Lee play?" Justine asked, her interest seemingly drawn back just a bit.

"Well, not with Willie. Lee liked to watch the bondage photography, but she turned down his entreaties for her to pose.[70] Man Ray had a story about Willie telephoning them to come by his studio in Montparnasse one evening. It seemed he was going out for the evening with Mink . . ."

"Who?" Justine snapped, peevishly.

"Willie's pet name for Marjorie. Anyway, it developed into a request that Man Ray and Lee baby-sit a girl whom Willie had chained to the newel of the staircase . . ."[71]

Uncomfortably similar to the night in Mississippi, I was interrupted as Justine grew distinctly agitated. This time, however, I was able to ascertain the ominous cause. We were at Hyde Park, and the road ran close again to the River. She was looking nervously about for the legendary River mansions. My enthusiasm for the story plunged, and she lapsed once more into that uncharacteristically moody reverie.

When, in the late afternoon, we gained the bridge across the mile-wide expanse of the Hudson, I felt we were being propelled, as by an elemental force, into the dark heart of the mystery. The law office was tucked away on North Front Street, overlooking the old Stockade historical district. That was the collection of stone structures that had survived the Revolution, when the Redcoats had burned Kingston to the ground.

---

70. Baldwin, Neil, *Man Ray, American Artist*, C.N. Potter, 1988, Da Capo Press, 1991, p. 166.

71. Man Ray, op. cit., pp. 153–156.

THE QUALITY OF THE SUNLIGHT had slightly but perceptibly shifted with the change in latitude. I was glad I had a jacket and was reminded that, not much farther up the road, beyond the time-haunted houses of Saugerties, lay the back door into New England—Stephen King country, H.P. Lovecraft country. As when "crossing the Styx" in the Mississippi night, I felt we had come to yet another edge of the known world.

That mind-set, perhaps coupled with the old houses we'd seen while driving up, was working on me when we did not find Roder in the office and were obliged to wait for a bit. From the window I surveyed the Stockade and reflected on possibly the only good lines of poetry Lovecraft ever wrote—of slanting sunlight on ancient stone structures, painting with life the shapes of the past. He'd imagined an aether in some old things that whispered of hidden dimensions.

"Even in his time, we still felt our connection to the Enlightenment. Americans regarded the 'Lords of Great Britain' as the enemy, or very dubious allies at the least," I felt called upon to pontificate on the Stockade's history. "That was before American dignitaries felt moved to bend the knee to their royalty, an act that in earlier time would have properly brought a charge of treason."

Justine was quite justifiably ignoring me, still lost in a world all her own. I looked back at the lowering sky and was struck by the effects of an unfamiliar place on one's psyche. The eccentricity of the views expressed was audible even as they came from my mouth. I'd never been an Anglophobe or particularly given to political symbology. I was debating whether the odd burst might not be mere avoidance of Lovecraft's final line: "In that strange light, I feel I am not far, from the fix't mass whose sides the ages are."

Roder, a large man, somewhat older than myself, arrived with profuse apologies for having made us wait. He kept glancing nervously at Justine as he ushered us to a conference table in the library. He then reminisced on the days when he'd been a young intern with the firm, and Seabrook had been still recalled as a colorful fixture of local history. The founding partners had regarded their continuing custodianship of his purported final work as a source of some small pride, a lingering connection with the past and to history, as it were.

Introduced as a vaguely defined friend of the family, I expressed the reverence in which Justine held the effects, extending appreciation for the firm's good stewardship over the decades. I inquired whether he had known the elder Justine.

"The old partners handled the important clients personally," he responded. "They did business with the Astors, the Dows, Van Dorens, Chapmans—all the old families." His eyes repeatedly appraised Justine as he talked. "I would only briefly glimpse her come and go, in the instances that she visited the office, back in the fifties and sixties."

He explained that he had to meet with Justine

personally to conclude a final bit of business. "I'm sorry that we could not forward the effects on to you. *Mais naturellement,* the ancillary device we have on file is unequivocal. The bequest is conditional upon receipt in person."

I began to assure him that the conditions were understood, but he cut me off and continued to Justine, "My dear, I am as you see, *Québécois.* I hope you will take my heritage into account and not be offended by a compliment. The way you carry yourself, so dignified while at the same time so sensuous—you remind me of her so much that the years roll away. You bring back, into this very room, the *ambiance* of the one circumstance when she met with me personally."

Roder seemed chagrined by his forwardness and, while Justine smiled gracefully, he possibly took the chill I was feeling as disapproval. He hastened to a huge old wall safe, returning with a large wrapped package, which he deposited before her.

"On her final visit, she asked to speak with me, as the youngest member of the firm. It was an exceptional conversation, *à la langue française*, by the way—at her pleasure. She instructed me to ensure a verbal message be delivered, designating the beneficiary of her estate, by whomever would eventually finalize this business."

Still exquisitely poised, Justine lifted an eyebrow, and Roder looked flustered, "It was a single phrase, all that I can remember her speaking *en bon anglais*, to be directed to you. But of course, you were not even born when—I can see her yet with the tears in her eyes—she bequeathed her legacy . . .

"'TO THE ONE WHO PERHAPS CARED THE MOST.'"

---

In the uncomfortable silence that followed, Roder busied himself with the wrappings, and I looked at Justine. She would only shrug, but the profound pain betrayed around her own eyes troubled me. He placed in her hands a large leather portfolio, beginning to crack with all the years. Her fingers trembled as she struggled with the old zipper.

Then she just stared at the stacks of notepads of every description, clipped bundles of loose scraps, and some typewritten sheets that lay exposed before her. Her vibrating fingertips moved over the array and stopped upon a small bundle of envelopes. They were tied in the old fashion with faded ribbons, not unlike those in her cedar chest at home. Seated close to her, I could feel the tension in her body as I read the front of the top one, addressed to Madeleine Leiris from William Seabrook.

As Justine struggled for control, I could see Roder's wonder at the degree to which the young heiress was moved by the touch of those long-ago people. Almost inaudibly, she asked about the manuscript itself. Taken aback, the attorney reddened and apologized for being derelict. He confessed that, knowing she would be coming for it soon, he'd been trying to read it. As he hurried to retrieve it from his office, Justine looked at me, brushing at the tears that had welled up.

"It hurts so much," she whispered, "and I don't even know why! It's as if the simple reality of these little pieces of their lives is too much to bear."

Roder returned to surrender the volume. Though it allegedly consisted of a narrative extracted from the notes, the elder Justine appeared to have treated it as a completed work by Willie. The typed sheets had been professionally bound inside a lavish, oversize set of covers.

Justine opened it to the front sheet, which could well have been typed on the old Underwood upright from her desk. It read simply, *The Fan-Shaped Destiny*. Visibly emotional, Justine excused herself and went unsteadily to find their facilities. Roder expressed nothing short of awe at such a young person being overcome by the matters of relatives she had never known.

"She's an exceptional young woman," I replied to him, with resignation more than pride.

"Without a doubt!" he exclaimed, eyes widening, his sense of the dramatic fully engaged. "*Écoutez*, she is like an image of the old lady. While I never knew that one so young, it is as though she is here again; I don't know how to express it."

After verifying that I already knew something of the nature of the old woman's business, Roder told me that she'd become a fable in select circles. While few had known her name, her power had become substantial throughout the South, and she'd not been one to be trifled with in New York either. I was inferring mob, something about which I'd wondered.

"We heard that her 'other' contacts were with families that went all the way back to the Black Hand. She'd known Huey Long. During that one conversation, she claimed to have been in the Arlington Hotel, in Hot Springs, when a meeting decided whether or not he would recover from his bullet wound. She was doing business in New Orleans during the time of Earl Long and Blaze Starr . . ."

Roder's vicarious enjoyment darkened, "There was also a *rumor* that she had psychic powers, and dabbled in voodoo . . . but listen." He spoke quickly before Justine could return, telling me that he doubted the publication value of the manuscript or its attendant notes. "I'm no critic, but I think that he must have been quite mad by the time he was writing this. At least, I could make no sense at all of what I read."

Assuring him that the value of the effects to Justine was not determined by their literary merit or lack of it, I would have learned more about the old woman's supposed later history. But Justine returned, more composed and ready to leave. Roder accompanied us to the car, supremely solicitous of her and inviting us to call again before we left. As he gallantly held the Lumina's door for her, she paused and drew herself erect.

No doubt an illusion of the lengthening shadows, as if they wrapped themselves about her—that she seemed to gain an inch or so of stature. Had the tresses that veiled her features likewise gone to darkened auburn, as she addressed him huskily?

"Believe me when I say that you have discharged

your commission admirably," she spoke over her shoulder, barely turning. "I hope our association continues. It's a comfort to find you're here, *m'vieux*, should I be needful." When I gave him a final nod, the gregarious Roder looked curiously speechless.

As we cruised through Kingston, Justine held like a baby the portfolio into which she'd replaced the bound manuscript. Her cheek against the old leather, she seemed truly at ease for the first time during the trip. We were booked on a return flight to Atlanta on Saturday. Our plan had been to prowl Rhinebeck Friday morning, then drive down and play in the City that evening. It had seemed only logical to view some of the old haunts of the Seabrook saga while we were on location.

I did still feel a degree of uneasiness as we drove the several miles to the bridge and crossed the Hudson to Rhinecliff and Rhinebeck. I had presumed that we would settle into the quaint little Rhinebeck bed-and-breakfast Roder had recommended, and Justine would begin to read the manuscript. But by the time we had finished checking in, she decided that she felt up for finding Seabrook's place right then. I was of divided mind.

I felt I was against the wall on this. Of course, after all the research I'd done, I was interested in seeing the actual locations of much of the story. Especially the barn where Willie had conducted his "experiments" with such as Aldous Huxley and Walter Duranty, as well as the Greenwich Village sites. Who knew when I might be back?

Still, the black thoughts from the trip up had not abated, so I tried to persuade her to wait until morning. She was insistent, pointing out that the weather was holding so far, and there was yet time before dark. She held that it was best to locate the old home then, in case the storm reached us before morning. I agreed, with the provision that we went immediately, before it got any later.

The River was just visible from the road. With the help of an address from the old envelopes, and some tourist brochures, we searched along a street that ran close to its bank. Some of the numbers along Morton Road were obscure, and we drove up and down, wandering some side streets. We glimpsed a number of large houses, the great round columns of the several mansions surprisingly resembling Southern plantation houses.

Willie had been released from the sanitarium in July of 1934, into the care of his psychoanalyst, Helen Montague. She was the wife of Columbia philosopher William Pepperell Montague, who was heavily into the influence of other dimensions on our experience. Seabrook had finished *White Monk* while in Bloomingdale, and wrote *Asylum* while staying with the Montagues after his release. Guests who had frequented the Montague farm at nearby Krumvallen were mostly Columbia colleagues and their spouses. Some of them had been around Willie's psychic experimentation in New York ten years earlier. A divorce from Katie was finalized.

In the fall, Marjorie obtained for them the place on

the Hudson. *Asylum* was quickly serialized and began to bring in money. The Depression was not so bad for people who had cash cows, and Willie was never without a book contract. The house had been a cottage on ten acres, with a huge barn. Willie had, indeed, subsequently converted it to house his studio and guest quarters, and to display the memorabilia of his travels, including the impressive collection of voodoo dolls.

It was next door to an estate where President Roosevelt frequently visited a favorite cousin, which I took to be the present-day Wilderstein Preservation. Nearby, Thomas Wolfe had written *Of Time and the River* just a few years earlier. Willie mixed in well with the locals of all classes, from Olin Dows to the local cab driver.

He and Marjorie were persuaded to marry by the local matriarch, Mrs. John Jay Chapman. I had wondered if that act of submission was related to Willie's masochistic shift. He had been impressed with some local lore about John Jay Chapman incinerating his hand to atone for a sin against a friend.

Willie and Marjorie were married in February of 1935, but kept it secret for some eight months, until after *Asylum* was published as a book and became a raging success. When they went public, it was also revealed that Katie had married Lyman Worthington, Marjorie's ex, at about the same time. As Lyman and Katie declined to give the date and place of their marriage, one might also wonder if a double ceremony might have been involved.

Even as I had studied the microfilm, making that notation, I'd seen the contradictions continuing. The alleged history of that Greenwich Village foursome, acknowledged even by Marjorie to some degree, constituted a further problem. There was scarcely any time in probable chronology for it to have existed. Seabrook followed up the success of *Asylum* by going undercover in a state institution for the criminally insane, writing an exposé on that end of mental health. His literary success with those endeavors would set off scores of imitators for decades, another unacknowledged impact. He was then forty-nine and Marjorie was thirty-six. The next three years were bucolic—garden shows and social life on the River.

He'd traveled some around the U.S. writing real mainstream fare for *American Magazine* and *Reader's Digest*. She was writing short stories for *Harper's*, *Mademoiselle*, and, herself also a Mencken creation, *American Mercury*. Marjorie had been happiest when they were both at their typewriters working. But then had come the infamous years of the barn, of *Witchcraft*.

I'd hoped to find the location by working from the old Dows estate and sometime girls' academy described in *No Hiding Place* and in Marjorie's book, but I was soon ready to give up until the morning. This was taking too long, and frankly, I'd not wanted to risk being out near the mansions after sunset. I felt slightly foolish for so yielding to superstition. Still, the descriptions in the old woman's *Testament* had been very vivid, and Justine's state of mind was too dicey for me to want to chance it.

We'd stopped in front of a seemingly vacant tract of land where I made one last effort to get our bearings. I was pointing out landmarks across the River, in the directions of Port Ewen and Hurley, which were denoted on our Chamber of Commerce map.

Justine had been expressing curiosity that I had little or no interest in that icon of my generation, Woodstock, and giggling about our being *"total tourists."*

". . . way up in the mountains over there is the gorge where Rip Van Winkle was supposed to have slept after meeting Henry Hudson's ghost crew." I laughed, enjoying, for my part, a certain feeling of normalcy.

She had followed my finger and begun playfully to debate whether that was *"really"* the location, or in the Blue Mountains closer to Woodstock, as some locals claimed. When she abruptly broke off, I looked back to see her scanning about and behind us. Without warning, she bolted around the car and disappeared into the high weeds and shrubbery. Startled, I had begun to follow, when the sound of her wounded cry quickened my pace.

I found her standing as you see the bereaved beside a fresh grave, one hand tight over her diaphragm and the other clutched to her lips, her shoulders tensed and shaking. As I reached her, she gave up a strangled sob. "Marjorie's little house is gone!" Some rubble at her feet suggested that a building had indeed once stood there, and debating whether this was the actual location of the cottage didn't seem appropriate. I started to put my arm around her.

"Well, the walls were built by the Indians and finished out by the Dutch," I began. "Nothing will endure forever, babe." The cloudy afternoon light dimmed abruptly, and I looked at the darkening, churning sky. There was a lot of circulation up there, and it was about to rain. With a sudden apprehension, I knew I'd made some ghastly mistake.

Maybe I was accustomed to the flat Texas horizon. Perhaps I had stupidly not thought of how, above the cloud deck, the sun might be setting just a hair earlier beyond Woodstock. While the higher Catskills weren't all that lofty, dusk seemed to settle much faster than anticipated. Whatever might be responsible for the effect, maybe only the slight change in latitude added to a mere degree of elevation—it was as though the shadow of the haunted hills was already coming down over Rhinebeck.

---

THE LEGENDS OF THE GORGES AND HOLLOWS were not whom I feared, however. I now think that I had known what to fear since reading Madeleine's *Testament*. Below us, toward the River, the lights had come on in some of the houses. Friendly lights, which might guide one home in a benign evening.

When I looked back to Justine, I was alarmed. She was biting her knuckle so hard that she had drawn blood, and her face was a mask of stark holy terror.

Her eyes had changed color and looked blind, to anything including me, seeing altogether *elsewhere*.

She whirled and ran madly up the hill behind us, oblivious to my calling after her, falling once, then scrambling on ahead. Oh shit, *I thought I knew her*. Despite everything, I'd continued to persuade myself of that. Then she pulls something like this! I'd pursued Linda on suicidal sprints toward highways more than once, but I'd been in much better shape back then. If this youngster was going to run amuck on me, I *did* have a problem.

Even so, I chased after her through the deepening gloom. In the fading light I almost collided with the wall of a large structure. Long, tall, and narrow, it was of the configuration that the old New Yorkers called a "saltbox barn." Sagging in abandonment with its paint long eroded, it was nonetheless evident from the various window casings at upper and lower levels that it had once been converted to habitation. There was no glass left in the staring windows, and a large front doorway yawned mutely empty.

Following Justine's hysterical weeping, I found her kneeling on a dirt floor, as if the cavernous space she was facing were a cathedral. The place had been entirely gutted, remnants of good Depression-era parquetry bearing silent testimony to the two missing floor levels. High above, I could see the darkening sky through tears in the roof. If this indeed had been Willie's barn, all trace of his loving work had been gone these many years.

"It's the dream," she moaned miserably as I knelt

beside her. "I forgot the dream, and now it's come after me." Gone were the faintest intonations of the young woman I'd known, and hearing nothing but the speech of the old Bronx was chilling. Thunder rumbled and lightning flashed away to the west. The crew of the *Half-Moon*, I thought crazily, remembering the legend, bowling with their ninepins up in the Catskills.

"I believed I'd awakened, but I kept waking up again, here," she cried with the terror of an abandoned child. "Oh, my Lord in heaven, please help me. Oh, help me wake up!" Her voice lapsed into a croaking whisper, seemingly akin to the dream experience of "silent screams," which one cannot seem to get out of one's throat.

The lightning flashed again, closer, and I could see that she had a profuse nosebleed. As in despair, she flung herself on the dirt and thrashed about, in a virtual *fugue* state. I endeavored to pin her down; there were certainly nails and God-knew-what in the debris around us. I'd succeeded in embracing her with a good grip when she threw up. Blood, snot, and then puke. I was getting the full treatment and hoped it was good for the soul, because I was not letting go. I noted with indifference my heart pounding to the unaccustomed exertion. If I were going to lose her there, I'd just as soon be dead, rather than face a meaningless world without her.

She had gone into full babble mode, and I frantically worked to decipher what it was she perceived. It seemed she believed herself on a parquet floor, adjacent to a bedroom where she'd gone to sleep; though other dream images and renderings continued to intrude. Some amber light source she was seeing, like a heating grate or a night-light, became the "scare furnace," and other distractions such as that.

She tried to squirm away from me, seeking after a vanished staircase. She was mumbling about plaster saints, African masks, and shelves of witches' dolls. Like a little child, she was terrified of looking at the painted faces—for fear of surprising them *looking back*.

The memory images were so intense that they were patently visible to her. I tried to help her recall that at least some of those memorabilia were packed away back home, but she would only keep begging, "Help me, help me. *Oh, Willie, à l'aide!* Wake me up, please wake me up . . ." Torturously, I pieced the thing together. She was not seeing merely where she wanted to be, but *where she thought she was!*

I had to stay with her, incoherent and out of it as she might be. If there were any hope of pulling her back, I had to go with it. I could only pray that there would be another day, when review of my interpretation of her semicoherent snatches had proven sufficient to the purpose. I cannot begin to recount the discursive bits and pieces from which I was obliged to frame an overall sense.

She rambled on about those other things Willie had kept upstairs, the witch's cradle, the rack. She longed to feel the chains from the rafters against her naked flesh. Even the thought of being placed on the torture instruments was comforting and desirable as compared with . . . The lightning flashes again defined the present moment, and I thought, *God help me, I know what's happening here!* The girl in my arms had never been in this place, but within her, no longer so deep, were the memories of how the other Justine had known it over the years, and especially on her last night together with Willie in 1945.

To her, it was as if she were sleeping here on that night, having a nightmare from which she couldn't awaken. Unconscious, her mind had drifted, as Dunne had theorized, into an unknown future and found . . . this present moment. To her, *this was the dream.* This nightmare—a world with her beloved Willie gone, the barn gutted, such a dark and sad place. She was trying with all her might to consolidate the memories that had defined that other self, fight her way back to an acceptable reality, *to him.*

I reacted as if to an evil demon, as Willie had perversely wanted to be seen, or perhaps feared that he might really be. "No, Seabrook, you bastard! You can't have her!" I screamed out, though maybe only in my mind; I'm not sure. "You didn't care for her before, and now she has another chance. Let go of her!"

But I could feel her slipping away, somehow detaching from the here-and-now. I knew she would joyfully quit this life if she imagined that she would wake in his arms on that other night. The war had ended, Uncle Sam was the last man standing and girding himself as the new Romulus. Her countrymen had imagined the dawn of a brave new world, but something within her would know that darkness had been closing over hers.

For the rest of her life, and into another, her unconscious mind would never escape the accusation of the unremembered dream—the prescient dream that had warned of their last chance. She would sacrifice anything to go back and change things. How could I, above anyone, fail to encompass the horror in that recognition? What else she might be going through as the memories that had composed another life slammed mercilessly into her mind, one thing was certain. That reality was not the horror to be escaped from; *it was this one.*

As I tried to pray, the lost ones of my own life closed in around me. The circle nearly complete, only my place was yet empty. I tried to believe that they would be waiting for me, and pleaded God to forgive my own hurtfulness and neglect. I thought I was going to vomit, too. I'd never been so conflicted, didn't even know for what the hell I was praying. To let her go was impossible. Yet comprehension of her pain was unbearable.

A maudlin little offering of my life for hers could not begin to touch the love that gripped Justine's soul, or divert its purpose. She had reawakened with a passion I had never known, even in my adoration of her. If she could not find him here, she would reach for that other night. Her youthful beauty, her brand-new future, were as nothing compared to the goal before her eyes. She would sacrifice her life, her self, her sanity, just to go back to that other night and make it different. *If she could not find him here . . .*

---

"MADELEINE!" I yelled in her face over the crashing thunder. "Justine," I corrected when I failed to immediately get her attention, "don't you know it's over, babe? The aching and the loneliness are over. The hurting can end now. We live in an otherworld, and I'll always be there to hold your hand. I promise you that, and may I be damned if I don't keep it."

The lightning flashed again, and I saw the green eyes were open, trying to make me out. There was no time to think this through. I knew that I might succeed in waking her into a state comparable to schizophrenia, but at least she would awaken. Without the only reality upon which she would let herself be grounded, I had no confidence that she would.

"Willie?" she asked faintly.

"It's me," I answered earnestly, wondering at the eerie notion that I might, somehow, have just damned us both.

Her hands sought my face in the darkness. "Oh my, you've grown a beard," she laughed weakly, "You always did look good with a beard." A prolonged electrical burst revealed us to each other, and she threw her arms around my neck with joy and relief so intense as it melded with my own. "And I've missed you so much. Oh, my dear, dear Willie!" I wondered at what incomprehensible image she might be seeing.

Was it like in a dream, where a figure might be two persons simultaneously?

The summer rain then came pouring through the holes in the roof above. At first she was deadweight as I lifted her, but she then more or less steadied herself. "We don't belong here, Justine. This is all gone, all past. It's behind us now, and we need to go on." I hoped I was sending the right message; at least she cooperated as I helped her from the barn. It was slow going back down the hill, but given our condition, I didn't mind a good soaking.

In the failing light, I could see that her new clothes were very much a total loss. There being no one about, I just stripped her down. She stood obediently and let the rain wash her while I got a suitcase from the trunk. When I turned back, her face was contorted with weeping, though her tears were lost in the rain.

"Oh dearest," she sobbed, "I lost our little girl." She sagged against the side of the car and I moved quickly to slide her inside. It took a moment for me to remember the matter of the second Justine's suicide, but then it required no psych degree to recognize the gravity of this lament.

"Hush," I whispered as I dried her off with some of my shirts. "I know; I know it wasn't your fault. I wasn't there to help." *Damn you, Willie,* I cursed silently. At least Beam Piper had the decency to apologize for the mess he was leaving behind. Even when he had shot himself to death, he had remained a gentleman.

"But she's *gone*!" This was so heartbreaking it was

unbearable, listening to pain that a soul had not been allowed to unburden across decades; or even, I now wondered, across lifetimes? Before my conception, my mother had lost a pair of twins shortly after their birth. Even with me as a comfort, she had grieved for them the rest of her life. I had no clue how to address this, and as I struggled her into her jeans and jacket, I was preoccupied with our situation.

Reality check: I was in an officially ambiguous relationship with a young woman of indeterminate means. Said young woman appeared to be thoroughly schized out and still bore the evidence that she had been beaten. Such family as she possessed could be counted upon to be unremittingly hostile, and any professionals whose attention might be aroused would merely draw interpretations that rationalized their paychecks.

All probable interpretations looked bad for me, and we were in an alien world where I had no contacts within the system. Even Roder represented an unknown quantity in these circumstances. As if on cue, a police car cruised slowly down the road. It didn't stop, but that just cinched my concerns. I started up and headed straight back to the bridge. Connecting with the Thruway on the Kingston side, I scrupulously observed every traffic regulation.

I'd as rather have gone to our lodgings for some rest and a better cleanup, but a bed-and-breakfast is not my usual speed of motel, where anything short of mayhem can go on with anonymity. I took the decision that our best course was to get back to the City as soon as feasible. There, at least, authority had not the time on its hands to become enthused with social concerns.

By the time I had settled back on the Interstate 87 run, Justine had dozed off. I gathered confidence that I had made the best judgment. We had not unpacked, and Rhinebeck held no further charms for me. As she slept away the miles, my mind was beset by brilliant memories and fantasies of my own. A strange composite from *The Château*: Justine being whipped, but with the elder Justine watching from the balcony? No, what was she watching? The blonde! It was the night I had bought the blonde, and I was holding out my hand, waiting for the girl to step down to me from the stage.

The road ahead was quite visible, but the steady rain dissolved the hard edges of reality. I remembered Justine on the escalator at the Marriott, moving away from me, as if seen from a ship leaving the shore. That conjured up an image of Willie on the gangway of the old *Berengaria*, holding out his hand to a timid young Madeleine-Justine, who was afraid to embark. He stood sidewise to her, waiting with his hand extended. I snapped on the dome light and checked on Justine. She was still dead to the world, but I could see from her eyelids that she was in REM sleep. Maybe another new wrinkle in this thing?

Years before, I had consorted for a while with Anton LaVey, the Aleister Crowley of the late century. He had remarked to me a proposition—that partners who sleep together may experience synchronization of elements of their endocrine glandular systems, much as women's menstrual cycles will match pace. He had speculated that this might explain occasional shared dreams and the like. Could Justine be projecting something? Even so, I suspected that the principle was intimately linked with the question of time. In any event, I knew that I could no longer deny the essential nature of the being beside me.

She awakened in about another hour. My peripheral vision is still good for my age, and I became aware that she was studying me. When I smiled at her she heaved a sigh. "Look it, when you're little and ask where you were before you were born? I know the answer to that now, believe you me. But everything else is a fright."

Her tone turned demanding, "Will you *please* tell me how long? I'm plainly all grown-up." Upon verification that she was twenty-six years old, she sniffed, as if slightly irked. "*Well!* I s'pose that's not as bad as it might of been. Oh dear, *you* did get old again, didn't you?" I wasn't expecting her to be up for tactfulness and tried to laugh it off. This was in spite of the distinct impression that in the woman I was now seeing there could well be a world-class bitch.

"We can't seem to keep from doing that, can we?" I tried to joke around it.

"Look it, fellow, lay off of the soft-soap. As if I can't tell you're ham-acting?" She asked quietly, but with an edge of steel, "You know that liars go to hell? I need a damned drink." I directed her attention to her purse. As she hefted the battered old hip flask, I had no doubt as to whom it had originally belonged. Bathtub gin! Like the curious combination of drugs in the old snuffbox, the clues had been there before me all along. Her remarks cut through the farce I'd felt obliged to perform. I knew precisely what she meant and responded in all seriousness.

"I believe that *you believe* I'm Willie. And now I have to believe that you are who and what you say. Isn't that enough for right now?" I wanted to touch bases with her present-life persona, and tried to get her to consider the association of her identity with a particular set of memories, but she wasn't up for it. Morphing into the likeness of a college girl on a mescaline trip, she drifted off into the molded dashboard and digital displays, as if everything was new and enchanting.

Before reaching the City, things continued on the edge of bizarre at a local "hot shop." I'd been thankful to avoid the presumably comforting, near-identical character of chain restaurants. Commercially contrived *déjà vu*, in our present circumstances, would only have moved me along toward a graver disorientation.

As I finally decided that I would have to fetch her out of the rest room, she emerged—putting her hairbrush into her purse. It occurred to me that I'd never seen Justine without a purse, even when in Goth drag. When I asked if she were all right, she haughtily announced that she did her hundred strokes at the same time every evening.

Then she wasted yet more time by insisting I feed

her the oatmeal I'd ordered to get something bland into her stomach. I got through this by presenting it as an obvious game for the perception of onlookers. It *was* an ordeal, infantilism not being my thing. But the way she took to the game gave me a further insight. Her conscious contents were overwhelmingly those of her predecessor, but she related to them as would a much younger person.

While I did not forget that she might contain *all* of the other Justine, at least up to 1945, including that woman's own youth, the behavior suggested that brain chemistry was a definite factor. I was further heartened when she giggled and apologized for "hurling" on me. There seemed reason to hope that the strong physical reality of the present might eventually reorganize the weakly connected past memories, rather than the reverse. I was thinking about this as we reached the City. Traversing the tunnel beneath the River, I felt her tense up again. Following her gaze to rivulets of moisture seeping down its sides, I sympathized.

The Manhattan traffic was manageable, so instead of going directly to the airport, I drove through the Village, chatting idly to her of the days of Kerouac and the Beats, and the times that had followed. I wondered at what it had been like in the earlier time, the Thomas Wolfe time, the Seabrook time. This turned out to be my second-worst idea of the day, hard after caving on the issue of seeking the Rhinebeck location near twilight.

Later I realized that she was being drawn, like a

moth to the flame, to confront the most emotionally charged contents of her predecessor's memory. The old woman had prescribed that she read the manuscript, and that's what we should have done, rather than have me start tinkering around. I asked her if there was anyplace she'd like to see. Her voice cracked as she cried angrily, "I'D LIKE TO STOP BY THE BREVOORT, AND DROP IN AT THE 156!"

---

"I'd like to breakfast at Mouquon's or play in the street, but I can't do that, can I?" She demanded that I turn onto West Twelfth and find a place to park, no small chore. "I remember you leading me up Fifth Avenue by a chain," she snickered, as we began to walk. "We'd gotten only as far as Fourteenth Street when some East Side Jewesses were coming out of Hearn's. They saw us and were shouting and pointing, when the big fat one got very angry and called you a Yiddish name, and then whacked you with her umbrella! We hopped into a taxi and came home quick. That was all that happened, really, but it *was* sorta exciting."

I tried to comfort myself that she had skimmed that story in Greene's book, but couldn't make my heart believe it as she drifted farther yet. It was awesome, and not a little spooky, hearing her describe the wide avenues empty except for a late streetcar and a couple of carriages. I knew that I was then hearing recollections from a childhood at the beginning of the century, when the buildings had been smaller and more widely spaced, and everything had been so, so quiet.

Listening to her made me feel, if we strolled just a bit further, maybe made a turn in some impossible direction, such would be exactly what we would find. In retrospect, I would wonder if, in the company of that being balanced between realities, might not I have been drawn to the margins of my own? We saw panhandlers, but they did not approach. A junkie, fixing up in an alley, we passed as ghosts in the summer night.

Walking back, we passed a church with an old bell tower. Scanning the second-story windows across the street, she wistfully recalled waking up to hear all the church bells ringing together. "I was frightened! Katie had been keeping me home, for fear of the epidemic. She put her arms around me, saying that it was for the Armistice. The War was over, and we were so happy . . ."

In the car, she doubled over and hugged her middle, grieved to the point of sickness. Justine's specific indifference to scenes of late-century ugliness around us revealed nostalgia as quite unrelated to the relative beauty of a given time. I'd never before thought of it like that. Our social ills did not impress a memory that contained sweatshops and Hell's Kitchen. No, it was something other that distressed her, and it was with foreboding that my attention focused on a number, well recalled from my research, on the other side of the street. With trepidation, I pointed out a location, which had come to house a realty firm.

She cupped her hands over her mouth. "I can't recognize it anymore." Profound tragedy was in her quavering voice. "Katie lit the window around the Christmas tree to make it easier for me to find my way. I didn't think—never imagined it like this," she sobbed. "The loss! I'm the same, but everything is gone!"

That was the conundrum, I discovered. The classic quandary of the immortal is only the human condition raised to a higher power. Oh God, we think so little; we view ourselves as priceless and value that about us so poorly. We strain toward the supposed potential of an unknown future. Then that future comes for us, and we find ourselves alone, in a strange and uncaring ghost-world.

Trying to seize the moment, I stressed to her that she was *not* the same. This was precisely why she must embrace, even magnify, her recent memories and persona, to whom this City would be a wonderful adventure. As we were talking Justine here, I was tempted to head uptown, attempt to divert her with the thriving sex industry. But comprehension paled when I would try to explain the simplest causal relationships. She broke down in sadness and frustration, like a coma victim who had awakened to a world that had passed her by. Immersed in the baseline reality of the other Justine, the jumbled contents of her present life were making little or no sense.

"I cannot construe what you're even talking about. This is Aldous's brave new world? It's *unmentionable*! *Quel cauchemar.* Let go of me, and I'm lost in a hellish nightmare." I tried again to reassure her that she had *not* remained the same. There was a part of her that was familiar with all this, could cope with it, but she was not to be consoled. Again, I swore never to abandon her. Even so, I was all too aware that I could be torn from her, and what would become of her then?

Minions of society all march to pretty much the same general orders: "If it looks different, shoot." A predictable commitment authorization from next of kin would have nothing whatsoever to do with any legitimate considerations. No help there. But taking her home to Atlanta, to shelter and isolation, left me uneasy.

I couldn't imagine that the elder Justine, planning for her successor to grow to maturity before recall, had intended a single-ended consolidation of personality. But maybe she had overlooked the traumatic effects of inputs such as we had just experienced. Locales that incessantly aroused feelings of regret and loss did not bode well for her integration and recovery.

At the barn, she'd longed for the security of her chains. Even around me, there was no calculating what she might do or say, but I could at least communicate with her. She would respond to me, even if delusional, as had my dying mother. I veered away from that awful comparison and applied the simplest of all tests.

"The President? I dunno, FDR? No, wait. I'm *still* doing that. Can you believe getting used to *President* Harry Truman?" That cinched it. I had to get her to a safe haven. Evidently, the entirely alien impacted less personally. JFK International merely intimidated rather than horrified. By then she was remembering who Joseph Kennedy's second son had been.

She stayed nestled under my arm, clutching her big portfolio, while I first attempted to change our reservations. Giving up on that, I bought us one-ways on a red-eye to Dallas–Fort Worth. It was either that or try to cope with more hours of waiting in the terminal, or finding our way to another, to get an Atlanta flight. Using the one credit card I carry for emergencies, I didn't even attempt to involve her in the process.

Then she spied a jumbo airliner taxiing beyond the plate glass. Even as the panic attack began, I remembered that the elder Justine had been afraid of flying. There was nothing else for it. I went into my pocket for the Valium, assuring her that the "strong sophoric" would keep her from being afraid.

"Speaking of Aldous's story? Well, this is like 'soma.'" At her body weight, what I gave her was actually going to knock her on her cute little butt. I had taken the decision that I would rather steer a zoned-out kid through security and onto the plane than one having a screaming fit.

As the drug took effect, I used a nearby phone to call Joe in Arlington, Texas. Justine had tried to be helpful with "wiring" him, then stared blankly at me as I explained that long-distance calls were commonplace. The agony of her frustration was visible. She would reach for a clarifying memory, but more often find only the dated assumptions of the other time.

She seemed to remember the *fact* of recent technology: "Keyboard, nothing. It's only typing, after all." But in the same breath she failed to comprehend how the great Western Union could have been reduced to consoles in the backs of check-cashing shops. It was ironic. Deutsch had proposed that past and future are merely special cases of alternate realities. In that light, the being under my arm had not only been able to use the "Everett phone"; with it, she'd called a goddamned cab!

Brief and to the point, I told Joe the ETA and flight number, that I was in an emergency situation, and that he might expect to find our young friend in a precarious emotional condition. It's very nice to have someone you can call like that in the middle of the night.

Drawing her against me as we sat in the gate's waiting area, I marveled at a subjective philosophical juxtaposition. On the one hand, there were the mysteries being unraveled: a vision of the fabric of the cosmic tapestry which boded a complexity undreamed of; on the other, a Zen-like clarity I had sought but never before found. One purpose, one reason for being; sitting there, stroking her hair.

# IX
# Ghost Years

JOE WAS WAITING FOR US, THANK GOD, AT THE GATE in the American terminal at Dallas–Fort Worth International. With Justine between us, and a good grip under each armpit, we were able to negotiate her down the ramps and outside. Such attention as we did attract was on the order of a few smirks from passengers and a dim eye from security, but as we were clearly leaving, there was no interference. Joe observed that they thought she was drunk, and I retorted that he should know. I'd had to peel him out of that same terminal, years before during his drinking days.

The circumstances of our "escape from New York" had left me paranoid about the details of logistics. We'd been able to embark owing only to being in a teeming monstrosity that gives not a damn—unless you block the flow of traffic. Californicated Texas, its much-vaunted tradition of individualism aside, has become the most intrusive and litigious place in the nation. Lawyers and social workers swing from trees.

Describing the restaurant adventure with his Justine, Seabrook had declared that no one interferes with a girl who's poised and happy. True now as well, but in his day the issue was the potential interference of individuals. In our time we are all in jeopardy of the benevolent "intervention" of the state.

At any rate, Justine was not presently poised and happy. Doped up, sporting numerous marks from our night at *The Château*, and still being impacted by vivid recollections that would be indistinguishable from schizophrenic hallucinations, she looked far too much the carrion upon which the social-service vultures feed. Joe's "suburban utility vehicle" was parked right outside, displaying a handicapped permit due to his wife Diane's disabilities. As we got Justine and our bags settled into the back, I told him flatly that we needed to go to ground for a few days.

Joe, who never worries about anything anymore, scolded me about being obsessed with what "might" happen. Without details which I was not even near being able or willing to give, he could have no clue as to the degree to which I could now be excused for *that*!

Living with a declining alcoholic renders one immune to public humiliation, and episodes from my experience with Linda had left me well equipped to handle the journey with a minimum of consternation. Once back in Texas, I possessed the contact resources to counter any but the most determined "intervention." Still, I was unwilling to risk the slightest possibility of her falling into the clutches of professional psych-hackers while her behavior was still dysfunctional. There was no way to gauge the damage that might be done by their ignorant meddling.

Another consideration was money. Justine would have to pull it back together before she could access her buffer, and I imagined that I had maxed out with the tickets for our sudden departure. I was grateful for Joe's largely unquestioning support, and to God for letting me get Justine to a less exposed place to recover.

I would not allow for any consideration that she might not recover, be unable to correlate the conflicting realities slamming into her memory. Just as well that she was crashed out in the back as we cruised the futuristic airport complex and the choked arteries into Arlington, now only a portion of the fabric of the sprawling D-FW Metroplex.

Insofar as I had a plan, it was to try to help reinforce, within the baseline, elements of her present-day persona. One that could cope with the sights and sounds of the alien landscape which had sent her antecedent self into a paroxysm of fear and disorientation. Her reactions to the Village suggested that an environment known to that other self, but radically changed, would not be very helpful. Just possibly, an unfamiliar but quiet suburban setting was the best I could provide.

The evidence was becoming overwhelming. I had no choice but to operate on the assumption that she *was* the other Justine, and always had been! But I was denied the luxury of elation at this potential discovery. Reflection on rational proof of continued existence must wait until I'd dealt with the remarkable, and rather terrifying, reality of the awakening process.

Her predecessor had indisputably contrived the conditions for her *anamnesis*, a "remembrance" or, more precisely, the negation of forgetfulness. She must have studied long on how her own preconscious buttons might be pushed. But something seemed amiss. The elder Justine's plan implied that her new incarnation would be gently reawakened by virtue of first living in her old home; then going to Rhinebeck; then reading the manuscript. That last had yet to be accomplished.

Had I messed up with the cathartic sadomasochistic activity at *The Château*, by taking her to the barn, or merely with my own inadvertent "intervention"? If so, then what of the confluence of synchronicity that bound me into this thing; whence did that come? All I could cling to was faith, and the few words from her *Testament*'s instructions to go to Rhinebeck, "for which I am so sorry . . ." Perhaps this reaction was not wholly unforeseen.

Before discussing the situation with Joe and Diane, I tucked Justine into bed in their guest room. Through her drugged fog, she seemed content with the chenille bedspread and oversize pillows, protected by the old wooden furniture and watched over by Di's wonderful collection of dolls. I could not escape the contrast of these friendly little figures with Willie's witch-dolls, which must have glowered over a woman called Justine on that last night in 1945.

---

I SECURED A NOTE TO A PILLOW with a safety pin, in case she should awaken: "Don't worry. I'm here. I love you." There was no predicting how long this process would take. While the memories of her antecedent self continued to self-organize into a separate persona, insisting on believing me to be her lost Willie, I would have to play that role to a greater or lesser extent.

There was irony here. Men have always projected desired images on women, demanding that they become what we need. Now, only by playing at being a man long dead, could I remain her bond with this present moment.

Contrary to how my young psych major might have been educated to self-diagnose, I was fearful. If this powerful personality from the past were to disintegrate, I believed that it stood to drag down with it into madness the less elaborate and fixed one of its successor. This was not some damned "complex" to be analyzed away, or, depending on your religion, exorcised. The two were really only a single Justine, and the breach needed time to heal . . . or so I hoped.

I took a hairbrush from the vanity and gently stroked the tangles from her red tresses. Watching them spread out on the pillows, I thought, *my angel, my chained lady*. I adored her as much as I had come to realize that I despised myself: myself and my world.

Had there been no real help for my poor Linda,

what could there be for an exotic creature like Justine? They'd stop short of burning her at the stake, but they'd gladly render her catatonic through drugs or electroshock to erase her inconvenient memories. Much of her education had been wasted; there is no science of the mind available today, only propaganda and self-serving bias masquerading as science.

I adjourned to the kitchen to drink coffee and offer some sort of explanation. Joe and I related by an understanding that was almost family, and Di is one of the kinder and less-judgmental people I've known. However, there is a limit to how much you can ask anyone to swallow in one gulp. In the tradition of Seabrook with his cannibal feast, I put together, for Di's benefit, an "alternative reality" that was true enough for the purpose. Having known Justine "a little while," I planned to marry her as soon as possible; some family problems due to the May-December aspect; had partied in New York with the wrong people. Joe looked at the ceiling and stayed quiet.

I would tell him later that I hoped the proposed marriage would be fulfilled when Justine was up for it. I preferred for that to be a *fait accompli* before I had to deal with her mother. I did neglect to mention just who her mother was! My only pure fiction was to invent a designer drug that tended to linger in the system with repeated flashbacks for a while. I didn't want them to be too disconcerted should Justine come out in period drag, looking for "Willie"!

After graciously acknowledging the most well-intentioned cautions to their crazy friend, I wandered outside for a smoke. Joe had offered me the use of one of his cars, and I reflected, in the markedly calm summer morning, that Lake Arlington was only a few miles away.

The thought of the place where this all appeared to have begun, at least for me, so many years before, had a curious effect. Rather than existing as I had previously thought of it, abstracted away into a superpotent archetypal domain, the memory blended quietly with the familiar atmosphere of the North Texas morning. In its heart was still a red-haired angel, but otherwise the memory seemed more a normal part of the fabric of my life.

I thought it likely that, in comparison with the extraordinary phenomenon sleeping inside, the whole thing about JJ was being reduced to more natural proportions. I couldn't go there immediately, risking being gone when Justine woke up, but decided that I would deal with it soon. Maybe going back there would shed some new light on my end of this weird business. I dropped a tranq myself, put out my pipe, and went to bed.

I was roused once, when Justine softly cried out and turned to burrow in against me. I gently wrapped her about me and dozed again.

Coming up again, this time from REM sleep, I brought back clear memory of my latest dream. Three of my familiar dreamscapes were superimposed, all locations along Interstate 35 and each featuring a highway interchange, which were also merged into one. I was amused to note that the big road's mile markers were delineated with numerical dates.

One branch of the intricate cloverleaf ran downhill into a dark place, like a bad neighborhood or a seedy little town. Justine had turned her ankle, and I went back and carried her uphill, walking on a graveled grade, which I associated with unpaved roads of the past. At the intersection, the rising sun was illuminating a newly completed highway link converging with my dream highway. I felt exultant, like an Orpheus triumphant, bringing his love again into the land of the living.

Coming fully awake, I abruptly recalled another dream, possibly from the previous sleep cycle. The drums beat in the jungle. Africa? No, maybe Haiti, for I recognized the chant as the one Seabrook had transcribed, "*Papa Legba, ouvrí barrière* . . . open the gate . . ."

I lay utterly still, fully engaged with the lingering impressions, consolidating all the memory I could. I knew that Legba is the Voudon *loa* of the crossroads, whose Catholic manifestation is Lazarus. His title is *Opener of the Gate Between the Worlds.*

The dim illumination sang that it was blue twilight beyond the drawn blinds. I was alone in the room. *Déjà vu à la Gulfport!* Panicking, I jumped up and jerked open the guest-room door. I ran, fully naked, through the silent house toward a light from the kitchen, but it was vacant as well. Joe should have been gone to his second-shift job by then, I knew, but where the hell was everyone else?

I tried to reassure myself that I would surely have been awakened had there been a crisis. I hurried back to the bedroom and pulled on my trousers, then fumbled for the light to find my other things. Finding myself without her, I had again to fight down the eerie fear that she was of a separate reality, so easily lost from my world. I spied my written reassurance, but saw that it had been removed and repinned to the bedspread. I registered that there was an additional notation beneath my scrawl.

---

*GONE SHOPPING*, IT READ, *LOVED YOU LONGER*, $J^2$

Shopping? The image of young Justine the mall monkey collided with the elegant, almost Spenserian, penmanship in which the abbreviated lines were written. I'd seen that handwriting recently, on yellowed letters and envelopes, from long before. But what seized me with wonder was her initial, boldly and lavishly inscribed, and attached to it the superscript digit two.

The message was ironic and profound. Her mother had been known as JJ. Thus, she was now seeing herself as Justine squared, Justine multiplied by herself, complex-conjugate Justine! I had to regard it as assurance that she was successfully integrating her psychic contents rather than being overwhelmed by the greater volume from her antecedent self.

As I poured coffee, sounds came from the garage attached to the kitchen, and I peeked through the door window to see Justine$^2$ helping Di with her crutches and several large plastic bags. They were laughing together about something, and I could see with a glance that Di had already adopted her. For some reason, I was reminded of the relationship between Linda and the elder Justine, nearly thirty years before, which had left me somewhat uneasy. Compared to that dark bond, this interaction came off decidedly healthy and wholesome.

I helped them through the kitchen door with the bags. Then Justine[2] threw her arms about my neck in a fierce embrace. Sensing her to be just a bit unsteady on her feet, I held her long, feeling relief that things seemed well enough. Di surveyed us over the top of her glasses as she put things away, saying nothing.

Justine[2] ran off to the bedroom with the bags containing her catch. Di had finished putting up and settled into the breakfast nook across from me when she returned, happily modeling a short skirt she'd found to match her leather vest. Her legs and midriff quite bare, the whip scratches were evident, and Di's look hardened. Even so, I couldn't conceive that as being a problem; Justine[2] was an adult, after all. Like Seabrook, I'd never made any secret of my sexual tastes, so Di shouldn't be surprised.

The girl pulled a chair over to the edge of the table and joined us. As she seated herself, I once again saw her palms sweep upward, lifting skirts that had not been there for decades. She looked down with confusion at her bare thighs, and an undeniable blush suffused all her exposed skin. She glanced at me almost furtively, and I had another revelation.

The antique patterns of acculturation in her mind would keep Justine[2], the exhibitionist, in a constant state of stimulation when in modern dress based on the sensation that she was practically naked. Regaining her composure, she chatted for a while and, though she looked especially young when she crossed her bare legs beneath her, the expression "happy and poised" came to mind.

After she excused herself, a slight but audible hint of the Bronx tainting her speech, I turned to Di. "What?" I demanded, wondering if I might be required to explain who "Willie" was or something.

"You're on probation with me, as of now." I waited to hear what was coming. "It's rare to meet a young woman that much in love, anymore, and with an old fart like you!" She shook her head. "I can't imagine why, but even the more distasteful things about you fascinate her. What she believes about you, it's just incredible." I frowned, but she waved off my incipient inquiry.

"Another time, but you had better take good care of her, or you'll deserve to go to hell." Di is a religious woman, but not of the sort who invokes hellfire. However, it wasn't the content of the conditional damnation that gave me sudden pause. It was the form, and I asked why she put it that way.

"I don't know. It could be the feeling I get that she's given up so much for you—so strong I have to speak my mind. Look, you're always coming around here, whining about wanting another chance." Her seriousness was frightening, "I think that somebody heard you."

There are not many people who can ream me out. I looked at Di, with her leg braces and all the suffering she'd endured, and it triggered again that devastating sense of shame. There was absolutely no sarcasm when I promised to do the right thing. It was not moral intimidation but the certainty of how deeply Di really could see into things which got me out of the room in a hurry. I was about to spill the whole bizarre story, as I'd told her all about JJ a couple of years earlier, and was sure she'd think me way over the top.

Justine[2] was at the guest-room vanity, outlining her lips in contemporary fashion. She had applied an eye mask, but instead of simply a dark band, it was composed of elaborate swirls and feathering with an *art nouveau* look. Her movements seemed more subdued, less bouncy; but she had been through a lot by any standard. I sat on the bed and watched, intrigued by the continuing merger of personas. "Does wearing next to nothing get you off? Not just your clit ring that keeps you horny, is it?"

"Please!" Her green eyes twinkled in the mirror. "Embarrassed much? Now I know why that's always done it for me. *Kewl*," she continued, "weird, yet cool." She sat back, appraising her cosmetic art. I had no clue as to how to delve further. I was afraid of doing something to upset what might yet well be a precarious balance. "Hey, you didn't do the bail thing"—she was smiling at me in the mirror, maybe a bit sadly—"when I showed my true colors."

"Why would you expect that of me?" Di was one

matter, but I now felt hurt and almost offended.

She didn't answer. "So it's like that." It was a question, though you wouldn't have known it through the flat punker assertiveness. "Di told me. The marriage thing?"

"You didn't give me an answer," I responded stiffly.

"You mean on the aeroplane, going to New York? *That* was a proposal?" She sighed. "I am sure I've only been waiting to hear one for eighty years, believe you me."

Justine$^2$'s speech varied, in part, with which sets of memories she was thinking about or associating. I didn't know when I should be concerned or even how to deal with the continuing identification of me with Willie. I guess it showed, because she dropped her hands in her lap and glanced nervously about the top of the vanity.

"I know; I'm sorry. I'm being touchious." She came to me and stood between my knees, and I pressed my lips against her shiny navel ornament. I took her hands and tried to explain my thoughts about the memories and integrating the personas, but was being distracted by her quivering belly. *"Non, non. Arrête!"* she teased when I pinned her wrists behind her back.

Emotion ran neck and neck with libido. I wanted her, yes, but as I was about to get on my knees anyway, I was moved to make an on-the-knees traditional proposal as well. She knew it, too.

"Babe, I can't doubt who you are, you're . . ." I was as unable to express anything as a teenager. ". . . you're everything. But I have to learn how to relate, don't you see? I'm terrified of even hearing how I looked through your eyes at *The Château* in sixty-nine. Whom do I know you *as*? Do you understand?"

"You know me. *You've always known me*," Justine$^2$ whispered, with a throaty hoarseness that struck a chord from those bygone nights. I knew then how stunned Roder must have been when a voice from the past had bade farewell to her "old friend."

Giggling at my disconcertion, she squirmed in my grip. "No way it's more gross than having to hear about that dried-up, perverted, old woman. Go and get me started, you know I'm insatiable. Swell gams, hunh?" I was pushed the rest of the way by a sweaty thigh thrown over my shoulder. "Gimme some sugar!" My face buried in her muff, I began to lick around her clit ring.

"It's all, y'know, about accessing new pathways to memories? Last night I pulled a real brainstorm. Now it's like Fibber McGee's closet in here—everything before that night in '45. The rest is defragmenting much more slowly, thank heaven. Oh," she moaned, "I'm gonna have so many stories to tell you!" I thrust my tongue deep into her, savoring her distinctive taste. Everyone has her own and Justine$^2$'s was slightly acerbic—it figured. Despite her heat, her attention was all over the place.

"Look it, think of me like a stroke victim or, play like I've been tortured with electroshock. That's no fun either, but it's farther up our alley. This feels like that, only the paths must be across time." She paused the motion of her hips and giggled mischievously. "I think you had more hair, didn't you?" As I lightly nipped at her navel, she switched channels again.

"Poor dear, don't fret," she cajoled, with the archaic inflection. "You've been so worried about being with a younger woman, and now it proves out that she's nearly a hundred years old. No, wait. Let me see. Centenarians *are* at our sexual peak," she laughed as I pinned her hips. "Better oughta get a cock ring . . ." She moaned as I sucked her clit between my teeth and worked on her with the tip of my tongue. "Or not!"

"Check it out. I would play like, a sex surrogate—for my girlfriends who were afraid of pregnancy, or flat afraid of sex, period? I would fuck their beaux so they didn't have to. Ooh. You like that, hunh? Make me hurt, *chéri, torturez-moi!*" We made love, as gently as she would allow. While an aroused Justine[2] heads directly for the edge, apart from more pinching and biting and fingernails in my butt, she was satisfied with "slow-processing."

I discovered that "fantasy" was another term whose normal meaning had expired. "Many men have had me," she moaned, "but only you did I wanna tell about it, to share everything." In the calm afterglow, she luxuriated in her recollections, and her language assimilated even further. Which was more amazing, to be inflamed by lucid erotic memories from other times, or their identity with the unacknowledged history of our own?

Regarding her grand indifference to questions of hygiene, she chided, "Lighten up. HIV is scary, but so were smallpox and scarlet fever. Say, syphilis before penicillin? What's the sense of immortality without some *savoir-faire?* Diphtheria? Been there, done that. Don't expect me to bat an eye at herpes or a silly yeast infection." There was nothing for it but to reinforce a state of mind that, all things considered, appeared healthy enough.

Neither of us could know whether she would experience a reversal. If I had any kind of handle on this, our trip to the barn had actualized a sort of psychic loop across time. She had plugged into that other Justine's precognitive nightmare in a major way. Cleaving so tightly to the assumptions of that long-ago moment, struggling to *be* that woman, had provoked an *anamnesis*.

She had been reeling from a sudden deluge of the psychic contents that had constituted her antecedent self—up until the night of that event. Still, there remained a quarter century of experience, which she seemed to be accruing at a more measured pace, if not as slowly as her gradual assimilation of bits and pieces before our ill-advised excursion to the barn.

Spiriting her away from settings that stressed her identity had been for the best, she agreed. "Worlds had someway collided, my worlds. The feelings were so strong . . ." she began, but I stopped her. Revisiting those feelings so soon seemed imprudent. I suspected that a fully coherent treatment of the *anamnesis* itself was improbable in any event.

She insisted that we begin to read the manuscript. "Even the fractions I've started to recall are like any book read a long time past. You only remember the content in general terms, and gotta be refreshed."

I asked if she could answer me as to whether she had foreseen meeting me, her book finding its way to me, any of the nexus of synchronicity. "Couldn't prove it by me"—she looked at me piercingly—"but my testament reads as though it were all about finding you, does it not? After discovering you at *The Château*, I must've prayed very hard."

Distraction was then of a different order. Though fully nude, she remained nonetheless poised, addressing me like a well-bred lady in an early-century drawing room. "Then, if I was not a part of your plan," I pressed, "how can you be sure I'm not just an interference, other than solely by your subjective feeling about the nature of our connection? And please, try to indulge me by distinguishing between Willie and me when you speak. It's confusing."

She nodded and slipped on her heels. It was evident that her unconscious impulse had not been toward the admitted sex appeal as she moved with what appeared a well-trained grace to get the big leather portfolio. She placed it on the bed and opened it, lifting out the distilled manuscript as though from among sacred relics.

"You . . . he," she corrected, "thought that 'coinky-dinks' are like lines of force in a field. Like metal shavings arranged around a magnet? As if, more like gravity? Effects of reciprocal histories interfering, or whatnot. Anytime you perceive them, or have the feeling of *déjà vu*, worlds have touched, or branched, on a scale visible in our lives, to say the least."

She laid a finger beside the ring in her nose. "These should not be seen as isolated little happenings. They're woven into the fabric of everything!" With that startlingly familiar pronouncement, she handed me the manuscript.

**FRAGMENTS FROM**
**THE FAN-SHAPED DESTINY**

August, 1945

. . . and so, I have been telling you that I have lived before. Not as a serial transmigration in a one-and-only universe, not in a "past" life, but the same one - in an otherworld, one which lies along another branch in the paths of my fan-shaped destiny. I believe that all of us may, now and again, slip just a bit off our well-beaten path. That is, unconsciously follow an adjacent route so nearly identical, on an incremental scale, as to remain beneath notice. From time to time, we might discover a discrepancy, which we promptly censor out as resulting from false memory.

Memories, and where they are stored, appear to be the ties which bind us to one actuality as opposed to another. This business of waking up at a prior moment and proceeding on a divergent course, a course determined in part by a substantial retention of my otherworldly memories, I believe that I could repeat almost never. Such a being would increasingly be set adrift from any particular actuality. I've had more than enough difficulty in sorting out the Brownie snapshots of moments from only two histories.

This is, perchance, the meaning of the waters of forgetfulness - that "draught of long oblivion" which the Poet tells us must be quaffed by all souls whom the gods have destined to descend again to the land of the living. The same general rule probably applies to transports to future or parallel moments. The human survival trait of clear causal reasoning would decree that memory should be so washed.

But every rule has its exceptions. I can never know, and consequently cannot try to tell you, how it came about that I woke up in Ella Baxter's boardinghouse in Augusta on that morning in 1907. It was as if a dirty film had been stripped away from the world. As if all things, visual and auditory, had been suddenly infused with an unearthly luminance. The colors on the quilt at my feet were abnormally vivid and made harmony. Why, I was almost afraid to lift my head or move, for fear it would all fade. You see, I had gone to sleep the night before, sunken in drink in my London rooms, in the deep December of 1940. At first, I thought I must have perished in that night's bombing, by just saying the hell with it and going to bed, rather than sanely hunkering down in the shelters.

Mayhap I did. When that war raged again, here in my second-chance world, I wanted to go over, but that was not to be. Had the destruction been terrible as I remembered from that other night, or merely in my own, eccentric, deranged eye? Could I comb the details of the Blitzkrieg destruction . . . but time for seeking answers has run out, again.

Remember that my dual, memory-conscious nicks-of-time spring from a single trunk, prior to that bright morning in Augusta. I have sometimes thought that the twisting and changing of a child's imageries and day-dreams, by my _faerie_ god-mother Piny, may have left me loosely connected to material reality. Late in the day, I believe once more, as I did before the gray walls of adulthood reared about me, that those eternal-in-the-now-hence-always-memory-lasting visions were no more dreams than these lives I have known. Surely, they must have been vestibules to otherworlds that my young grandmother opened, in love and pity, for another little soul who, like herself, found ordinary life unbearable.

So many questions still. Is physical death requisite for a complete transport to another history? I know for a certain fact that one may double back and re-enter upon a path, consequently commencing an other life, at a point other than at birth. And what is the nature of these points, these bits of destiny action? While boarding at Ella's place, I had now and then gazed hypnotically at candles, trying to read my future. This would produce some strange moments, slits that I might have been able to return through later, which is as may be.

Conversely, symmetry would seem to deny death a monopoly on exits. If so, what would be left behind by a departing Self? Or is that entity coterminous with each diversified one of our selves, and all that's involved is a matter of sharpening an alternate focus? Where I'm hopefully bound, I may learn some more of the answers. My friend awaits me on the bank of the Cavally River, but there may first be an unavoidable bath in the Lethe.

It may be objected that I but faintly touched on this in my books. I've had the privilege of bughouse psychic therapies, thank you, a point that begs no further enlargement. I hinted at what I could.[72] Though the message is there, for those who

72. Seabrook, *Witchcraft*, p. 268. "It can be that this whole thing has happened before." He then quotes the mathematician Cassius Jackson Keyser of Columbia, "Simultaneity of events is relative, not absolute; the sense of time is only an imperfect sense of the fourth dimension in space." A possible example of Seabrook hinting at what he could.

have eyes, I constrained myself to publishers' and readers' expectations. The result was that my effort on witchcraft was hardly an illuminating contribution to any science of the paranormal.

What effects there have been on my writing are nothing I can shout about. I found it almost impossible to keep to a proper chronology and, every so often, advanced patently contradictory views. Imagine the retention within one's mind of similar yet not identical sets of memories. Throw enough time on a given series or episode, and it becomes difficult to recall which of its variants applies.

More important was that over time, I would say by about age forty, the otherworldly memories had dimmed, as do all old recollections. After a point, I would no longer be able readily to assign a given recollection between the slightly differing sequences. The most intense remained as warnings and did influence my conduct. They were as astral dreams, burned into my mind, yet of a different order of reality. Logically, I could not always square them with what the facts of this life assured me to be real, but neither dared I ignore them. They accused me, as has the voice of my dead brother.

The most terrible was that of standing at the window after the sirens had gone up over blacked-out London. As I had before and would again, I'd run away to war, leaving behind a Katie who would follow after me "no more forevermore forever" because she was no more, her blithe spirit extinguished in drink. Back at home were Lyman and Mink, doing each other to death because I wouldn't take her hand when Mink's need had been greatest. Lyman was no excuse for me, quite the contrary. Following after Katie like a puppy, he'd been more than ready to do her better, had only the bad old bear been willing to let her go.

I had been drinking alone in my rooms on the last Sunday in December. A moonless night had fallen early. The propaganda had assured us that the hellish attacks of the autumn had abated. The Battle of Britain would essentially be over but some had thought otherwise. Ambassador Kennedy, persuaded that England was finished, had resigned and returned home. I'd heard that more Londoners than usual had retired to the deep shelters that evening. What had prompted their foreboding? Had angels walked among them to spread the warning? Had they flown in across the Channel to raise the alarm that the Valkyries were aloft? If so, none had been inclined to waste his energies on this patently lost soul.

The sky had been completely dark by six o'clock. Even before the sirens had gone up in the southwest, I had heard the droning of the Heinkels' and Junkers' engines, also seemingly far more than customary. In minutes, the first bombs had fallen on Southwark, across the Thames. The beams of the kettle lights sought the intruders. I watched the gaudy white sparklers of the incendiaries and felt the reverberating thuds from the high explosive bombs. As the frequency of the strikes increased, there had begun a curious lull from the anti-aircraft guns. I remember wondering if the city's defenses were failing when, at a quarter of seven, the electricity had gone off.

---

Indeed, "the lamps had gone out all over Europe," but Justine's little candle had been snuffed out long before. Somewhere in France, even as I had listened to the wail of the sirens that London evening, the boots of the Reich might have been slogging over her muddy grave. If my life had ended, I knew that it had been because I'd lost my link with the divine. God help me, I had brought her to that, <u>thrown her away</u>! Thrown up the corporeal incarnation of the archetype I'd conjured with Piny's aid, the lady-in-chains who had always been there for me.

I had inherited her from the hand of Aleister Crowley in 1919, after he'd branded his

Star into her fair hide and then abandoned her. Taking her to Europe, I'd displayed her, only succeeding in handling her carelessly - as had my mentor, the "Great Beast," might he burn alongside me in hell! Poised and pretty as a picture, alert and sensitive, and a slave to her senses, she had been an instant hit in the Paris of the Lost Generation. When I later let her slip away at Evenos, I temporized, persuading myself that she had found her element. The dissolute intelligentsia of that world had been absorbed with the figure and philosophy of the "divine Marquis." Noted <u>artistes</u> had helped to outfit Justine with all the accoutrements to scandalize and titillate a bored society.

She had been initiated by the cultists of sexual slavery, at a restored castle by the sea, overlooking the haunted hills and ravines of ancient <u>Var</u>. Katie and I had watched with voyeuristic delight from the balcony above the banquet hall while Justine, wearing only her high silver collar, had been put through her paces. We would talk most of the night of how the girl had registered. Trembling with anticipation, she had been led to the enclosure at the top of the spiral iron staircase - the strong room, where her cries, both of pain and pleasure, had no place to go except the dark depths of the Mediterranean.

If I had made her a plaything, Katie had loved her, and I believe that it had been reciprocated. She had not wanted me to leave Justine in France, no matter how the girl herself had cleaved to that dark destiny. Months had passed, then a year and more, while I'd begun to realize that I had made a terrible mistake. The books I had dreamed would lie unwritten, just as I would never even try to get to Samarkand, or any of the other fabulous places that I had wanted to see.

Without the lady-in-chains who forever had been linked to my writing, without my Muse, all that had been without meaning. Katie had done her best, albeit through her own pain, to be as Justine to me. But Katie had always been a different kind of love, a different sort of warmth. She would submit to my childish demands, endure to coddle my cloying needs. But she could never inspire me to be more than a hack reporter. As for myself, I think that I had never even known how to love.

We had resolved to find Justine, but already sin piled upon sin. Around Halloween of 1925, I'd met Marjorie Worthington at a card party. We had been about to sail for Europe, and Mink would join us in April. Another applicant to fill the chains and bracelets of Justine. And Mink, so oddly prim in many ways, had been decidedly unsuited to the role. Before Marjorie could reach us, it had come to light that Justine had killed herself - after I had gone away. At that given moment, far too late, I made an unseemly grasp at "repentance." On my knees, I had abased myself before God and half of Paris, begging, screaming, pleading to be forgiven. Then it was that Katie, unbeknownst even to herself, had truly begun to hate me. While she could not touch my self-loathing, the hell I had made for myself had only just begun.

Mink had arrived, and in time we returned to New York. For the next several years, in a pact of misfortune and common upset, we sought surcease in sex, dope, and liquor. Contacts I had had, with such as Morand and Ford Madox Ford, I let wither. Even as I would use her body, I pushed Mink's devoted spirit away, while her husband had pined hopelessly after tragic Katie. Our gay foursome, lionized by Village life as colorful nonconformism in the mode of Byron and the Shelleys, had been to me dark, and sad, and empty.

---

A dozen more years of a deepening hell on Earth would drag by, of which I've told some and will yet relate a bit more. But now you will understand why that last night had arrived as an almost welcome apocalypse. The orange incandescence had spread about the entire horizon, but the sight recalled me only to the color of her hair. How to make you understand what I mean? When a man attempts suicide, it means he still wants something. There's still an avenue of escape. But total despair means there is no hope, no way out. I had never attempted to follow Justine from that farthest circle of hell. Instead, I guzzled another slug from the bottle on the nightstand. Sinking faster, I thought there probably would be little need to expedite things. Blood red clouds silhouetted the barrage balloons above the city, while the glowing pyres below illuminated the dome of St. Paul's. The bomb strikes had increased to every few seconds.

Had I prayed for oblivion, it certainly would not have been upon those brave souls down below, but for the end of my pathetic world. The final thought I can remember, from that sodden night, may have been the fortuitous trigger, when I imagined myself illumined with a sort of mystical, if not maudlin, exaltation. Concocted from the imagination of hindsight? It glowed benignly, like the precisely right quantity of hashish, the third pipe of opium, the perfect balance of cocaine and heroin. And at the center of it was to wonder if, far away in the deep heavens, millions of light-years from that dying city, there might not be a new constellation;

the Lady-In-Chains, whom the angels called Justine.

---

MY EYES WOULD HAVE CLOUDED anyway at that heartrending plaint; the recognition, far too late in life, of what had really mattered. This would have been the case even had I regarded it all as sheer delusion, a fantasy fueled by Willie's futile desire to escape—to war, to a happier past, whenever. Yet her eyes told me that I knew very well at what I was looking. I sought mere relief through technical analysis, through levity. The meaning behind the source was at hand, but all the vastness of space-time could not dispel the tragedy of that one damned soul.

I read a bit further and then looked at Justine[2] with fresh esteem as I comprehended the remarkable meaning of the meandering, sinuous narrative. I was genuinely impressed that she had been able to distill the contents of Willie's thoughts and notes at all. The characterizations in Justine's *Testament* had been generous. While she had labored for years, painstakingly separating apples from oranges and rendering a semblance of coherent chronology, uncertainties still abounded.

More memory returned when she was able to point out, from time to time, a possible resolution, or make a clarification. But a man who claimed not two sequential lives but simply the same life in two versions had compiled the original notes. I jest: there was nothing "simple" about it, because, to a great degree, he had *written it that way*—as though both histories had occurred simultaneously!

"If he hadn't killed himself, he should have been shot for *this*," I grumbled as I saw what he had done. That amused even Justine[2]. Making matters still worse were marginal indications that he believed himself aware of yet other realities, branching from or converging with those about which he had written.

Willie Seabrook had been riding a wilder nightmare than his friend Ward, called "Jimmy," could have imagined. From early on it became evident that Greene's book had not been purely fiction. The only fiction, in fact, seemed to be that covering Willie's life to about age twenty-three, when they had worked together on the *Atlanta Journal*.

It had been during many drunken nights in Atlanta, no doubt, that Willie had spilled out to Jimmy nothing less than a future history. Rather, a history of the futures of choices *not* made from the time the paths had branched a few years earlier. At the least, Greene had chronicled particular matters on which Willie had been fixated, from a future he imagined that he recalled. If he had heard the full scope of events relating to Justine, Katie, and the others, Greene had chosen not to believe it all or otherwise to remain silent.

"We have all the time in the world to ponder the literary implications," said Justine[2], "but you maybe gotta take a rain-check on a few. Some questions may always be mysteries"—she smiled benignly—"like, in 'real life'?"

Justine[2] eventually put on some clothes, and we relocated to the front porch. We continued to examine *The Fan-Shaped Destiny*, the lost manuscript of William Seabrook, which the other Justine had lovingly pieced together from the thread of narration running through the notes from the barn experiments. We read through the night, ate and slept, and kept on reading, welcoming each other's arms and hearts being there when the going sometimes got too heavy.

---

I awoke the next morning to an other life. Certainly it took a while to believe that it was real, that I was actually twenty-one years old again on a bright sunny morning in Augusta, Georgia, with my whole life in front of me. But I soon found out that I could stump my toe against it, and Dr. Johnson's criterion for the refutation of Berkeley came into play: If it can kick back, it exists! The horses of Augusta could most definitely kick and, while enraptured with these shapes of the past, freshly painted with new life, mine almost ended abruptly. The half dozen of the Augustan gentry, who were thus far playing with the new horseless toys, had not yet learned to steer them very well.

Persuaded that the world wasn't going to go away, I would finger my godawful stiff collar in an unaccustomed warmth and wonder if my memories would vanish. Had it all been a dream? Was it possible to experience a nightmare that subjectively seemed to have been over thirty years long? But recollection faded only to the degree one would "normally" expect. Gingerly exploring my baffling hodgepodge of acquired recollections, I acutely watched everything about me with a sort of puzzled fascination.

Simply put, it was life. No angels came about to lecture me on lessons I should be drawing. They weren't about to let me into heaven anyway and, as I saw it, I had had my time in hell. Buds were bursting, doves came. I continued to feel good and happy, though I felt slightly scornful about it. I suspected that such a state of grace was too good to be true - turning earth into heaven, myself into a sort of saint, a patent absurdity. "Elation" is a pleasant, agreeable term in common parlance, but in cold psychiatric jargon, not nearly so pretty.

It simply was; no choice but to let it ride. The only stupid, decent thing to do seemed to be to make the best of it, while trying to puzzle out what had happened. And, by ding! I was also going to live. Scraping together a couple of hundred dollars, I set about to realize an unfulfilled dream and embarked steerage to Cherbourg, to tramp about Europe. Geneva, my final destination, was a natural enough place for a young man of Lutheran background to consult with the great scientific minds.

I do not suggest that, in the year that followed, the construction of a working hypothesis was all that was on my mind. I reckoned that Madeleine, my Justine-to-be, was yet a little girl in pinafores and plaited hair, behooving me to leave her to complain that her play-like cowboys should not be rescuing her from the Apaches so promptly. It would be the better portion of a decade before she was ready for me. A young Atlantan society miss would be waiting in the nearer present. While I was resolved that the errors of the time before were not to be repeated, I had a lot of regrets over joys not tasted to get out of my system.

Nineteen-ought-eight was a great year for science and philosophy. Freud and Jung had commenced their collaboration, and the Geneva campus was all abuzz about Minkowski's recent address presenting the broad implications of Einstein's relativity. All this was grist for my mill but, even knowing how the English engineer Dunne would try to adapt this to explain time and the mind, my purpose was frustrated by my own uninitiate aptitudes. The construction of even a simple, relativity-based model was too difficult without the proper mathematical foundation. Holding what we Americans called "degrees" back then, in philosophy, I got ambitious and wrote a post-graduate paper on time, space, and causality.

Working at a nearby table in the library was a young Russian *emigre* who looked older than his years. He had been so impressed by the goings-on in the physical sciences, since the discovery of the electron a few years earlier, that he had taken time out from his revolution to write a book detailing the philosophical implications. I was able to converse with him in French, holding long confabs and even debates. I was initially surprised to discover that his thoroughgoing Marxian materialism did not at all blind him to the complexities of questions of reality. His point was that solipsistic denial of the material arises in every generation, always purporting to be a new discovery, the result of "recent science." It would be precisely through plumbing the "inexhaustibility" of the material, as he called it, that the true magnitude of the cosmos and wealth of worlds would be discovered.

"Your countrymen, as I have met them, have no strong faith in the existence of even a single past." He had pursed his lips and looked down his nose like a stuffy professor demanding "what else can you show me?" "The Amerikansk lives in a sort of ahistorical millennial revelation, a viewpoint more appropriate either to the savage or, dialectically, to the citizen of a truly revolutionary regime. Your vision of reciprocal histories, if it does not deny the material, then raises it to the nth degree. The Great Powers will not find such an annihilation of Berkeley to be in their interests, unless so presented that the oppressed classes embrace it as an escapist dream." I queried him further, seeking light on things from a psychoanalytic standpoint, so to speak. "I do not so speak," he snorted.

He felt that better than a century would elapse before science attained a level even to reasonably discuss the problems obsessing me. In the meantime, he applied Dr. Johnson's criterion with a vengeance, most particularly where the Czar was concerned, and argued to me that the various solipsisms were invariably devices of the ruling classes. I had suddenly realized, by way of the grapevine telegraph, that the young man was none other than the mysterious Lenin, already something of a fable to the avant-garde. While he sounded genuinely fond of me, in spite of what he called my "insufferably decadent bourgeois mentality," it began occurring to me - for the first time - that the better part of discretion would be to keep my distance from such a man of his own destiny.

Debating with the Russian had given me fresh insight as to how problematical are the mechanisms of change. While nominally minimizing the role of the individual, he himself was destined to become a pivotal figure in history. Were it indeed possible inadvertently to effect the course of major events, then most of the collateral chains would follow suit, and, Q.E.D., I might no longer possess even limited foreknowledge. Not to mention changing the assumptions which I could anticipate in my loved ones. Radical change might erase my predictable influence. The rational man in my extraordinary situation should approach, only with the greatest trepidation, the creation of a world where the shape of things to come may surprise him unawares. I retreated into my studies, and the Russian soon moved on in the conduct of his own affairs.[73]

---

While loafing about Washington Square, the time before, I had played with the ancient Chinese book known as The Changes of Chou. In

73. Lenin, V.I., *Materialism and Empirio-Criticism,* 1909. The work on physics and philosophy Lenin was writing in Geneva.

Geneva, I speculated upon the body of lore that alleged it could open the gate to otherworlds. Dismissed by most scholars as superstition from the days of the dark Han dynasty, that interpretation obviously begged for review by me. I learned of a related tome by a nobleman who had written fiction, a despised genre in China, under the name of Ts'ui Pen.

Said to be bound in yellow silk, it sounded as though it might be the template for a work which the romance novelist Chambers had fictionalized in horrific terms. I've always preferred the company of Dostoevsky, Poe, and the like. Chambers penned some lines that will be granite when most of our current so-called literature is tinsel dust. I first read his work as a boy. In this life of mine, I have found it as very disturbing as the legendary play it purports to descry. Chambers understood that the image of a man haunting Paris streets, expecting to discover the lifeless body of his love, was more ghastly than any of the demons he had conjured from other dimensions. No matter how many times I read it, I've always wept for him.[74]

---

74. Chambers, Robert W., *The King in Yellow*, 1895. The story referenced, "The Street of the First Shell" is set in the Paris of the Franco-Prussian War. As "shop-girl fiction," its inclusion with outré tales related to the "Hastur cycle" of Bierce and Machen has been, possibly unjustly, criticized for a century.

The yellow volume's reported concept held a beguiling similarity to those branching paths of destiny whose traces I sought. My search was to no avail, save stimulating the interest of others, which is as may be. While searching the European libraries, however, I was able to study the source materials of Michelet, which had seduced my ancestor Peter Boehler into tinkering with witchcraft. Over time, I swung far from science and philosophy into the dervish direction of the occult.[75]

While some aspects of this life have seemed peculiarly difficult to abrogate, other changes have unleashed a cascade of chaos. I have to report that a given material actuality is as little malleable to the heart's desire as any other. Fate has often been temperamental, if not downright pettish. My impotence to avert the death of my brother Charlie gave me pause that haunts me yet. I have dwelt past the point of distraction on what further subtle changes I might have wrought.

Does the cosmos exact payment-in-kind for a change in the balance? Was Charlie's life the price for one saved? It is true that the night the deal was done, regarding my sepa-

---

75. Seabrook, *No Hiding Place*, p. 370. Principal authorities (fourteenth through nineteenth centuries) that Seabrook may have studied in Geneva are listed in Michelet's 1856 book on demonology and witchcraft.

ration from Katie, was also the first occasion that I found myself literally unable to stop drinking. Did I take her otherworldly destiny upon myself or was my sickness the spawn of my own divided soul? Will yet another have to pay the price for a living Justine?

The years went by while I implemented a plan, its early phases remaining similar to the progression of events I had already known. Experience indicated that caution might be moderated. I ran away to war, as the script required, but earlier and with a volunteer military organization from which I could return when desired. While I did swallow some chlorine gas at Verdun, I was able to come back in the posture of a visionary idealist and hero, never having come as near to death as with our army the time before.

In the fullness of time, I was on hand in New York to meet Justine, comfortably before Crowley had her in his power to mistreat her. I never told Katie the entire story, lest she think me shell-shocked, but I was able to exercise a moral or immoral suasion, holding that we had something like a sacred obligation to the young girl. I already knew that when Katie met her, she would fall in love with her as well.

But the very resilience of the timeline that allowed the small modifications brought me near to panic, when Justine continued, repeatedly, to be almost preternaturally drawn in Crowley's direction. That business, in the summer of 1918, when Sarg pimped her to A.C. for his river trip, was the worst. It felt as though malignant spirits were at work to confound my best efforts toward her survival. I did not cast A.C. as the villain of what could be her hapless melodrama, knowing only too well what a vile world it really was and what a flawed, all-too-human pig I knew myself to be, but I saw him as an essential link. He keyed the situation, supplied its texture. I am writing about a man whom I liked, and who liked me; of whom I had made a friend, but would have killed, if necessary, just to break the chain. It is consequently impossible to expect me to be objective or fair.

On the day that I went to his rooms at One University Place, to watch him brand a naked girl with a hot sword, only then did I finally believe that she was going to live. It was a stranger, a little schoolteacher who, you see, was kneeling on the carpet in the identical circumstances under which I had first seen Justine the time before.[76] That evening I wept histrionically and did not

76. Greene, op cit, p. 118. Compare *Witchcraft*, p. 218. Seabrook identifies the girl branded with the Star as Hirsig, but to Greene she was a "Justine."

ever want to let Justine go. I kept touching, again and again, the place on her breast where that awful Star would never be seen, and felt that a curse had been lifted. She must have found it so queer. Scarcely could she have imagined that, even as I was loving her, I was giving thanks to a God I hadn't known I believed in for granting a dispensation of which I knew I was not worthy.

Even so, my confidence that others would inevitably continue to take her sacrificial place was limited. On her first trip to Europe, she amazed me when her precognitive vision of a little street circus came true before our very eyes in Avignon. At the tintinnabulations of the bells that had so maddeningly irritated Rabelais, the elderly lion took umbrage, nonchalantly pissing on the front row of spectators, and I clicked on something about her demonstrated "psychic" facility previously unknown to me. That final detail recalled my attendance at that same circus, in the company of a Justine lost, the time before.

In a fit of morbid curiosity, I drove her by the <u>Chateau d'Evenos</u>, which I was gratefully surprised to find still in ruins. But it was nothing short of horrifying as Justine cooed with a nostalgic vision of how wonderful it would look restored. Could this be the true explanation of precognition and other visionary phenomena, a link with the perceptions of our diversified selves on other paths? Nothing magic, occult, or incredible about it? From then on, I was adamant about keeping a close eye on her in France. Knowing that I'd best speak to Katie about it, I found her mystified as was Justine, but I demanded her agreement. If she loved Justine, she would back me up.

In later years, we would meet a woman, like Santolina Marr a mystery in any world, whom I recognized from among the slavery cultists. It's always difficult to identify someone met out of the context in which you've known them, so you may imagine the difficulties I've encountered along those lines! As it happened, she was a close friend and anima of my friend Paul Morand, and contact with her was inescapable. When I broached the subject, pleading my case for protecting Justine, she appeared not to recognize what I was talking about and demanded the whole story before agreeing to anything. I've seldom confessed so much, but she listened with close attention to detail, allowing that, should I ever write something about it, she surely would be keen to read it . . .

---

I HAD TO LAY THE MANUSCRIPT DOWN for a while, partially due to the emotional cost to the artist who was spilling out his soul. Even were this pure fiction, it had to have been as difficult to dredge all this up as to read it. I reminded myself that at least some of the key branching-worlds fiction had been published before 1945. Greene's book came out in 1930, and it was even conceivable that Willie might have obtained access to an early English translation of "The Garden of Forking Paths."

It may have been only the subjects and the setting, but the latest paragraph had made me think of *The Story of O*. Had the real reason that Willie leased the château been so that a "Roissy" he remembered helping to destroy his beloved Justine could never exist there?

These implications were astounding enough in themselves, let alone the difficulty of confronting the bizarre explanation this lent to the memoirs in old Justine's *Testament*. Worse, the limits of my ability to deny recognition were also being strained by the turn of phrase, the private thought, the spooky parallel. His autobiography had also eaten my lunch, but to no degree compared with *this*.

It was like a hall of distorted mirrors on the midway of Linda's childhood, as the image of Willie and Katie watching Justine's initiation from the balcony superimposed upon an older Justine and myself in another *"Château"* in 1969. Only days before, I had been looking back up at that same spot while a new Justine suffered; it was maddening.

Willie's fascination with the reincarnation doctrine of the *Druse* intruded, and I began to doubt this identification less than I feared it.[77] Oh God, I did not *want* to be him; that was it! I was haunted by a semi-facetious warning from the ghost of Big Richard, the gentle giant of a biker; *that girl Karma, she's a bitch, man. She'll get you.*

*Please God, make it didn't happen.* Let this cup pass. That this might even possibly be what my life was about, brought to this moment to face the music for the sins of multiple lifetimes, along with my own well-stocked one; that was intolerable.

Placing that aside, how could I doubt the veracity of Willie's story when I was required to look up and address myself to none other than Justine[2]? She was easily as extraordinary a creature as he claimed to be. I tried to find relief by focusing on the material reality of the "real" world around me, but the cicadas and honeysuckle perfume of the summer night just carried me to the lake. It called from a few miles and many years away, back to JJ, and when I would again look up, I had to know those tortured green eyes were also those of her daughter.

"By God, Justine, how you must have looked to him in those last moments!" It was not insensitivity

---

77. Seabrook, *Adventures in Arabia*, pp. 214–217. "The Druses undoubtedly got it from India, but have developed it into something quite different . . . a Druse soul flies at the moment of death into the body of a new-born Druse baby . . . the survival of personal memory was rare . . . not one Druse in ten thousand recalled anything of his former state . . . Obviously the Druses are a 'closed corporation.' According to their doctrine the number of Druse souls is fixed." It is interesting that Seabrook neglects mention of a similar belief in "metempsychosis" shared by the Yezidis. That Kurdish sect survives today in the Middle East, former Soviet Central Asia, and a German diaspora.

that made me wonder back to lines in her *Testament*, and exclaim, "Watching you walk away, knowing it was the last time he'd see you in this life, you must have looked so beautiful. The simple reality of your existence, your survival, represented everything worthwhile he felt he'd accomplished."

"How did I rate living with *that* for the rest of my enduring life?" Her pain was profound. "You spoke to me of the agony of life. Is it s'pose to hurt, and hurt, and hurt, forever? It was agonizing as any torture to realize that, to know . . ." She put her fist to her lips and moaned softly, her speech betraying the flood of new memories drowning her.

"To know that I had but to turn around and grab ahold, and refuse to let go. I cursed myself for delaying in sorting out the fragments; only a day or so less and I would of found the suicidal message and dashed up there. That was unthinkable! Even as I came to believe that there really might be another chance, it would be at the price of there never being peace. I would never forget the hurting, not even after death."

I cradled her in my arms until the remembered heartaches passed. She was not alone. Again, I was thinking of Richard, and the night that I had been out sporting, and avoiding another tedious session with him, when I could have saved his life. Had a frightened woman, who hadn't known him long enough to dismiss his bullshit, shot him as believed? Or had they been involved in a drug deal gone bad? Which it had been never mattered. The bottom line was that I had not been there to talk him down, when he had left

Kong in my yard and gone sadly away, for the last time. I, his best friend, would never have to listen to his problems again—only wish that I might—for the rest of my life.

---

"POOR MINK!" Justine[2] had collected herself and, rubbing her eyes, jarred me back from my own brooding. "Can you imagine how she felt, for the love of her life to have killed himself on their anniversary? Any wonder she couldn't get over it?" She glanced up, reproaching me even more strangely, "At least she had her writing," I followed after the apparent contradiction rather than her discomforting insinuation.

"No, babe," I was bewildered, "they were married in February."

"It was *observed* in the fall," she scolded, "on the day the marriage was announced to the world." Even short that information, I was mildly aghast that, in all the months I'd spent picking over the details of their lives, I'd not noticed the coincidence of the twentieth of September. It was the little psych major who inquired with a piercing stare, "The fact of that oversight doesn't tell you anything?" She shrugged and drifted back to that other place.

"The temptation to end my life first became harder to resist. Katie saved me, pulled me back many more times than she knew. We never know, do we, when just being there makes all the difference?" I looked away, trying to fight down the horror at my own guilt. *Oh Richard, I am so sorry.*

"Then," she continued, "an idea began to grow that would've been alien to me when I was younger. It became a certitude that I was like, Willie's creation, his Galatea. I was to tarry here, to testify to his life. To give up, to die the pathetic wreck they wanted me to be, would've been to hook up with those bent on destroying his work. Once I saw through that, I never would've done it."

She looked up at me expectantly. My bemusement deepened with the levels being plumbed. She had not just loved this man; she'd quite literally worshiped him. And, there was no way in hell he had been deserving. Even so, I nodded. "I can get behind that, babe. Lately, I've had thoughts about values that I've never seriously entertained in my life."

Even while breaking for food, we talked on about the phenomenon. The most visible difference in dealing with Justine$^2$ was her growing ability to access the substantial learning of her antecedent self. The old woman had, after all, grown far beyond the young dilettante of 1917. For years she had studied all those books accumulated in her home and more, as well as delved into truly arcane wisdom. While I remained, presumably, better versed in the physical advances of the last twenty-five years, Justine$^2$ was more deeply grounded in the fundamentals than I had ever been.

". . . here's my thing," she was saying, while ravening a microwave pizza, "Willie, like myself, really would only recall snippets; hey, that's our memory anytime. We can only hold so much immediately available to conscious recall. Sort out all the variables of any real-world situation, and what he wanted to affect would like, have already gone down? Whatever his 'foreknowledge' from a similar path, he was still looking at only another world defined by multiple powers of uncertainty . . ."

I had been riveted by her battle with the stringy cheese and tomato sauce, sitting with her legs crossed under her oversize sweater and looking for all the world like a typical postadolescent. All along, I'd been witnessing some degree of a split personality, certainly in tastes. The young Justine had bounced between french fries and *haute cuisine* with equivalent zest. No doubt, still other vacillations had gone right by me.

"That's *any* given world at any point of contact. Only in *all* the worlds, taken together so that every possibility occurs, are things for sure. We got another chance. A chance, that's all there is, ever—in one world or many."

I had been wanting to ask something that had been on my mind for a while. "Is it correct to regard you and him as the same phenomenon?" I reached with a napkin to delete from her chin a smear of sauce that was driving me crazy. "Willie came from another path on a branching timeline, whereas you are the product of a transmigration along the same path."

"Are you, or I for that matter, way sure it's the same one?" She appraised me. "All that muck about the Longs that you said Roder told you—I'm not finding any recollection of such things, the Kingfish . . . As if I'd not remember Blaze Starr! It may be I was playing head games with a young lawyer or, it could be that the past I remember and that of the old lady you met in '69 are not quite the same. That Brit physicist—what he said?"

For the purposes of my personal obsession, the most striking of Deutsch's observations had been his elucidation of the quantum concept of time. "The branching paths are only a simple schematic. The reality would be more in the way of a vast number of decks of cards, all shuffled up together. Each card is a snapshot of a 'moment,' however that is conceived, in the sequence of its particular deck." Deutsch had written:

> To a first approximation, the multiverse is like a very large number of co-existing and slightly interacting spacetimes. . . . There is no such thing as which snapshot from another universe happens "at the same moment" as a particular snapshot in our universe, for that would imply an overarching framework of time . . . There is no such framework. Therefore there is no fundamental demarcation between snapshots of other times and snapshots of other universes. This is the distinctive core of the quantum concept of time: OTHER TIMES ARE JUST SPECIAL CASES OF OTHER UNIVERSES.[78]

---

"In that magic lantern show," she said quietly, studying her food, "the illusion of Willie's to-and-fro across

78. Deutsch, op. cit., p. 275, 278.

time, and that of mine, would both be quick sketches of more complicated happenings. Hey, no time travel as such, yea? The 'Kodak moments' whose 'arrow of time' leads to our present moment—*'our'* past? Can't go there." The green eyes hardened with comprehension three steps in anticipation of where I'd left off. "Those instances are all—about inputs that they like, *did* receive, and still were able to point here, to a future that is our present moment."

"Well, I guess that takes care of me," I sighed ruefully. "I must agree that, whatever explanations of psychic phenomena we find, physical law is never violated." She saw me beginning to grasp, finally, that these notions had never been difficult for her. I'd attempted days before, in my vanity, to snow her with concepts encompassed decades past—by a woman from whom the logic and loss of life had demanded embrace of the incredible.

She looked up mischievously, "Like, I ought to know?"

"Don't pull rank. Your transit was from about the time of"—the words kind of stuck in my throat—"your death. Otherwise, you would only remember things before the 1945 encounter with the dream-loop, which was responsible for your awakening in the barn. We might even see that *anamnesis* as a partial transit. But all this is based on Willie's 'science'; Dunne's ideas plus the branching paths. What did the *mambos* add to your equation? How did they modify his process to arrive at an event like reincarnation?"

She shrugged, uncomfortably. "Lookit, I haven't remembered much. They had initiated me into Voudon. There was a ritual, invoking Legba, down in d' bayous by an old French graveyard. Y' know, where they bury the dead people up above d' ground?" She rolled her wide eyes in a mode previously unseen and shuddered.

"When I crashed, two who were still living came and tended me, till I went away. But I was way off-line by then. That's why, with not knowing what they did 'fore I was outta there?" I watched her vacillate amongst personas within the course of single phrases.

"Why do you suppose, out of all possible worlds, you chose this: to awaken as your descendant? You presumably could conceive avenues that were more direct. If the method is embodied in these notes, you could have just started over, like Willie."

"Mightn't I of found a whereabouts and shape there was no possibility an old reprobate like you could resist?" She giggled nervously.

"You don't remember your actual death?"

She silently shrugged a negative, but then looked up. The green eyes were terrifying as they burned into my soul. "I know that, with my last breath, I was still loving you." These wounds were severe, and I didn't want to open them, so I backed off. She made as if to speak again, then all shades of sophistication evaporated as she burst out, with inflections that were near to Cajun, "Nay, pleaze! I don' wanna go there. Lez nawt talk 'bout grave-yawrds!"

I suspected she was copping out, but, as she well

knew, I would not push it. I backtracked to, I thought, safer ground, Willie's "cascade of chaos." "With a 'forward' transition, at least you don't need to be concerned with those problems. From day one, in a branching world that started from a 'past' moment, he inevitably would have been behaving differently—even if trying to suppress his familiarity with a similar possible history. Effects would have propagated exponentially." Benford had visualized causality waves looping between the past and future, the paradoxes they produced giving a new kind of physics—a wave function that didn't describe mere possibilities, but spoke of different universes.

"Surely, after first yourself, then Katie, and even Willie were living on beyond your otherworldly death dates, he knew that the advantage of his foreknowledge was exhausted."

"*I* knew that"—she shakily unwound and grinned slightly—"fifty years ago. You can't relive the totally same past, or you would've already remembered so doing. Total *déjà vu*, an eternal return along the same loop, *way* hellish!" Then she inquired cagily, "What are we thinking, about all that 'payment-in-kind,' death for a life, and so forth?"

"I don't believe that. Talk about a concept that's simplistic! But I can understand how he might have turned superstitious under the pressure of everything that had befallen him." I saw that this seemed to be of crucial importance to her.

"You think? Pos?"

Then I remembered, *"Will yet another have to pay*

*the price for a living Justine?*" I grasped her hand. "No, babe, no. Maybe his bloodline carried a suicidal gene. Or, remember what you wrote about being 'loosely attached'? There is no principle in the cosmos that demanded your daughter's life." She smiled gratefully, but the dubious look wasn't banished. "Or, your grandmother's life, depending on how you choose to regard it."

For once, my efforts to lighten things up were successful.

We went to bed still talking. I thought about Rhinebeck and old New York, their gaslight shining through the eyes of Justine[2]. What sorts of messages and perceptions might be possible across worlds, which were also across time? All kinds of sightings, ghosts, temporal anomalies, et cetera were newly explicable. Just assume Polchinski's math did describe something real . . . but she had drifted off.

I lay awake for a while, thinking of September 1945—the war ended and the past already being denied. The ghosts of darkening yesterday lingered on verandas or beside wrought-iron railings to witness memory of them being abolished. Two months before my conception, Willie had killed himself. Then the light-world of my eyes had opened upon an art deco hospital's rounded-cornered wards and tiled hallways, beginning my lifelong sequence of impressions.

I was now reminded of an essential truth, recalling H. Beam Piper, who had been, even then, crafting his first tale of alternate realities. That truth was simple and yet profound—that I, too, had been born into another time, an otherworld. *As always are we all!* The revenants of our pasts await us in adjacent rooms; doors within our hearts remain forever ajar, begging just the right nudges. And should the mind perceive that truth to be more literal than psychological?

Could it really be? I thought of Marjorie, struggling bravely twenty years later to preserve the memory of a man who had been so cruelly thoughtless. How I wished that I had discovered Seabrook's work back in my youth. I *knew* I'd have found its significance. Me, at eighteen, or even fifteen, reading something like "Justine in the Mask"? A chapter heading like that would have jumped off the page at me!

*Believe* that I would have been in Fort Lauderdale, where Marjorie lived, for my first Spring Break. I might have become her friend, maybe helped her with her book, maybe met Justine five years before *The Château* . . . Ye gods, what was I thinking? To still the wave of emotional vertigo, I turned and embraced Justine[2]. With incredulity and a nagging fear, I had discovered that holding my "world in my arms" had ceased to be merely a romantic expression.

---

By the 1937 of that other life, I was over fifty and washed up, certainly in my own eyes. King Features having long since recognized my want of some essential ingredient for creative writing, I had returned to The New York Times. I was deemed too mediocre an artisan to be heroically competitive with stars like Walter Duranty, but my only other option for earning a living would have been to accept Lyman's offer to get me into advertising. In that case, never yet having cared much for the idea of suicide, doubting that I would like being dead any better than being alive, I had accepted a Times posting to London.

One evening I happened to attend J.B. Priestley's play, Time and the Conways. Opening to rave reviews, it was just the thing for a moment when all feared that war was again approaching with inexorable step. In that world as in this one, how pitifully brief had been the mere score of years between the great wars! Those, whose fathers, husbands, and sons had been devoured, watched the great beast turn again for them, their children, and grandchildren.

The play had riveted me with masochistic rapture. The Conway family, brother, sisters, and lovers had survived the War to End All Wars, and celebrated in Act I their hopes for a happy future. The tableaux of their little party were picture postcards of Hope and Love. Act II had moved ahead past eighteen dismal years of failure and disillusion to visit the surviving characters in their regret, recrimination, and hopelessness.

Thence, in Act III, Priestley had employed his novel time-shift concept. It opened at the moment the first act had ended, at the happy family party. As the young figures continued to express their naive aspirations, foreknowledge of their fates became excruciating to the audience.

The lead character, Kay, portrayed as an aspiring young writer with a slight prescience, would be damned to sense the despair that lay ahead. Near the end of Act II, mourning their happy young selves then lost forever, she cried out to her brother, "There's a great devil in the universe, and we call it Time." You may think it maudlin, but the play intimately caressed the unspoken fears of the coming holocaust, and many of that staid English audience wept outright. It struck like a prize-fighter's fist into the very heart of me, I can remember that.

Kay Conway had been comforted in the second act by her brother's recitation of a theory he had read, that time and reality are other than they seem. ". . . and when we come to the end of this life, all those selves, all our time, will be us - the real you, the real me. And then perhaps we'll find ourselves in another time, which is only another kind of dream."[79] But, as the third act ended, the comforting words were still lost in that

79. Priestley, John B., *Time and the Conways*, NY: Harper and Brothers, 1938, pp. 75–76.

bleak future. Owing to the time shift, they had yet to be written. I used my press credentials to go backstage after the final curtain. I found myself somehow unwilling for the play to be finished. I, too, had wished for the characters' impossible dream - of grasping that happy little moment and holding it forever.

I'd been surprised to find the cast assembled by Priestley around a little man with a large drawing pad on an easel. It developed that he was none other than John William Dunne, the engineer who had built the first British warplane. He had retired from his career to become the dean of Serialism, which, a sense of kindliness in his soft voice, he had been endeavoring to explain to the cast. The actors listened politely as Dunne talked and drew diagrams and equations, illustrating the concepts that had inspired the play they'd just performed, the concepts alluded to in the lines of Kay's brother. I confess that I had begun to drift as well. Dunne's ideas went far to resolve the paradoxes of relativity but, in themselves, did little to address the inescapable lot of mankind trapped in a linear time.

The actress Jean Robertson, who had portrayed Kay Conway, shared the limelight with Priestley. I remember thinking that he loved her. Our eyes met, and she gave me the ghost of a smile, reminiscent of Katie in her better days. Then it all twisted back eighteen of my own years to memories of the best Christmas Eve ever, standing by the gaily lighted window of our brownstone flat, watching for Justine.

The fantasy had such a compelling texture; momentarily it sounded plausible that, somewhere in time, she was still skipping up the street to be with us. The relief ended, but I had remained detached. The cast members were a small, closed set, with whom I could no more group than could I slip the bonds of time. The sense of meaningfulness evaporated. Standing on the edge of that warm and happy circle, which I couldn't enter, had become just too painful.

Another portent had been awaiting me in the lobby. Near the doors, I spied the writer of scientific romance, Olaf Stapledon. He was in the company of the radical scientist Haldane, the friend and mentor of Huxley. That mob were people I had always wanted to know but, as I'd squandered my potential, had never even gotten to meet.

They had been talking with a woman journalist I'd seen about. At that weird moment, she reminded me of my long-ago young grandmother Piny, who had given me the only fleeting relief I'd ever known from this slaughterhouse of a world we're encaged in.

Somehow, I managed to click with Miss Constance Kuhr, and we spent some time together before she left for a United Press posting in Vienna. She introduced me to Stapledon, from whom I learned of the fledgling variant of scientific romance in my own country. Through him, I became acquainted with Haldane, and the brilliant young physicist J.D. Bernal.

Miss Kuhr, as intriguingly hard and brittle as the other women I'd loved had been pliant, also introduced me to the great Paul Dirac. I'd learned of the new field of quantum mechanics and the outlandish speculations which its creators privately entertained. These excursions of the greatest scientific minds had gone unknown to the public, largely due to the new, dark quality of mystery, with which the governments had swathed scientific research in preparation for war.

Not long afterward, I was sent to Spain and tried to get myself killed. Missing the big journalistic battles, I nevertheless covered the heroic *Brigadas* defending that doomed Republic, as they fell back time and again before the onslaught of the dark legions. I suppose that there, whatever my moral failings, candid and complete indifference to my well-being satisfied me that I was not a physical coward, at the least. Yet, it was before the fall of Madrid that I had returned stateside.[80]

During that visit, the great devil Time had come for Katie. Long anticipating this, I'd thought myself prepared, but the actuality of burying her at last was devastating. The book had closed, never to be reopened. My inquiries, into exotic realms of science and philosophy, had given me scant comfort. They sounded to be but mere notions, without substance in the face of the awful reality of meaningless death. They might have been fleshed out, had I begun sooner. The saddest words in any language are "if only." Their whispers follow me still, from that ever-receding far-away.

---

80. Clark, VèVè A., with Millicent Hodson and Catrina Neiman, *The Legend of Maya Deren, A Documentary Biography and Collected Works, Volume One*, NY: Anthology Film Archives, 1984, p. 407: "Before coming to Rhinebeck, Seabrook had fought in the Spanish Civil War . . ." On location in Rhinebeck in the summer of 1975, they reiterate this nonsense in the course of interviews with locals: "others knew he had fought with communist forces against Franco in Spain." (p. 408) The Spanish Civil War began with the fascist rising of mid-July, 1936. International Brigades were deployed by the fall, with the American "Lincoln Brigade" reaching Spain by the winter. Franco's final victory was declared on 1 April 1939. The authors themselves had dated Seabrook's residence at the Rhinebeck property from 1935, well before the war. In other words, the absurd quotations above would have Willie's neighbors convinced that he was a participant in events, which were taking place in Spain, even as he was residing among them! Why the authors of a scholarly work would include these as statements of fact is a dilemma that pleads for comparison with the content of this "Fragment."

After the funeral, when there had been nothing left to do in New York except drink, I'd been moved to investigate an event taking place in conjunction with the World Fair. At a hotel in Midtown, it was billed as the World Convention of Science Fiction, a number of the writers directed to my attention by Stapledon in attendance. It had proven an effective distraction.

I'd been surprised to discover that Will Jenkins, known to me as a feature writer, had been writing scientific romance under the *nom de plume* of Murray Leinster. Over lunch, he expressed intrigue with speculations I'd heard from the English scientists. He ruminated about the vague old notion of diverse actualities, inherited from the Gothic, but untouched by the new genre.

One evening, we had *aperitifs* with a Pennsy railroad detective, an aspiring writer with the interesting name of Beam Piper. A lean fellow with hard and intelligent eyes who didn't fraternize much, Piper told us that he had been attempting to write stories in this vein. Very much a gentleman of the old school as he lighted his pipe, he nevertheless confided, after a few drinks, his belief that he himself had been born in another reality and had, in his writing, been seeking an explanation.

Literate as to everything readable from

the classics to the modern Ulysses, he was sore about the apparently calculated neglect, even of classical philosophical speculation on the plurality of worlds. "Not even to mention the folklore of many cultures, Gaelic, African, Arabian, which get a short shrift from official science. All those people," he had stroked his thin mustache and the flinty eyes twinkled with shrewd amusement, "are savages, you understand. It's not tolerated that we should learn anything of value from them."

"But, Judas Priest, man! Surely heaven fills the bill as another reality? A concept, compatible with physical law, that gives to reasoned belief, why, belief in human immortality . . ." I had begun.

"Would be as well received as the 'good news' of the Apostles," he'd laughed diffidently. "You can forget institutional learning. Only in a literary ghetto such as ours can such radical ideas be propagated. Nevertheless, we need the raw materials, the research of science. It's too bad that some adventurer hasn't taken up the challenge of going to the deserts and jungles to ferret out the wisdom from time immemorial."

In the clubby atmosphere around the billiard tables, Piper had waxed effusive on his subject - uncharacteristically, Jenkins had whispered to me. He detailed plans for books, including the notion of volitional suicide as a means of transport between actualities. I asked if he meant reincarnation.

"Don't like that term," he complained, "but we may be stuck with it in writing for the public. It's an approximation of a Sanskrit word that's far too vague. The Greeks had a more exacting concept, metempsychosis, the transference or transmigration of the soul." I'd wanted to explore Piper's odd assertion that he'd experienced multiple realities, but he was back on track of the reasons their genre was so queerly despised in America.

"There hasn't been enough science worth spitting at in the States," Jenkins had interjected, "only technology. We'll get real scientists - now that they're fleeing Europe." But he held that conditions for scientific romance would not change for a long while more. "The rancid blanket of state security is coming down over speculation as well as science itself." He confided, in low tones, rumors of bureaus conceived during the World War, mandated to contain information in an emergency. When war came, the "emergency" measures might become permanent.

"Patriotic caution," he'd warned, "becomes an obsession for control that may inhibit popular comprehension for the rest of the century. Your friends Bernal and Haldane have already landed on the sedition list," he'd nodded to me, "for trying to democratize scientific information, as much as for their pinko politics."

As we had taken our leave, I recalled Piper's comparison with the Gospels, and asked his thoughts about religion's attitude toward such questions. "Say, fellow," he'd chuckled sadly. "Priestcraft has hope reserved to the somehow-good. You know . . . the Scopes trial was just jake with them, wasn't it? The Church <u>contains</u> inquiry, religious and otherwise. It's a strange thing about the mentalities that take such comfort in a vague belief that 'everything happens for a reason.' Spell those reasons out, and all you see are backsides headed out the door!"

The encounter with Piper was so pregnant with shades of meaning for me, in an other life, that I've quoted as much as I can recall. I'm in his debt, in any world, and I wish him well. I believe he was in the same boat as me, and would recall his thought, that in the magic of distant jungles and deserts might lie answers as pertinent as in the halls of physics.

I had managed to be reposted to London, in hopes of getting back to a front. There had been some talk of making the convention an annual event but, as it adjourned, the Wehrmacht had begun to roll across Poland.

In a few days, even as I hurried back to my post, England had declared war. The Chicago Tribune had sent Miss Kuhr to Poland, and I'd lost track of her. I guessed that I might grieve for Constance along with all the others, if not dead, then lost to me as if she had been. Like a ghost from that past that never was, Constance would find me again, late in an other life. But, I will hold to myself what was between us. Here, she is the mother of my son, the widow I leave behind.

Some pleasant diversion was offered, in the company of a young-old fashion-photographer-turning-war-correspondent. Her grim and glorious pictures of the Blitz were gaining fame both in England and at home. Through the shrouded streets of the London night, she seemed to carry the sunshine with her. Her aggressive intelligence did not put me off; Constance had given me the cure for that little conceit. The wear and tear of a frenetic early life had left her perhaps a mite too haggard to excite me. More likely, it was just a matter of my candle fizzling out. She would reach out. I would retreat. At last, she had drifted back to her lover.

In that otherworld, I had no one left to leave, so I then stood vigil with all the brave Conways of London, as they awaited the coming of the Luftwaffe's Valkyries. I pray that they, too, prevailed in the end. Was it only as seen through the lens of my own hopelessness, that the dawn seemed a thousand years removed? By that final night, I was through, and I knew it, as far as any effort to save myself was concerned. It had been so late, too late for me with Mink, or to find another Katie. And never, or ever again, could there be another Justine. At the last, I would invite oblivion, but it would be something else that answered.

# X

# The Fan-Shaped Destiny

In this life that we have succeeded in building amongst ourselves, things have gone differently. I'm sure you will agree, better - however much flawed, we did do that. But by the fall of 1928, I was disconsolate over the prospect of soon parting ways with Katie. You should know that my unconscious had compounded the thirty-three "ghost years" along with the rest, in establishing my sense of duration. I reckoned time spans, consequently, as might a man of seventy-five years. Our sixteen years together, this time around, sounded so pathetically brief. Perceiving the early traces of Katie's erosion, under the battering of my neurasthenic temperament, I exerted myself to find another way.

Might not the changes I had wrought be sufficient? I had become a successful author by the age of forty-two, with a couple of best-sellers under my belt and preparing to produce a third. We had had exotic years in Haiti and Arabia, where Katie had many wonderful adventures. At home and abroad, we'd go de luxe and group with the most interesting people. Why, in this world, the club at 156 Waverly even belonged to her, and was a far cry from the dingy Cubbyhole.[81] Most and dearest of all, our darling Justine still lived and loved with us. Might not she, alone, make up for the shortcomings of life with me?

After a morbid attraction to their wedding almost resulted in an unwanted encounter in the spring of 1923, I had heroically avoided even so much as meeting, much less becoming involved with, Mr. and Mrs. Lyman Worthington. I would run across Mink around the Village, but would quickly cross the street, avoiding contact. I had managed to forget all about the meeting that had never happened. Then my friend Don McKee, aware that I was in the doldrums, invited me to make a fourth at bridge one night late in October.

Appalled to discover that I seemed to have been maneuvered, into spending the evening across a card table from Mrs. Worthington, I

81. Seabrook, *No Hiding Place*, p. 212. Compare with Greene, op. cit., p. 106. The Cubbyhole corresponds to the name of a nightspot in Greene's fiction.

still thought I might get through it gracefully. Rather, I found I couldn't keep my eyes off of her. Never conventionally beautiful, Marjorie was always striking. She _registered_, and the attempt to confront a person and body that I had known so intimately, as if just casually met, was excruciating. How often had I twined that luxuriant dark mane around my . . . well, you get the idea.

Thus distracted, I was undone by the simplest thing. Beginning to relax, imagining that I was in control of the situation, I slipped. I addressed her as "Mink," the pet name I had for her the time before. When she dropped her cards, I had an inkling of what had clicked. My fears would be confirmed when I went around to see her later. She had, indeed, harbored ambitions toward encountering the notorious writer and adventurer. The convenience of Don's card party aroused no misgivings or forebodings; it had just turned out that way. Yet, ever afterward, she would remain beset by spells of queerly distorted _deja vu_. Glimpsing an otherworld, whether she had experienced it or was, God forbid, as yet to experience it, dream polluted her reality thenceforth.

Life with Marjorie would educate me to additional dangers of our peculiar existence. Later, when we were living in the _Villa Les Roseaux_ near Toulon, I had to employ extreme measures to shoo away a phony cleric, a dangerous dabbler in the esoteric, who was always mooching about. He had deeply affected her, and I wouldn't stand for it a minute. I gratified his curiosity by educating him in the darker aspects of the fan-shaped destiny! Resistant to comprehension of their true nature, Mink remained so heartbreakingly, pathetically vulnerable to the power of her sporadic episodes. She would insist, years later, on having followed me abroad in 1926, even though she could never recall much, in the way of events, which might give flesh to the two missing ghost years.

---

As always, I first tried to flee. Katie and I were due in Paris in November to put together, with Paul Morand, the African expedition he'd made possible. There, I hoped to find that which I had sought from the mountains of Kurdistan to the Haitian forests. Katie just laughed at my flight from still another peccadillo, though I suspected that the pain hidden by her mirth rivaled my own. This is all detailed in my writings, including the body of my association with Wamba. From that insolent young witch, I finally learned the lore of the branching paths, and its African origin. Wamba's last words to me, however, have gone unreported until now.

On the day of leave-taking, as our party readied to cross the Cavally River, Wamba spoke in her mix of French and Bambara, "I say no adieu, for you are not seeing your last of me. Would that I were there now, on a day you do not cross over, but stay here and live with me." She gazed off into the haze of the African morning. In my heart I doubted that I should again return, whatever vision she had conjured. Giving me her bland, disturbing smile, she went on in the pidjin mix, garnished with Yafouba terms, of which my understanding was unsure.[82]

"I have seen such a day." She held out her hands as if in benediction. "You walk this path a while, then were it like a dream that dissolves with the morning mist." Like a sign, a burst of rays broke through the hazy dawn. She nodded with emphasis. "On this same morning, you would not cross the river." I stared at her, I think not daring to comprehend. Her voice returns now, which is as may be, the one and only solace I hope to find. She concluded the litany with an even less comprehensible prophecy.

"I bethink how you turn this way again,

82. Though unorthodox as to tense, the account of Wamba's farewell is linguistically compatible with a translation from the simple syntax and vocabulary of the pidgin mix cited. *The Fragments*, overall, contain certain idiosyncratic spellings and stylistic usages typical of William Seabrook's known writings.

farther along the path. Before I go on ahead, I shall send the message to my sisters across the sea. Should they cross your path in years to come, then shall you remember your old friend." I watched after her until she disappeared into the forest. The sunbeams, refracting through the haze, were disorienting. There were kaleidoscopic moments when I couldn't tell whether I was approaching the river or following Wamba.

But cross I did, and went away into the country of the Guere. On Christmas Eve, lost in the forest of Khabara en route to Timbuctoo, I suffered my first recurrent dream of Wamba's farewell. I've never been able to shake the feeling that, better than Jimmy, or Walter, or Paul's friend to whom I've blurted out portions of the shameful truth, she was able to see into the darkness of my secret heart. I believe that I now understand whence followed Wamba's affection for me. I think that she was another creature like myself, a consciousness molded by metempsychosis - a "metem" who had walked amongst the worlds, from a place where she had known me very long and well.

I first met her in this life, but I think she insisted upon becoming my guide owing to having first met me in another. If God will tolerate my impertinence yet one more time, I will try to live up to whatever first impression gave birth to such friendship. For the longest, for fifteen years, I've dreamed of Wamba walking away into the forest. Then, as happens in dreams, the scene would shift to a crisper morning than in Africa, a morning much like today, and it would be Justine walking away.

I would wake up in the melancholia I'd known before. I didn't know then, and I don't know now; must it be always so, as it was with Katie? Sounding reconciled to our parting, once I had delivered the promised trip to Africa, she was fine about it. It was Justine who had raised wildcat hell. Like the time before, Marjorie had come to France to find me, and I conceded that I had obligations and unfinished business with her as well.

Lest I leave the silly suggestion that it was self-sacrifice moving me from woman to woman, I ask you. Could anyone, save Wamba, have imagined the nature of my bond with Mink? The unnatural conviction of destiny, with which her spells imbued her passion for me, would certainly have let me ruin her life again, had I not acknowledged us. But the passion was returned in full measure. Neither was it any fault of Mink's that my drinking was getting out of hand.

God forbid that any part of this record become a temperance lecture! No man has ever been a victim of whiskey - only of his own weakness. Determined as I was of the correctness of my course, much as I enjoyed to be with Mink, any excuse would suffice. Letters from Katie, samples of her writing, as though for my critique. Colette and Baba in Timbuctoo,[83] indeed! News of her slutting around in Mexico, with another member of the Estranged Wives Club, would move me to crack open the next bottle.[84]

Once Mink's divorce was final, I even wrote the presumptuous letter of all time to Lyman, demanding why didn't he make Katie an honest woman? Eventually, he would. Justine, I continued to keep at arm's length. Mink and I were living in Toulon. A demon, which I couldn't exorcise as easily as I had the "Abbe Penhoel," was the one reminding me that France had held mortal danger for Justine. Perhaps it was irrational, but I had the same sexual tastes, grouped with even wilder sets, and Justine would always go to extremes, push things too far. So how could I know, I ask you?

It might have been fortunate that Justine

---

83. Seabrook, Mrs. Katherine, *Colette and Baba in Timbuctoo*, 1933. Katie's second children's book.

84. Spratling, William, *File on Spratling*, NY: Little, Brown, 1932, pp. 57–58. Katie was in Mexico in 1932 with Clare Spencer, wife of Harrison Smith of Cape and Smith, visiting Bill Spratling in Taxco. Hal Smith, who would later send the "ouanga" bag to Seabrook, then deleted Spratling from his list of authors.

chose to despise Marjorie as much as she loved Katie. For play beyond that which Mink could accommodate, there were always others. Hell's bells, sometimes I just ran ads! Popular misconception aside, it's never difficult to find girls, like my young friend Eleanor,[85] who will volunteer to be chained and whipped. The dearth is of men able to distinguish this practice from mindless brutality.

---

85. Concerning the belief that Eleanora (Maya) Deren had been one of Seabrook's "research girls": is the *Fragments'* "Eleanor" actually Deren? Her employment by Seabrook, in a research and secretarial capacity during the term of the "barn experiments," is confirmed in *The Legend of Maya Deren*, Clark et al. Her chroniclers present, on pp. 411–416, a letter from Deren to Herbert Passin, later a professor of anthropology at Columbia, dated 16 Feb. 1940. It contains an account of meeting Seabrook at Martha's Vineyard, during the summer of 1939, while she was working for and living at the home of writer and critic Max Eastman. Confirming literary research she had done for Seabrook's *Witchcraft*, which she included in her resumés, she goes on to describe a trip to Rhinebeck earlier in that week of mid-February. With a major blizzard settling in, she had read portions of the manuscript, specifically mentioning material from the chapters on "Justine," finding them "reasonable and interesting." Subsequently, however, she recounts being put off by Willie's categorically sadomasochistic proposals and deciding to return to New York. Willie was not exercised, as more young women were due to arrive that weekend. The letter is low-key, even comical, in comparison to Passin's lurid and fantastic recollections of Deren's alleged verbal account of her experiences in the Hudson Valley. Her chroniclers carry on as though they had discovered something highly illicit. The thread of their 1975 investigation into the genesis of her interest in Voudon, during this employment by its earlier authority, is lost.

Seeking self-definition throughout her short life, Deren had variously styled herself "Elinor, Elinka, Eleanora," and ultimately the nickname "Maya." While her chroniclers assert that Deren documented the period 1 Jun. 1939–29 April 1940 in detail, there exist conflicts regarding Deren's activities while she was with Willie's friend Eastman (a

---

Returning to France, after the publication of my book on Africa, we visited my friend Walter Duranty at his wife Jeannot's St. Tropez home. Walter had just made the coup of his historic interview with Stalin, and was basking in the admiration and brilliant accolades of the smart set. Some were bemused by our camaraderie, ignorant of Walter having been more deeply involved, in his youth, with

---

devotee of open marriage) through her association with Seabrook. *The Legend of Maya Deren*, p. 304 compares her soft berth with Eastman to her subsequent employers: "She would not be as fortunate working for Seabrook and Dunham, each of whose careers dominated Eleanora's own." The chroniclers had initially sought the genesis of her obsession with Voudon, which was to consume much of her career. It was even rumored to be involved with her early death, from a cerebral hemorrhage, in 1961. It appears that Seabrook, the foremost white authority on Voudon in the early century, was declared a dead end due to implications that the chroniclers regarded as inappropriate. While citing Worthington, *Strange World*, pp. 221–22, they ignore pp. 218–219. After disposing of Hal Smith's "ouanga" bag by fire, Marjorie wrote: ". . . three 'Lizzies' have decided to come one at a time! That will teach me to fool around with magic . . . It was the middle of February, and soon after Lizzie Number One arrived, the snow began to fall, and by the next day had worked itself up into a blizzard . . . Willie came down from the barn at intervals. The first Lizzie, a girl he had hired a year ago and who had returned for more, wasn't working out. She was not, he said, 'the flaming thing she was last summer.' She seemed tired and he felt sorry for her, so he let her go after a day or two." The notes from Marjorie's Journal continue, with the next "Lizzie" working out well as of Friday, 16 Feb. 1940. On that same day, Deren was back in New York City, writing her account of the visit for Passin. It is reasonable to conclude that "Lizzie Number One" was Eleanora Deren. While providing no definitive answer, this suggests a different picture from those presented by either her or the chroniclers.

Aleister Crowley than ever was I. Comparing lives touched by the Great Beast, checking them on each other, had led us to believe from early on that I was not alone in my conscious congress with otherworlds.

Walter had rounded up the journalist George Seldes in the company of a recently acquired, beautiful blonde leftist from Texas, of all places. As my friend Max has always contended, Texan Communists are of a different cut - more anarchist than red, and open to anything. To George's amazement, I promptly persuaded her to spend some time, exquisitely suffering, in a cage in my Toulon loft.

The real fly in George's ointment was Walter, with whom I was sharing the girl's attentions. A brouhaha started up at dinner, Walter surprising everyone with a very serious proposal that she return with him to Moscow. Jeannot threw a large fish across his face, and then ordered us all out of the house. Walter put the blonde up at a hotel and asked me to look after her, so I moved her into the loft. George, by that point, sounded relieved.

Mink, on the other hand, got sore and drunk on rum. Out of humor with these "Lizzies-in-chains," as she called all my substitute Justines, she promptly ran the girl off - at the point of one of my Damascus blades. I'm sure she never understood why I was so amused, taking her out for her favorite dinner and wine. A reserved and easily embarrassed person, Mink is generally mute when she first meets people. Intimidated by waiters and clerks, switchboard operators, haughty saleswomen, guests at teas and literary cocktail parties - even her own publisher, or so it seemed - but you'd never have made that blonde believe it.

Across the table, I contemplated her fine manners, the perfect antithesis of undeniably other-than-decorous Justine, and my renewed fondness and appreciation were bittersweet. Why, it was simply that the holy terror I'd just witnessed, uncharacteristic of sweet-natured and polite Marjorie, was so reminiscent of my red-haired angel herself!

Justine had last been in France the previous summer, in 1930, about the time I became acquainted with the artist Man Ray, who shared my interests, if only aesthetically. One evening, when Justine was staying at my Paris flat, Mink and I had to attend a banquet where I was the guest of honor. I telephoned Man Ray and asked if he and his date, Lee Miller, a good-looker recently arrived from the States, would drop by and visit with Justine.

Lee was so young then! She'd begun outraging taboos a couple of years earlier when, at age twenty-one, she'd been the first photography model to appear, elegantly gowned in

McCall's magazine - in a Kotex advertisement. The supercilious mortification of our countrymen had prompted her to sail for the more sophisticated climes of Europe, where she would become a brilliant photographer in her own right. There must be poetic justice that a woman I had foolishly rejected the time before would not, this time around, have any interest whatsoever in me.

I could scarcely believe that I had seen her as too old and worn, at thirty-three! Meeting her again, a decade earlier, my foreknowledge of how she would begin to season made her youthful vibrancy only the more precious. Youth wasted on the young? More honest, though a less colorful piece of reporting, is for me to concede; to that young Lee, I was but a degenerate old soak.

On the other hand, the time before might have been only of a moment, which was as may never be; of the Blitz, or a spat with her lover. Today, promoted by her skill, the Army, and Vogue magazine into the love-idol photojournalist of the Western Front, she seems to have come into this more than I had intended. I do hope Roland Penrose appreciates what he's getting.

In truth, I did have ulterior motives, beyond disliking Justine to be on the streets of Paris in a mood. While Man Ray and Lee enjoyed our company, Lee had declined to participate in our photography sessions, though she liked watching them. To Man Ray, Justine in her leather bonds would look good enough to eat. I hoped she would register with Lee sufficiently to get her out of her clothes during our next session.

Justine, accustomed to going everywhere with me when I was with Katie, chose to see it in a different light. She threw one of her ferocious tantrums, tearing off her clothes and screaming that, if she had to have baby-sitters, they would damned well see the whole show. She insisted that she be found chained to the newel post and would accept only the compromise of a loincloth. Mink, typically, was mortified, though I was amused.

Still, I sent her home again, ostensibly because of her friction with Mink - that convenient fiction being a mere fig leaf for my fear. Three years later, my trepidation would be confirmed in New York. Marjorie had written a novel, entitled Scarlet Josephine, that had overtones of D.H. Lawrence.[86] Interestingly, it was about a bookish woman writer who became obsessed with a reciprocal life and inadvertently brought it into being.

Mink appeared at a party celebrating its publication wearing her collar of two pieces

86. Worthington, Marjorie, *Scarlet Josephine*, NY: Alfred Knopf, 1933. An alternate realities tale, in its own fashion.

of hinged silver with shiny knobs that snapped into place about her neck as her one and only adornment. The wearer had to hold her head high and was unable to turn it, producing a regal appearance. A slinky black gown matching her luxuriant mane, Mink created a sensation. When asked about the collar's unusual design, her replies were the customary dumb, polite banalities.

In Paris, I'd labored long in its production, sending Man Ray exact measurements of her neck and chin by way of _pneumatique_ mail. His little silversmith, who lived way over by the Buttes Chaumont, had made repeated bus trips to my Montparnasse studio, with his satchel of tiny anvils and hammers, before he got the _art moderne_ collar and its companion bracelets to fit just right.

It was my stupidity for having invited Justine, allowing the poor girl to be taken, when she made a row, for behaving like a jealous child. It was my burden alone to understand the veracity of her impossible contention that the tailored collar somehow belonged to her. I endeavored to handle her so gently, for only I could know of a design the time before, in a world where it _had_ been hers, where our play had helped cost her precious life.

Only after her altered destiny had been assured, did I fully confront its uncertainty. Her new fate would be as indetermi-

`nate as that of any other man or woman. Of the one I loved most, I would no longer have foreknowledge, and I feared the effect of my own continuing influence. I suppose it fortunate that she had given birth to a beautiful little girl and, consequently, was otherwise occupied. Now, there was a mirror into which I could not begin to look. By then, my drinking had gotten to the point that it was to be either a stretch in Dr. Caligari's Cabinet, or the graveyard . . .`

---

"VIVIDLY! WE WERE AT THE PLACE DE L'ODÉON when you commissioned it!" she hissed when I asked her if she remembered those incidents. Her pale green eyes burned like a magnesium flame, and she flushed with remembered rage. "I'd been sizzlin' at you being wise at my expense, explaining me to the press as your fuckin' *mascot*, of all things. After you left me alone with them, you can believe me when I say that I talked some shit!"

In her anger, her speech was vacillating wildly between personas, so I avoided inflaming her by making any comment on the total identification of me with Willie. I couldn't distinguish whether there was fragmentation, or its reverse, an emotional involvement of the whole combined entity.

"I told them I was a ho' and that you played this game so that you could like, *may-be* get it up. If you couldn't get into her pants, you have *me* to thank. You can be so goddamned sure I fucked you! And, you can sit on your heartfelt little alibis and rotate. If I had known that it was indeed true, that you had Man Ray make *my* slave collar *for Marjorie*, I'd of slapped your ears off!"

I was blown away, not by the barrage, but its implications. Saying nothing, I went inside and retrieved my copied pages of Man Ray's memoirs. When I returned, she seemed to have calmed a bit. She looked at them and shrugged, "Yea, I remember how he got all journalistic on your ass. Aw-hunh, good enough for you. *Hein!*" She stopped short. "If this isn't some kinda shit."

The pages I'd handed her were from the later, 1988 republication, with additional illustrations. She was staring at the black-and-white photos, taken in Seabrook's Paris apartment circa 1930, which could easily have been modern bondage and discipline shots. They were the ones that featured a naked woman trussed up on the carpet with leather straps. Her legs appeared shaven, though her armpits were not. She could be seen as quite pretty, even through the stylized twenties' makeup. A masked woman, costumed in a leather apron, was kneeling above her.

"You know them?" My own astonishment was rising. While the bound girl's curls looked oily and disheveled, they could easily have been red, compared to the black mane of the woman who knelt over her. The emotion in Justine's timbre had morphed into an unspeakable pathos, coming from somewhere apart from the normal spectrum.

"Go on with you, now," she whispered. "I only

looked at that face in the mirror every day." I marveled at the longing in her eyes, knowing I could not comprehend what she must be feeling. Reviewing pictures of our younger selves often can be bad enough. Reflection upon the image of flesh that had ceased to be one's own might be akin to a sort of "postpartum" grief, as at loss of self—or of a child. That paradox, from which she had sought release at *The Château*, she must confront as established fact. Observing oneself from outside; *who is observing?*

I studied the image of the original Justine, then looked again at Justine$^2$, then back to the picture of her great-grandmother nearly as young as she. Emotionally, I felt the "hall of mirrors" effect again, with the old woman I'd met in '69 lurking behind, and ahead, and in-between the worlds.

"My God, this is you? You were thirty-something when this was taken! Are there more like this?"

"Oh yes, thirty 'something,' *indeed. Damn!"* Her voice cut like a steel razor. "Could you be any more annoying? Yes, a lot more, if you can find them. You can be sure that *I'm* a babe anytime. *Lee* thought so," speaking of Man Ray's free-spirited young *protégée*, "and *believe* that I had a rave on for *her*.

"But, he'd be first saying 'go, girl,' then, 'stop.' Like when she did Cocteau's film? Think I didn't know that sniffing after her was the real reason for that silly idea of going to war again—and pushing sixty, of all things! As if you *even* had a chance with the future Lady Penrose, you old fool!

"Say, what if I told you that she played with me,

pulled stuff on me that he wouldn't write about and didn't tell you? How would that make you feel? Like, her reaching beneath my loincloth, and using her fingernails to . . ." Momentarily, I would snap that this thoroughly weird tease had been calculated, but she succeeded in getting past me again. I felt a hot surge around my neck and a tingling in my loins.

"Jealousy wedded to voyeuristic arousal," I conceded. "Point taken, but how much of the rest of this . . ." I revisited the implications, about Marjorie having sensed a repetition of their other-life meeting, and Justine glimpsing an alternate reality while driving by the *Château d'Evenos.* "Are we supposed to be accepting the proposition of a group of souls traveling together through times and worlds? Stuck with each other, as it were?"

"Not like a totally new idea, I'm sure. Jews, *hasidim*, go with it—and what about the 'closed corporation' of the *Druse*? Besides, isn't this all, y'know, compatible with your research, like with Marjorie's weird time sequences?" I assented that, short of checking notes, I was reasonably sure that was so.

"Telepathy"—I was grasping at another paranormal straw—"or clairvoyance; observing and remembering without actually experiencing. Could that not be the story behind all of this in some fashion? Arguably, you could have obtained the basis for much, though not all, of this from my mind."

"Hel-lo? I'm accessing your mind, my great-grandmother's memories, or observing her experiences—but without having experienced them for 'myself'? Sweetie, even *I* don't believe I'm all that!" She was demonstrably still far ahead of me, cataloging all sufficient reductions of the phenomena we'd observed. "What's the idea? You still have this thing going on where my baseline identity is someway apart from her?

"Process this: I continue to reconfigure into something like a mental replicant of her"—she held up the picture of the bound woman—"with *all* of her contents." She raised an eyebrow licentiously. "How would you define the difference, philosophically, so to speak?"

The entire situation was mind-bending. "It's not going to be easy to live with you," I laughed with resignation. "A brat, with a classical education and the worldly wisdom of an old madam."

She snickered evilly. "Don't forget the whiff of Goth for spice." The quip made me think of something that just might test her psychic potential. I went into Joe's computer room, pulling down from the wall a small scimitar, which he'd picked up while working in Saudi Arabia. I took it back and handed it to Justine$^2$.

"Do anything for you?" She handled the little sword in its red-and-black scabbard curiously. I explained that, when Joe had first shown it to Linda and me, Linda had a sort of vision. Barefoot in the sand, before an adobe-like house with slanted walls, she could feel a rough garment against her skin. She'd had the vision before, but this object made it particularly intense.

Justine$^2$ pressed the scabbard against her cheek

and briefly caressed it with her lips, "It's the smell from the oil and leather," she murmured softly. "She remembered the goat smell." I acknowledged her prescience, briefly elated that I might have touched on an alternative, possibly tidier, explanation. I told her how the vision would recur whenever Linda drank goat's milk.

---

"OR FETA CHEESE, at an all-night Greek restaurant in Atlanta," Justine$^2$ whispered. She closed her eyes and knitted her brow, pressing the scabbard against her middle, as against a pain. I started to go to her, but she waved me back, sitting quietly with her bowed head jerking ever so slightly and tears streaming silently down her cheeks. *My God,* I thought, *will I ever learn to stop screwing around?* It was evident that, again, my indulgence of a whim had opened another floodgate of memory.

The eerie thing was the way I knew this. While she was immersed in some distraction from Atlanta, so, too, an image had wafted among my own thoughts—of staring across the bridge at Laredo into the big Mexican night, wondering about a place Linda had longed to visit, an art colony in a town called Taxco . . . I could feel within myself, as in the tunnel underneath another River, droplets of association began to form. This could not be the issue of Linda's vision alone. Watching Justine$^2$'s agony, I felt helpless. I wanted to hold her, but she would only allow this process to be between her present and former selves.

She opened her eyes and drew in a long, shaky breath. Then she took both my hands and sank down on her knees. I followed her lead, relieved that this experience didn't seem to entail the devastating effects of that in the barn. Seating us knee to knee, she gripped my hands painfully tight. "It's just not cricket—checking up happy memories to be as hurtful as the sad. I s'pose it's that they remind us of the grand times that are all gone, is it not?"

Her anachronisms were in full bloom. I started to respond, but she reached up and gently pressed my lips. "Hush, dearest," she whispered, "not to dread, it's not a bad thing." Her eyes burned through their moisture like some bioluminescent sea creature rising from the depths. "Think way back in the day, to *The Château*. I told your Linda that she reminded me of someone?"

I'd very nearly gotten used to Justine[2] talking, as the old woman, in the first person. "It was in response to her asking if you would take a whipping for her. It was a bit out of the blue."

"Not betwixt us." With a strained rasp, "Can't you remember how we were together, an old woman and the so very young dancer?"

"Like you were lovers," I admitted, "and back then that was a bit much, even for me."

"Oh, my love," her grip tightened on my fingers, "I've remembered how I knew for certain, on that first night when we went out for breakfast. Even before I was sure I had recognized you. I am so sorry, but I really and truly believe that. Dearest, I had known her before as well, known her as our Katie."

"It's not possible!" I'd not seen this one coming, and my mind and heart rebelled. Certainly, we had carried this thing beyond all rational comprehension. "Surely Katie was still alive when Linda was born, wasn't she?" My grasping was audible. Katie and Lyman had vanished from public life after their marriage. Apart from their purchase of a home in rural Pennsylvania, my research had turned up zip on their further histories.[87]

"It is so," she nodded, speaking with a tenderness that her younger persona tried to hide under the punker armor. "Katie passed away"—she choked slightly on the words, as though the bereavement was still felt as a recent one—"in the spring of 1966, up near Trenton. At Christmastime, Lyman got really blue and, he shot himself in his apartment."[88] Her features screamed of tragedy. "I did so hope that he had time to read Mink's book, but I don't think he did!" she cried out.

87. *The New York Times*, 20 Sep. 1935. Included in the story on Seabrook's marriage to Marjorie Worthington, is a mention that Lyman ". . . had married the former Mrs. Seabrook 'six or eight months ago,' but declined to give the date or place." Also see Worthington, Marjorie, *Strange World*, p. 202, in a 24 Feb. 1939 quotation from her journal: "News of Lyman and Katie. They have bought a remodeled farmhouse in Bucks County and seem to be happy."

88. Lyman Worthington's date of death is confirmed as 20 Dec. 1966—from obituaries in *The New York Times* 22 Dec. 1966, Trenton Times 21 Dec. 1966, and *Hightstown Herald*. He was found dead in his Hightstown apartment of an apparently self-inflicted gunshot wound. He had been reported despondent over the death of his wife about eight months prior. Our appreciation to Rebecca, of the Hightstown Public Library, and Lynn, of the Trenton Public Library.

Her cry was a blow straight to my heart, and the madness I was listening to aside, there was something going on in me that I couldn't get around. Nor was this feeling new; it had been with me since early in this odd quest. Months before, there had been some strange moments in the University of Texas library. While seeking just this information, I'd located an indexed obituary that I had felt sure must be Katie's.

But I'd procrastinated long while scrolling down the microfilm. When I'd eventually brought the item up and read of a woman who was clearly *not* the object of my search, I had been mystified by my feelings of relief. I had surmised that all of this had gotten involved with my feelings about Linda's death, for it had been as though I'd not *wanted* confirmation. It seemed that never seeing it would somehow keep Katie alive, like Schrödinger's kitty; letting me imagine that she lived on—even though that would have made her over a century old.

But this! I couldn't deny there was something more. Lyman, dead by his own hand. How ironic that he and Willie, who had married each other's former wives, should share suicide as well. Like gracious old H. Beam Piper, and the first Justine's little girl. The hurt inside was as great as for the dearly departed of my own life. At least Katie and Lyman, like Marjorie, had lived fairly long. Instead of moving ahead to address the impossible assertions, I discovered that one question twisted me up inside.

---

"WERE THEY HAPPY?"

"Lyman was kind, and he had always loved her so. He never made fun of her." She wouldn't look at me, her brilliant tresses covering her face. I waited for her to spell out the accusation that hung in the air. "*Écoutez*, her writing *did* matter. It hurt her so that the one writer who rated had ridiculed her for writing for children. She never wrote anything again."

Again, as on the pier, the burn of the whip; again the terror of responsibility, but not so acute as the simple disappointment at the ugliness I was hearing. *The bastard,* I thought, *that twisted, cruel, demented bastard!* Had I not thought all along that a link of some sort existed? There was no question that, at the least, I'd heavily identified with him—so what did that, in itself, say about me?

"Justine, I know what you imagine you see going on with me, and I will admit that there are some feelings about all this that are, as you would say, *way weird.* But now I'm hearing some things that I just can't accept." Does anyone ever believe a denial?

She was not to be deterred. "*Pourquoi pas?* We don't know what all may be possible, outside linear rules. You, I'm sorry, I mean Willie, went 'back,' to become himself as a young man. I hopped 'forward,' to become another at birth. It may be that Katie could go 'back,' reconfigure as another, one who would be involved with you. This direction thing we have going on is really all about 'sidewise' worlds, only someways like the ones 'before' or 'behind' us."

I remembered Heinlein's story "Elsewhen," in

which some of Dr. Frost's cross-world travelers had become transmuted into entirely different entities. Why not, indeed? We may often dream of ourselves as altogether different beings, complete with other sets of memories. That other, unconscious self has no problem with it. But I was still feeling absolutely reactive.

"Anything other than at birth would constitute out-and-out possession of a developed consciousness, an intrusion I cannot accept. But even this scheme has Katie's subsequent manifestation *coexistent* with her for fifteen years, in the same reality, the same space-time continuum."

"So it sounds kinda out there. Where is it written that she couldn't?" A touch of "young" Justine had come to the fore. "Why can't two versions of a self coexist in the same space-time? How identical are the selves of identical twins, not even to mention clones? I've yet to meet any traffic cops policing the to-and-fro on the nonlinear superhighway, looking to get their phases entangled with my drawers.

"As if another world converged, one with a history like Willie's 'otherworld,' where Katie was dead long before Linda was born? I don't have all your damned answers," she pouted. "I only know what I experienced, beginning with Linda's recounting to me a vision, which I knew to be identical with one of Katie's happiest moments in Timbuktu."

I was not prepared to give the same degree of credence to Justine$^2$'s memories of subjective impressions and beliefs as to her more solid recollections of actual events. Proofs to which this assertion could be subjected, even in principle, were few to none. Still, mad as it sounded, the melding of the feelings I had long repressed with her fantastic scenario was uncanny. I uneasily recalled Linda's episodic efforts to paint, and the probable transparency of my appraisal.

"You would have me believe that I loved her more than you, that I sought her out instead? And worse, that it was futile, that it went down worse than the last time?"

"Nay, please! How could I judge you for finding our Katie, for trying again?" More often, the fusion of her personas' language seemed melodious rather than fragmented. Whenever this happened, the sweet and caring woman inside the tough little babe continued to become more visible. Drawn into the fantasy, I wasn't easily consoled.

"And failing again? She had been best left with Lyman, who kept her alive. In this ugly picture, I do no good for her at all. If I'm with her, it happens all over, just the same way."

She leaned into me, tearfully hugging my neck. "No, dearest, not the same way. As if I can't imagine how it was to stay to the very end. *Unmentionable!* Do you remember, our first morning together, how I got all teary?"

I looked up with curiosity. "I'd said that Kong would go to heaven for being Linda's loyal friend. I thought that I had maybe hit a nerve in you—loss of a favorite pet or something."

A cold cloud descended. "I only had pets once. One night, my drunken step-pig stomped the kitten to death. Finding the broken little bodies, I could see how the brave puppy had run to try to help when his little friend was in trouble, and that bastard had killed him, too. Not like seeing a man kicked to death, but I am here to testify that it looked very like as horrid to a little girl's eyes. I wondered for a long time if life wasn't but a momentary flicker; if existence was not muchly dead meat."

*Sweet Jesus,* I thought, *how can she remain sane?* All the hurts of another life melding with those of this one, frequently reinforcing and exacerbating each other. Without her psych training, she might not have survived this. Was that preordained? If so, were the cruelties and suffering likewise predestined? What complex of experience must have shaped her, that she might inherit an entire personality?

She came around, shaking it off. "I couldn't know yet, that morning. Like, I was wiggin' that I was so extreme up on you, not knowing from whence that came. Preconsciously, the part of me that was still sleeping had known that Kong had not been the only loyal and faithful soul. I was moved by seeing that you weren't quite the man who wrote this manuscript. No longer bailing out; not as if pushing me away, either." I was listening to her find support in the resources of her antecedent self.

I remembered my wild thoughts as I'd watched her, caught up in the dream-loop at the barn, grasping after her last night with Willie. Imagining Henry Hudson's ghost crew in the storm. Like the spectral nude upon the Avignon Bridge, the Rip Van Winkle association was now obvious. *The sleeper had awakened!* The evidence I'd seen, the knowledge she possessed, could not be doubted, whatever personal delusional baggage she had carried along with her. But the way she looked at me, again as to a light in the darkness, brought a crushing responsibility.

"Justine, my darling"—I stroked her hair—"if being him, being Willie, is what you will continue to need from me, then I want more than anything for that to be so. But it scares the shit out of me. I'm nobody's hero, and neither was he! If I'm in any way ahead of him, it's just that I learned that a little sooner."

"As if I didn't know, back in the day, that you were full of baloney?" She had a new thought. "Tristan; a hero there?"

"As in *Tristan and Isolde?* I'm only familiar with Wagner's score. A lot of opera in old New York, right?" I conjectured.

"New York, nothing. The University of Texas, Austin, 1994. Your cousin was there; she knew German, I didn't."

"She's colder than me." I reflected, lighting my pipe, "I don't like tragedy—it may be art, but I find no beauty in sadness. So I'm a wuss?"

"Whatever." She picked up her thread. "Tristan is clued that he's condemned himself by loving Isolde, who's betrothed to the king. His thing is, if by his death is meant the punishment, to be suffered if they're discovered, he accepts it.

*"But,"* she accentuated, "if by his death is meant everlasting torment in the fires of hell—a belief the people who created the saga really had going on—

hey, he accepts that as well." The green eyes burned like those same fires. "What do you think of *that?*" she virtually snarled.

"Love with an attitude?"

"*Fuckin' A!* The cosmos of the Romantics is not for wussies. I shan't get past putting attitude on JJ, don't you know? How could it be other? I would welcome the tortures of the damned to be with you. You'd better believe I'll get tacky on her ass."

"You'd probably enjoy hell, Justine." She did not smile. "Babe, I'm not worth that. Of course you tempt me to play into it . . ." The sarcastic twist of her mouth told me I had better not be caught dissembling. "I just don't know."

"For now, only one of us has to," she sighed and squirmed against me. After a while, we returned to *The Fan-Shaped Destiny*, and Justine[2] began to remember and locate notes from the continuing barn experiments, supplementing the narrative. Willie had remained centered on techniques for inducing pain and physical stress in female volunteers, never bothering to deny the sexually sadistic roots of his obsession.

From the very outset, however, it had escalated into something more, due to his first subject having been Justine. The endorphin acceleration, sexual stimulation, and selective deprivation of the senses other than tactile had seemed to stimulate her brain chemistry, exciting her high psychic potential. The striking phenomena this generated, perhaps involving glimpses of alternate realities, brought him to appreciate the greater depths his practices touched upon.

---

BY THE SUMMER OF 1923, Willie had sent a young Russian *emigrée*, a Balieff singer who had known Rasputin, through a psychic "slit in time." Distilling down Aleister Crowley's baroque symbology, he added a few components to the torturous regimen. He'd focused her attention on a six-line *kua* from the ancient Chinese *I Ching*, known to him as *The Changes of Chou*. He had happened upon some tortoise-shell divining wands and, researching their use, came across a German translation of the book. At John Bannister's studio in Washington Square, after hours in a painful kneeling position, she had "slipped across" to psychically visit an alternate reality where she was a wolf on the northern tundra.

The hypnotic device was more evidence of Seabrook's possible impact on science fiction. Phil Dick had credited no other source for his inspiration than Carl Jung, who would prepare a foreword to an English translation in 1949 (the same version I'd stumbled upon and stolen in Fort Worth in 1962). Richard Wilhelm had only been completing the German version in Peking during that same summer of 1923, so it was unlikely that could have been the German version Seabrook recalled. The point is: No one but Dick had employed the *I Ching* as a presumed conduit to alternate realities. No one except Seabrook.

There was no equivocation about the foundation of Willie's experiments having been torture, though this typically amounted only to extended periods of uncomfortable bondage. The next year, in the Middle East, he studied the more extreme techniques of the *Rufai* Dervishes. His adventures with the occult and the paranormal continued for a decade, until chronic alcoholism took him near to dementia.

In 1938, recovering, he observed the experiments at Duke University and began his activities in the barn, resolving to take the work of J.B. Rhine and put some hair on it. Much of this saga had been recounted in his autobiography, which mentioned the involvement of Walter Duranty in the activities at the barn. The manuscript before us suggested that Walter, knowledgeable of the workings of Crowley, had contributed much to the focusing symbolism of Willie's rituals.

The relationship of Willie, who remained an elitist Republican, with Walter, for decades the *New York Times*'s man in Moscow, continued to amuse me. "Babe, if I'm Willie, I certainly didn't carry the politics along with me. Most of my life, I've been seen as something of a Red, more likely a *'metem'* of Walter than Willie." My little joke only served to open another door.

"Pos that Walter hadn't made his point? Say, you were an old Southerner, but you were never personally a bigot. By the twenties, you were a liberal on race and, hey, like Wamba? I'm *way* sure. Walter was your conscience, and Max as well." She thought, "Do you believe in karma, like you said your friend Richard warned you?" Her anachronistic speech sounded pained, "Jimmy told off on that horrid little joke you played at the expense of a poor transient.

Oh, I do remember it, unfortunately. You hotsy-totsy guys with all your money—for shame!"

I held up my hand, and she broke off, "I'm sorry; I know," her anger abated. "You can't go there yet. But, the concept that you might've had some things to pay for? Process that!" She didn't understand that was the notion from which I most recoiled.

I attempted to get off the troubling identification and back to the subject at hand. "Why do you think he remarked later that he wished he'd never written *Witchcraft?*"

"*He* was still living with Mink," she quipped, "and I'm so sorry, but whatever her good points, she was not an ideal prescription for a man suffering from chronic guilt. Walter was better suited to handle her, much. You know that affair went on like, *for-ev-er*, after Willie was totally dead? Really and truly, I don't know, unless it connected with his paranoia."

As we read further, she observed, "You're so right; once he was way dead, it was open season on his work. Hey, what's up with this? Here are the laced bondage gloves that were made along with the mask. Like you told me that dude used, when he described us in the restaurant, and gave me Katie's name? Tell me there wasn't something going on there?"

A tedious, overly long treatise followed, declaiming on the scientific appropriateness of young, athletically fit females to endure prolonged torture. We looked at each other, and I kept a straight face. "Yeah, *right*."

She looked innocent. "He said that; yes, he really did. Fifty years ago it didn't sound so absurd, it truly didn't."

Late in the barn experiments, Willie had added, with Walter's input, a final element to his eclectic witch's brew. The unoffending hypercube, an octagonal figure, represents a cube extended into four dimensions. Each side of the eight constituent cubes is coterminous with another surface, a self-enclosed system with no "outside."

Willie had labored to designate *I Ching kua* to each set of intersecting corners, in relationships prescribed by the ancient book's patterns of changes. In his extreme variation on psychic parlor games, it served as a mandala, on which his subjects focused while their endorphin levels rose. One rendering, very artistically shaded, enhanced the optical-illusion properties, so that the cubes seemed to extend off the paper.

---

THIS LATEST BIT OF WEIRD FAMILIARITY, I would identify only much later as related to a dream that had followed our night at *The Château*. At that moment, I wondered at how it would feel to be inside such a figure. I likened it to a hall of mirrors, in which Justines watched Justines off into infinity, each somewhat different. I expressed my thoughts, as she watched me, watching it.

"I was thinking that it feels like your bedroom in San Antonio, where there's another room on every side. It's the space betwixt the worlds, which Willie believed was the same as the dreamspace. I'm afraid I wasn't much of a visionary those nights in the barn. I was either sexually aroused, or busy trying to manipulate, or"—she gave a little shrug—"I was distracted by pain. I was starting to get too old for the rough stuff, and when I tried to play like I once did, I would be hurting too much to concentrate."

"A long damn way from the polite parlor telepathy of Mr. and Mrs. Upton Sinclair."

"Oh, they were so *over* by then! They didn't come around, nay. Huxley, yea. You can be so sure *he* was there."

The visions observed and reported by numerous suffering "research girls," through many dark nights in the Rhinebeck barn, had begun to lead Willie in the direction he felt he would ultimately have to go—to find the "older magic" that he believed represented what had happened when he had awakened in Augusta in 1907. But late in the game, he had abandoned his approach through subjects, beginning to experiment on himself. He seemed to be looking for a new application, a view of attacking the problems from a different angle.

"That was the take the *mambos* had on it when I told them I'd found you again, back in '69. Wamba, by-the-by, had become a legendary figure in the West African sorcerer societies. Her words were known even 'across the sea,' in America. And, she had kept her promise." She paused and took my hand.

"Dearest, they knew of Willie's life when Santolina first took me to them. What was truly strange, they knew of mine, too, and our little girl's, in detail that Santolina couldn't have given them. When I laid my plans, they warned me that such fine-tuning was barking up the wrong tree. Like anything else in life, you're apt to opt for whatever you can access. Ofttimes, it may be like 'any port in a storm.'"

"What was the role of Voudon in all this, for you?" I revisited my earlier queries, sensing that she might then be prepared to deal with them. "For all of his background, collection of witch dolls and all that, Willie didn't seem to incorporate it in his technique."

"He knew its power, and was a bit afraid of it, as Mink described in her little book.[89] They know some-

89. Justine's direct reference is to *Strange World*, pp. 216–18, including its quotation from *Magic Island*. However, Seabrook's respect for Voudon may only be appreciated by reading *Magic Island* in toto. See Seabrook, William, *The Magic Island*, NY: Harcourt Brace, 1929; also Wirkus, Faustin and Taney Dudley, *The White King of La Gonave*, Garden City, NY: Doubleday, Doran, and Company, 1931, introduction by Wm. Seabrook. Haiti and La Gonave were not the full extent of Seabrook's brushes with Voudon. Worthington, *Strange World*, pp. 216–18, describes his fearful reaction, in early 1940, to a present of a Haitian "ouanga" bag from Harrison (Hal) Smith. It appears that his alienation from Smith and his partner Jonathan Cape had wilder dimensions than a mere dispute over contracts. See *No Hiding Place*, p. 281. Also *The New York Times Review of Books*, 6 Jan. 1929. Oddly coincidental, *The Magic Island* was being reissued in Paris (also D'ailleurs, Phébus) in 1997. Even as the events of this narration unfolded, Seabrook was being rediscovered by his beloved France.

Of course, perspective is relative. See Davis, Wade, *Passage of Darkness: The Ethnobiology of the Haitian Zombie*, University of North Carolina Press, 1988, pp. 71–72. "The most notorious of these publications was a book, *The Magic Island* . . . (Seabrook) presents as fact the reputed use of nine zombies in the fields of the Haitian-American Sugar Company . . in many ways the author was remarkably sympathetic to the peasants and the Voudon religion. This sympathy, of course, only made it that much worse . . ." We may only speculate why, sixty years later, the exploiters of the Haitian Occupation would be actively defended against such an ostensibly ludicrous charge.

thing about finding points of convergence. The rituals they performed seemed, to me, as a giant transformer, boosting the power of my purpose, someways helping to direct it. Coolest thing was, the initiation of *metem*, if I may use your word for the process itself, into one's own genetic line was not unknown to them, commonsensical, even."

I'd not had time to properly digest Deutsch's intriguing chapter "The Significance of Life," in which he visualized the DNA codons bearing their information in a self-replicating pattern across the worlds. In a perhaps not so remote association, I described how various New Age thinkers regarded the *I Ching*'s sixty-four *kua* as representing a pattern in the woof and warp of the cosmos. They had also correlated the *kua* with the DNA codons. That thought led back around to Phil Dick's use of the *I Ching*.

"For argument's sake"—I resolved to confront the implications—"let's have Willie's 'self' reborn as me, only months after his death in this world, though he may have spent an indeterminate period in yet another reality. I understand that, according to your scenario, we don't attach any particular significance to the timing. You met me years later, and thought you knew whom he had become. So, what did you try to do, then?"

"It was way harsh, meeting you and Linda, when I was already ill and it was far too late for me? What I wished for, ever so much, was a world where I was JJ. If only I were she, then we could all be together again, our *partie de trois*. Don't you see? If I could remember enough to avoid JJ's mistake, then seek out our Katie as well . . ."

"But that's not what happened," I interrupted with another reach for humorous relief. "And I'm confident that you were not at all deterred by possible Freudian implications." It was such a subtle, yet bizarre, juxtaposition for her to acerbically flip me off without breaking stride.

"The *mambos* had their own way of looking at things," she continued. "They didn't much relish the idea of retrograde transits. It may be that, since you—Willie, I mean, had gone to meet Wamba, they saw me going back to change things as someway an interference with her. They were more supportive of sequential schemes that moved me, more or less, 'forward.' *Semilinear!*"

She looked reflective. "They bade me scan for such a location. There was a vision of a little girl playing in front of the house where JJ was raised. Shown where I must go, it never even occurred, at first, that the little redheaded girl might be other than her. Later I learned that it was *her* little girl." Tears welled up, and she dropped her head. I touched her in a silent query.

"We must go by there, please?" She peeked up tentatively, "I didn't realize till just now. Why that visit to my grandparents' house, that is to say, Mother's stepparents, is one of my few good childhood memories? I was so deliriously happy, because I must've been touched by the other part of myself, and knew I had succeeded! Say, it's a powerful, but hardly exact, science."

What I was witnessing was both awesome and chilling. Her perspective was attaching to first one then the other of the symbiotic selves, but the cycles seemed incrementally channeling down toward unity. "At the least, you're looking at the basis for a whole new school of psychology here."

"Nay, some have played with this, they really have. Like, in grief therapy? 'Healing the dead,' imaging a world where things went down better is all about an intuitive grasp of this. But the profession won't permit it to be pushed very far. There are over three hundred separate schools of psychology as it is."

I couldn't resist. "They've got that right. We need another about like we need more lawyers."

The chilling component was more personal. How many times over the years, before my ill-fated reunion with JJ, had I driven by that same old house whose specter had just revisited Justine[2], dreaming of a different outcome? How often, after we'd finally met and failed again, had I tortured myself for failing to inquire after her in those earlier years before it was too late?

---

HOW WIDE MIGHT A PHASE-ENTANGLED GHOST have cast her net? Whose body and soul had I missed so dearly? Had my "little red-haired girl" been JJ, after all? By God, I thought; I could even have seen Justine playing in that yard as a child. My mind recoiled from the numinous images, but the suspicions they incited only ran on, into other areas.

What if this was all true? How profoundly might it have affected my life? Other thoughts encroached, which I realized I'd been driving back. While the main objectives of such experiments would remain unprovable and untraceable, the accompanying synchronicity storms could be quite visible, affecting the outcome of many observations.

"Jung had a clue, early on, that analytical psychology couldn't ignore those effects," she agreed. And that was not the only arena where avoidance could not be practiced.

I described to her the weird circumstances following the murder, in the summer of 1967, of my friend George. His death had early influenced my continuing interest in the nature of reality. The circumstances had been widely believed a political assassination. An investigation had followed the inadvertent arrest of the triggerman, some fourteen years later, on other charges. It had revealed a network of remote associations among the principals in the case, defying all laws of probability. It had gone to the point of the DA's Office calling a halt, demanding simplification of the case sufficient to be credible to a jury.

The perpetrator had been convicted in an unusual courtroom drama which included, among other things, the first successful use of hypnotically retrieved memories in witness testimony. Though he received an effective life sentence, the jurors never had any idea of the complexities surrounding the evidence they had examined. That was another story, however. The germane point, which struck me with the same quality as Justine[2]'s experience at her mother's old home, was one that had returned to haunt the back of my mind months before. While doing the Seabrook research, I had been transfixed by an impression of Walter Duranty's Moscow days.

After George's murder, the things we had seen made his young widow Mariann and me, like many of our contemporaries, despair of our country. In the fall, we had journeyed to the then–Soviet Union for a few months. One November evening, we had stopped for a drink at the Metropol Hotel, across the square from the Bolshoi. I noticed a balding man in a black overcoat, either an American or a Brit, who occasionally spoke in English, declaiming loudly to a group of Muscovites. Those were the days of the Brezhnev reforms, but old habits were still in place, and the Russians seemed nervous at his forthrightness on whatever issue he was debating.

We'd met many more American expatriates in Soviet Russia than our press would have had us believe existed and had been curious about the man, but it had been time to leave for the ballet. On the way out, I'd been startled as he emphasized a point, striking the floor with an ornate cane.

Returning from the ballet about midnight, we crossed the square just as a light snow began to fall. I remembered we were having a fine time, whistling "Midnight in Moscow," a big hit not many years before. As with Willie refraining from discussing Constance, what was between Mariann and me, I will hold to myself. The world does not need to know.

Then, across the square, an apparition in a dark overcoat and fur hat, the like of which only foreigners and peasants were still wearing, exited the Metropol. Walking with the stiff gait that characterizes a prosthetic limb, it was immediately recognizable as our loud friend by the ornate stick with which he assisted himself.

The snow thickened as we approached the hotel, but I could still see the figure, as it stopped and seemed to watch us down the deserted square. The image remained of an arm raising the cane, as in salute, before vanishing into the snowy darkness. Remained for years, to stun me as I read a description of Duranty, with his artificial leg and elaborate stick, holding forth at the Metropol Hotel.

That night in 1967 was easily thirty years after his drunken debates, and a decade after Duranty's death. Reality, according to Justine[2], would allow for two or three equally outrageous explanations of what that represented; Dunnesian precognition of something I would read thirty years later being the simplest.

"Willie was never in Russia, dearest, so you needn't fear being asked to own past life memories. A *metem* beholding and saluting another, though; I do believe that happens. The educated hobo on the Savannah River? Willie's dread of being part of that man's dreams wasn't a philosophical metaphor. He never escaped the feeling that he was linked to him, that, someway, he *was* that man." She raised that emblematic eyebrow. "Like you felt, after you got into researching Willie, muchly?"

"You think you can do that, recognize beings like yourself?" I asked. "Did you notice something while you were out shopping?"

---

"I HAVE BEEN DOING IT, SWEETIE," SHE RETORTED ACIDLY.

As always, the meat that I could get my teeth into was the synchronistic aspect. Thinking of that in association with Duranty led me to revisit another concern. Should a synchronicity storm brew around anything deemed to affect state security, it probably *would* tend to excite the interest of a number of bureaucrats.

I sketched for her the story of the federal raid on the offices of *Astounding Science Fiction* in March of 1944. A story they had published was judged to imply unusual insight on atomic research. John Campbell, the editor, had hinted to the writer that he might be perceived as knowing too much about actual projects—the Manhattan Project, as it developed.

If Willie had known Will Jenkins in this life also, he might have appreciated the situation through Jenkins-Leinster's contacts with the bunch at the Philadelphia Naval Yards. The manuscript did confirm that by mid-1945, Walter, his friend and Mink's new lover, was warning him that aspects of his activities were unappreciated by some government circles.

The FBI had been shadowing Duranty virtually all the years of his association with Seabrook, acquaintances reporting regularly on his activities and beliefs.

It was probable that the barn adventures had not gone unnoted. I shared with Justine[2] my assumption that this worry had prompted him to secure his notes, wherein he had chosen to embed his farewell, with her.

She shrugged, smiling slightly. "There are other considerations." She slowly lit a cigarette in a manner that only could be described as genteel.

Thinking I might anticipate her, I went on, "Look, they were ending a world war and preparing for the next one. Certainly governments would have a great interest in experiments with precognition. Whatever Willie's personal paranoia, should any research girl ever have been reported to have persuasively demonstrated probable foresight . . .

"Why, even today there would be an interest in co-opting minds that could correlate the variables of possible outcomes beyond the capabilities of the most powerful computers?" I involuntarily ended my pontification in a question as I watched her expression of tolerant amusement. The new persona had consolidated further. The modern young woman was not gone, but tempered with wisdom and experience a century wide.

"But it's the *past*, don't you know?" she breathed. "The 'research girls' had singularly few experiences of precognition. I can count mine on one hand. A biggie, like the street circus, may have gone down precisely through receiving reinforcement from *here*, from being significant way down the branches of many possible paths. It's all about *retrocognition*, detailed hindsight, if only of one or two sets of possible past moments.

"If you hadn't already crashed when Orwell's book was published, you would've instantly recognized some of his ideas. Controlling the here-and-now by redefining and limiting the past is old as Egypt, as Sumer. Establishments are skeptical of any who hold on to even approximate living memory of what has shaped the present moment."

Genuinely humbled, I assured her, "We will protect you. Couldn't let anything happen to my pretty teacher, could I?"

Still smiling, though with a sweet sadness, she answered, "If you but knew, when you have said something like that before." I would not injure the moment by protesting being saddled with memories of things apart from my reality. If nothing else, it was becoming rather convenient to accept a linkage of some sort.

She seemed to gaze far away, and whispered, "I think we are necessary. If temporal hypocrisies must be served by putting the quietus on the most commonsensical trivialities of another day, how much more so for matters of great moment? History is butchered to the point that there would be no continuity at all, were there not always some of us with long memory. Either physical immortals, of some variety, exist in linear time, or it is *we* who own the past, insofar as it's intuited to be someway 'real.'"

I grimaced. "In fact, there are always some fools in academia who are wanting to announce the 'end of history.'"

"That's poorly understood, but . . . Check it out:

The set of all moments that, even remotely, *could* have led to the present state of affairs—somewhere, *somewhen*, really did happen. Let the swells construe the past as other than unitary, and limiting the possibilities to those supportive of the status quo is a short trip. You get bent about them excluding or marginalizing the rest of the set, yea? This revisionism is also about, y'know, including moments from other sets that, while they existed, too, could not have led here."

"What about creativity?" I snapped to the perplexing implications. "Maybe our concept of imagination is all wrong. It could be simply the faculty of perception across the worlds, and the ability to agitate that in others, like Jimmy Greene, the loyal friend. However he may have disapproved, he knew that Willie's behavior was not without meaning. He was even moved to make it into a novel."

"We will teach each other, as we've done before." She looked at me with unabashed adoration. "*Mon compagnon d'âme, je t'aime.* And I'll say it again, *chéri*. I've missed you so much!" How could I feel other than undeserving, under that withering warmth from an intellect of such magnitude?

"Babe, I would accept it all, if only I could find one 'snippet,' as you say; one memory of my own that supports it—I would willingly let you direct me to the rest."

"Where is it written that you won't? Here"—she handed me back *The Fan-Shaped Destiny*—"finish your lesson."

---

And now the book is nearly ended, and I prepare to leave this reportorial record with my trusted friend, my <u>ame soeur</u>; to do a sort of belated justice to the one, who of all the kith and kindred who remain alive, perhaps cared the most. Interspersed with these notes is a methodology, which I suspect is only one among many, for effectuating the transport. In this, at least, my eccentric flashings have not been in vain. Should, in a forgetfulness cruel or kindly, I fail to find you, it may be that you will deign to restore yourself to me.

Your most unworthy companion in eternity prays for this. You cannot know what contrition in this plea for yet another chance. I have been forced to look, sober for the larger part, at a miserable panorama of flight, miles and years wide, all over the map, running away from myself. At the end of my dismal time before, I knew that it was ever you who had blessed my poor life with what meaning it possessed. I was nothing without you. One would have thought, extended an unbelievable grace, I would have done my damnedest to handle you with more care.

Things have turned rather queer for me in the later years. I was successful in spite of myself, had my adventures, wrote my books. That is to say, I invented plausible reasons for my obsessions and they produced by-products. Yet, every so often, this world has seemed as if it resents my presence, would deny my existence, as the physiology rejects a foreign intrusion. The scientific romance of this world elaborates reciprocal histories, and physics will eventually follow suit, even did it come out of Africa and through the pen of a sadist. But neither my name nor that of Wamba will be heralded.

Hollywood has made millions, and will make untold more, off voodoo and zombies, but the name of the man who filed the first English reports has been expunged. Those credited are the very hidebound scholastics who tried and failed to debunk my accounts. In the literature of the paranormal, I am but a vanishing footnote; in that of the erotic, I exist not at all.

While I was not a great writer, this time I was a remarkably competent one. Jimmy Greene gives me his highest praise: that I got on with the job of being a good reporter. Yet Harcourt refuses my manuscripts and my books cease to be reprinted in the face of still-existing demand. I predict that, once I am gone, I will be forgotten in record time. It seems like everything about me is questionable. Does it sound plausible, to be too controversial and yet beneath commentary simultaneously, I ask you? I fear such contretemps say much - about our brave new world that will follow upon the heels of the recent war.

Questions to which you will put this dark present; how a man in his sixtieth year - though it is to me like a century - and who has recently fathered his only son, would arrive at such a denouement? I could not satisfy that, were I to count all the ways that I landed myself in this trap. Even my second chance, in common with all my flights and attempted escapes, too often proved futile, echoing with regrets. I am willing to relinquish my will, my life; give over my self into hands stronger and wiser than my own. Wamba, I feel sure, lives still in this world, but I need our moment in time, and I need her old teacher, the Ogoun who remembered the magic in which time was folded backward.

Pray God I may yet be different for my brother Charlie, for all of you. Some who subscribe to the doctrine of metempsychosis hold that souls naturally travel together in sets. If so, I think it is less a regimented Roman march through a linear time than a melding of some lives into others, an overlapping.

So, as with Walter's stock joke, "On ne fait pas d'omelette sans casser d'oeufs," which we wore thin, we broke a lot of eggs but it was not a bad omelette, was it? At least you are all still here. In my mind's eye I can see Marjorie at her desk writing; she was happiest when we were both working thus. Ever and anon, she may turn and look for me, but Walter will be there. Katie is safe with Lyman. Tell her, won't you, that it was never something hateful about her writing? When I read Gao of the Ivory Coast,[90] and thought of how our little monkey, whom I still had with me, had loved her - I was dead drunk for four days.

Justine, God bless you, Justine, the cosmic contradiction. Striding away with your bracelets and chains still tinkling like bells, yet always fierce and determined. And so alive! At the last, there is perhaps cowardice in it. Wanting honestly to be as honest as I can, sans cribbing or weasel words, were there not a chance in a million threatening you, could I have taken the littlest chance? My angel, I could not have lived to see you die again.

I trust that you will go on to new happiness, but to paraphrase Michelet, you are still living and working on as always. It is well. You will not be bowed down with the grief of losing me; you can do quite well without me. The ranks will close up again,

---

90. Seabrook, Katherine (Edmondson,) *Gao of the Ivory Coast* NY: Coward-McCann, 1931. Reissued by Negro Universities Press, Westport, Connecticut, 1970.

the vacant place be obliterated. The house that was mine will be full of life, and I bless its prosperity . . . but I, I can never forget you!

I promise that if I see you again, be it in another time or an otherworld, I will cherish you. God willing that I become less of a child and less contemptibly frail, I will try to love you better. Somehow, we dream the worlds we live in and, without love, there are no dreams.

Farewell, to meet again,

W.B.S.

# XI
# The Lake

BESIDES MY ADOLESCENT RASH OF PRECOGNITIVE dreams, I had pondered whether some recurring dreams during early childhood might have signified the end of a previous life. But their content had been something like being run over by a big oily machine in an open field. Going back to my earliest days, neither dreams nor memories revealed anything that pointed recognizably to William Seabrook.

Still, this extraordinary week had revealed many other things that defied explanation. Its central fixture was my seemingly fated connection with the *gens* of the Justines, a line we now believed might be infused with Willie's genetics. It began with meeting JJ that long-ago night at the lake, concurrent with the birth of my interest in the same alternate-world fiction whose inspiration I had lately traced to Seabrook.

A full thirty-five years later, it had culminated in my involvement with her daughter, to whom I had been led blindly through my search for Willie's story. Which story had, in its turn, been generated by a late-life renewal of my early obsessions. And what a host of tantalizing convergence in the interim, mostly unrecognized for years. The convulsive reunion with JJ, accompanied by the matter of The Ring, seemed an icon of a principle. If it is possible for a universe to split into two slightly different realities by a quantum-mechanical event, then symmetry demands that two slightly different universes may converge and become identical in the same fashion.

Then there had been the dark, bizarre involvement of Linda and myself with the woman now known to have been Willie's Justine, without a clue of her being JJ's grandmother!

With grateful wonder, I had begun to comprehend that her course of action, resulting in Justine$^2$'s present configuration, had been partially prompted by that meeting. Justine$^2$, before whom the elder Justine's treasured copy of Willie's autobiography had flown to me like a harbinger of destiny.

Leaving aside the question of my being a *metem* of the forgotten author of all this, it appeared that convergence with his influence, and even progeny, had greatly impacted my own personal history. My superstitious fear of having to answer for a multiplicity of trespasses, most likely a projection of my own unconscious issues, had given way to a fatalistic *qué será, será*. I now knew that I would have to explore to exhaustion the significance of such an incredible nexus, wherever it might lead.

More subjective was my uncanny affinity with Willie's work. In contrast to my experience with the classic science fiction, I had not found a single Seabrook passage that I had memory of reading before. Yet each book and article was infused with a texture that intimately caressed my psyche.

Why, the very absence of recognition was significant! At least a couple of his works had to have been on my mother's bookshelves when I was a boy. Not even to mention the copy of *Witchcraft* that seemed to have lain inexplicably among Charles's possessions for decades. How the hell had I missed him? It seemed as though it would have required preconscious avoidance.

Finally, *No Hiding Place* had arrived in my hand, like an ominous bird, complete with its little news clipping. Never had I found the story of another man so psychologically kindred, both for good and ill. I couldn't plumb his deepest feelings without an emotional storm of my own.

Even then I had known that the bottom line came early in his story, when he cried out in sorrow and remorse after his lost brother. In one little line, from the work originally entitled *My Brother Charlie*, he had offered up a lament—which is the deepest, most fervent prayer of all mankind, would we only admit it:

---

"OH GOD, IF I COULD GO BACK to that other night and be different." No mindless wimp, this man, I'd thought. Not one to drug himself with psych-excuses and deny the horror of responsibility. True, he had taken it too far. His brother had died from natural causes, but he could find guilt in anything, Charlie's life twisted by Willie's failure to stand up for him against a domineering mother—and a consequent weakened will to live—Willie took all onto his own shoulders. Now *The Fan-Shaped Destiny* had shown me the true gravity of a failure-haunted life. Given another chance, he must have believed that he could fix everything.

He had been sufficiently different for Justine, for Katie, and Marjorie, but persisted in the belief that he had somehow failed Charlie. Despite his grasp of the paths of high probabilities' resilience, he had felt himself damned. To the end of this life, he had ". . . heard another voice, and hear it always. 'If you had liked me, Will, it might have been some use.'"

I had such a dead brother in my friend Richard, from whose fate I could excuse myself a hundred times over, except for "that night" when, if I had been there, it would have been different. Also Willie's first-life Katie in Linda, if only on a psychological plane. But all this could be easily explained away as the universal human condition. Unless, I was surprised by a thought that then captivated me—unless enlaced worlds and lives might, *itself*, be a part of the human condition!

I'd spoken with Justine[2] of going around my old haunts, though fearful that projecting morbid fascinations of my own might have unexpected impacts on her. Yet the logic of our involvement, the linkages I'd been mulling over, surely couldn't be entirely one-way. Consider the plan for her antecedent self, returning along the timeline, to become an "improved" version of JJ.

"Be cool. I'm good to go to town here. It's grand that you're putting me into your picture." She had been applying elaborate feathering from the corners of her eyes, sweeping up to connect with the ends of her arched eyebrows and shading in between. It looked like something Man Ray might have drawn, or perhaps Dali.

She put on her sexy leather vest and skirt with high heels, then put her hair up in a fifties ponytail. The eclectic combination of styles meshed strikingly. We started messing around, like a pair of kids, when she insisted on tying my thinning mane back similarly. Di looked in and went on by, shaking her head in continuing disbelief.

We drove to Fort Worth along old US Route 80, passing the site of old Top-O-The-Hill, the infamous casino and brothel. For years occupied by a Baptist seminary, it was long forgotten and gone, except for the stone gatehouse and pillars I pointed out to her. I wondered, semifacetiously, at whether she might have had any business acquaintance with the place.

"Maybe *l'Autre*," she shrugged. Justine[2] still did not fully identify with the legend of the later Madeleine as related by Roder. Those portions she had not yet consciously recalled, she referenced as belonging to "the other."

We passed by Rose Hill Cemetery, final resting

place of a man named Lee Harvey Oswald, who had spirited all of us off down a treacherous branch in the paths of destiny. Beyond the high school that I had attended with JJ, we cruised the still-spooky road through a surviving stretch of undeveloped river bottoms. I pulled over where a gravel path still ascended to a preferred "parking" location we'd called Grasshopper Hill. There, I drifted into a matter-of-fact account of making love to JJ, of interludes become as mythic to me as colorful pulp-fiction sagas. Justine[2] displayed sincere interest and didn't bat an eye, certain testimony to her being a tad beyond the commonly human. Imagine a young woman who could listen to all that without irritation or boredom!

She'd kicked off her shoes and was sitting, typically, with her butt between her feet, in what therapists call the "W-sit" position. Dropping the seat back, she looked at me mirthfully out of the corner of a feathered eye, "Checking me out?"

"Not really." I was a bit chagrined. "In fact, I was just realizing that I don't know why I'm doing this." She sighed and stretched herself, displaying her figure. With her muscles on stretch, the nerve impulses would rebound from her bent knees back up the inner thighs, serving as a degree of self-arousal.

"Hey, you're getting me all kinds of hot. Rewind that part where you fucked her in the autumn leaves. Was she wearing her green jacket? I'll bet you a dollar she kept it on."

She laughed at my shocked pause. "Razzing you! That jacket, believe it or not, was still around when I was little. She takes good care of her things," Justine² mused with actual fondness, "and it was her favorite. No, wait. Let me see. No, I'm reading your mind, I really am."

I wasn't laughing. "We could assume that you're now perpetually functioning a bit out of linear time," I talked fast. I was blushing hotly, for the first time in decades, from some weird embarrassment. "Do you suppose that there can be some phase entanglement of our wave functions?"

"You slay me. Are you a card or what? I'll entangle your functions, later—you can believe that!" Trying to control her giggling, she grasped my arm. "Don't be so solemn. It's just fine about JJ. I'm gonna get the best part of you."

"God, babe, if only that were so."

Driving deeper into the old, decaying east side, I talked of the joys and hurts of youth, and the horrors of meaningless, abbreviated endings. I told her more of my parents, particularly my schoolteacher mother. Strong, self-assured, she had empowered herself without benefit of society's dubious blessings.

"Sounds like Myra," Justine² suggested.

"Like her in some respects, perhaps." I glanced at her with a hint of chastisement at the comparison with Willie's mother. "She was never the tyrant that Myra became."

"Sounds like she didn't need to be," she teased, getting the giggles again.

"Brat."

We made the promised stop by JJ's childhood

home in a neighborhood that had truly gone to hell. Still, the late-afternoon light was benign, and the slanting sunbeams did most tenderly paint with life the "shapes which lingered still."

The sight of the run-down old home made my heart ache in spite of all that had transpired. She became more subdued, reminiscing on her long-ago playtime and the *mambos'* assurance that she must aspire to that prescient vision. I listened to a little girl's joy at the first touch of what was to become, and had perhaps sustained, Justine[2].

An air of normality around those reflections furthered acceptance of the circumstances as believable parts of life. She deliberated over a semiconscious equation, which had persisted through this life, of that experience with her hope of finding her longed-for father. Something awful leapt unbidden from the shadows of the dark arc in my memory.

It had been the one time I *had* stopped, and almost gone to the door. I'd been transfixed by a little girl playing in a pile of leaves that had been raked up in the crisp autumn. Hair like a maple tree in flame had made me believe that she must be JJ's child. Justine[2] watched me in a hushed tension while I confessed the repressed recollection.

I was close to nausea as I admitted to standing immobilized when JJ's stepmother had called the child to come away from the strange man. JJ's "mom" had not, of course, seen me for a decade at that time. Then I'd run away from that house, and from the little girl who, in all childish innocence, had approached to show me the pretty colors—in the patina that the years and earth had emblazoned *onto an ancient, dirt-filled Coke bottle* from her grandmother's yard.

"For God's sake, Justine, say something!" I demanded of her pensive silence. Would she hate me for that, for not finding a means to force myself into her early life?

"It may shed some light on my decision to live here," she considered calmly. "Say, this was probably not at the very same moment as my vision loop. There was no *anamnesis* involved. But if I did behold you, and at some level recognized you from *The Château*, that would've totally clinched the deal. If so, something will come back to me." I continued to agonize over the picture she had made me draw of the shape of my concern.

"Dearest, the larger part of me didn't come looking for you so that you could be my father. Pos it's not this thing you have going on that you're someway screwing your daughter? You're way more touchious about that than I am."

Then it was she who was lightening the mood, persuading me that we were merely looking at another aspect of the storm of synchronicity. Worse than at any time in this affair, I felt any sense of bedrock present reality slipping from my grasp. Looking at the window JJ used to crawl out at night, I found myself at last believing that "somewhere in time" she was still so doing.

"Surprised if you were to see her? Not," Justine$^2$ replied to my contemplation. "You love her, you miss her. She lived here. The heart sees many things that the eyes do not. How's that for a pithy statement? People *can* someways see those they love in familiar settings. Why not? The heart longs for them, the heart sees them." It was the only time since we'd met that she had sounded like her mother. While I admired the dark angel within, I adored her the more for not entirely abolishing the influence of my little lost love.

---

DUSK WAS SETTLING as we parked in the lot of an elderly strip center eight blocks away. It sat across the street and half a block from my old home. Neighborhood assistance offices and a storefront church, trying to arrest the decline, now occupied its spaces. This was the place where JJ and I shared that impossible memory of my adolescent gallantry, offering to marry her with whomever's child. That conversation, which for a variety of reasons, could not have occurred anytime close to her actual pregnancy.

"JJ remembers that she met with me after I'd passed her a note in class. One of those long letters, you know, on folded-up notebook paper. But it's impossible. I'd gone to another school by then. I can remember writing it and giving it to her, and even a bit of what was in it. But it just can't be!"

"You don't get it?" she asked gently. "Time was right, but the world was wrong. Here, you were losing her, and what you wanted more than anything was another chance. So much, that what you remembered was a moment glimpsed from a world where there *was* another chance."

"But, damn it, babe, she remembers it, too!"

"It may be, deep in her soul, she too wanted another chance," she mused softly, looking into the deepening twilight. "A world where you didn't leave, where you passed on the *smart* life you led to marry the little high-school girl when she was abandoned . . . No, wait." She shook off the empathy and snapped, "I'm so fucking sorry! If she could believe that was in you, even if only in a strange memory, and not take your hand? Hey, she was some kinda fool, like I always thought."

She hopped out of the car, slamming the door, and pranced up the sidewalk as if knowing exactly where she was going. *Way weird*, I thought, hastening to catch up with her through the deep blue twilight. More, there was ceasing to be any delineation among patterns of speech, cadence, or language. As her persona tended toward unity, the question of whom I was addressing was becoming moot, but this opened new areas of confusion.

"Like you always thought your mother to be, or your granddaughter?" That was not a joke.

"All that." She turned to me. "I can remember how I carried girls, many of them friends, to the abortion mill. I visited them at those horrible 'homes for unwed mothers' and walk-up flats with swinish husbands and squalling brats; seeing how oh, so *happy* they were—like their teeth hurt. Babies aren't bad, but the trap was brutal. JJ had a fucking cakewalk!"

She had not. JJ's tragedy had not been that many

years later, only almost at the end of the reaction. All those conventions had still been in place. Their apostles were even more vicious and fanatic, sensing their time was almost ended. She had been among the later victims of the final campaign to break the progress of women.

I was trying to puzzle this curious blind spot in her preternatural understanding when, turning to continue along the walk, she blurted out, "Why'd *I* survive, when I was so much worse than them?" I said nothing, but mulled over the sudden insight that some things take more than a lifetime to resolve. Young Justine, the psychologist, had her work cut out, having to carry Madeleine's baggage as well.

The house lights along the street reminded me of the window lights in Georgia, the little lights in every window . . . She began to recite from, I sensed, farther memory.

"Y'know, Willie had been a big adventurer. He'd wandered through the Arabian deserts, sought out the secrets of island jungles and darkest Africa." Ardently, she went on, "It made him so mad when a critic said that, all the time, like many roaring adventurers, he was only running farther away from home—shouting and crying in the dark because he was lost." My cornea reflected a flaring of the lights, as her voice clutched at me.

---

"AT LAST, IN DESPAIR, HE HUNG IT UP AND CAME HOME."

She had stopped in front of the old house where I'd

grown up, still in good repair and much the same as always. The forest green shutters were now painted darker, maybe even black. But that little change made all the difference. Justine[2] gripped my arm and urged me up the walk, and the last thing I wanted was for her to let go. For this looked like the dream, my last adolescent precognition, and the one that, above all, I had believed to be impossible.

Justine[2] ignored the bell and struck the heavy brass doorknocker, to whose specific sound I had a conditioned childhood reflex of alertness. Hearing that loud metallic rap after so many years startled me. She was eager, as if it were she having a homecoming, and a very happy one at that. As for me, I was imagining approaching footsteps.

Who might open that door, looking as huge to me as when I had been a child? Who might be sitting in an armchair in the study, which I would be able to see off the foyer when the door opened—working a crossword puzzle in the evening paper? Upstairs, I had dreamed my dreams. Up there, my friends and I had played with hypnosis and pushed hard to open a gate to the future, the past; like any teens, to anywhere but here!

It did not open. We waited, and Justine[2] knocked again. Then I rang the doorbell, and we waited some more. We just kept standing there, both of us, expecting *something* to happen. When we could no longer deny that there was no one home, we reluctantly retreated.

Crossing the street, I looked back at the treetops

upon which I had meditated from that darkened upstairs room. That had been after my phase of staring at candles, when discovery of the slow diffusion of Eastern disciplines across America had inspired me to imagine that I, too, could attain higher wisdom. As before, the higher wisdom eluded me when I stumbled on the curb and nearly fell on my face.

I looked at the offending concrete with confusion. Then I remembered that it had not always been on the edge of the street. There had been head-in parking there, with an indentation all the way to the sidewalk. In the years since, it had been eliminated, the curb brought on out to the street. But the indentation had been there in the dream. This was not the dream.

In front of the old drugstore location, I paused to light my pipe. Richard and I would linger long at the lunch counter, reading the pulp science fiction off the rack so we didn't have to pay for it. Even were the store still there, it would exist for me only to house Richard and "that other night."

It was true that there, reflected in the plate glass, stood a better-preserved approximation of my father. My focus channeled down to Justine[2]. With her hair tied back, she momentarily looked so much like the JJ of years before.

But even in her surreal, reflected image, a second glance revealed the feathered eyes, the nose ring, the kinky-looking leather outfit, complete with the braided thong band biting into her thigh. Passionately reciting nothing beyond what Willie had said of himself, she had revealed what she hoped for me to find there.

I had actually come closer to her vision than to my own. She was my goddess-in-chains, the meaning of my life. Yet, she was visibly Justine[2] the *metem*, a creature from another world. Despite her youth, she could not be the sweet innocent who had opened the dream-door. She had never been, at least since before the First World War!

Had I not, from being blown before the hormonal storms of my early maturation, always remained somewhat disconnected and waiting? Did it matter that there may have been a glimpse of yet another world in which she might have been my daughter? It was not dissimilar to the "false memory" of the parking lot, of a world where JJ had perhaps accepted me due to an early pregnancy. Possibly those worlds were one and the same.

Now it seemed that we might all have such episodes with regularity. It could be that such glimpses of cosmic consanguinity, kinship across the multiverse, as it were, might serve to strengthen our bonds in this reality.

A Prussian deputation of psychoanalysts could prattle in my ear forever and yet fail to make the simplest fact of all go away. Why demand this miracle conform to an interpretation of a past vision? Why was I always continuing to look backward?

When we reached the car I hugged her tight against me, trying to pull myself back to the present moment, to shake off the ambiance that had settled over everything like a numinous fog. I lightly ran my fingernails around her smooth thighs in a way I knew would please her, and she squirmed against me. But there was more than eroticism going on.

"All there has ever been was waiting, just waiting. For decades, waiting for you," I breathed in her ear. "No matter what else it might all mean; we are together and, for whatever incredible reason, you are mine. Nothing else matters, nothing else *ever* mattered." I didn't know what else I could say to her, or tell you. There is no way to articulate something like that. What if it had happened to you? How would you describe what it felt like?

I got into the car feeling like one of Willie's zombies and fumbled for my keys. Down at the corner with Lancaster Avenue, the highway to Dallas in farther time, a ratty little convenience store occupied the location of the old Lone Star Drive-in. Had I seen Richard and Marilyn drinking a Coke beneath a corrugated metal canopy, it would have added nothing to this sensation of existing altogether apart from time as we know it.

At the intersection, my gaze wandered to the west, recalling the amber flash of the Texas sunset in times of fewer pollutants and city lights. It had always seemed like Halloween, in that final moment when the setting sun had burned like an orange fire among black clouds on the horizon, and the night had fallen all at once.

I turned east and slowly cruised down Lancaster, vaguely following a route of conditioned reflexes from the nearer past. The wide boulevard itself had changed little in all the years of my life. Our windows were down and the early Sunday evening was abnormally quiet with scant traffic. In my dreamy state of mind, the quiet world around us seemed *empty*. Like there was as little press about us of human presence and activity as in those long-ago years on which I'd been focused.

"Like a thing where your mind is reaching across time?" Justine[2] agreed. "I'm down with that, I felt so in the Village." After a reflective pause she queried, "The oldest memories you have? *Raconte!*"

---

ASSOCIATING WITH THE FIERY SUNSETS, I described some very early childhood impressions of the last great wildfire that swept close to Fort Worth, perhaps back around 1949. It had taken out an old farmstead that my parents had still owned outside town. They had bundled me up and driven out that night in our old Dodge. I could still remember watching the burning sweep across a wide arc of the flat horizon.

In my distracted wandering, I'd turned off Lancaster onto the spur road that skirted the lake, then had automatically turned again. I stopped in confusion when a chain-link fence blocked our way. I recognized with some embarrassment that I'd been driving to the lake, but the old road over the dam had been closed years before. I turned back toward the thoroughfare that now routed traffic to approach from the east through Arlington.

She pressed me to continue, like my story was going somewhere. "The next day, we went out again for my father to pick over what was left of the old farm. I wandered away in a terrible fascination with the blackened debris.

"A rooster ran by, like from out of nowhere. His colors were bright against all the black and gray ash. I ran after him and found a glass jar full of hard candy that had somehow survived the fire. The candy looked like jewels to my eyes. It was funny. I was convinced that the rooster had directed me to the treasure and was giving it to me!" I laughed, enjoying the intimacy of sharing this early part of myself with her.

While I talked, Justine[2] was content to continue cruising the route to the lake. Finally, I asked about this, "We don't have to go there, you know?" Slow to begin to understand my own motivations, I was chagrined that she had been able to see through to so many of them.

"I'm still good to go. I wanna see it." She watched everything intently as we pulled into the little lakefront park with its piers and small marina. The old trees still circled the shelter house, though they were now a small stand separated by asphalt parking from residences, rather than the outriders of woods bordering on the lake. Remarkably, though, the vista toward and across the lake would seem to have hardly changed. It was now the dark of night.

"We're at a nexus in your life, when you're strongly entangled across the years and the worlds." My discomfiture was growing.

"Don't you understand that I've spent my life

wanting to go back and make things different, somehow set things right? Like Willie did?" I still struggled with that fresh probability. Facing her, in that memory-haunted place, I was backed into a corner and had no choice but to confess my doubts and fears.

"I'm not pining over JJ and the past anymore. I want to be here with you."

The smile turned wicked, and with it returned a tinge of the Justine I'd first met. "It's all kinds of gratifying to hear you 'fess up to that," she gloated. "But seriously, it's not about her. This is about us, and about the young boy that you were."

"I don't think I could look myself in the eye, knowing what life put him through, knowing what *I* put him through. Anyway, I can't possibly want to change the past, a path that led to you."

"You're still not getting it." She was impatiently urging me toward the old shelter house. "Our moment is concrete, it won't go away." She hesitated, then continued, though a bit uneasily, "You could leave it, though I pray you mean what you say, but this world abides."

Standing in the shelter house, lit by the green fluorescence from outside, this conversation was eerie to the extreme. The old wooden benches and tables had surrendered to one-piece steel, and the area was now open on all sides.

In earlier time, rest-room cubicles had walled up the north end. These had been replaced by modern facilities nearby, though the covered plumbing apertures were visible in the concrete slab. I noted to her that it was the same old roof above. Small square light fixtures, painted over and unused for years, remained embedded in the ceiling.

"Let's go someplace else," decided Justine[2] with a nervous impatience. "Say, I wanna hear more about the magic rooster! Do some regress, here. As if I can learn to use it to recover some more of my shit." The punker cadence and vulgarity were wedded oddly to the Bronx accent that had generally accompanied more formal speech.

I was quite malleable at that moment. At her urging, I lay back on one of the metal benches and explained how she might assist with the hypnotic suggestions. I focused on the nature sounds, the breeze in the trees, wavelets against the piers, and occasional quacking of the local ducks.

Her unique eclectic speech now familiar and comforting, I visualized the numerals of the years rolling away backward like mile markers on a highway—the image from my recent dream. This variation on my usual approach to regressive self-hypnosis soon had me concentrating on the image of the rooster.

I described its colorful feathers, including the almost prismatic iridescence on its breast, the legs like polished brass. I began to feel something untoward when I had to compare its appearance with the giant roosters to which Willie's laudanum-addicted grandmother had introduced him over a century before. True, my rooster had been large, but not that huge! I had been a very small child then, after all.

Captivated by the clarity of this childhood distraction, I went on with the recollection. "My mother came and got me, upset because I had wandered off. She led me away, and I didn't see the rooster anymore. I bawled about it, later on, when I wanted the candy and remembered that she had taken it with us. I guessed that she thought it was probably ruined and threw it away.

"Years later, she would maintain nothing like that had happened, that I must have dreamed it. But why would an adult remember such a small thing anyway? I'm not even sure why it made such a heavy impression on me."

I felt Justine[2] take my hand. "Dearest, look again. Go back and look carefully as your mother leads you away. Don't be afraid." Why afraid, I wondered? Even as I knew I was. But this was not a fearful memory—it was a fun one. The recognition grew that my fear was not at all about some suppressed trauma, but in the here-and-now.

The pressure of her fingers recalled that long-ago hand-holding, and I remembered looking up, looking up at some impossibly long skirts with . . . with curious ribbons below the waist, contrived to resemble a *bustle*, of all things. I had looked up into the elfin features, not of my mother, but . . .

I drew back from the image in utter confusion. "It wasn't my mother!" I exclaimed with consternation.

Her grip tightened. "Just remember your promise—nothing matters except that we've found each other." I could hear concern in her voice, blended with tension as though something exciting were at hand, and . . . joy.

I wasn't feeling particularly joyful. "It was my *grandmother*," I whispered. But that could not be, for I had never known a grandparent. The branches of my line procreate late, if at all, and those people had been gone for years before I was born. What could this be? An early glimpse of yet another alternate reality, one in which I had known my grandmother?

At that moment, I *knew*! I bolted up from the trance so abruptly I almost fell off the bench. My throat was paralyzed, and I could only stare at Justine[2] in my shock. As if coming from her sweet lips, I might be able to accept that which I couldn't bring myself to say.

She obliged me. "I'd heard this story the time before, *chéri*. It was your Grandma Piny, wasn't it?"

So there it was. As I had leapt into full consciousness, I'd dragged along a further association that took minutes to blossom into real memory. I had to move around, and we walked down toward the piers, across the paved boat landing that bordered the lapping wavelets.

There *had* indeed been terror back then, on *the night before*. In a dark and scary place, a fiery horizon haunting him like a half-remembered London hell, a small boy had been frightened out of his wits. The next day, his mind had run away for a moment to the refuge of a little boy in another life. The consoling memory had been integrated with events and assumptions of this life I thought I knew, never guessing it had been of a different order.

How many such things might we hold in our minds without notice, except that they may be so strangely compelling as to persist a lifetime? The glimpses that followed may have been partially constructed, fleshed out by having read *The Fan-Shaped Destiny*. Nonetheless, they were elaborations on a truth.

The girl who had been the woman who had loyally defied time and death to reach a man who, over and over, had treated her precious life with him as lightly as a petulant child, reached up and stroked the back of my thinning hair. Once more, a dream from another life was intruding upon this one.

It was not remorse alone that brought me to my knees. I *had* to get my cheek against her legs, as with the lady-in-chains in Piny's tower; as when, learning that she had died and knowing it was his sin, the man I was had once prayed hopelessly on a quay beside the Seine.

There may never be more than the glimpses. I think I will learn yet a bit, because the jungle drums still beat somewhere and lead on to something, but even this much was, at last, enough. Because I was finally able to tell her the truth that had taken more than one lifetime to find a voice.

"Justine, oh Christ! Justine, my darling, I am sorry. I'm so, so sorry. Do whatever you want with me. Please just be willing to forgive, I don't have your endurance; I'm not as strong as you. If you leave me, if I lose you again, I'll go mad." I wasn't able to stop. I had kept on repeating my remorse.

---

"IT'S ALL RIGHT, C'EST MOI, C'EST MOI . . ." She, in turn, had just kept on stroking my hair and repeating that ancient formula of comfort. Finally, the catharsis abating, we found our way back to the shelter house. Words cannot express how it felt to *see*, after nearly half a century, into that dark arc where I'd never been able to look.

"*Believe* that now you know what you had going on?" She feigned wickedness, "Don't you know that you *have* gone mad, and more than once? It was ever only yourself who wouldn't forgive."

Drawing me to sit again beside her on a steel bench, she continued, "You made it just fine, didn't you ever believe that? I'll bet it was Wamba who showed you how to stop running, to turn around and come back where you belonged. And, y'know? It may have been only symbolic, but I'm glad I always made sure to leave the lights on for you." I was nearly overcome again at that image, knowing now whence sprang that devastating sense of shame, seeing myself as the little boy finally giving up and going home.

"*Enfin!* It may be that someday you'll own to yourself," she elbowed me playfully, "how indebted you always seem to be to women. Let's find out what else is back in the day." Having obtained such an enormous revelation, I had now the confidence to accede to her enthusiasm, so I lay back and let her help take me down again.

I described to her the burning horizon, the black pillars of smoke, and the red clouds underlit by the fires. The last night in London, of course! I also recovered an entirely forgotten childhood fear of the kettle lights and the dark shape in the sky of sporting events to which my father would take me. The unoffending Goodyear blimp must have recalled the shape of the barrage balloons among the pencils of light seeking the German bombers.

"Go on with you, now," she urged after I had seen all of this, and I had trusted nothing in my life more than I now trusted the sound of her voice. "There may be more places you can see into. Oh look, isn't this where the party was?" I could hear her moving about, but that was okay, too. Everything was. "Wouldn't you like to go to the party? See if there's anything you haven't remembered?"

I was amazed at how brilliantly I could remember it now. Where I had first laid eyes on JJ when another guy and I had "switched dates," learning only later that the swap had been at the girls' contrivance. Where I had stood, where she had stood, sizing me up with that little mischievous smile that her daughter would inherit. I wondered aloud whether that look had come down from "the ghosts of Justines past."

"Just *go* with it . . ." I registered Justine$^2$'s snicker, but the vision distracted me from her continuing murmuring.

I described all of it, unwinding behind my eyelids like a movie. The piers much as they appear now, except for the illumination of the mercury vapor, jutting out into darkness toward the lights of the power plant across the lake. Only intermittent bare bulbs beneath metal reflectors had illuminated the trees behind us, in that time before condominiums had been built nearly to the lakefront. I sighed nostalgically and opened my eyes, looking up at the ceiling.

A trick of reflection, I thought, that an old painted-over light fixture seemed to glow dimly yellow. I got up off the bench to look more closely, feeling a nip from the breezy night air. That was no reflection, that thing was *on*! My astonished gaze slid down, to be blocked by the partition walls at the north end. Out of the corner of my eye, I could see distant headlights on the road across the dam. I looked around in confusion, at the little blue-and-white 45-rpm record player on a wooden table, the wooden bench behind me, and at a girl with her flaming red hair pulled back into a ponytail.

Momentarily, it seemed I was that boy who had stood transfixed by JJ. So young, so slight, and trying so hard to look tough in my first leather jacket. Memories, memories that would have to be put away and forgotten. Strange glimpses of a life yet to be lived, which had charged that night with a sense of destiny and, if dwelt on, would pollute reality. The moment passed and I was no longer he. But a girl's green-vinyl jacket was not a leather vest. And there were still no condos encroaching on the park, only trees and the night.

Awareness returned of the sounds around me, of lesser volume than I would have imagined. The party seemed much smaller than I'd remembered, fewer than twenty kids, who looked so goddamned *young*. I barely recognized them, and didn't remember any of their names. I stared stupidly at a boy who was speaking to me. Then I realized he was Tony, one of my friends back then. I was perplexed to recognize how my memory had adjusted chronology.

This was real! I was "back in the day," more precisely, *the night*. In real time, Charles, Richard, and the others who were to become permanent fixtures of my life were people whom I had not yet even met. More eerie was the knowledge that Tony was doomed to die in Vietnam a few years later. That thought probably helped frame my ignoble first words in my new reality.

"I got to take a piss." Which was most literally the case, I assure you. In the john, I was careful to relieve myself before looking in the mirror, though what I could see and feel of my clothes and body had already told me the story. Things in my life have made me afraid, but none could compare with the terror of looking into my own young eyes. A single bare bulb dimly illuminated my gnarled feelings.

I spoke brokenly to the stricken young face, "Oh my God, Justine, what have we done?"

I thought of the moment when I had felt myself to *be* that boy, even to abrupt recall of the long-forgotten intrusion of bizarre thoughts, thoughts whose nature was beyond his comprehension. In that strange moment, I had consolidated my awareness, my self, toward the assumptions of his time and place. I remembered the account of Willie's moment of "exaltation" on that fateful night in London, before he awakened back in Augusta from a lucid dream some thirty-odd years in duration. Unintentionally, I seemed to have discovered the key to transit, for this was unlike even the clearest regression vision. But, *damn it*! At the barn, Justine had *wanted* to return, and I'd been able to hold her back from even that fierce obsession.

The moment that my world had divided in a major way now lay behind me. There had surely been a jillion variant subatomic events since then, every tiny junction farther removing me from the path I had lived. Had I made a pathetic sprint for the rest room, when I'd first laid eyes on JJ, I'd not likely stood transfixed by this damned mirror. Certainly not stood there talking to a love lost not only in time, but also on an entirely different branching path of reality. I remembered her coaxing tone as she had finessed me to the house, then the lake, and back into the past. A softly murmured phrase consolidated itself into clarity: "PAPA LEGBA, OUVRÍ BARRIÈRE . . ."

---

God, no! She couldn't have ditched me, could she? Might she have gently scraped off her old lover, rewarding me with the fulfillment of my most precious fantasy? But I remembered her reassurances and could not bring myself to believe that this was other than a horrible irony. I was sick at heart. More horrific yet, might I have *died* at the point of transit? My heart ached at the thought of Justine$^2$ crying over her lover's death yet again. And what were the odds that Justine$^2$ would emerge in this reality at all?

Feeling ill, I drew a deep breath and something else kicked in. On one level, it didn't *feel* like I'd *gone* anywhere. It was more like I'd been there all along, my attention having taken an excursion on which I'd seen many wondrous things—then returned to this place along the same path by which it had left. The air was sweeter, the smells more intense, their associations arousing feelings long forgotten. Most likely, it was merely a matter of a body and brain that properly processed oxygen, producing a wave of euphoria that softened the impact of black thoughts.

A long-admired, if not emulated, philosophy of "play it like it lays" came to mind. I nodded to the boy in the mirror, "At least, I don't have to let *you* down again." But there was more. The germ of an idea was sprouting into consciousness, a slender reed that I might grasp against the dark tide of desperation and panic. A large proportion of my fantasy life had prepared for precisely this impossible moment. I apparently had another lifetime to deal with my own issues, and the time for action was *now*. Bolting for the rest-room had likely been advisable. Meeting the young JJ with soaking trousers would have not done at all.

I went back out to see JJ chatting conspiratorially with a girl in a tight sweater and flared skirt. Dressed for easy access, I thought with cheap amusement, for I could also recognize Shirley, my official date. Shirley had a magnificent run as the high-school 'slut' ahead of her. If you happened not to know Shirley's reputation, she would be more than happy to tell you all about it. Which, of course, was precisely why I had asked her to the dance, where I was destined to meet, instead, with the fatal attraction of the century. A hormonal rush surged in response to my thoughts. Lord, I'd forgotten how easily triggered it was. No mystery that adolescents are so desperate.

I stopped by an ice-filled tub and pulled up a NeHi Orange. I fumbled stupidly with the cap until I comprehended that twist-off technology had not yet arrived, going back in search of a bottle opener. There was no doubt that this was a very material world, and all that I knew indicated that there was nothing for it except to make the best, to use what I had. Soon, I would have to put my mind to outlining my "future memories" as completely as possible, study what spin I could put on matters affecting me without disrupting the larger configuration of the "map."

Shirley soon moved off with Gene, the slightly older boy with whom I knew she wanted to rendezvous, him having a car and all. The love of my lifetime came off like a little girl against the angel I was missing, for whom I yearned with every aching breath. But my growing concept calmed my labored breathing as I proffered her preferred soft drink to the girl who, in an other life at least, was destined to become *the mother of my Justine.*

We then went for our long-remembered walk down to the pier, and I went directly to work on the agenda. With no illusions of exactly replicating how this had gone down, I carefully, so as not to frighten, used my unnatural advantage to neatly push all of her buttons as I remembered them. It helped that she, thirty years down the line, had confessed all that I hadn't known about her initially. The boy who had taken her away in that world, and would here if things remained equal, had been a smooth talker. But he would play hell competing with *this*, if he even ever got to meet her.

With accelerating confidence, I shamelessly demonstrated seemingly paranormal guesses about her family background, then about her own young pain that bordered on the suicidal, to take things deeper and heavier. Could she become as enticing to me as memory had served? Perhaps more so, for reasons I was only beginning to understand. I gently took her hand and looked at it, knowing it was destined for painful arthritis, and felt an unexpected tenderness.

That I was going to make love to her had never been in question. With one kiss I was hard as a rock, and I knew that she was similarly aroused, as well as being completely snowed. The only glitch was rediscovering the zipper hidden along the left hip of her slacks. The ease of the conquest detracted not at all. I knew only too well that my real challenges were far ahead.

When I slipped off her panties and went down on her, an act *almost* beyond her fourteen-year-old imagination, the issue was decided. When she still had the presence of mind to insist on a condom, I was able to oblige. I had come armed for a date with the notorious Shirley, after all. Donning the rubber in the dark, it was awfully easy for one's thumbnail to puncture the tip . . . Along with foreknowledge of her typical responses, I found enough control of this body to get her a couple of presentable orgasms before I climaxed. More, I experienced the almost-forgotten novelty of staying erect for a while afterward!

The rest was love talk and a long stroll on the graveled shoreline, discussing "what does this *mean* and what will we do now?" Cosmic concerns of teenagers, just as if they possessed some command of a larger picture. During all the years that I'd run this fantasy tape in my head, I'd mused about the presumed issue of intellectual disparity in the imaginary situation. It proved to be no large problem. Placed in the reality, my own mode of relating turned out to have an unexpected resemblance to that of my earlier self.

I had fancied that any unavoidable whiff of maturity would make me all the more attractive, but it was something other that emerged to serve me. Adolescent mannerisms were reclaimed with an unflattering ease, seeming not at all unnatural. Excessively emboldened, I attempted a tentative brush with the actuality underlying our situation. Her comprehension quickly faded.

"Do I sound flipped out?" She was looking at me with growing skepticism. "You know, crazy, 'lost all my marbles'?" I had taken care to guard my speech against unknown usages, such as overly casual profanity, but less obvious anachronisms kept slipping out.

"That's a new one on me. No, but, isn't learning from the mistakes of the past about all you can do with it? You could be right on the mark about all the 'why-fors,' but it's another one of those things . . . interesting, but in the grand scheme of things, means nothing to the average person. It 'won't put food on the table,' you know? Worrying about time going all haywire wouldn't be a big deal to most people. They have to live their everyday lives; don't have time or interest."

Here it came. I could hear the socially correct, self-censorial mechanism kicking in. I was not about to engage in debate that would only provide ignorant adolescent detractors, and flatly stupid adults, with something to chew on. I could only faintly recall, from the time before, the issue of an argument related to the permissible limits of speculation.

Having no life as yet, I'd read Voltaire's *Candide* and inappropriately wanted to share my no-doubt poorly understood discovery. That my excursion into a larger world of ideas had not been well received by another teenager was understandable. Less excusable had been a similar reaction from a teacher; a sad commentary on our crippling background. I remembered thinking that it was a matter of JJ being childish. Of course, I had managed to overlook the small detail that we *were* children.

She chattered on about our capacity to choose the general perspective from which we would live our lives. Looking ahead with joy and optimism or looking back with sadness and regret. Her song of praise for the eternal present did not strike me with the tedium that it might have in that other life. The difference was within myself. I had seen the days when this little summer flower would wilt—when she would have to struggle every day to look forward. My foreknowledge of that inevitable daily struggle was excruciating.

That her opinionated harangues were incompatible with my selective recollections was perhaps due to the softening of their edges. They were studiedly tractable, seeking to not offend. She was such a sweet girl. Not yet burned and brutalized by life, intimidated into stultifying her mind, she was still more interested in the content of ideas than in questioning whether she could allow herself to have them. I had arrived in her life sufficiently early—there was yet time!

". . . no matter how much you want to, you can't go back and change a thing. Yesterday is past. Tomorrow may never come. There is only today, which is a gift. That's why we call it 'the present.' I know it sounds real square, but that's the main thing to me." Remaining quiet, I just smiled at her little lecture. I made a promise to myself that I would never condescend or abuse the gift of compliance.

I knew that she yearned for a college education that her stepparents would not be able to afford, so I assured her that mine could send us both. Not quite the truth; they could help *start* both of us, especially if she were the mother of the grandchild I'd never given them in the other world. I'd have to work, but you can't have everything. In this life, I *might* become a science fiction writer, predicting the shape of the future with uncanny accuracy. I almost got the hysterical giggles, imagining the publication of *Labor Rep from Dimension J*!

For various reasons, I'd determined that we should not ride home with Gene and Shirley. As it happened, we missed all rides. Returning to the shelter house, we found ourselves alone. I was satisfied, calculating that setting us up for being out all night just about cinched what would have to follow. My original plan in motion, another had been growing inside it like a psychic embryo.

True enough, in this time and place, I could mechanic an early pregnancy to guarantee a marriage. Overall, I had every intention of forcing us from the conventional assumptions as soon as possible, for this society did not trouble to police strata it had declared marginal. To this end, I would not eschew any device, even very cheap tricks. But there was so much more.

We stood again on the pier, amidst the wavelets and ducks, as in a San Antonio park during our melancholy adult reunion—in a world we were never now to know. The die was cast. By whatever point the worlds had divided, a replay leading me to Justine[2] in the fashion I remembered would have been patently hopeless, even were I sufficiently masochistic to walk that path.

Even at that moment, a spermatozoon of destiny might be wiggling toward a branch in the paths. I could relax and reflect on my alternate course. Many things might change now, the friends and lovers to come might not have to hurt so much, or die so young. Why, maybe that boy Tony could live as well! I remembered him as a young man of deep commitment. Might he not fight for peace, rather than die for a government that would just be playing a goddamned game?

Soon I must confront the beloved dead: my parents, my mother most of all. While this prospect gave me serious pause, it was inevitable. And only she, even if with some careful handling, might believe and accept what I was. I'd been her late-life "miracle child," after all. To her I'd always been so special. I needed some friend to whom I could talk, and no one else in this whole wide world . . . but then, my thoughts smashed head-on into something I'd overlooked. The plan was derivative of a long-term fantasy, ignoring the realities that had given it flesh.

---

THE BELOVED DEAD OF AN OTHER LIFE WERE YET LIVING HERE!

I had no direct memory of them and did not feel inclined to inflict myself on them in their waning years. Incongruously, I remembered the root of my fantasy of going to Fort Lauderdale. Tony and I had talked about such a prospect for months after drooling over Connie Francis and Yvette Mimieaux in *Where the Boys Are*. This boy I had become was a different person, a different life. Could I really befriend Marjorie, or make up anything to her and Katie?

I especially feared the thought of watching Katie die in a few years, if Justine[2] had been correct about her connection to Linda. Linda was another responsibility I had to work into this agenda, damn it. All that I'd speculated about the burning memories of other lives proved to be a fearful truth. Bedrock reality was going to be my life with JJ, yet these beloved ghosts who would haunt the corners of my vision could never be safely relegated to the realm of "imagination."

And the one who had to be reckoned with, who had shamefully only then occurred to me as an existing reality, was the elder Justine. My knees weakened at words echoing from *The Fan-Shaped Destiny*, ". . . to the one who, of all the kith and kindred who remain alive, perhaps cared the most."

I looked at JJ, who smiled at me uncertainly, though full of trust. But all I could see was the color of her hair, and a band of shadow across her eyes like the punker makeup of a possible future. Then it was that I knew what had generated the anomaly of a nostalgia-haunted life, which even in adolescence, had my eyes firmly fixed on the past. I knew why I would have to have fixated on JJ in any world. It was so simple, her resemblance not alone to a daughter yet unborn, but to her grandmother. To the woman bound naked on the carpet of the *Hôtel Place de L'Odéon*. Madeleine Leiris, my true, original Justine.

Like golden bells, a goddess had laughed out loud at me. I was startled by a *memory* that had no continuity with the life I'd known. Not recalled since, since *a time before*, I recognized the classic profile of the sun goddess, smirking derisively as she had turned back to her camera. It had been I who was fairly humiliated by an arrogant young photographer, not the model in the familiar old leather straps who had glanced up at me accusingly.

It was her still—it had always been her. Most of the

time, when the path divides, when your essential life is defined, the meaning of your existence is determined—it is by little things you see only in hindsight. Sometimes not.

I thought, maybe for the first time in my life, really thought about the consequences of what I was about to do. I remembered the warning from *The Fan-Shaped Destiny*, "The rational man in my extraordinary situation should approach, only with the greatest trepidation, the creation of a world where the shape of things to come may surprise him unawares."

I could have no idea what acting to involve Justine in our lives would mean. That she would ever do ill to me or her granddaughter was inconceivable—even while I had come to understand that nothing would stop a Justine until she had what she wanted—in any world. Life with any Justine is little but surprises, and I suspected that, at least in my personal life, I would enjoy precious little pretense of precognition. This life would quickly become radically different from that which I remembered.

I'd modified my original scheme to try to make myself the father of JJ's child, who might be destined to become the vehicle of Justine's *metem*. But even as I had woven the threads to become the father of Justine$^2$, the simplest chronology of the lifelines had eluded me. How could I wait here now and ignore her, compound my original sins, even if I couldn't remember them firsthand—sins for which I had only just begged forgiveness?

A fond smile at the thoughts of her incorrigibility

was wiped from my lips as I comprehended that the Justine of this world and time had less than a decade to live. The black realization caused my throat to seize up and my guts to tremble. I had no choice; I *had* to be with her, perhaps even to love her. It mattered naught that she was old and would soon be ill; *it was still her inside.*

I'd been recently graced with the dubious blessings of many moments of truth, but this was the mother of them all. Back flew a shattering recollection that had mystified me on the pier in Gulfport. Oh God, were our possible futures, as well as our alternate pasts, all potentially visible to us, with no means of distinction? Had I heard the echo of a heartbroken plea from this life I was entering? I looked once more at JJ. She smiled again, tentatively, sensing my pain. I tried to give a reassuring look and placed my hand over hers. With her grandmother's help, she would be a good mother; all would be well.

But it rang in my head like a cry from hell, *"It's still me inside!"* I averted my eyes, my glance freezing on the power plant across the lake, brightly lit in gay blue, yellow, and red. Could there have been more not admitted in the manuscript, lied about by omission in shame and sadness? In whichever worlds she might have pleaded those terrible words, I swore to God that she would never utter them again, never be left to cry alone in the dark.

I watched the lights and fought against the buffeting of the emotional storm. In my mind's eye, they became the lights of Lake Charles, driving through the Southern night with young Justine by my side, wishing that we could just drive on forever. They became the lights that shone even now, this very night, from her home far away outside Atlanta. Then I utterly lost it, thinking of *our* home, as it had been since she had happily run up the steps to display her lights for me. In this world, as in that other, she had grown old there; sitting high up under its tin roof, hoping and praying *for me*. Could I again betray the cheerful hope celebrated by those little lights, knowing now the meaning of her horror of the Rhinebeck darkness?

A poet said, "In dreams begin responsibilities," and the bludgeoning of this truth did not end. So young she must have been before, running gaily up a street in the Village, alongside vanishing carriages and the growing horde of horseless carriages, scanning the second stories of the brownstones through the snowy night, searching for the more modest Christmas lights to guide her home. Would this remain my penance, to chase her through the times and worlds, waiting for her to grow up, or waiting to die to be with her once more?

---

I STOOD, PHYSICALLY, IN THE DEFINING FANTASY OF A LIFETIME, finding that it was only "the goal in sight again." I did love JJ, how could I not? I must always have seen Justine in her, and now I believed she might even become the mother of Justine[2]. But, as the *Lakota* would say, my destiny was "written in the spirit world." I could do naught but the necessary to reach her, to be with her again.

"Am I going to get clobbered." JJ fretted. "I'm going to be grounded, probably forever!" It must have been very late, there were no more cars on the road over the dam.

"Forever is a long time," I answered. I was still watching the lights, darkness hiding the tears streaming down my cheeks. "Until forever, I can run over and you can crawl out your bedroom window most any night. Dig it?" She laughed with delight, due to yet another of my "prescient" insights of her habits. "Anyway, it'll give you plenty of time to write your grandmother about us. She'll approve of us, and your stepmother won't defy her."

"Wait up! Is this for laughs? Far be it from me to pop off about my own grandmother"—she had turned incredulous—"but she is one strange old bird. Why would you think she'd even care?"

"You can believe that she cares, baby. Perhaps she's the one . . . *the one who cares the most.*" My voice caught as I spoke the fatal words. "Tell her I said exactly that." Would I ever know what it meant that, in every time, somewhere along every path, she was waiting for me? No turning back, I rushed on.

"Tell her that Wamba, that's *W-a-m-b-a*, has sent her friend back where he belongs. Trust me that will mean something to her. She'll know what to do and want to meet me, and she'll help us. Here, I'll write it down." I fished for a pen, then laughed shakily at myself when I realized that I didn't yet habitually carry one. Then I found it, nonetheless.

When I looked up, I was alone, my abrupt solitude easily confirmed as the pier was well lit in the green of mercury vapor. It was on the lake, yet it wasn't. Behind the pier lay a broad expanse of cement, the gravel we had walked on throughout the evening escaping like dreams that flee even as we grasp for them. It was still that long-remembered night, but not. The first hint of dawn was lightening the eastern sky behind the condos.

Now what was *that?* I wondered stupidly. What was *that* all about? For a fleeting instant, in a scene more surrealistic than familiar, a young boy reached to embrace a girl from a darker time. She had become the real-world incarnation of the angel he would never forget, from a strange waking dream, the lady with the flaming hair whom he knew had somehow been with him always.

The moment passed, and all was again familiar, but would have been a descent into hell had I not been able to immediately focus on the silhouette in the very short skirt. She sat, legs crossed, elbow on knee, and casually smoking a cigarette as she watched me from the shelter house. I wanted to run up the pier, but quickly decided to accommodate a more abused cardiovascular, and walked up instead.

"Hey." At her flat punker greeting, I wondered whether another monosyllabic monotone had ever resonated as sweetly. "I was afraid," she gasped, as I roughly seized her up in my arms, "you were gonna make me come after you again."

Assuming she spoke of the other world, I shuddered, "Never. Never again, not even in death!"

"Scary, aw-hunh?" she rubbed in the obvious comparison. I had no bitch with the chastisement. I knew even more certainly that I would accept anything in lieu of the pain of separation. I collapsed down beside her in a surprised exhaustion. I was amazed that the entire night had passed in our reality.

"How is it we weren't rousted by the park cops?" In our time there was a curfew to keep drug deals at a minimum.

She shrugged, "We were all—about staying quiet in the dark, and they went away." Then she silently smoked another cigarette while I told my story of the temporary transit. Toward the end, Justine[2] snickered, "She won't gotta crawl out that window, much, before she gets knocked up."

So overwhelmed by what my memory told me I'd just experienced, I only then began to think through finding myself on the pier. "Was I acting all that out, walking through the scene?" Then a more embarrassing consideration, "Do you think he'll remember his first time, or did I take that away from him?"

"There's a no-brainer," she laughed. "I'd like to think that *you* experienced something even better." She drew my hand beneath her skirt to feel the stickiness between her legs. "You found me delightful, I am *way* sure!"

"He was here? His consciousness was consolidated in my present body?" Somehow, I'd not thought of that. God forbid that happened in every transit.

Throwing the consciousness of an innocent into a body at life's end was reprehensible. I thought of those instants in the transits when I felt superimposed with another, perhaps many others.

"You should get down with that. And stop referring to yourself in the third person; it's *way* weird! You'd better believe that I've been patiently listening, to '*he*' this and '*he*' that, all damned night. It's one thing when you don't remember being *l'Autre*, like with Willie's experiences? But this is another wrinkle, and it's seriously creepy. Everything that boy was, is still a major part of your self. Deep inside, you are all that. When you went back, you like freed it all up." She was giving me a consoling rationale in conventional psychological terms.

"But what did you say to him?" At her raised eyebrow, I corrected myself, "Or, say to me?"

"Who you really are, and how to learn more. By 'chance,' I prepared you, for the thing you had going on back there, and it wasn't hard. You were a bright kid, not resistant to ideas. My thing is, I liked you that way. I hope you let me see more of all that. Check it out. The memories you retrieved are stored there, not here." She tapped my forehead.

"To describe that someway improbable past to me, you had to first scan the memories from there, from the physical brain and nervous system that recorded them. What you've imprinted here, now, is a memory of memory. Say, that's not even 'your past' now, it's another world."

"You needn't have wigged," she mused. "That you

could retrieve your own history was proof positive that the link with the here and now was in place." Her Bronx accent and period speech were creeping back and mingling with the other.

"You'd better oughta keep your heart open, believe you me. Be sure that you really and truly wanna help your self retain access to the locations where the memories of tonight are stored." I looked at the comfortable seriousness in her eyes, seeing metaphor in the cosmetic feathering that had replaced the punker mask. As in her speech, she was coming close to complete integration. "You'd be barking up the wrong tree by shutting it down—for dread of losing me or the vertigo of balancing among the realities."

Understanding was growing in step with the breaking dawn. I remembered my thoughts and feelings just before being drawn back. Damned little psych major! Rely on Justine[2] to turn the bottom line into an imperative that I learn to love myself as much as I loved her. She was looking at me with compassion, and the intimacy was near overwhelming. With her, there was little possibility of simple privacy, much less secrets.

I touched her bare thigh. "What was it like, tonight?"

She threw back her head in laughter, "Aw-hunh!"

---

"WE ALSO DISCOVER A NEW DIMENSION IN VOYEURISM! Nothing doing! I'm gonna torture you and make you wait on the story, till I can get you up by telling. But believe me when I say, these performance difficulties you're always fretting do not appear to be a fixture of the physical organism."

"You were frightened, at first," she went on, "but when I figured out to whom I was talking, I fixed that in a jif. You had already read enough science fiction to be down for it. Then you kept wandering around, playing with your beard, and wanting to *look* at everything, like you were stoned.

"I had to keep coming after you; thought I was gonna have to sit on your face to keep your attention. You were mesmerized by the condominiums, so I tried to explain about condos and yuppies, MBAs, and BMWs. But when you took me to mean that yuppies all ride motorcycles, I told you that there are some things it's better not to know!"

Then she knocked off the comedy. "Yes, dearest, about the possible future, which is our past; the waste and the grief, the heartache, and the futility." She went on in some detail, and it was hard to listen to, but I could tell that it had been as painful to deliver. Barely growing into a young man, he would always have been looking back, at what might have been. The most well-intentioned efforts of his time and place could not have addressed that. Without her preparation, he would have lived his life that way, too often sacrificing the joy of the moment, as had his counterpart who had grown into myself.

I looked at the slab beneath my feet, holding her hand. "I wish someone had told me." It was not a joke.

With some emotion she continued, "You asked, if

you did the things I advised, would you become the man I loved. I couldn't look at you when I bade you not be concerned, that it would be a better life you would lead." Her face was averted from me then, as well. "I told all I could remember you saying, about your friends' destinies—how you might help them."

They had talked long into the night, while I had strolled with JJ, in that same deserted place. Our steps must have woven ghostly tapestries, crossing and recrossing as we'd walked and talked, "separated only by time." She'd tutored him as to probable large events in the world, let him see a bit of the future, and how to relate to it. Of Willie, of Katie-Linda, of how to find her own other self and the manuscript in that snapshot of time. Unlike my handling of JJ, she had presented that last as an option to be used a few years later if things went badly in spite of everything.

Then she had instructed him in what he thought he wanted most, how to win and hold JJ. She had talked seriously about what he would have to sacrifice, to what degree he must stop playing the rebel and pretend to be more sedate. But, being Justine[2], she also advised him of the times for other methods, slight degrees of terror that would intimidate his competition, and the various "inappropriate" behaviors which at JJ's age, time, and place would be taken as confirmation of true love.

I rolled my tongue in my cheek, "Then again, some things never change."

"Bite me! Did I tell you wrong?"

"Not exactly sticking to the high road, were you?"

"You said the very same thing last night. How long ago did you hone that sardonic attitude into a primo defense mechanism? No, wait! Did you want her, muchly? If she was all that, you'd be, y'know, about any means necessary? Seduce her into behavior that would disgust the peers; you and she being seen as despicable by everyone, so fuckin' what? You'd get her. You'd be taking her to a whole different world, pardon the pun, and this stupid town would be nothing but a bad dream."

"You're sure I was paying close attention?"

"I gave you a 'pop quiz.' I wasn't a mean old schoolmarm, and I'm sure I don't have your mother's persuasive skills, so I bribed you," she said snottily. "For another go betwixt my gams, I made you recite everything back." *God,* I thought, *I'd love to be a fly on the wall when that world's Justine comes to "help."*

Responding as to whether she was ever concerned that the exchange might be permanent: "Even getting it done, I could feel you were all about being back there. Though you were so up on me as to think it might be a good trade," she bragged. "I believed it must connect with what you had going on there, that I could feel time"—she shrugged—"or *what-ev-er,* running out.

"So I said: Buy her if you could, or knock her up. *Merde!* Every worthless bastard in the world proclaims his desire for fatherhood, when all it's about is to shackle a girl. Anyone ever give you a medal for being better?" She reflected, "Don't worry, I told you it was only a Band-Aid; then it would be up to you, building a life that was something other than a brutal trap."

I was silent. The close dovetailing of her agenda with the one I had worked on JJ was eerie, in that I knew that mine had evolved even as it had been acted out. She turned her face away again, but her voice softened. She'd told him that they must have a little girl and name her Justine; that JJ's grandmother would explain all later.

He would have everything necessary, even be armed with the second chances foreknowledge would provide. It was chilling to hear her recount the warning that, if he ever abandoned them, he would only be able to wish he could go to hell to pay for it. The real horror, I'd now seen, had been the belief that I *couldn't* make amends.

"I asked you whether you'd had the dream in which the girl answers the door at your house. The look on your face said that you had. It also told me that the compact I made tonight was sealed, but to be sure I made you describe every detail. Then I warned that you must keep the old house, at least till the daughter is grown."

Justine[2] seemed always to be two steps ahead of me. At my question, she turned and laid her hand on my chest. "My poor dear, you must be so tired." She patiently pointed out that before the night when the worlds divided, his reality and mine were one. I thought I understood.

"The dream set me on the path to my destiny, which, in turn, brought me to loop back and 'reconfigure' the events? The dream is vital?" This part was almost classic Dunnesian stuff.

She spelled it out, as she had for him. "You must have the daughter, in the house, to go to the door one evening for whatever reason. Because up in your room, separated from you by only quanta of space-time, the still-younger boy that you were is watching through the dream." I stared at her, speechless, as I recalled the final lines from *The Fan-Shaped Destiny*, "Somehow, we dream the worlds we live in . . ." I admitted that I had believed that to be only another colorful turn of phrase.

"The last thing I said to you was, and I'm sorry, not about you, save indirectly. It was, I'm afraid, a personal indulgence only for myself." Emotion rose in her speech, and it was the last time I was to hear that purely archaic style.

"I asked you to do one last thing for me. That when you believed your wonderful life with JJ irreversible, when you recalled me only as a friendly ghost from a world of might've-been; on some lovely evening bring your little family to the lake, back here where it began . . . AND, REMEMBER ME TO HER."

---

That last was delivered in broken sobs, and tough little Justine[2] shook all over, burying her face in her hands. I pulled her against me and rocked her gently. "That was beautiful. You've accused me of being a wordsmith, but that was beautiful." There were no appropriate words for this, but I was trying to tell her that I understood, God forgive me—I understood at last the broken heart of what had been going on! That child to be born to them was *not about* another life for her.

"Could you possibly have been just a little bit more insensible?" she lashed out at me in her pain, but I didn't mind. "Did you truly believe it was only about vehicles for our continuation, or healing the wounds that kept us separated across the void? Did you think you were the only one who had to make amends? *Do you get it now?*"

I got it. Yes, I've been a pig, I told you that before. Old Justine's original ambition, to become JJ, had been far more profound than Justine$^2$ had been willing to admit, or would ever fully remember, or perhaps, than her antecedent self had consciously comprehended.

Would she, or had she, achieved that in an otherworld? Had it been a *metem* of Madeleine-Justine that would, once again, give birth to a lost daughter? The Justine who, due to whatever causes, had ended her young life in 1947? What I had hitherto thought was happening had never been her agenda for that situation. Nor, I suspected, thinking back on my dreams, had it really been mine.

"Did you believe that, when you said it would be a better life that I would lead?" My unspoken question was obvious—whether it was a better man the boy would become. Justine$^2$ was recovering her composure. "I don't know." She appraised me with flat honesty. "But one of you had to believe it."

"It wasn't in the vein of a plan," she went on. "I didn't know what had to happen till tonight. I knew that the dream had been so important to you, it must affect us someway. Then, being confronted with you as you had been, made me remember the might've-beens you spilled out at *The Château*.

"When you pined to me about JJ years ago, when it was too late for you, or for me in that life—I do believe that framed my original notion." She paused and chose her words carefully, "My late memories were mercifully vague. It was only tonight that I recalled the *mambos* prophesied that we could only help her when you weren't always bailing out."

We walked down on the pier. The sequential colors of the sunrise, pink to gold to white, battled for control of the wavelets. As they clashed, my fatigued eyes interpreted them as a multitude of little warriors, literally slugging it out. I thought with amusement that quasi-schizophrenic poets might possibly see exactly the metaphors they employ. As a wave of the little light-beings danced near the pier, a swirling eddy spun them into a circle like the ritual dancers.

"We did what had to be done, the only way it could have been done," I offered quietly, my heart become so full I thought it would burst. "I know myself then, including the flip side of my early cynicism. I'd have done the right thing, simply because someone had finally told me why." I watched the wavelets and the ducks, whose distant ancestors I'd listened to throughout the night.

"Hey, this part is gonna take some getting used to. I could've lived with you being my father—though for now, I kinda think I like this better." She playfully pinched me. "But I never thought of it in terms of you really starting to grow up!"

# XII
# Hindsight

BY THE TIME WE AWOKE FROM SLEEPING AWAY THE day beneath the watchful vigil of the dolls, Justine$^2$ and I had known each other for *one week*—as those around us reckon time. As space is measured, we had circumnavigated a large part of eastern North America. But between us, in another sense, we had spanned the apocalyptic twentieth century and touched other continents, not to mention bouncing off an alternate universe or two . . .

Justine$^2$ had, or would recover, actual memory of most of it. But in some world's "darkest Africa," I had lost my conscious memories. I remain skeptical that I shall ever recall the larger part of them. Maybe just as well. Perhaps the pain of the guilt that took lifetimes to unburden, acknowledged in bits and pieces and always too late, had become too great.

Or maybe forgiving myself will reopen possibilities. I've thought that I'm beginning to recall the grinning countenance of Wamba, and hope someday to meet again she who was the best friend anyone could ever have. In any event, there are no longer any doubts that it is true.

The *mambos* knew something, beyond simply the techniques they employed to assist Justine, directing her transit into *metempsychosis* to become her great-granddaughter. Through a network of the initiates, Wamba had sent the message to her sisters across the sea of something she recalled from another life—that she had sent her friend back where he belonged. Decades later they would meet the woman Justine, who was following after him.

That part is no longer a great mystery to me; neither is their "clairvoyant" knowledge of our child. It seems so simple now. Much of precognition and retrocognition is revealed to be but "qubits" spilling across the times and worlds—a possible function of Polchinski's mathematical "weak connection." Perhaps someone had merely recounted a strange dream—about a pretty spirit who would willingly have gone to hell in search of her prodigal love.

It would be only vanity to seek a chain of causal explanations in a single universe. Ultimately, one had come among the voodoo women who knew of our story. To some other wandering soul, as yet unidentified, we owe an inexpressible debt of gratitude—and to a wise *mambo* who, living always in expectation of synchronistic events, had paused to listen closely. There was no divination by chicken entrails, or anything of the sort, just a knock on the door.

There had been a critical moment that long-ago night on the darkened pier, a moment that made all the difference, which decisively divided the worlds. Certainly there had been innumerable variances during all those dark hours but, in Justine$^{2}$'s view, none of them had produced a divergent timeline that could not eventually become again identical and converge, disappearing except for a lingering trace of strange memory.

"Your undisputed artfulness, I am so sure, was in vain," she had explained in her oddly integrated speech. "Like, in most of the paths branching off before the last moment, JJ was never reconciled to the weird hookup. You repressed and altered the event so as to make it compatible with the reality you knew."

I had to ruefully admit the probability. Beyond my first sight of JJ, my memories from that night were likely a selective sampling. Loving her could as easily have been combined with being in the arms of Justine$^{2}$. The impact of that experience, involving revelations of our once and future selves, would certainly have sufficed to generate a lifetime obsession!

My extreme sense of hurt over losing JJ would have been compounded by the loss of my magical friends; the red-haired angel, and perhaps glimpses of my other, older self, who had nodded to me in passing. I wondered at how many more mistaken worlds, as full of sadness as this we'd known, we had created before arriving at the present accommodation.

"Not so many as to get bent about. Most would converge again within days or weeks. The paths of higher probability do seem, like, more resistant than we imagined? Some, like the world of the two-pearl ring, existed separately for months. But the fact that JJ remembers that one proves it spilled into ours as well. For sure, divergent histories don't prevent worlds from becoming similar enough to converge."

So what was critical? What constituted the triggering moment? I recapitulated how Dr. Benford had speculated on the necessary conditions for a message across time that could alter a history.

"He wrote of some minimum impulse necessary to trigger a paradox. When some critical volume of space-time was tweaked, then the disturbance would propagate outward instantaneously, with enough amplitude to matter. You could change the past regularly as long as you didn't create paradoxes with large amplitude. He visualized a multiverse with a single wave function, scattering into new states of being as paradoxes formed inside it like kernels of ideas."

"*C'est ça*; he said it!" Justine[2] beamed. "I was sure it had to be your determination to make the dream come true that I'd prepared in you. Or not. Persuading JJ to direct events toward me by invoking Wamba's name and quoting from the manuscript? No, wait. You did do a bang-up job. Hearing that would've had me all over the situation like stink. I would've come to you immediately, and no interference would've been brooked, however well intentioned. *Emmerde!* You launched serious preemptive stink."

She sobered, "What truly appalls me is that it

required even that much to keep your appearance in her life from escaping my attention. I must've been as dreadfully neglectful of JJ as I was of my little Justine."

"Don't *you* start beating yourself up, now. You couldn't have monitored every boy in your granddaughter's life from a thousand miles away if you'd tried. She was deliciously promiscuous—sufficient for *me* to fall in love with her. So, we theorize that turning her thoughts toward contacting you was the 'bit of destiny action,' a quantum flash in JJ's brain, at a moment when it could have gone either way?"

"Where it went *both* ways. We are living on a path where it was all disregarded. On that other path, she wrote the letter or made the call." I questioned her certitude, and she looked exasperated. "Oh, men! Like, intuition? When I saw the commitment in your eyes, I knew that it was done. You didn't doubt the dream so much, back in that day. You knew it was of something terribly real," as she tried to cite Priestley's critique of Dunne, her voice betrayed her continuing pain, "as real as a dead child."

"What reconsolidated the parts of my self to its respective worlds," I persisted, "and at the critical moments?" I thought about her partial transit in the barn, that I feared might have become consummated had I not been there to pull against the dream-loop drawing her to 1945—finally only accelerating the *anamnesis* that confirmed her *metem*. I compared the particulars to my temporary transit, which she believed was also associated with a dream-loop.

For the first time, I saw in Justine[2] something

approaching humility. "You, you make me feel . . . so *proud*; outing with it, like it's from your heart and you haven't even thought it through. If love doesn't 'steer the stars,' at least we know it affects quantum events."

"Come again?"

She dropped her eyes, and said quietly, "The manuscript? What were your last thoughts of that horrid night in London, and the way you said good-bye after the second time around? It was all about what rated more than anything."

She looked up and there was so much love in her eyes that it was frightening. "*O, je t'aime!* When you found your moment of truth, the closest me was *here*. It was easier to reach across quanta of space-time than across a thousand miles. Besides, though you couldn't know it, I would've tried to send you away, near the end of that life, when I was sick and it got very bad."

"Vanity, thy name is woman." I shook my head. "You couldn't have kept me away. And how do you explain the dovetailing of our agendas, played out separately at both ends? More, how do these, ostensibly romantic, obsessions move inevitably toward the creation of a world for our child?"

"Lookit, a child's world begins with the love of a man and woman for each other? Hey, *that's* a radical idea! If you demand a causal answer for that, we'd better oughta start going to church again, like we did back in the twenties? *How* is courtesy of synchronicity, but that magic word gives no answer as to *why*."

Thus, I discovered my passion to exchange realities to have been like one of Wamba's masks, putting another face on the burning need to tie up the loose ends from less-spectacular escapes. Willie had contemplated his future at Lausanne and then struggled for acceptance when it came true, *again*. Had a limping specter in a snowy Moscow night signaled a sequential past of which I would become aware only decades later?

As I move toward the end of this account, my curious tendency to lapse into a god-awful Victorian-Edwardian writing style is no longer lost on me. This conceit, from which Willie and his contemporaries had laboriously worked to free themselves, is utterly incompatible with my late-century education and reading interests. I now know why this, long a mystery to others and myself, has been with me always. It must be like Justine$^2$'s integrated speech.

Later that quiet morning, I studied the sleeping girl. What silly insecurity it had been, feeling too old, in the hands of someone with a century of combined life experience. In Justine$^2$, I could also see the old woman. It now shamed me to realize that, at *The Château* in 1969, I probably could not have loved her. That early in this life, I had been too young and stupid. How many wonderful partners do we miss, poisoned by petty differences and presumed imperfections that mean nothing, not a thing?

I could also see the image of the woman, as if from the forties, whose aspect I had glimpsed in San Antonio, in the strange light of the hotel bar. I suspected that was as Willie had last seen her near the end.

The loveliness that had torn his heart out as she

walked away for that last time is, I have come to believe, a memory rather than a construction. The Justines are all one, and all beautiful. I felt redeemed that, *in extremis*, I had reached for her in whichever form. I recalled the rest of Borges's verse, which I'd not been able or ready to remember in the predawn rain on Wednesday:

---

". . . AND THE SHEER CONTEMPLATION OF THAT FACE . . . will be, for the rejected, an Inferno, and, for the elected, Paradise."

I acknowledged Justine as my wife in the old shelter house at the lake. In light of the above, such a ceremony may seem something of a redundancy, but it fulfilled, for her, an ambition of terrifying longevity and endless frustrations. My friends were in attendance, and I could see her looking them over, evaluating whether she might already know some of them. I hoped there were also others, if only in spirit, those lost to meet again.

My glance kept straying to certain spots on the floor, to an old light fixture, down toward the pier. At a table outside, not far away, a young couple was picnicking with their children. Had my transit really not been Justine$^{2}$'s plan? What was the most likely meaning of the phrase she'd murmured as I attempted regression?

*"Papa Legba, ouvrí barrière pour ce, ma p'tite . . ."* (". . . open wide the gate for this, my little one? My darling?")

I thought about a young family from another world. "God bless them," I whispered, "God bless our little girl." Justine[2] gripped my arm so hard that she might have drawn blood, smiling through tears that our friends thought were the emotion of the moment. I trust her absolutely—to be Justine. Will she eventually tell me what she meant by what I can pull back?

Going on to San Antonio to pick up Kong, we made an effort to at least talk with her mother. Justine[2] had immediately presented us as a unit, the subject not open for discussion, and damned near got the door slammed in our faces for our trouble. Relenting, JJ apprehensively avoided the circumstances with a depressing litany of her arthritis and other maladies.

". . . pressing on nerves running to my legs, causing me to be unsteady on my feet most of the time. Balance is important, one problem on each side," she laughed nervously. "I'm considering acupuncture, but haven't worked up the courage yet."

In my mind, I had yet to come to terms with JJ as the little grandmother before me. I did not want to lose the hot young babe. Not a "good girl," but a *real* girl, in nineties' eyes, and it didn't help matters that I remembered making love to that young girl so "recently"!

As JJ was thanking me for what she took to be empathetic concern, Justine[2] rudely interrupted with an ill-advised attempt to discuss the past; specifically, my relationship with JJ. Her mother listened with a tense politeness, then responded with her typical clichés, some tending toward the cryptic.

"All we can do is to love well those whom we love." That seemed to exhaust her capacity for the personal, and JJ waxed philosophical. "Our lives are little drops of water, but they can come together into a mighty 'river of good.' No one person can have a big effect on such a large world, good or bad, but together we can—and it's up to us to make sure we're in the right river."

She looked at me, and I confess to uncertainty as to what was being discussed. Stupidly, that "right river" intrigued me sufficiently to venture into the conversation. I recalled to her our shared anomalies, the ring, the parking lot, my long-ago dreams. After a while, she sighed.

"You've explained much of this to me before. These things were a *very* long time ago, and I've never had your capacity to remember everything I've ever heard or was said to me. My memory continues to diminish about almost everything except the trivial stuff. It sometimes seems that the more trivial, the more likely I am to retain it. The more important it is, especially if it has to do with me personally, the less likely. It's frustrating.

"You know that I've never been the type to pick apart a conversation, or dream, to identify and understand every nuance of it. Not only do I not have the capacity to do it; I don't have the interest. Folding in upon myself and obsessively analyzing everything I've done, or what has been done to me, is not something I care to do. I'm not in denial about it—I can hear *you* saying that already," she tossed at Justine.

"You have to have some basic understanding of the

past, but once you reach a level you can live with—mine is obviously considerably shallower than yours—you have to move on and hope to make better choices in the future. I don't dismiss the depth of your involvement." Her green eyes scanned both Justine[2] and me meaningfully, though without their old sparkle. "I just don't think it's very healthy.

"Is this the deal with the dream you once told me about? Where you and I got together and had a family? You saw this 'daughter' in a dream that was so vivid you had to accept it as truth because you'd had other dreams that proved true. Is that right?" I was speechless. What could I say? If it were anything, it was indeed *"the deal with the dream"*!

"You found yourself a daughter"—with a wounded resignation—"and you did it by taking mine." She turned to Justine[2]. "I have many regrets about the choices and decisions I've made in my past, like most people. But I must accept them and the results they produced." I saw Justine[2]'s nose ring flash as her nostrils began to flare. "I have to accept that what's done cannot be changed." I just shook my head, hoping the girl would not feel called to revisit past sins in painful detail.

"What do you expect to accomplish by understanding all the 'why-fors'? Inner peace? *That* would be a healthy goal. What would you be able to change if you did completely understand every nuance? How would it change how you live the rest of your life? No matter how much you 'pick the scab' to see what's underneath, it will not change anything or help anyone." I had to wonder again at the levels being trolled. Justine[2] might have every right to be getting hot.

"I think, as one grows older, one has to move past the 'what-ifs' of life. You can strangle on them, like your great-grandmother. Justine, she could be such a pill. I guess you would say, she projected everything. She imagined that a great-grandchild she'd never know, or have to relate to, would somehow carry on for her. She became such an obsessive mentality that, if she were here today, would say . . ."

*"Screw you. I've got my own issues!"* Snarling dismissal of the lecture, with its possible innuendoes, the bitchy side of Justine[2]'s antecedent self surprised me. I registered her mother's shock—at the faintly discernible, doubtless remotely familiar, taint of the old Bronx. Being JJ, she had the eerie moment cached, in its appropriate 'box,' in record time.

"Oh, sweetie, you are so much like her! It was only right for you to be her heir. But please, don't carry on the pain and bitterness. I do believe that it is inescapable human nature to have regrets about the past—wrong actions, missed chances, bad decisions." I was feeling sure veiled contrition was being proffered. Then she continued, plainly including me.

"You can expend all your mental and emotional energy on regret. Life will pass you by, and that would be a tragedy. Longing for the chance to relive the past makes us miserable. It keeps us from doing what we were put here to do. Please don't keep on hurting yourself.

"You, *like others who should know better*"—JJ gave

me a scathing look—"are caught like a fly in the spiderweb of your past, unable to get free and fly away. You are struggling hard, and that's good. But you do need to fly away from that web."

JJ turned to me and, rescinding the hateful expression, sighed. "Most of us don't change a lot as we get older, do we? We only become ourselves squared to the second power, both the good aspects and the bad. That's like the truism that you can't change another person. Life is full of hard lessons, don't you think? If we're lucky, we get past much of this by midlife. That makes the rest of the trip a bit easier."

Taking umbrage at the remarks directed at me, Justine[2] was on her feet, fists on hips, and tapping her foot. A quick appraisal was that her stance bespoke combat. I made hurried farewells as I swept her out the door, ignoring her protests. It was not that I doubted this weathered JJ's ability to hold her own with "Madeleine." I had seen, even within the limitations of her vision, why she was yet the pivot—the rock around which the radicals, the exotics like Justine[2] and me, must orbit.

I had begun to understand how all my efforts to illumine the times I had shared with JJ had come to nothing. It was natural enough for Justine[2] to feel, like a member of any younger generation, that all possible histories supported her harsh judgments of her mother. Not so easily anticipated was that, far from bestowing additional perspective on JJ's fatalistic acceptance, the dark, early-century Bohemian beneath would only reinforce the nineties gal!

JJ would never see the reflections of Justine[2] or Madeleine in her mirror. Still, I had come to suspect that our little red hen, with her pithy clichés, might have been the conciliator for many contentious inner voices. But Justine[2] was not going to be having much of that, not for a long, long time.

The superimposition of her antecedent self on a tacky mother-daughter spat did not much concern me. If at all, it was in the shape of uncertainty as to how the stresses might affect the still-fresh integration of personas in Justine[2].

Rather, it was JJ's metaphor about ourselves, *"squared to the second power,"* that moved me out of there. The slight prescience recalled Justine and Marjorie's *déjà vu* across the worlds. I was not in the market for any new paranormal ramifications for at least a while.

"*That* went well! A world where you and her could stay together and raise children would be some kinda shit to see," Justine[2] spat, as I encouraged her across the lawn. *"What-ev-er!"* When I admonished her for not being gentler, she snapped with only a bit of sadness, "She'll either own it or she won't."

"Maybe in another life," I remarked without thinking, and we looked at each other and laughed at the unexpected entendre. The bottom line was that we could do little about JJ's misery in this life. I thought again of a young family at a lake. Such things tend to become family stories, and our legends shape us. I suggested that telling her children about the night that the good angel had visited their father might convince even the teller that she, too, deserved happiness.

---

"THE GOOD ANGEL? AS IF!"

Justine[2] was almost rolling on the ground.

"Or fairy godmother. Heaven help you; you know that's what it will turn into in the telling. Don't forget that we've cast JJ in a pivotal role in this cosmic soap opera. She just wanted a normal life with everything neatly ordered in little boxes, and look what we've done to her!

"In this world she gave birth to her grandmother, who then took up with JJ's teenage lover, who was the *metem* of her grandfather. Over there, she's going to mate with her grandfather to give birth to her own mother. Unless, of course, that JJ is somehow really *you*; in which case, things might get just a little bit complicated. She deserves better from the cosmos than being merely a brood cow for The Lost Generation of Space-Time!"

"It's that male mind thing you have going on. Even at your best, you don't easily get it. What has haunted JJ's entire life? It's her mother—the legacy embodied in her name. When you and she bring little Justine into that world, you can believe she will know all has been made right, *tout va bien*; most of what's wrong for her goes away." She caught me watching, absent her mother in her face, the morphing of her sarcasm into that sweet sadness of hers. "It's a woman-thing, you wouldn't understand."

All defensive levity aside, I wondered whether my little joke had been so far off the mark after all. Could it be that *metem*, with greater or lesser degrees of recall, may serve as the "guardian angels" of their genetic lineage? Might they be guided among the branching paths by following the lines of their human progeny? Could there be literal truth when those about to depart have sometimes promised to be with us forever?

David Deutsch must have been thinking about Schrödinger's little book, *What Is Life?*, which defined genetic structures in a single world as "aperiodic crystals." They would be recognizable extensions across many worlds because they would vary less, in their detailed internal structures, than would non-organic matter.

Each *metem* engaged in its own quest to tie up loose ends, these immortal beings would fare amongst the worlds, inexorably creating greater order where; otherwise, there would have been lesser. These continuing selves would generate yet more of the "negative entropy," upon which Schrödinger believed the crystalline structure of life feeds.

I admitted my uncertainty as to exactly where the events we'd set in motion in the other world would finally lead, and expressed regret that our daughter might not be born to us here. "To be brutally frank, you're a little old." Then she surprised me again. "Hey, I don't think she'd be ready for *metem* as a boy. If you impregnate me, we'll have a son, and it's only fortunate we're from Texas, because I can't see any way around having to name him 'Justin.'"

"Woman's intuition again?" The look I got reminded me that, coming from Justine[2], this was no idle threat. Her expertise as regards possible futures had to count for something. "Would he be one of *us?*"

"I hope to goodness not! A tree doesn't grow very high without any new branches." This might suggest a way out of an impasse she presents to me. I cannot yet reconcile myself with her hellish determination toward wasting her young life, by not allowing me to leave her behind when my physical form is exhausted.

"Want me to live a long time, you'd better oughta take good care of yourself," she threatened, referencing her suicide in a life she knows only from the manuscript, supplemented by a few glimpses. She emphasized her point. "Don't *even* think about doing something like you did in 1945 to me again, or I'll roast you alive. *Believe* that I can stay peeved *for-ev-er*!"

If not to accept, it became a bit easier to cope with, when I understood that she cannot be measured by ordinary standards of sanity; nor could any self-aware *metem*. She functions upon some seventy years of conscious life experiences that are not, strictly speaking, part of our reality. While I understand that, there are limitations on what I can handle. I think the promise of immortality should liberate one to fulfill the immediate incarnation. She supposedly learned that before, but I have to take her present viewpoint with deadly seriousness.

I've had nightmares of rolling over on my

deathbed and looking into her impish grin as she lies beside me with a toxic IV in her arm. I've no intention of seeing this hideous presentiment actualized, at least by these entities we try to regard as our discrete selves. This demands some careful thought, and I know that Justine[2] could never abandon her child.

She was ever the eroticist and, with a brand-new body, she will doubtless continue to be an erotic being raised to a higher power, inclusive of her appetite for all forms of sensation. So we're probably going to witness some outrageous displays. While advancing age will naturally render me more voyeuristic, she'll engage in the forbidden just because she can. While I want to build to please her, I questioned some of this. We no longer require physical stress for transit or *anamnesis*. Isn't there a time for the hurting, metaphor for the agony of life, to stop?

"Not *liking* this! Guilt from other lives is expiated, but I still get hot at the thought of a whip across my bare ass. For cripe's sake, will you ever leave off whining? If you're gonna start flogging yourself, *now*, over the suffering of women, you've gotta wait for symmetry to provide you with the alternative."

I tried to point out the conditions of Willie's life after 1942, but got nowhere. "*What-ev-er* that amounted to does not *even* relate. You would need to be a submissive woman, not a submissive man. It's not *even* the same." She went on at tedious length with her theory that gender and sex-role changes must be incremental. "If I took *metem* into a male identity right now, I'd probably turn out a submissive male." She made a face. "Hurl!"

I retorted that she was being a bigot, ignoring probable effects of the different brain chemistry, et cetera. "Despite the continuity of your personal experience, I question sex roles being as fundamental as gender itself. Look at the degree to which historical patterns are involved. You won't find many African Americans inclined to play with our whips and chains, and that's not all. Go figure personal environment, the degree to which I might be trying to control a powerful mother-figure." Remembering the fact of Myra Seabrook, I added, "or mothers."

The downside of Justine[2] lay in contemplation of how many centuries she might be disposed to bicker. "So it's like that? *I'm* the fuzzy-thinking psych grad here? Don't even ask me to believe you've come through one more life, still slavishly kissing Freud's bourgeois ass! Say, haven't these times chosen to regard sexual orientation as fundamental?"

"Point, but I still disagree. People, heavily weighted to the ends of the dominance-submission spectrum, may more easily encompass a gender change. I can tell you that, whether they admit it or not, there is not a male dominant who hasn't, at one time or another, wished he could experience the woman's position."

I knew I had talked myself into a corner, even as it came out of my mouth. *"Kewl,"* Justine[2] grinned triumphantly. "I had a dream last night that you were whipping me but, someway, I was you. So, we have only to arrange the other end of the loop, and we can explore that, can't we? *Foutettez-moi, chéri!*"

We'll no doubt have many more years of philosophical debates over the creation of and continuing interaction with alternate realities, than it would amuse the readers of this account to contemplate. Isn't it sheer hubris to speak as if that otherworld were dependent on our intervention? Did it not inevitably exist anyway, along with every other possibility? And the whole set of questions, about the relationship of identities to memories to physical beings, that sort of thing? It would doubtless have been better, had these events befallen a physicist and a neurologist, rather than a psych grad and a playlike lawyer. But this was *our* story—we, whatever we are.

Consider the ancient question as to the nature of the Self. In what sense might I be Willie, or Justine[2] the original Madeleine? In the strange line of the Justines, one might posit some form of genetic memory, though logically such should only pass on data from point of conception to point of conception. As far as I know, I have no genetic kinship, though Willie certainly liked to imply that he spread his seed far and wide. I only know what I have seen and felt, plus a few memories that I can explain in no other way. And, I am convinced I have his woman, who assures me that I am he.

Who are these beings that we call "ourselves," who seem to move across times and worlds, endlessly duplicated and approximated, yet believing our selves to be discrete entities? With every thought we share "qubits" of data with knowledge-bearing matter throughout the branches of the multiversal wave function. "The more it changes, the more it stays the same, and the hand just rearranges the players in the Game."

This, too, exonerates Justine$^2$ from an ordinary standard of sanity. We hold sanity to inhere in the degree to which we can objectify ourselves, see ourselves as only the characters of our story and not as its author. Is that truly sane? It is, after all, that "other," unconscious self who more often has precognitive experiences, and no difficulty in regarding itself as an immortal being, free of linear space-time. True, that self makes little distinction among its psychic contents; memories, alternate worlds, spirits, and fantasies are all the same to it.

The confidence of Justine$^2$'s convictions is contagious. Does my child by JJ in the otherworld truly represent the lost daughter of her antecedent self? Were that mere wish fulfillment, it would seem that she would be equally emphatic in asserting an identification of herself with that JJ. Rather, she dubiously points out that the conditions of her 1969 encounter with me, which had generated that scheme in this world, were radically changed. With all that subsumed into another scenario, she believes she would have chosen an alternate course. I had no sense of that young JJ *being* Justine—other than via a strong genetic kinship.

Is there some symmetry principle behind JJ birthing a vehicle for her lost mother as she did in this world for her grandmother? The perpetuation of the name seems more than merely symbolic. The whole curiosity of the *gens* of the Justines suggests a far more involved mind-body connection than we have yet imagined. Deutsch had identified the basis:

> But now we have come almost full circle. We can see that the ancient idea that living matter has special physical properties was almost true: it is not living matter but knowledge-bearing matter that is physically special. Within one universe it looks irregular; across universes it has a regular structure, like a crystal in the multiverse . . . [91]

*Like a diamond*, if you will, its iridescent glory shining into the skies of many worlds.

> In such places, objects extend recognizably across large numbers of universes . . . as the location of the processes—life, and thought—that have generated the largest distinctive structures in the multiverse.[92]

So, we could see knowledge-bearing matter, immortal in the sense that it's replicated across many worlds, and thus across time, as inextricably bound up with destiny. The life-cycle of organic beings, all the

---

91. Deutsch, op. cit., p. 190.

92. Deutsch, ibid., p. 192.

possible patterns of our genetic identities, is our portion of those great structures!

We could, probably will, go on endlessly. The Fan-Shaped Destiny spreads out over infinity. We will continue to explore it, like adventurers on the unknown footpaths of late colonial Africa or Arabia. But we are at best explorers. Our elongated memories give us only a slight advantage, not ultimate answers. And they tell us more about humanity than about nature.

And so, at last, this book is nearly finished. I am preparing to print out this epilogue from the PC on Justine's desk. It sits above the elderly Underwood, still nestled in the desk well below. I reach out to caress the cover of her old copy of *No Hiding Place*. I think that synchronicity may be as close to the hand of God as we will ever see. I've wanted no more than to be at home with her while we completed the account and digitized *The Fan-Shaped Destiny*. It contains the method for effectuating the transit, the heart of which Seabrook brought out of Africa, inspiring literature and, perchance, some of science itself.

I have thought long, and can conceive of no greater tribute to those who inspired that body of work, than what I'm about to do. Justine[2] is hell-and-be-damned that, in this life, I should take her to live in the south of France to redress what she felt denied before. Her means are hardly inexhaustible, but it's not out of the question. We will be leaving soon.

Tonight, after my printout is finished, we will insert the other disk and begin to upload *The Fan-Shaped Destiny* onto the Internet. If Willie's fear of dark, suppressive forces was right, what a wonderful thing this late-century technology may be. No longer may books be burned or thinkers consigned to oblivion. From a satellite sailing across the constellations, it again comes back to you, you whom it has actually been with always.

Kong has gone on ahead of us now. His passing made me reflect that I cannot persuade myself that all sentience does not share in the miracle. Somewhere, Linda has found him. Somewhen, I will have done with looking to the past. On that day, I would like to go with my Justine to a new place, let the waters of Lethe close over us, and awaken in a bright new morning where we can be children together. This is a prayer, as has been my recounting of this whole strange saga. Perhaps, finally, I'm still as far from having seen it all as I ever was.

Justine$^2$, with her high "psychic" potential, has indeed been able to recognize many more like ourselves than is surmised, even among the devotees of *metempsychosis*. A part of what she does is the mere application of common sense to manner or speech distinctly out of place, to the unguarded assumption that doesn't fit in time and space. Look at the reality about us with a new eye, and you will witness much of this for yourselves. She says they move anonymously, attending to their own affairs and, no doubt, avoiding the generation of large paradoxes. She thinks that most have memories of paths through spacetimes closely related to this one, though a few may recall very different worlds.

I wonder, too, if there may not be broader meanings to some old religious concepts. Might "born again" have denoted, not a subjective catharsis, but a literal answer to that universal prayer for yet another chance?

Don't misunderstand me. We were not and are not saints, and have no ambition to become such in any foreseeable lifetime. If you regard our condition as a blessing rather than a curse, and wonder that people as unworthy as ourselves should receive it, we would first question where the hell you get off—presuming dominion over to whom the grace of God is extended?

Men and women presumably can make incremental progress during even one life. To our eyes now, our other selves appear cruel and shallow. We are better now and, in the eternity ahead, and behind, and sidewise, the "better angels of our nature" will continue to sit upon our shoulders. Sometimes not so gently.

It is true; we recall no suffering in villages ridden with Ebola, or of starving in a refugee camp. Our remembered trials were very personal. Let me assure you, that is no guarantee against bleeding out from a hole in the heart. We do not claim to have deserved anything; *this is the human condition*, consciously recalled or not. "In my Father's house, there are many mansions."

It is New Year's Eve, the century along with the Millennium draws to its close, and we're going down to Peachtree Street to celebrate. Justine[2] just dropped through, again, to model her scandalous attire for the evening, pleasantly annoying me to remind you that she thinks the numbers of the "born again" among us seem to be growing. Maybe mankind is special after all. Maybe our ability to see the otherworlds, even through a glass darkly, is what distinguishes us.

*Maybe something wonderful is happening.*

http://www.geocities.com/FanShapedDestiny
uploading: sat, 31 dec 2000 18:45:20 est

# Selected Bibliography

## Physical Science and Related Topics

Deutsch, David. *The Fabric of Reality*. NY: Penguin, 1997.

DeWitt, Bryce and R. Neill Graham, editors. *The Many-Worlds Interpretation of Quantum Mechanics*, Princeton Series in Physics, Princeton University Press, 1973. Contains the original Everett and Wheeler papers, first popularizations by Everett and DeWitt, plus other material.

Dunne, John William. *An Experiment with Time*. NY: Macmillan, 1927.

———. *The Serial Universe*. Macmillan, 1938, London: Faber & Faber, 1934.

———. *The New Immortality*. London: Faber & Faber, 1938.

———. *Nothing Dies*. London: Faber & Faber, 1940 (rev. ed. 1951).

———. *Intrusions*. London: Faber & Faber, 1955 (finished and published posthumously by Dunne's wife).

Polchinski, Joseph. "Weinberg's Nonlinear Quantum

Mechanics and the Einstein-Podolsky-Rosen Paradox," in *Physical Review Letters*, Jan. 28, 1991.

Schrödinger, Erwin. "What is Life?" and "Mind and Matter," Cambridge University Press, 1967 (first published 1944) pp. 65, 75. Based on lectures delivered under the auspices of the Dublin Institute for Advanced Studies at Trinity College, Dublin, in Feb. 1943.

Weinberg, Steven. "Testing Quantum Mechanics," in *Annals of Physics*, Volume 194, Mar. 6, 1989.

———. *Dreams of a Final Theory*. 1992 NY: Vintage, 1993–94.

Wolf, Fred Alan, works, especially *Star Wave*, NY: Macmillan 1984.

## Selected Classic Science Fiction Predating the Everett Theory

de Camp, L. Sprague, and Fletcher Pratt. "The Incomplete Enchanter." In *Unknown*, May and Aug. 1940, first published in book form by NY: Doubleday, 1941.

Heinlein, Robert A. "Elsewhere." In *Astounding Science Fiction*, Sep. 1941. Title was changed to "Elsewhen" in the collection *Assignment in Eternity*, NY: Signet, 1953.

Leinster, Murray (Will F. Jenkins). "Sidewise in Time." In *Astounding Science Fiction*, Jun. 1934. Published in various collections.

Moore, Ward. *Bring the Jubilee*. NY: Del Rey, 1955.

Piper, Horace Beam. "Time and Time Again." In *Astounding Science Fiction*, April 1947. Various collections.

Stapledon, William Olaf. *Star Maker*. London: Methune, 1937.

## Selected Pertinent Fiction

Benford, Gregory. *Timescape*. NY: Simon and Schuster, 1980. Afterword by Susan Stone-Blackburn. Winner of SFWA 1980 Nebula Award.

Borges, Jorge Luis. "The Garden of Forking Paths." 1941. English publication 1956, various collections.

Dick, Philip K. *The Man in the High Castle*. NY: Putnam, 1962 (won the science fiction Hugo Award in 1963).

Greene, Ward. *Ride the Nightmare*. New York and London: Jonathan Cape and Harrison Smith, 1930. Reissued by Avon in 1949 as *Life and Loves of a Modern Mister Bluebeard*.

Matheson, Richard. *Bid Time Return*. 1975, retitled *Somewhere in Time*, as was the film. Features Priestley's work as Priestley features Dunne's.

Priestley, John B. *Time and the Conways*. NY: Harper and Brothers, 1938.

———. *Man and Time*. NY: Doubleday, 1964 (Crescent, 1987), nonfiction work including the theories of J.W. Dunne.

## Nonfiction, Biography, and Memoirs

Benford, Gregory. Commenting on Everett and Leinster. In *The Magazine of Fantasy and Science Fiction* Jul. 1993, p. 96.

Selected Bibliography

Clark, VèVè A. with Millicent Hodson and Catrina Neiman. *The Legend of Maya Deren: A documentary biography and collected works, Volume One*. NY: Anthology Film Archives, 1984.

Man Ray. *Self Portrait*. NY: Little, Brown and Company, 1963. Reissued in 1988 with new illustrations from the Man Ray Trust.

Seabrook, William B. *Adventures in Arabia*. NY: Harcourt Brace, 1927.

———. *The Magic Island*. Harcourt Brace, 1929.

———. *Jungle Ways*. Harcourt Brace, 1931.

———. *Asylum*. Harcourt Brace, 1935.

———. *Witchcraft*. Harcourt Brace, 1940.

———. *No Hiding Place* (autobiography). NY: Lippincott, 1942.

Seldes, George. *Witness to a Century*. NY: Ballantine, Random House, 1987.

Symonds, John and Kenneth Grant, editors. *The Confessions of Aleister Crowley*. NY: Hill and Wang, 1970.

Taylor, S.J. *Stalin's Apologist*. NY: Oxford University Press, 1990. On the life and career of Walter Duranty.

Worthington, Marjorie. *The Strange World of Willie Seabrook*. NY: Harcourt Brace, 1966. A hope, a prayer.

*The New York Times*, 1927–76 for news items, feature stories, marriage notices and obituaries concerning William Seabrook, Katherine Edmondson Seabrook-Worthington, Lyman Worthington, Marjorie Muir Worthington-Seabrook, and Ward Greene.

Printed in the United States
220603BV00001B/57/A

9 780759 550391